THE BURNT HOUSE

THE

BURNT

HOUSE

FAYE KELLERMAN

HarperCollins*Publishers*

HarperCollins*Publishers*
77–85 Fulham Palace Road, London W6 8JB

www.harpercollins.co.uk

1

Published by HarperCollins*Publishers* 2007

Faye Kellerman asserts the moral right to
be identified as the author of this work

A catalogue record for this book
is available from the British Library

ISBN: 978 0 00 724320 4 (Hardback)
ISBN: 978 0 00 724321 1 (Trade Paperback)

Printed and bound in Great Britain by
Clays Ltd, St Ives plc

To Jonathan, my on-the-spot editor and shrink

And a very special thanks to Bill Kurtis for all his help

THE BURNT HOUSE

PROLOGUE

AT EIGHT-FIFTEEN IN the morning on a balmy Los Angeles winter's day, a 282 Lucent Industry Aircraft, better known as WestAir flight 1324, took off from Burbank Airport holding forty-seven commuters. The ETA to its final destination, San Jose, California, was one hour and six minutes and the ride was expected to be smooth and uneventful. The skies were blue, the wind gentle, and the heavens' visibility was unobstructed in all directions. Sixty-seven seconds later, with its nose still headed skyward, it inexplicably yawed to the left, did a 360 rotation on its axis, and began to plunge down until it clipped a power line, thundered its last hurrah, and burst into flames, the explosion so great that it was heard five miles away.

The main bulk of the fiery fuselage landed on a three-story apartment house in the Granada Hills section of the

West Valley, transferring its inferno to the residential structure. Windows shattered, gas pipes detonated, and electrical wires arced blue lightning through the skies. The eighteen-unit building crafted from stucco and wood was swallowed by flames that spanned every color of the rainbow. The noise was so deafening that it drowned out the human screams. The stench of fire, smoke, and fuel oil that infused the air was toxic and suffocating. Oxygen was choked out of the atmosphere. Flesh burned alongside metal and leather. Debris were scattered and windblown for hundreds of feet. Within a heartbeat of time, a green suburban landscape had been transformed into an unimaginable holocaust of hell.

1

HE CEREAL SPOON stopped midair. Rina turned to her husband. "What was that?"

"I don't know." The lights flickered and died along with the TV, the refrigerator, and probably everything in the house electrical. Decker reached over and picked up the portable phone. He punched in one of the landlines but got no response.

Rina lowered the spoon into the cereal bowl. "Dead?"

"Yep." Decker flicked the light switch on and off, a futile gesture of hope. It was eight in the morning and the kitchen was bathed in eastern light that didn't require electrical augmentation. "Something blew. Probably a major transformer." He frowned. "That shouldn't affect the phone lines, though." He pulled out his cell and tried to contact someone on a landline at work. With no response coming from the other end, Decker knew that the damage was widespread.

The Los Angeles Police Department's West Valley substation—Devonshire Division in another age—was a few miles away from where Decker lived. When this kind of thing happened, the place was a madhouse, a switchboard of panicked people with emergency lines ringing off the hook. "I should go to work."

"You didn't eat," Rina said.

"I'll grab something from the machines."

"Peter, if it's just a transformer, there isn't anything you can do about it. You'll probably have a long day. I think you should fuel up."

There was logic to that. Decker sat back down and poured some skim milk into his cereal bowl, already laden with strawberries and bananas. "I suppose the squad room can wait another five minutes." They ate in silence for two bites. He noticed the wrinkle in Rina's brow. "You're concerned about Hannah."

"A little."

"I'll stop by the school on my way to work."

"I'd appreciate it." Rina tried to think of something to say to distract both of them. The default conversation was the kids. "Cindy called yesterday. She and Koby are coming over Friday night for dinner."

"Great." A pause as Decker finished his cereal. "How are the boys?"

"I talked to Sammy yesterday. He's fine. Jacob only calls before Shabbos or if he's upset. Since he hasn't called, I'm assuming everything's okay."

Decker nodded, although his mind was racing through emergency procedure. He stood and tried the land phone again. The machine was still lifeless. "Is the den computer still plugged into a battery pack?"

"I think so."

"Let me try something." Decker unplugged the small, portable, kitchen TV and lugged it into the back den. Rina followed and watched her husband drop to the floor and insert the electrical cord into one of the empty sockets. The seven-inch screen sprang to life. Decker tried one of the local stations. The TV was color but showed only images in shades of black and gray.

"What are we looking at?" Rina asked.

"A fire." As if to underscore Decker's pronouncement, a billowing cloud of orange flames materialized. His cell jumped to life. "Decker."

"Strapp here. Where are you?"

For the captain to be calling him on his cell, something was really wrong. "At home. I'm just about to leave—"

"Don't come into the station. We've got a dire situation. Plane crash on Seacrest Drive between Hobart and Macon—"

"*Good Lord*—"

"What?" Rina asked.

Frantically, Decker waved her off.

"Is it Hannah?"

Decker shook his head while trying to digest the captain's words. ". . . took down an apartment building. A few firefighters are already at the scene, but the local units are going to need reinforcements ASAP. All units are being directed to Seacrest and Belarose. We're planning tactical."

"I'm ten minutes away."

"You got a roof light in your vehicle?"

"Yes."

"Use it!" The captain hung up.

"*What?*" Rina was pale.

"Plane crash—"

"Oh my God!" Rina gasped.

"It landed on an apartment—" Decker stopped talking, his ears picking up the wail of the background sirens. He glanced back at the TV screen.

"Where?"

"Seacrest—"

"Where on Seacrest?"

"Between Hobart and Macon."

"Peter, that's about five minutes from Hannah's school!"

"Go get the Volvo. I'll convoy you over with the siren in the unmarked and then go out to the scene."

Rina's eyes were still glued to the TV screen. Unceremoniously, Decker turned it off. "You can listen on the radio. Let's go!"

Rina snapped out of her stupor, realizing the extent of what was to follow. A very long day followed by a very, very long night. She wasn't going to see him for the next twenty-four hours. But unlike the people on the plane, she would see him again. Her heart started racing, her throat clogged up with emotions, but words escaped her.

Once they were outside, she found her voice. "Be careful, Peter."

He nodded, but he wasn't paying attention. He opened the car door for her and she slipped inside. "I love you."

"Love you, too. And yes, I will be careful."

"Thank you. I didn't think you heard me."

"Normally, I probably wouldn't have, but right now I could hear a butterfly. That's what happens when overdrive kicks in. All senses suddenly warp speed to hyperalert."

LIKE MOST PRIVATE schools, Beth Jacob Hebrew Academy High School—grades nine through twelve—had recently flexed its flaccid muscles against its overindulged adolescent inhabitants. Teachers, tired of beeps, whistles, and ring tones interrupting lessons, complained to the administration that in turn passed a *draconian* law—according to fourteen-year-old Hannah Decker—that prohibited the possession of any electronic gadgets, the sole exception being calculators for advanced math. The ordinance had gone into effect three weeks prior—a case of poor timing because with the land phones out, the school was frantically trying to reach parents on the limited cell phones that it had.

Most of the parents had an inkling that something was wrong, so by the time Decker and Rina pulled up, there was already a line of SUVs waiting to haul away the children.

Decker got out of the unmarked and walked over to Rina's Volvo. His nostrils flared at the acrid smell of smoke, his eyes watering from floating ash. He put his hand over his mouth and motioned for her to roll down the window. "How's our food and water supply in the house?"

"You know me. We have enough for the entire neighborhood."

"Good. Go home and don't go out. The air's horrible and is only going to get worse in the afternoon when the winds pick up. Are you going to be okay?"

"Absolutely," Rina said. "Go, Peter. And thanks for getting me here so quickly."

"She's my daughter, too. Give her a kiss and tell her I love her."

"I will."

Decker returned to the unmarked, now sandwiched between Rina's Volvo and a Lincoln Navigator. He turned on the siren, it squawked, and the car behind him gave him an inch of backup room. A minute later, he was on the boulevard, using his wipers to clear white ash from his windshield. Even with the siren, the normally five-minute drive took much longer. All the traffic signals were out and the roadways were clogged with vehicles. Weaving in and out of the tiny spaces allotted to him by his siren, Decker managed to reach ten blocks from the appointed spot before he espied the yellow police barricade tape. Miraculously, he found a parking space that didn't block the street or any driveway. The scorched atmosphere was thick with ash falling like rain. Even with the door closed and the windows up, there was a sickening, permeating stink of jet fuel and molten metal and wood that burned his throat.

As a detective lieutenant, Decker was choosy about his field visits when a crime was called in. But he was always prepared, and that meant he had latex gloves and face masks in the console of his car. He slipped on the mask, wishing he had goggles as he opened the door.

Immediately his face was hit by a heavy slap of hot air. The sky billowed with black smoke and the occasional leap of an orange flame. He showed his badge to a uniform, also wearing a face mask, whose assignment was to patrol the borders of the yellow tape. The kid's eyes were jumpy as Decker stepped over the tape.

God, they made them young these days.

As he edged closer to the disaster, visibility was reduced to soup, the fire's roar pounding in his ears like crashing waves. He could make out a plethora of fire trucks: departments of every stripe had been called down to the scene. There were ambulances of all colors and makes.

Sirens wailed and strobe lights flashed through the misty darkness. Human figures skittered about like gnats.

When he got within a half block of the rendezvous location, he spotted a trio that could have been anyone, but by their height and shape, Decker surmised that they were Marge Dunn, Scott Oliver, and Wanda Bontemps. With every forward step, the stench grew stronger—fuel oil, charred wood, boiling metal. He could barely hear himself think because of the screech of lapping flames, sirens, and human screams. Trained as a medic in Vietnam, Decker had seen destruction and chaos, but none of his war experiences could have prepared him for this.

When he was within striking distance, Decker saw that his identity assumptions had been correct. Marge Dunn, Scott Oliver, and Wanda Bontemps were sweating under protective gear—slicker coats, mouth masks, and goggles. Marge waved Decker over and handed him a slicker and a pair of goggles. She shouted, "Strapp told me to bring these for you."

"Smart thinking," Decker shouted back. "How long have you been here?"

"About three minutes and that's too long," Marge hollered. She was a tall woman but seemed bent over and consumptive under the weight of smoke and a heavy protective coat. Her forehead was soaked and dirty.

Decker said, "Does anyone know what crashed?"

"WestAir out of Burbank," Wanda Bontemps screamed. "A commuter airlines. I heard there were around forty-five aboard?"

"God, that's awful," Decker said. "Terrorism or mechanical failure?"

Shrugs all around. Stupid question. How the hell should they know? His mouth was speaking before the brain kicked in. Decker felt a vibration on his chest. His cell was ringing. He shouted into the receiver. "Scream or I won't be able to hear you."

It was Strapp, and even though the captain was shouting, Decker could barely make out his words. He plugged up his other ear with his finger. "Okay . . . will do . . . I've got it." He returned the cell to his pocket. "He's stuck in traffic from a tactical meeting. First thing we need to do is evacuate the residential area in an orderly fashion. Let's work within a ten-block radius outside the yellow tape line. The fire marshals are clearing the area within the barricades."

Decker managed to extract a notepad from his suit jacket.

"First, let's get the ghouls and the lookie-loos out of here. Wanda, if you take care of that, we get some clear lanes for emergency vehicles. Anyone who doesn't leave immediately is subject to arrest. Marge, you coordinate with traffic. Take a bunch of uniforms, station them at every other intersection, and set up some kind of traffic escape route. Oliver, let's work out an orderly grid of the area. I'll start grabbing as many detectives and officers as I can so we can start knocking on doors."

As expected in the ensuing pandemonium, the biggest problem was cars jamming up the streets. Panicked folk were packing cherished belongings, stuffing their valuables into cars, trucks, and vans. This particular vicinity was a neighborhood of solid homes with dens, big TVs, and lots of electronics. Some of the houses had pools, and decks and barbecues. All of that could be replaced. It was all the silly items abandoned inside that made people weep: the photo albums, vacation souvenirs, the knickknacks, and the curios.

As soon as Oliver got a decent grid map, Decker made his assignments to his waiting detectives, saving the evacuation of the area nearest to the crash for himself. There was a bullhorn on each block telling people that they had to leave their homes now. That was fine for people with cars, but what about those who were without transportation? What about the sick and the elderly?

Decker began to knock on doors.

The first house in his area belonged to a woman with two small children. She was very thin, her dark hair covered with ash, turning it gray. She coughed as she cried, hauling out a brown box filled with items that were obviously important to her. Her two small children were already strapped into car seats.

Decker said, "You must evacuate now. It's not safe for your children and you to breathe in this air."

"I have to lock the door."

"Give the keys to me and get in the car."

The woman complied, slipping into the driver's seat. Decker returned with her keys and helped her back out of her driveway and into a lane of cars.

Banging on the door to the second house, Decker got no response, but he could hear frantic barking. Looking through the cyclone fence that delineated a backyard, he spotted a small ivory-colored toy poodle, forlorn and incarcerated. He opened the gate and picked up the pooch, carrying it to the next house.

That house was occupied by a young Hispanic woman in a maid's uniform and small Caucasian preschoolers. He told her she must leave with the children. "Do you have a car?" Decker asked her in English.

"I try calling Missy. The phone no work."

Decker switched to Spanish. "You have to leave the house. You carry the little girl; I'll get the big one." He hoisted a boy of around four into his arm while holding the crying poodle. "Come on. Let's get out of here."

"What about Missy?" the housekeeper asked frantically.

"Tell your boss that the police made you leave." Decker spied the neighbor across the street loading his family into his van. He darted across the street with the kid and the dog in his arms. He spoke to a man who appeared to be in his forties. "Take the woman and children with you. They're stuck without transportation out of here."

"There's no room," the neighbor said, folding his arms across his chest.

"Then take out the boxes and make room!" Decker shouted.

The man backed down and found room in the car. "Not the dog," the man insisted. "I'm allergic."

Decker didn't press the dog. As he crossed back, he knocked on the hood of a sedan driven by a young mother. Her baby was in the back. She rolled down the window. Decker said, "Can you take the dog? The owners aren't home."

"Is it friendly? I have a baby."

Decker knew the dog was scared and sometimes fearful animals bite. He told the woman he'd try someone else and finally managed to palm off the mutt on a mother with a teenage boy who was home, sick with the flu.

The door-banging on the next three houses went unanswered, but he did rescue another small dog and two cats. He was forced to leave behind several big dogs, trapped inside the houses or behind fences. His main concerns were humans, not animals, but it made him feel sick to leave these poor, pathetic pets. But he—like everyone else—would deal with that later.

His throat was scorched with dry heat, his eyes burning behind the goggles.

The next residence on Decker's list was occupied by a woman carrying suitcases to her car. After giving her orders to leave immediately, he asked her if she could transport the pets he was holding. She agreed without hesitation and left her house, sobbing as she started up her car.

Smoke clouded any remnants of sunshine. The sky was dark charcoal and all Decker could make out were the pinpoint beams of headlights as cars filed out of the neighborhood. Mechanically, he jogged from one house to another, picking up any stray pet he could tote and giving them to the fleeing residents in the area, checking off address after address to make sure that no one was left behind.

An hour into his searching, he knocked on the door of a wood-sided one-story shingle. At first, it appeared that no one was home. But when he knocked again, Decker thought that he might have heard something, a muffled scream or yelp. It could have been animal, it could have been his imagination, but it could have been human. Something in his gut told him to go inside.

Lowering his shoulder, he rammed the door several times until the lock splintered and the door swung open.

The interior of the house was dark clouds of smoke.

"Anyone home here?" he shouted.

The response was a strangled cry: it seemed to be coming from the back. He made his way through the acrid hallway and found an elderly, bedridden, sweat-soaked woman who must have been in her nineties.

It was nothing short of a miracle that she was still breathing. The woman's wheelchair was folded and tucked into the corner. She was trapped and as scared as a treed squirrel.

"Thank God!" the woman mouthed, tears pouring from her eyes.

Decker unfolded the chair, lifted the sticks-and-bones woman from the bed, and eased her into the chair. Her nightgown was wet with sweat, urine, and runny feces. She was shivering even though it was close to a hundred degrees inside. He found a clean blanket and draped it over her skeletal frame. Then he noticed a pharmacy's worth of medication resting on her nightstand and stuffed the vials into his pockets. "Don't worry. I'll get you out of here."

"Thank God!" the woman said again.

As he wheeled her through the smoke-laden living room, he said, "You're all alone here, ma'am?"

"My nurse."

"What about your nurse?"

"We heard a terrible crash . . ." The woman was trembling as if she had palsy. "She said she'd be back for me."

"How long ago was that?"

"A long time . . ."

"Does she have a car?"

"Yes . . . in the driveway."

There wasn't any car in the driveway. The nurse had probably fled as soon as she saw the flames. Decker wheeled the old lady outside, pushed her in her chair for half a block until he found a van stuck in traffic on the road. He knocked on the driver's window and a startled woman looked at him and then quickly away. He knocked again and presented his badge. She rolled down the glass.

"I need you to take this woman out of here. She was abandoned in her house." Decker pulled out the medication from his pockets. "Take these with you."

The woman didn't respond, dulled by panic and fright. Eventually, as Decker kept talking, she comprehended what he was asking her to do. She depressed the unlock button and Decker opened the back door.

He belted the old lady inside next to the woman's five-year-old boy. The child gave the old woman a shy smile and then, in an act of altruism, offered her his lollipop.

The old woman cried. She grabbed on to Decker's hand. "God bless you."

"You, too." He hefted the woman's wheelchair into the back of the van and thanked the driver, who was still too scared and too stunned to respond verbally.

After he had finished his initial list, he moved on to residences that were farther down the road but still very much in the sweep of the firestorm. With all that jet fuel to burn and broken gas lines to feed the inferno, it would be a long, long time before things were under control.

The fire marshals wanted to clear a two-mile radius. A residential area like this one included not only private homes but condos and apartment buildings. That amounted to a lot of people and a lot of cars. Decker regrouped with his detectives and made new assignments.

Hundreds of remaining doors to knock on: the terrified eyes, soot-streaked arms holding boxes, fingers gripping suitcases. Forms flitted from house to house, vehicle to vehicle. Loose animals roamed the streets, crying out with choked and desperate barks, visibility close to nil.

It wasn't hell but it was a good facsimile.

He worked without interruption as the fire burned deep into the night.

2

THE POLICE TOOK eighteen-hour shifts. Somewhere Decker got down enough food to calm his stomach, although he had no memory of eating. The crash information that filtered through to the emergency crews was incomplete and contradictory. With the passing of the first twenty-four hours, no radical terrorist group came forward to take responsibility and that seemed to soothe frazzled nerves. Decker thought it was quite a world when everyone was rooting for mechanical failure. From the eyewitness accounts, it appeared that the plane had been in trouble from takeoff. Ascent was never fully realized, and a few moments later, it nose-dived. No one remembered seeing a midair explosion, and so far, no videos of the crash had surfaced.

Thirty-seven hours after WestAir flight 1324 plummeted into 7624 Seacrest Drive, the fire department declared that the inferno had been contained, although it was far from out. Jet fuel was still stoking the flames, and even in the areas where active fire had died out, there were still flare-ups. It would take days before residents could come home. The Gov had come down, declaring the site a disaster area, making it easier for the surviving residents to get federal aid and loans.

From the snippets of data that went in and out of Decker's ears, he surmised that the casualties numbered around sixty to seventy, of which forty-seven came from the hapless travelers on the plane. Ground casualties were still being assessed.

Decker was dismissed from duty after forty-two straight hours of work. If he drove home, he didn't openly remember operating a vehicle. Nor did he recall seeing his wife and his teenage daughter, or taking a shower. Exhaustion had robbed any recollection of his falling asleep. His first conscious memory was Rina waking him up at nine in the morning. He was confused but not ungrateful. His dreams had been disturbing. He wiped his sweat-soaked face with the sleeve of his pajamas, leaving behind a gray streak of soot.

Rina handed him the phone. "It's Captain Strapp."

Decker took the phone and depressed the hold button. Electricity and phone service had been restored sometime between when he had left and when he had come home.

"We're getting calls, Pete. Family of loved ones that lived in the burnt house or in the area: relatives wanting to know if their kin is alive or dead. I want you to set up a task force and collect as many names as possible. Also, get the dental X-rays so that when the coroner's investigators go in for recovery, we can provide them a list of names and the X-rays for identification. We'll be one step ahead."

Decker understood the words as English, but it took him a few moments to grab the meaning. "Uh . . . do we have a list of the ground deaths?"

Strapp's voice was strained. "Did you just wake up?"

"My wife just woke me up. I've only been home for"—he looked at the clock—"a little under eight hours."

"How long did you work?"

"About forty-two hours."

"Good grief! That's a lot of overtime."

"I suppose it is." Decker hoped he had kept the sarcasm out of his voice.

"In answer to your question, we don't have a list of ground deaths. That's what I want you to work on. I want your task force to contact the families of the suspected ground deaths and gather names. You can act as a liaison between the bereaved families *and* the NTSB *and* the coroner's office. I'm calling for a town-hall meeting to assess what the community needs. The first thing we need to do is to set up a system so that worried families can access information."

Decker's brain was beginning to work. Strapp was spot on target. The charred bodies of the crash belonged to the coroner's office, the wreckage of the plane belonged to the National Transportation and Safety Board, but the community belonged to the police. Working with bereaved families was bound to be a gut-wrenching assignment, meaning it would be a job that he'd do personally.

Another long day.

Strapp was talking. ". . . less immediate note, there have been reports of graffiti and looting in the affected areas. I want those investigated as well."

Decker sat up. "Who's reporting the looting? The residents haven't been allowed back in."

"That's what I want you to find out."

Decker exhaled. "All right. I'll try to make it down in about thirty to forty minutes."

"See you then."

The receiver clicked off. Decker gave his wife the phone. "I've got to take a shower and go to work."

She didn't even bother to protest. "I'll make you breakfast."

"Food . . . that sounds *real* good." Decker swung his legs over the bed, stood up, and stretched his six-foot-four frame. Over the years he had gained a few pounds, topping out around 225, but for a guy in his fifties, he carried his weight well. "Is Hannah in school?"

"School is in the hot zone. It's been temporarily canceled until the board can find facilities where the kids can inhale without clogging their bronchioles with ash. We're going to my parents for Shabbat, by the way. The air isn't pristine over there, but it's a lot better in Beverly Hills than it is here."

"That could apply to a lot of things. That sounds fine. I'd love to see your parents."

"You would?"

Decker smiled. "After witnessing such harrowing events, I look forward to a night with the in-laws and their mundane problems. Besides, your mother is a phenomenal cook."

"That she is."

"What about Cindy and Koby? Weren't they supposed to come over on Saturday?"

"Friday night, actually, and Mama was gracious enough to invite them as well. Hannah, by the way, is thrilled. Not so much because she's going to see her grandparents, but because she gets to see her friends that live in the city for a change."

"It's the age."

"That's true. Hannah lives for her friends. She's either IMing someone or on the phone or doing both at the same time."

"I hope I can make dinner this weekend." Decker kissed his wife on the forehead. "This public servant may be doing overtime for a while. At least it'll mean more cash in the till."

"I'd rather have you." Rina stroked his face and Decker realized how lovely she looked. His hormones shot through his lower body, but it was all for naught. He didn't have the time.

After he showered and dressed, he sat down to pancakes and a cheese omelet. He drank four cups of coffee and two glasses of juice. He could have eaten more but the clock was ticking. When he announced that he had to go, Rina didn't try to hold him back.

"Are you safe behind a wheel?"

"Safe and completely fueled."

"I packed you a lunch while you were showering—four sandwiches and various side dishes. What you can't eat, you can share with your brethren in blue."

"I'm sure they will be grateful for any morsel I throw to them." He kissed his wife chastely on the lips, deciding that this wasn't at all satisfactory. The next kiss was long and deep. "I really do need to retire from my job."

"You keep threatening, but for me it's not a threat. First of all, I love you. Second of all, I've been collecting a list of projects that we've jawed about over the last four years. I'm ready when you're ready."

He knew what she was referring to. They'd conversed endlessly about adding more space to their eighteen-hundred-square-foot home, although the house had been losing occupants rather than gaining them. For the last few months, they'd been cutting out articles in design magazines. Rina's pet project was a sumptuous master bathroom. Decker had been saving articles that dealt with media rooms and home theaters. Everything was still in the dream stage, but it made for interesting reading over the weekend.

Fantasy was the stuff of life.

AT HIS DESK, Decker sorted through the list of names and numbers. "This should keep me busy for a while."

"Why not call a conference for all of them to come in?" Marge asked him.

"Because I think initial contact should be personal. These people lost loved ones in a horrible way. Besides, it shouldn't take me all that long to make the phone calls. As the families start dropping off the dental X-rays, we'll set up a schedule. There needs to be someone manning the desk all the time to deal with the bereaved until we've got all the bodies accounted for."

"I can do that."

"We should also contact several professionals who can offer support."

"I'll call social services and see what they can do for us."

"Great." Decker regarded his favorite detective—over forty and young at heart. They had worked together for over twenty years. As bedraggled as he felt, she looked fresh and alert. "How many hours of sleep did you get?"

"About five. Why? Do I look that bad?"

"On the contrary, you look chipper."

"It's the coral blouse," Marge told him. "All women look good in coral."

"What about men?"

"Men should wear black. It makes them look mysterious. In your case, Pete, black would set off your red hair very nicely."

"It's more gray than red," Decker grumped.

"It's still has plenty of red in it. So does your mustache. And you've got a lot of it . . . head hair. What you really need to look hip is a soul patch."

"I'm beyond trying to look hip. All I want is to look appropriate so I don't embarrass my teenage daughter."

"I thought that was the purpose of parents of teenagers, to embarrass them."

She had a definite point. Nothing was as much fun as to see his kids squirm at his misbehaviors. "So what's going on with the graffiti and the looting?"

"We've gotten calls about homes being tagged."

"How did that happen with units patrolling the area twenty-four/ seven?"

"The taggers are wily guys. They're also not afraid of heights. We found signatures on the 405 Freeway overpass, and a couple of twenty-foot-high billboards. There's also one on the top of the Parker/Doddard building, which has to be seven stories high."

"Criminal Sherpas. Send them out to Everest where they can do some good."

"I don't think we'd like to see their signature in the snow, especially if we think what they might use to write with."

Decker let go with a deep laugh. It felt good. "Not a pretty image. So what's going on with the looting? Who's reporting the activity?"

"Anonymous phone calls." Marge laughed. "Since the residents aren't back in the area to substantiate the claims, I'm thinking that may be thieves reporting on other thieves."

"Any arrests?"

"A few for burglary, but that hasn't deterred the felons. You know how it is, Loo. If houses are left unattended, crime is going to happen even with a strong police presence. The bad boys love to take chances. It's like the tented houses when the owner fumigates for termites. There are always one or two yutzes who think they can beat the system and make it out before poisonous gas renders them unconscious."

"How many looting complaints have been called in?"

"About a dozen."

"Okay. Assign someone to call up the owners of the looted houses and have someone meet them there. Do a quick search inside to see if something is missing. That way if something has been stolen, they can contact their insurance agency right away."

"I'll get to it right away."

"Thanks, Marge."

"Leave the door open?"

"Absolutely."

After she left, Decker looked around his private space. It was small, with used furniture, but it had walls that reached the ceiling and a door that made it an office as opposed to a cubicle. He was even lucky enough to have an outside window, although it didn't open. It wasn't big, but it usually let in enough light to add a pinch of cheer. Today the sash framed a gunmetal-gray sky. Ash had collected on the sill. He ran his hands through his gray-yet-still-red-according-to-Marge hair. He was still tired, but didn't dare bitch about it, not when he looked down at all the message slips.

His fingers dialed the first number. A young male voice answered the call. Decker introduced himself and asked for Estelle Greenberg. The voice told him to hold on a second and then it called out, "Ma, police are on the phone."

The woman who came on the line spoke before he uttered a word. "You found her!"

"Mrs. Greenberg, this Lieutenant Peter Decker of the Los Angeles Police—"

"Yes, yes . . . did you find my daughter?"

"And your daughter is . . ."

"Oh, for heaven's sake! Why are you calling me if you don't even know why I called?"

So much displaced anger. Decker rode with it. "I was just given a message. I'm sorry to upset you. Believe me, that isn't my intention."

"Did you find my daughter?" She was yelling over the phone.

"We haven't recovered any bodies from the affected area," Decker explained. "It's just too hot and dangerous to search."

"Then why are you wasting my time?" The fury in her voice barely overlay her desperation.

"First of all, I want to tell you how sorry I am. Second, I want to explain why I called you. I'm trying to gather information so that when the investigators do go into the area, they'll know who they're looking for. From this conversation, am I correct in assuming that your daughter lived in the affected building?"

The answer didn't come right away. When it did, it was laced with tears. "Yes."

"All right. May I please have her name?"

"Delia Greenberg. Apartment 3C."

"I know the next couple of questions are going to sound moronic and insensitive, but I have to ask them anyway. So please forgive me if I upset you. I take it you haven't heard from Delia since the incident."

"No."

"Does she have a cell phone?"

"I tried it a thousand times . . ." She was weeping. "It goes directly to her voice mail."

"Okay. Did Delia live with anyone?"

"Alone."

"So there was no one with her when it happened?"

"I don't know! There might have been. She had friends stay over sometimes."

"All right. Do you have any names, perhaps?"

"I don't know! I can't think right now!"

"You're really helping me a lot, Mrs. Greenberg. Thank you for talking to me. One more thing regarding Delia. Do you think that you could obtain a copy of her dental records for identification purposes?"

The request was met with a long, long pause. "Probably," she whispered.

"They can be sent directly to me or you can bring them in person. You are welcome to come in to the station house at any time or any hour and talk to one of us. There will always be someone here who'll be familiar with your situation. I'm going to give you my cell number. Feel free to call it at any time."

"Thank you," she said without emotion.

Decker rattled off several sets of numbers. Whether the woman was writing any of it down was anyone's guess. "Is there anything you want to ask me?"

"Who am I talking to again?"

"Lieutenant Peter Decker."

"You're a lieutenant?"

"Yes, ma'am."

"Your captain couldn't have given me a call?"

"He'd be happy to call you, Mrs. Greenberg."

"But he didn't. You did."

"Yes. If you want to set up an appointment with Captain Strapp—"

"Why should I want to set up an appointment if the man doesn't have the decency to call me?" She was sobbing. "When do you want the X-rays?"

"How about if I come to your house and we'll go to the dentist together?"

The woman didn't answer. All Decker heard was weeping. Then she said, "All right. Do you know where I live?"

"No, but I can take down an address."

"I don't live so close to my daughter. She wanted her privacy. I'm all the way in the city."

"I have a car, I can drive. What's the address?"

She gave him the street address. "When can you come?"

"How about tomorrow morning around eleven?"

"Eleven would be all right. What do you look like?"

"I'm very tall and have red hair." *That's turning gray very quickly.* "I'll show you ID at your door. I'll see you tomorrow."

"Thank you, Lieutenant. I know you're trying to be nice. It's just ..."

She was crying again. Decker could have said, "I know ..." Decker could have said, "I understand." But he didn't know and he didn't understand.

Thank God.

3

$\jmath\ell$

I T WAS A hard time for the West San Fernando Valley. Even the
news that the crash had likely been caused by mechanical failure
didn't stave off the increase in emergency calls, of reported heart attacks, asthma attacks, and fainting spells.

The week of the crash, Decker had worked on casino time, never
seeing the light of day, never knowing what time it was. He never made
it to Rina's parents' for Friday-night dinner, nor did he make it over the
hill for Shabbat Saturday lunch. There was just too much to do. He did
manage to cram in a phone call to his married daughter. Cindy was a
grand-theft-auto detective over the hill in Hollywood, and had been
doing double duty because so many of the uniformed officers had been
diverted to the crash area.

But all things must pass, and eventually the terrible incident that
had grabbed headlines in the local papers for two weeks running became old news. Coverage faded and fell to page three, then to page five,
then to the back of the front section. Eventually it was relegated to local
news until it became yesterday's news. With the coroner's investigators

working nonstop on the body recoveries, and the NTSB working nonstop on plane and fuselage recovery, the police were permitted to go back to doing police work.

No one would have definitive answers for many months. Maybe it would even be years before the total puzzle was put back together. The nature of the beast required time and patience. Rina had told him that immediately after the crash, people in the area had seemed to move a bit slower, taking more time to smile and say hello. Traffic had been sparser and much more polite. And despite the initial looting and break-ins that had happened directly after the crash, overall monthly crime had actually taken a drop.

A temporary aberration it seemed, because the statisticians reported that the following month, life and crime in the San Fernando Valley had returned to their precrash status.

FORTY-SIX DAYS AFTER the crash, as Decker was looking over the upcoming court cases of his detectives, his extension rang. It was Marissa Kornblatt, one of the three department secretaries who manned the front desk for the squad room. Over the intercom, her voice sounded tentative.

"Excuse me, Lieutenant. I have someone on the line who is demanding to speak to the head honcho."

"Head honcho?"

"His words, Lieutenant, not mine. His name is Farley Lodestone, and as far as I could make out, he's ranting about his missing daughter."

"How old is his daughter?"

"Twenty-eight."

"Twenty-eight?"

"I told him our standard policy is thirty-six hours before we file a report, but then he said he's been waiting over a month and he has had enough."

The man sounded like a nutcase. Decker said, "Why don't you patch the call to Matt Thurgood and have him take a missing-persons report—"

"Lieutenant, Mr. Lodestone is screaming that it's a homicide. I don't think he's going to be happy with an MP report . . . sir."

"I'll take it." Decker punched the blinking light. "Lieutenant Decker."

"Lieutenant?" The voice was surprised. "Finally! Now we're getting somewhere! You know how many phone calls I've made over the last few days?"

"How can I help you, sir?"

"Farley Lodestone is the name and you certainly can help me, Lieutenant Deckman. My stepdaughter's missing. Me and her mom haven't heard from her in forty-six days. We thought about it and thought about it and came to the same conclusion. That sumbitch husband of hers finally went out and did it."

"Did it?"

"You know what I mean, Deckman. The sumbitch finally *killed* her!"

Decker looked at the phone monitor and took down the calling number. It appeared to be a cell phone and was from an out-of-the-city area code. "Mr. Lodestone, why don't you come in to the station house and we can talk about this? Things that are this serious shouldn't be discussed over the phone."

There was a long pause. "You think so?"

"Yes, sir, I do. I could see you in about an hour. How does that sound?"

"Too quick! It'll take time for me and the missus to get over there."

"Where are you calling from, Mr. Lodestone?"

"Fresno."

One hundred and eighty-six miles away as the crow flies. "And you're calling this station house because your stepdaughter lives in this area?"

"Two-three-one-one-six Octavia Avenue. That's where you'll find the sumbitch."

"And who is this sumbitch?"

"Ivan Dresden. He's a broker for Merrill Lynch in Porter Ranch. My stepdaughter's name is Roseanne. Roseanne Dresden."

Decker tucked the receiver under his chin as he wrote it down. As he saw Roseanne's name in print, he realized he wasn't reading it for the first time. "Her name is familiar. Would there be any reason that I might know her?"

"Well, you mighta probably read her name in the papers saying she was on that WestAir flight that crashed down on the apartment building."

That was it! Decker's mind was racing, trying to understand the purpose of the call. "Mr. Lodestone, are you saying that your stepdaughter wasn't on that WestAir flight?"

"That's exactly what I'm saying."

"But the papers reported her as one of the victims."

"Young man, I'm sure someone somewhere musta told you that you should never believe what you read in the papers."

THEY MATERIALIZED AT the station house at ten minutes to five in the afternoon. Farley and Shareen Lodestone were dressed in their Sunday finest, the man in a decently fitting gray suit with a white shirt and a tie, and Shareen in a flowered dress and low heels. She had taken the time to put on rouge and lipstick. Blond and blue-eyed, with good skin, at one time the woman had been attractive, but grief had deepened her eyes and depressed their light, giving her face a beetle brow.

Farley was thin and of average height with a mop of white hair. Yet Decker had seen enough of these guys to know that they were deceptively strong and wiry. He knew that beneath that jacket and shirt were some stringy arms with good grip strength. The man looked more mad than upset, but that was often a man's way of coping with heartache.

Decker got them both cups of coffee and settled them into two seats opposite his desk. After closing the door, he sat down and took out a notepad, although he suspected that what they were going to tell him was a case of extreme denial. He said, "Before we get started, Mr. and

Mrs. Lodestone, I want to express my condolences. I am very sorry for your loss."

"Yeah, I am, too," Lodestone grunted out. "So if you want to help, you'll put that sumbitch behind bars."

"I always had a queasy feeling about him," Shareen added.

"Him . . . meaning your son-in-law?"

"That's right," Shareen said. "Ivan Dresden."

Decker wrote down the name. "And you suspect . . . what?"

"That Ivan killed her."

"Didn't I already tell you that?" Lodestone butted in.

"Yes, you did." Decker paused. "Before you came in, I called up WestAir. They verified that Roseanne had been on the flight."

"Yeah, verified in what way?" Lodestone said. "They haven't found her body."

"They haven't finished all the recovery, Mr. Lodestone."

"They finished most of it," Shareen added. "They got thirty-eight so far."

"Then maybe we should wait until they have all forty-seven."

"They aren't gonna find forty-seven bodies, Lieutenant," Farley said. "Besides, it don't matter if they do find everyone on the passenger list because WestAir didn't issue her a ticket."

That threw Decker momentarily off guard. "They didn't?"

"No, they didn't!" Farley said triumphantly. "So how the hell did they know she was on the flight?"

Decker didn't answer. He wrote down *no ticket?* while stalling for time.

Shareen rescued him. "Let me start from the beginning, Lieutenant. Roseanne was a flight attendant for WestAir. After the crash, when we couldn't get hold of Roseanne, we called up the airlines. But WestAir told us she wasn't working on flight 1324. Then the company called us up a couple of days later and backtracked. No, she wasn't working 1324, but she was on the plane, hopping a ride to San Jose to work the route up there for a couple of nights . . . which is why they claimed they didn't issue her a ticket."

"Wait a minute." Decker started to take notes in earnest. "I thought every passenger who flew on an airline had to be issued a ticket."

"That's what I thought," Shareen said. "But I was wrong. This was told to me by one of Roseanne's friends, so I hope I'm getting this right." She took a deep breath. "Okay. Here we go. I think if you work for the airlines and you're flying to work at a destination, you don't have to be issued a ticket even if you're not working the flight."

Decker nodded. "So it was possible for her to be on the flight and for the airlines not to have a record of it. But then they'd have a record of the assignment, wouldn't they?"

"They should have a record," Shareen said. "But they're not telling me yes, they have one, or no, they don't have one."

"Right now they're not saying nothing without their lawyer," Lodestone said.

Shareen said, "Roseanne used to work San Jose. So I figure that maybe WestAir was shorthanded in San Jose. So I called up San Jose, and asked if Roseanne was scheduled to work some routes up there. First they tell me no, then they tell me yes, then they tell me that if I want to talk to them again, they'll put me in contact with their attorneys."

"Same old, same old," Lodestone said.

Shareen patted her husband's knee. "Their hemming and hawing was making us very suspicious."

Decker nodded. It did sound funny on the surface, but the airline was probably in disarray.

"I talked to Ivan," Shareen said. "I just didn't like what he told me."

"What did he tell you?"

"That at the last minute, Roseanne changed her plans to work in San Jose. He told me emphatically that she was on the plane and he was upset enough without me making up stories about her not being on the plane. Then he said, in the long run, we were hurting not helping and that he and several other people had lawsuits pending, so we should kindly shut up."

"He told you to shut up?"

"Not in those exact words, but that's what he said between the lines. Then he told me I was in denial." The old woman's eyes watered. "I'm not in denial, Lieutenant. I know in my heart of hearts that Roseanne is dead. I just don't think it was the crash that killed her."

"You said Roseanne had worked San Jose before," Decker said. "Could she have gone up to San Jose to visit someone?"

"Who, sir?" Lodestone said. "She's married."

"I was thinking about a friend."

Shareen said, "If she was hitching a ride to visit someone, then WestAir would have had to issue her a ticket. The only way she could have boarded the plane without a ticket is if she was working the flight—which WestAir admitted to me that she wasn't."

"But then they backtracked," Decker said.

"They're lying," Lodestone insisted. "They haven't found her body! You know why they haven't found her body? 'Cause it isn't there. If that isn't proof enough of something's wrong, then I don't know what is."

"Mr. Lodestone, I don't want to sound like a broken record, but neither the coroner's office nor the NTSB has claimed to recover all the bodies. And even with those that they have recovered, it takes time to do positive identification."

"Lieutenant, I talked to the sumbitch and asked him point blank why they haven't dug up her body. You know what the sumbitch told me?"

"No, Mr. Lodestone, what did he tell you?"

"That they just didn't dig deep enough. Can you believe that?"

Maybe it was true. Piles of debris still hampered much of the recovery operations. Still, it was a strange remark. Decker nodded sympathetically.

"Does that sound like a grieving husband to you?" Lodestone asked him.

It didn't, but Decker had stopped trying to pigeonhole grief long ago.

Shareen said, "The only reason that Roseanne's name is on the list is because Ivan Dresden called the newspapers and told them to put her down on the list."

Decker didn't like the sound of that. "Are you certain about that?"

Shareen backed down. "Well, that's what I think."

Lodestone said, "When he found out about the plane crash, he finally found a way to kill her and hide it. You know, I wouldn't be surprised if he blew up the plane on purpose."

Decker had heard people say outlandish things when upset, so his accusations fell on deaf ears. None of the vehemence surprised him, although the intricacy of the fabrication that they had created to explain their daughter's death was beyond the pale. "Has Ivan Dresden ever threatened your daughter before?"

"He was having an affair." Shareen had neatly sidestepped the question. "She was going to divorce him."

"The condo's in her name," Lodestone told him. "I helped her buy it. He was gonna lose everything if the divorce went through."

"And what did he do for a living again?" Decker asked. "Something with finance?"

"Broker for Merrill Lynch. That's a fancy title for a salesman."

"And what do you do, Mr. Lodestone?"

"Hardware . . . three stores and every single one of 'em is profitable." A smile bisected his face. "Used to bother Mr. High and Mighty that I make more money with my nails and screws than he does with his fancy stocks and bonds."

Shareen said, "No one has seen or heard from Roseanne since the crash, Lieutenant."

That's because she has disintegrated into dust. There was denial and there was this kind of denial, people so horrified and filled with rage that they actively hunted for an object to absorb their venom. Their anger was so encompassing that it blocked out not only the anguish, but also reason.

Decker said, "And you're *sure* that she wasn't on the airplane?"

"I called up a few of her friends," Shareen responded. "No one remembers anything about Roseanne working San Jose."

"Can you tell me the names of the friends you talked to, Mrs. Lodestone?"

"Certainly." She picked up a purse and opened it. "I have a list in my handbag."

Lodestone clapped his hands. "Now we're getting somewhere."

Decker held out his palm to slow the old man down. "One step at a time." After Shareen handed him the list, he took a moment to look over the names. "And this is everyone you've talked to?"

"Yes, sir, and the addresses and phone numbers are current."

An efficient woman. "Well, I suppose this is as good a place to start as any."

Moisture in the woman's eyes ran over the lower lids and down her cheeks. "Thank you, Lieutenant, for taking us seriously."

Decker patted her hand. "In return, I want you to do me a favor, Mr. and Mrs. Lodestone. After investigating these leads, if I feel that Roseanne was definitely on that plane, I'd like you to understand when I say that I can't do any more."

"Fair enough," Lodestone answered. "What are you gonna do besides call up those people on Shareen's list?"

"I've got a few options."

"Like what?" Lodestone pushed.

"I'll talk to the airlines . . . talk to the flight attendants who worked the desk to see if anyone remembers seeing Roseanne board the flight."

"That's good because we tried doing that," Lodestone said. "WestAir wouldn't return our phone calls."

Shareen said, "If you could push them hard enough, I'd bet my bottom dollar that you'll find out she wasn't scheduled to work San Jose."

"Maybe it was a last-minute change in schedule."

"I don't think so. There's something fishy going on and WestAir isn't talking."

"I'm sure they're worried about lawsuits," Decker said.

"They should be worried," Lodestone told him. "If my plane crashed and killed a bunch of people, I'd be worried, too. They can be worried all they want, but they don't have to worry about a lawsuit from us 'cause they didn't kill Rosie. That sumbitch did it and that's all I have to say."

4

THE NEXT MORNING, Decker called in Marge Dunn. She had just come back from a spirited weekend with a man she had declared to be a keeper. Will Barnes was in his late fifties—a detective out of Berkeley who was divorced with no children, but got along well with Marge's adopted daughter, Vega, now a young adult studying astrophysics at Caltech. For the last six months, Barnes and Dunn had seemed perfectly content with a long-distance relationship. As of a couple of weeks ago, Barnes was telling Marge about an opening in the Santa Barbara Police Department—less pay but about two hundred miles closer to L.A. That meant the relationship would be within commuting distance.

As Decker related his conversation with the Lodestones, Marge nodded in the appropriate places. Today, she had donned a white shirt, olive slacks, and a brown jacket. The neutral coloring would have normally washed out her complexion, but her skin glowed with a deep weekend tan. Her brown eyes sparkled with *love*.

At the end of the tale, Decker raked his hair and took a sip of water, giving her a moment to absorb everything. As he was summing up the story, he realized how weird the Lodestones' accusations had been. "Pretty bizarre."

Marge raised an eyebrow. "Beyond bizarre, Pete. I'd say we're into the realm of fiction." She flipped through her notebook. "So let me make sure I have this one down correctly. Roseanne Dresden was a flight attendant for WestAir."

"Yes."

"Her husband claimed that Roseanne had made a last-minute schedule change that put her on the doomed WestAir flight 1324."

"Yes."

"She was not working flight 1324 but was en route to San Jose to work some WestAir flights up north."

"Yes."

"Therefore, because she was on a flight for work, she was not issued a ticket."

"Yes."

"Now her stepfather and her mother are insisting that Roseanne's husband, Ivan . . . as in Ivan the Terrible . . . heard about the crash, and suddenly decided that this presented an opportune time to kill his wife."

"Yes. She was contemplating divorce and he stood to lose financially, according to Farley Lodestone."

"The stepfather who owns three hardware stores."

"And every single one of them makes money."

Marge continued: "So Ivan killed Roseanne once he heard about the crash. Then he called up the newspapers and told them that Roseanne had been on the ill-fated flight, and that her name should be added to the list of crash victims."

"That about sums it up."

"And so far, her body has not been recovered."

"Farley Lodestone made a point of telling me that three times," Decker said.

"Yes. But as of this morning, there are still bodies that have not been accounted for. So why don't we wait until the recovery operation is complete?"

"Lodestone is tired of waiting."

"And we have to capitulate to this man, who probably harbors some irrational grudge against his son-in-law?"

Decker shrugged.

"May I ask why?"

"You may and I will try to answer you because I've thought about it myself. If it were just Farley's accusation, I wouldn't bother. But there's something earnest about the mother, Shareen. She knows that Roseanne is dead, so she's not in denial. I know the smartest thing to do is to stall them until the body is recovered, but these folks are suffering. If months go by and recovery doesn't locate Roseanne, we're just that much further away from what actually happened. Things get lost, people move away. If it is a homicide, it would be good to have a jump start."

"If."

"I know. The big *if*."

Marge smiled. "What do you want me to do, Rabbi?"

"Make a couple of calls to WestAir. See if you can't get some written confirmation that Roseanne was actually on the flight—a computer printout that showed Roseanne's work schedule, a memo or a slip of paper: anything that puts Roseanne working in San Jose. The Lodestones were trying to do that on their own, but right now WestAir isn't directly talking to any of the families."

"Probably worried about lawsuits."

"That and also busy trying to figure out what went wrong. If we could find the assignment sheet, maybe we could give the parents some peace of mind."

"And what if there's no written record of a schedule change?"

"There has to be, Marge. She couldn't just show up in uniform and hop a plane."

"Why not?"

Decker sighed. "Well, maybe she could do it, but why would she do it?"

Marge conceded the point. Roseanne must have gotten the assignment and there must be a record of it. "All right. I have some time in the afternoon. I'll make a few phone calls."

"Thanks."

"If the airline refuses to cooperate, is there anyone else I can talk to who might verify Ivan the Terrible's account of what happened to his wife?"

"As a matter of fact . . ." Decker pulled out the list that Shareen Lodestone had given her. "What I have is a list of FORs—friends of Roseanne. For what it's worth, they told Shareen Lodestone that Ivan the Terrible's version of what happened was pure horseshit."

"Have *you* called anyone?"

"No. I am the lieutenant. You are the sergeant." He handed her the list. "Now, as the sergeant, you may assign this task to someone else."

"Who do you have in mind?"

"You choose."

Marge stepped outside Decker's office and looked around the squad room. Most of the detectives were already in the field and the few who were loitering around their desks were making a good pretense of looking busy.

All except Scott Oliver.

The thirty-year veteran detective was busy cleaning his nails. He had obviously showered this morning because his face was shaved pink and baby smooth. His black hair was combed straight back and kept in place by gel. His clothes were meticulous: a gray linen suit, a starch-pressed white shirt and a cherry-red tie, with lizard-skin loafers on his feet.

But somehow, even with all that morning grooming, he had missed his nails.

She walked over to his desk.

"I see you're busy," she told him.

"*Qué pasa?*" he asked without looking up.

"I have an assignment for you."

"Hit it, babe."

"You can either call a list of people or you can call up WestAir and deal with bureaucracy."

Oliver looked up and frowned. "How many people on the list?"

"Around eight."

He took the list and scanned the names. "Info, please?"

"A flight attendant named Roseanne Dresden was listed as one of the people who died on WestAir 1324. Her parents think she wasn't on the flight, but instead was murdered opportunistically by her husband, Ivan, who then called in her death to the newspapers, saying that she had a last-minute schedule change and was on the flight."

Oliver stopped filing his nails, his eyes dazed. "What?"

"You want to take out a notepad, Scotty. It might help your aging memory."

As Oliver put away the manicure set, Marge explained the Lodestones' theories. When she was done with them, she realized that the story still sounded absurd. "Look, what would help close this out is finding someone who saw Roseanne board the flight or an official work order that says that Roseanne had flown up on 1324. Because she wasn't issued a ticket."

"She wasn't?"

"No. If you're a flight attendant and you're working the flight, or you're on your way to work a flight, you don't have to be issued a ticket. I'm thinking that it shouldn't take more than an hour to clear up this mess and give the parents some peace of mind."

"You think this won't take more than an hour? Can I quote you on that, Dunn?"

"No, you may not quote me on that, Oliver, because I've been fooled before."

PHONE CALLS TO the airlines went nowhere. Marge went from one division to another with no one anxious to talk to her, let alone give her any information.

"I can't help you with that. Let me try another department."

"I think we have a task force dealing with the crash. I'll transfer you there."

"I have no way of knowing that. You might want to call up human resources."

"I wouldn't have that information. You'll have to call up Burbank."

"Sorry, I can't give you that information without a written request from the employee."

"The employee is dead," Marge told her.

"Then I'll need a written request from the next of kin."

Next of kin was Ivan Dresden, who, in Marge's opinion, might not be inclined to give written consent.

She was spinning her wheels and that was the problem with the phone. It was hard to be charming and disarming without the visuals. She hung up the receiver and went over to Oliver's desk.

"How's it going with the list?"

"They're at work, Dunn. I left messages and kept them vague. If they have something illuminating to tell me about Ivan the Terrible, I don't want to scare them off. Furthermore, I don't want it to get back to the husband that we're looking into his wife's death. I would surmise that such action would displease him. How's it coming with you and WestAir?"

"The phone is good for some things, but not so hot for others. How would you like to come with me and pay a visit to WestAir?"

"And what makes you think that the company will talk to us?"

"Our gold shields. They're very shiny."

"Where are the offices?"

"Burbank." Marge checked her watch. "We can grab some lunch then attempt to wade through the corporate morass. I have a few names. By the way, the women I spoke with over the phone *sounded* young and beautiful."

"Sure, dangle that carrot in front of me." But Oliver was already on his feet, straightening his tie. "What the heck. I'm kind of hungry anyway."

———

THE BOB HOPE Airport—formerly Hollywood-Burbank—was one of those smaller, suburban airfields that attempted to drain air traffic from LAX. Originally associated with Lockheed, the Hollywood-Burbank/Bob Hope was a convenient locale for the residents of the San Fernando Valley. The field was way more Burbank than Hollywood. For years, Burbank's biggest claim to fame was NBC studios. Recently, the city had been trying to gentrify, with boutique theaters, funky vintage clothing shops, café restaurants, and tree-lined jogging paths. But the strip malls still abounded. So did the car dealerships, the outlets, and the cheap electronic wholesalers dealing out of storefronts.

Turning onto Hollywood Way, Oliver and Marge passed several business hotels, several franchise restaurants, and a business park of soulless glass structures—all windows but very little light. WestAir corporate offices were located in a bank building on the fifth floor. There was an adjacent parking lot for the structure and Oliver chose to park on the top level, even though there were plenty of spaces on the other three tiers. This was his usual habit. His rationale was that if the big earthquake should hit and the parking structure pancaked, his car, sitting on the top level, would stand a better chance of surviving.

Just as Marge pushed the elevator button, her cell rang. She looked at the phone's window and the number staring back startled her.

It was Vega's cell.

Vega, now living in one of Caltech's dorms, called every night precisely at eight o'clock, come hell or high water. It didn't matter where she was and it never mattered where Marge was. Vega called at eight because Marge had asked her to call every day. Not necessarily at eight o'clock, but that was Vega—a rule and a schedule for everything.

So her calling now signaled an emergency.

"I've got to take this," Marge said.

Over the line, Vega's voice was panicked.

"Oh, Mother Marge, I am so sorry to be bothering you. This is going to sound very silly, but I don't know what to do."

"Tell me, honey."

"Mother Marge, I work with a man named Joshua Wong. He's in my particles class. He's a very nice man." She took a deep breath. "He asked me to come with him to a *party* tonight. I was so shocked that I said yes."

A grin stretched Marge's mouth. "Honey, that's *wonderful*."

"Mother Marge, I don't know what to do."

"Just have a good time, Vega."

"I don't know how to have a good time. I don't even know what a good time is."

Her voice was one step away from tears. Marge knew her daughter's radical statements were completely true. Vega had grown up in a cult: all work and absolutely no play. When the cult was raided and destroyed, the teen had been left an orphan. Marge had taken her in and they had developed a special relationship. Most definitely, the girl knew how to love, but no matter how much Marge tried, the kid was socially blunted.

"I don't know how to act at a party. I don't know what to say. Joshua is going to think that I'm stupid."

"That's not possible."

"What do I say, Mother Marge? I am so sick and dizzy about this that I can't work. I'm afraid to go but I'm also afraid to cancel. I like Joshua. I don't want him to hate me."

"First of all, no one could hate you." She looked up and Oliver was making fake yawns. She glared at him. Then she took a deep breath.

Talk to Vega in a language she can understand.

"Are you in front of your computer?"

"I have my laptop, as always."

"Okay. I'm going to give you some instructions. Write them down."

"Right away, Mother Marge, I'm ready."

Her voice had perked up at the sound of an assignment. "Clothing. Go out and buy a nice pair of black slacks and a black top. No turtleneck, Vega, make it a scoop neck."

"Long- or short-sleeved?"

"Either one. Shoes can be anything black. I'd wear your combat boots. That would show that you're not afraid to be an individual."

"Okay, but they're dirty. I'll polish them. What else?"

"Do you still have that gold necklace I gave you?"

"Of course. I treasure it."

"Don't treasure it, wear it."

"I will do that."

"Fine. Do you have any perfume, Vega?"

"No."

"Go buy some . . . wait, not perfume. Eau de cologne. It's cheaper."

"What kind?"

"Uh . . . any kind that smells good." She glanced at Oliver, who was tapping his watch. "Now, instructions for the party. Listen closely."

"I am listening."

"Good. If you ask people questions and look like you're interested in their answers, people will talk to you. People love to talk about themselves."

"But what if they ask me a question, Mother Marge? That's what I'm afraid of. Or rather . . . that's of what I am afraid."

Marge sighed. She'd been taught the king's English and that made her weird. "Vega, if they ask about your background, tell them you were adopted at a young age by a single mother who was a cop. Usually, the word *cop* shuts people up. Do *not* tell them about the cult and Father Jupiter. If you do, they will ask you many, many questions, Vega. You don't want that."

"Yes, you're right."

"Sweetheart, just be your own sweet self. Talk about the weather, talk about politics, talk about your work. It's a party of Caltech people, right?"

"Yes."

"Then I'm sure you'll know some of the people and I bet quite a few will have some understanding of astrophysics and your current research."

"I can ask them about their research?"

"Absolutely."

A big sigh. "All right. I'm going to do this, Mother Marge. Where should I buy the clothing? Is the Gap suitable?"

"Yes, the Gap is fine."

"Good." Another exhalation. "Thank you so much. I feel so much better. My stomach pains are gone. I love you, Mother Marge."

"I love you, too. Let me know how it goes."

"Of course. I'll call you at eight o'clock tonight."

"Sweetheart, if you're in the middle of the party, you don't have to call me."

"No, I will call you. If I don't, I will be very anxious."

"Then I'll be waiting for your call. Now go shop."

"Yes. Thank you. Good-bye."

"Bye, honey." She stowed the cell in her pocket. "Let's go."

"Some geek asked her out?"

"Some smart person asked her out," Marge corrected.

"Is she freaking out?"

"Vega never freaks out. But she is a little nervous."

"How old is she?"

"In her twenties." She glared at Oliver. "No wiseacre comments, please. Just be happy for her, okay?"

Oliver looped his arm around Marge. "I am happy for her. And I'm happy for you. It's going to be fine."

"I sure hope so. I just want her to be happy. I want her to have a nice, normal social experience. God, I hope it goes well and he's not a jerk."

"I'm sure he's a very nice young man. And even if he is a jerk, that's part of the experience, too, right?"

"I suppose so." She smiled at him. "Yeah, you're right. I can't protect her anymore. She's an adult."

"Exactly. Now take a deep breath and please stop biting your nails. We have to con an airline into thinking we're important."

5

AT THE RECEPTION desk, a twentysomething, exotic-looking woman of mixed race scrutinized the badges presented to her while ignoring the ringing phone lines. She peeled her eyes away from the shields, looking up at their faces, then flipped a sheet of black hair over her shoulders and checked her log. "And your appointment is with . . ."

Oliver said, "It's not down there?"

"I don't see it." Exotic Woman shook her head. "Hold on a moment." She pushed a button. "WestAir. How may I direct your call? One moment." She depressed a buzzer and mumbled softly into her headset. Then she looked at Oliver.

"Who was your appointment with?"

"Jeez, I forgot the name." Oliver tapped his forehead. "Someone in human resources. If you name a couple of names, I'm sure I could recognize—"

"The director is Melvin O'Leary and he's not in right now." Down went another blinking button. "WestAir. How may I direct your call?"

Marge spoke up. "Someone must be working in human resources. Can you give the department a call and tell them that Detectives Dunn and Oliver are here?"

"In a minute." Another line. "WestAir. How may I direct your call?"

"Hey!" Marge shouted.

Shocked brown eyes beelined toward her face. *"Excuse me?"*

"We're investigating a homicide, ma'am, and *you're* impeding it! Do you want to help us out or do you want to cause WestAir more bad publicity?"

Pissed but nonetheless chastised, Twentysomething regarded a directory. "I'll see if Nancy Pratt is able to help you."

"Thank you."

She shoved down a button and asked for Ms. Pratt. When she spoke into her headset, her voice was barely above a whisper. She regarded Oliver, not daring to make eye contact with Marge. "Your names, please?"

Marge reiterated slowly, "Homicide Detectives Dunn and Oliver."

"Thank you." Mumbling into the headset. "Ms. Pratt will be with you in just a moment. You can take a seat." Back to her phone lines. "WestAir, how may I direct your call?"

The two detectives sat on sling-back chairs. Oliver leaned over and whispered, "What's the game plan?"

"Maybe Pratt can direct us to the right department."

"Hope so. Be nice to get Dresden's work schedule and be done with this silly case. It's a waste of our time."

"I agree."

"So why are we doing this?"

"I think Decker felt sorry for the parents and the story had just enough intrigue that he wants to make sure that she was on the plane."

"Is there any doubt?"

"Oliver, it doesn't pay to get ahead of ourselves." At the sound of heels clicking onto the floor, Marge looked down the long hallway to see a woman approaching. Tall and big-boned, with clipped blond hair, she appeared to be in her forties and wore a black suit, white shirt, and sensible pumps. The two detectives stood, and when she was within greeting distance, she held out her hand. "Nancy Pratt. Elizabeth tells me you're from homicide."

"Yes, ma'am, we are." Marge introduced the two of them. "Is there a place we can talk privately?"

"Absolutely. Come this way." She led them down a black granite corridor, and opened a door that connected to another hallway, except this one had Berber carpeting. The foyer had cubicles on one side and offices on the other, hushed except for the occasional shuffling of papers or fingers clicking against a keyboard. The insides of WestAir looked like Corporate Office, U.S.A.

Nancy Pratt turned the handles of several locked doors until she found one that was open. The room was small and sterile, with a single table and four chairs. It was also frigid, with air-conditioning that roared as it escaped the vent. She motioned for them to sit, then took a chair, folded her hands, and waited for one of them to talk.

"Actually, we're not sure who to contact, but we figured human resources is a good start," Oliver said.

Nancy looked pleased. "So how can I help?"

"Our needs are simple," Oliver said. "Which department assigns the work schedules for WestAir flight attendants?"

Nancy's smile was patronizing. "Before I can direct you to the right department, maybe you can tell me what you want?"

"All we need is a copy of the work schedule for one of your flight attendants."

Pratt clucked her tongue. "I'm sure you know that I can't give you that."

Marge said, "The employee in question is deceased. Roseanne Dresden. She was on flight 1324 and, apparently, WestAir had assigned her to work San Jose field just that morning. All we're looking for is verification of that assign—"

Pratt held up her palm as a stop sign. "I'm sorry, Detectives, but I can't help you with that or anything about Roseanne Dresden. All questions about flight 1324 must be directed to the flight 1324 task force."

"Look, Ms. Pratt, I know that's the company policy and I know you have to worry about lawsuits, but what we're asking for is a very simple thing. We just want some kind of written verification that Roseanne Dresden was on the flight because she wasn't officially working the flight. But she wasn't issued a ticket, either, which means she had to be on assignment, correct?"

"Detective . . ." A sigh. "It sounds simple to you, but it isn't simple. Anything with regard to flight 1324 must be handled by the task force, period."

All right." Marge gave up. "Where can we find the task force and who should we speak with?"

Nancy Pratt was already on her feet. "If you could wait here for a moment, I'll see if anyone's available to help you. It may take a few moments."

"No problem," Marge said. "My throat's a little dry. Would you happen to have a glass of water?"

Nancy's expression matched the arctic temperature in the room. "I'll see what I can do."

After she left the room, Oliver said, "I don't think she likes us."

"I don't think WestAir likes anyone poking around in their business."

"You know we're not going to get anywhere without warrants. And we have no cause to get warrants. This is a total waste of time."

"Let's just play it out and say we tried."

Neither of them spoke for a minute, Oliver shaking his leg, Marge rubbing her arms. The knock at the door was a welcome distraction. A young man came inside holding a paper cup and a plastic bottle. He was slight in build, with blue-black eyes, zits and pits on his cheeks, and a tentative attitude. Marge surmised that this was his first job and he was trying really hard not to screw it up.

"Excuse me, but someone wanted water?"

"That would be me," Marge said. "Thank you very much."

"You're welcome. Anything else?"

"Not really," Oliver answered, "unless you want to break into some files for us."

The boyish man looked aghast.

"I'm kidding," Oliver said. "I'm from the police. Think I'd have you do something illegal?"

"I wouldn't answer that if I were you," Marge told him. She opened the bottle of water and poured half of it in the cup. "It could only work against you."

The kid gave a small smile. Being one of the gang seemed like a new experience for him, so Marge took a big chance. "Relax, sir. You don't want to end up like your boss, do you?"

"You mean Ms. Pratt?"

"She seems a little humorless." She drank the cup dry then moved on to the rest of the bottle. "Or maybe it's just that WestAir has been under tremendous tension."

"That's for certain."

Oliver joined in. "And when everyone gets testy, I bet I know who they take it out on."

The blue-black eyes became wary. "Anything else I can do for you?"

"What's your name?" Oliver asked.

"Henson."

"Okay, Mr. Henson. I'm Detective Oliver and this is Detective Sergeant Dunn. Now we're officially introduced."

"Nice to meet you, but my first name is Henson. Henson Manning. My mother was a big Muppets fan and had a whacky sense of humor, ha ha."

Poor kid, Oliver thought. Not only was he saddled with no muscle and bad acne, but he also had a weird name.

Marge gave him her most sincere smile. "Henson, thank you very much for the water. You're the first smile we've seen all day."

Henson nodded. "You polished that off pretty quickly. Can I get you another bottle?"

"No, I'm fine, thanks," Marge said. "But you look like you want to ask me something. Are you wondering why the police are here?"

Henson's shrug was noncommittal, so Marge had to talk fast. "We're looking for the work assignment schedule for a flight attendant named

Roseanne Dresden. Supposedly, she was on flight 1324 but wasn't issued a ticket."

Oliver added, "Any ideas?"

"Flight attendants aren't issued tickets."

Marge said, "She wasn't officially working the flight but was en route to work in San Jose."

Oliver said, "All we need is her work schedule and we're out of WestAir's life."

"Can I ask why?"

"Insurance fraud," Oliver lied.

"I thought you were from homicide," Henson countered.

"Slow week for murder, we're moonlighting," Oliver said. "The point is we tried getting the paper faxed to us, but no one can seem to find Roseanne Dresden's work schedule."

"Or doesn't want to find it," Marge said. "Did you ever meet Roseanne?"

"No."

"Shame. I hear she was a lovely person."

He stood guard by the door, looking sideways as he talked to the detectives out of the corner of his mouth. "Company policy is that if anyone asks us about flight 1324, we should direct them to the special flight task force." He dropped his voice. "Management doesn't want any of us talking about it."

"Lots of lawsuits, I bet," Marge said.

The kid didn't bite. "I'm sure the task force will find what you're looking for."

"I'm sure it could if they made it a priority," Marge said. "But I don't think they will."

Oliver said, "Just too many other issues to worry about. Would you know who keeps the paperwork for job assignments?"

"Everything's computerized here. I'm sure they could find it easily."

"If they want to," Marge said.

"I've got to go." Henson crooked a thumb in the door's direction. "Good luck."

Nancy Pratt knocked into his shoulder as he left. "Ow." She glared at the gofer. "Could you kindly watch where you're going?"

"I'm sorry, Ms. Pratt."

"What's your name again?"

"Henson Manning."

"Well, now that you dislocated my shoulder, go get me water and an Advil."

"I'm so sorry."

"Now, please."

As he left, Nancy muttered "stupid kid," but none too softly. Then she turned her attention to the detectives. "I'm sorry, but there's no one on the task force that can help you at this time. I've brought in some forms. If you'll fill them out, giving us a written request of precisely what you're looking for, someone more knowledgeable than I will get back to you with some answers."

Marge said, "Actually, all we need is written verification that Roseanne Dresden was assigned to work in San Jose and was on flight 1324. That shouldn't be hard to find."

"I'm sure it isn't, but I can't help you. You can fill out the forms and mail them back to us. I've enclosed a self-addressed stamped envelope for your convenience."

"That was thoughtful," Oliver said.

Nancy took his words at face value even though the tone was snide. "We try our best." She opened the door as wide as she could, almost smacking Henson in the face. "Well, you're just everywhere, aren't you."

The young man looked mortified. "Here's the water and the Advil."

"Thank you." She popped the pills in her mouth and swallowed, giving him back the paper cup. "Now could you be so kind as to show the detectives to the exit?" She smiled tightly at Marge and Oliver. "Sometimes when people are distracted, it's hard to find."

She departed in a huff, leaving them with Henson and the paper cup.

Marge whispered, "Cheer up. You'll probably outlive her by a good thirty years."

For the first time, Henson gave a genuine smile. "Do you need your parking validated?"

"Uh, yes, thanks," Oliver said.

"Wait here. I'll get the stickers." Henson returned a few minutes later. "Did you get what you needed?"

"'Fraid not," Marge said.

"All we got is the old bureaucratic runaround and a very polite but unhelpful 'we'll see what we can do.'" Oliver held up the papers Nancy had given them. "And a bunch of forms to fill out."

"This way." Henson led them back through the carpeted hallway into the lobby. Phones were still beeping but the exotic woman named Elizabeth was nowhere to be seen. The young man dropped his voice. "Look . . . if you give me your card, I'll see what I can do."

Marge shook her head and whispered back, "Stay out of it. I don't want you getting in trouble for doing anything illegal."

Oliver's card was already out of his pocket. "However, if you want to ask around, I won't object."

"Detective, if I ask around, I'll bring attention to myself. Right now I'm the invisible whipping boy."

"That's a bummer," Marge said.

"I don't care. It's decent pay for a summer job and I can ride my bike."

"You go to college?" Marge asked.

"Cooper Union in New York."

"Science or design?" Henson stared at her. Marge said, "My daughter's at Caltech. She looked at Cooper Union, but wanted to live closer to home."

He nodded. "Yeah, I can understand that. New York is a big city." He pushed the elevator button. Still talking softly, he said, "I'm pretty good with a keyboard, if you know what I mean."

"I don't want to hear this," Marge said.

The elevator doors parted and the two detectives stepped inside. As the doors closed, Henson said, "I'll get back to you within the hour."

As they rode down, Marge said, "I sure hope we don't get the kid into trouble."

"C'mon, Margie, did you see the look in his eyes? With a single stroke, he's morphed from a nerd to Tom Cruise in *Mission Impossible*." Oliver smiled. "Good with a keyboard . . ." He laughed. "The kid'll have our answer in ten minutes."

On the way to the parking lot, Oliver dumped the request forms along with the SASE into the nearest trash can.

6

THE COFFEE WAS strong and bad, unlike the news, which was just plain bad. Decker winced as he attempted to down the black mud. Then, placing the mug on his desk, he decided it wasn't worth the rotgut just to get the caffeine jolt. A computer printout lay on his desk: a list of victims from flight 1324, and Roseanne Dresden's name wasn't on it.

Marge was seated, but Oliver was standing near the door. Both were waiting for his next set of instructions. Decker said, "So then tell me again. What exactly is this?"

As if his asking would change the picture. Marge said, "This is what we're assuming is WestAir's *original* list of the people aboard flight 1324. Oliver and I checked it against the original *newspaper* list from the *Times*. That one *had* Roseanne's name on it."

"And this came from Henson the Hacker?"

"Yes."

"How reliable is this kid?"

"I don't think he made this up, if that's what you're asking. I think he retrieved this little nugget somewhere within the bowels of WestAir's microchips."

"So it's possible that he doesn't have the entire picture," Decker said.

"It's probable that he doesn't have the entire picture," Oliver answered. "This was just the shit he was able to pull up within an hour or so before closing time. There's probably a slew of material he can't get access to."

Marge said, "You also have to keep in mind that lists change . . . like when there's a baby or a toddler that wasn't ticketed. Roseanne wasn't ticketed, so it could be something like that."

Decker said, "So somewhere between the crash and the printing of the *Times* edition, Roseanne's name was added. The question is: Who added the name?" Mutual shrugs answered his question. The crash was still using its long tentacles to give Decker a massive headache. "While Henson the Hacker was doing his mischief, did he happen to find any work order that nails Roseanne being on the flight?"

Marge shook her head no.

"Then the two of you are going to have to go back to WestAir and go through official channels. Find the official list and Roseanne's work order. Without it, we have nothing."

"With it, we'll have nothing," Oliver stated.

Decker became irritated. "Just go back to WestAir and find what we're looking for, Scott. It seems to me that neither the *Times* nor WestAir would put her on the official victims list without being able to verify it. It would open them up to lawsuits."

"Not if the husband, Ivan the Terrible, called up the airline and told them to do it," Marge said. "Besides, he's already suing the airline."

Decker said, "This should be easy to settle once we have the work order. Oliver, did any one of Roseanne's friends call you back?"

Oliver took a small notebook from his pants pocket. "Two: David Rottiger and Arielle Toombs."

"Two out of eight?"

"Not a terrible batting average considering that all the names on the list work for WestAir, and the airline's official policy is that anything to do with flight 1324 goes through the flight task force."

Marge said, "After having visited the corporate offices, it was probably pretty brave of these two to call back. If management finds out they talked to us, it could be bad for them."

"So set up interviews before they change their minds," Decker said.

Oliver said, "I've already made an appointment with Rottiger. He lives in West Hollywood, and since I'm going into the city tonight, I asked if I could stop by around six. He agreed, but he sounded cautious."

"And what about Toombs? Where does she live?"

"Studio City."

"Do you have time to talk to Arielle Toombs tonight?" Decker asked Marge.

"If I do some rearranging. I was going to meet Vega at six."

"The girl's actually going out on a date—"

"Scott, you're not being nice." Marge looked at Decker for support. "A guy asked her to a party tonight. She wanted to meet me before the party, but I could meet her afterward."

"No way, this is a big deal in Vega's life and you've got to be there."

"Thanks, Pete. I really appreciate that."

It was four in the afternoon. If Decker could set up something with Toombs in the early evening, then he'd take the family out for dinner at Golan. His mouth watered as he thought of shwarma and baba ghanoush with warm pita bread. Even if he couldn't set something up with Toombs, dinner at the restaurant still sounded good. "Give me Toombs's phone number and I'll make an appointment with her."

Oliver gave him a set of digits. He looked uncomfortable and Decker asked what was wrong.

"I don't know . . ." A forced exhalation. "Just where are we going with this Dresden thing? Do you *really* think that her husband heard about the crash and magically decided to bump her off and use the flight as an alibi?"

"Maybe they had a fight or something," Marge suggested. "They didn't get along, according to Roseanne's parents."

"Yes, exactly," Oliver said. "According to Roseanne's *parents*. And we're going along with their craziness because they're grieving and in denial?"

Decker said, "I'm still reserving judgment, Scotty. Find out as much information as you can about Roseanne Dresden and the official WestAir policy about putting flight attendants on planes without tickets. Marge, you call up the *Times* and see if you can't find their original list. Then see if it matches the one given to you by Henson the Hacker. And if it does, who at the *Times* added Roseanne's name to the victims list or was it called in by WestAir. And if it was WestAir, who specifically called it in."

"No problem, but I doubt L.A. *Times* will have anyone there at four in the afternoon."

"Then leave your number and do a follow-up call tomorrow. Plus, I want both of you to go back to WestAir to find the work order."

"All the airline is going to do is give us forms to fill out."

"So fill them out and press for more."

"It might hold more weight if you were there with us, Decker," Oliver said.

"My shield's the same color as yours."

"But your title's higher."

"That's true. Which is why at this stage of my career, I don't do bureaucracies other than LAPD."

THE STREET WAS located behind a major supermarket, the address corresponding to a set of bungalows that shared a common lot, the only distinguishing feature between the four structures being the A, B, C, or D tacked onto the address. The outside area was a wee brick square patio hosting a faded teak table and chairs and surrounded by assorted ceramic pots filled with leafy plants and flowers dripping with blooms.

A man in jeans, a gray T-shirt, and flip-flops held a steel watering can, bending low as rivulets poured out the spout and rained down on bright red begonias in a terra-cotta container. He was medium height, and just a smidge short of stocky. His hair was deep red and his complexion was a map of freckles. His demeanor suggested that he was unbothered by Oliver's presence.

"Excuse me," Oliver said. "I'm looking for David Rottiger."

The man continued to water his plants. "I'm David." He finally looked up with eyes round and brown. "Is it Detective Oliver or Detective Scott?"

"It's Scott Oliver. Either one is okay. And thanks for agreeing to talk to me."

"I'll probably get fired in the process."

"I certainly hope not."

"I don't even care anymore. You can't imagine how tense the atmosphere has been since it happened."

"I'm sure it's been very unpleasant."

"Unpleasant doesn't cover the range of emotions that you feel when your friends die and you know in your heart of hearts it could have been you." His lip trembled. "Where are my manners? Can I get you some water or a cup of coffee? Something stronger?"

"Whatever you're drinking, Mr. Rottiger, sounds fine to me."

"I have a wonderful Syrah that I opened last night. Have a seat, then. I'll be right back."

"Take your time. It's beautiful out here."

"Isn't it, though? My one refuge is gardening, but it's a good one." A few minutes later he came back carrying two red-wine glasses filled almost to the brim. He handed one to Scott and the two men drank in silence.

Oliver said, "Excellent texture. Very smooth. Do you mind if we talk some inside, where it's little more private?"

"It's fine with me, but you know that I'm not allowed to talk about flight 1324. We've been instructed to refer all questions to the task force or to WestAir's lawyers. So anything about the flight is off-limits."

"I understand," Oliver answered. "Actually, I'd like to talk to you about Roseanne Dresden." He stood up. "Which unit is yours?"

"C as in *crash*." He gave off a weak smile. "Morbid humor. It helps to get you through the day."

"I've used it many times myself."

Rottiger opened the unlocked front door. The place couldn't have been more than six hundred square feet, but it was done up to perfection: high ceilings with crossbeams, gleaming bamboo floors, and lots of light. The walls were painted pale green and were hung with Japanese scrolls and minimalist pen-and-ink abstracts. Since the unit had only one bedroom and one bath, the double-wide couch made for comfortable sleeping quarters for guests, Rottiger explained. A black granite counter separated the living room from the kitchen. It was a stark surface except for an obsidian vase of bloodred roses. One of the kitchen cabinets was open, exposing a thirty-inch plasma TV. Oliver was impressed . . . especially with the TV.

"Is that HD?"

"But of course. When I watch baseball, I can see the players spit chaw in 3-D." Rottiger pulled out a bar stool from under the counter and sat down. "So what can I do for you?"

"I'm sure this is going to sound a little funny, but Roseanne's parents have contacted us. They don't believe that she was actually on flight 1324."

Rottiger stared out the window while sipping wine.

Oliver said, "What do you think about that?"

"I think it's hard for them to accept some things."

"So you think Roseanne was on the flight?"

"I didn't say that."

"On a small plane like flight 1324, are there enough jump seats for working flight attendants plus an extra like Roseanne?" Oliver asked.

"I'm sorry, Detective, but these are technical questions. You really should be discussing these issues with the WestAir lawyers or the task force. I can't discuss policy with you."

"WestAir doesn't seem to want to talk to us."

"I'm sorry, but I can't talk to the police. If it gets back to management, I'll lose my job." He took a long sip of wine. "The only reason I'm talking to you at all is curiosity. Why is a homicide detective interested in Roseanne? Surely you don't believe Mrs. Lodestone's story, do you?"

"I understand you were very good friends with Roseanne. What was she like?"

"Are you profiling Roseanne?"

"In a way. Tell me about her."

"Have you ever seen a picture of her?"

Oliver shook his head no. Rottiger held up a finger and came back a few minutes later with a photograph of eight WestAir flight attendants. He pointed to a tall willowy blonde in the middle. "That's her."

Oliver whistled. "Beautiful woman."

"Yes, she was. It's amazing that she was so naive about men."

"How so?"

"She grew up in a small town up north, with Bible parents in a Bible community."

"She was religious?"

"No, she gave all that up. But she still carried that farm-girl innocence. Her faith in her husband defied credulity. It took her catching him in the act for it to finally sink in what a shit he was. Even then, she agreed to therapy and mediation."

"How was that working out?"

"Not well." He turned to Oliver. "You don't think she was on flight 1324, do you? You think that bastard did her in and blamed it on the flight."

Oliver scratched his cheek. "Right now I'm just getting information, sir. And when you're doing that, you've got to keep an open mind. What do you think?"

"Put it this way. The condo they were living in was in her name. So was the bank account, the car, the furniture, and just about everything of value that they owned. After catching him red-handed, Roseanne started talking about divorce. Poor little Ivan. Now how was he going to pay his lap dancers if he had to make rent and car payments, too?"

"Lap dancers?"

"Ever heard of Leather and Lace?"

Oliver faked naïveté.

"It's a 'gentleman's' club." Rottiger made quotes with his fingers. "I have a good friend who works there as an exotic dancer." When the man saw Oliver's facial expression, he said, "It's not like you think. She's only doing it for the money."

"That's usually why girls lap dance," Oliver said. "Anyway, what about her?"

"She met Rosie and Ivan at one of my famous patio parties." A look of disgust washed over his face. "When Roseanne wasn't looking, Ivan came on to her."

"Does your lap-dancer friend have a name?"

"She does but I'm not comfortable giving it to you, right now. Especially after what happened with Ivan. I work very hard at putting my parties together. I don't need idiots like Ivan making my friends feel uncomfortable. But there's a punch line to this."

"Go on."

"Two weeks later Ivan shows up at Leather and Lace, stuffing twenties into my friend's thong."

"And did the relationship between the two of them . . . uh, improve?"

"That isn't the point!" Rottiger bristled. "The point is he was spending lots of money on his bad habits. Roseanne's money, no doubt. She finally had enough!"

"So Roseanne was contemplating divorce."

"Yes. *Finally.*"

"And where was Roseanne living while she thought about divorce?"

"In her condo."

"And Ivan? Where was he living?"

"They were still living together, but I think she was about to kick him out. She told me if *anyone* was going to temporarily move out, it was going to be him."

"Because the condo was in her name."

"Exactly."

"Didn't her husband have a job?"

"Some kind of low-level job in finance. I know they were living off Roseanne's money as a flight attendant because Rosie complained about it."

Oliver thought that it would be helpful to get into Roseanne's bank accounts to see whose signatures were on the household expense checks. Maybe Ivan was skimming money from his wife's bank account and that was the last straw. So far, the only thing working against Ivan the Terrible was bad behavior. And if that was a crime, Oliver was in deep, deep shit.

Rottiger said, "You know that the bastard is going to get a lot of insurance money now that Rosie's dead. She had a life insurance policy from the company, and on top of that, I'm sure he'll get a settlement from the airline. She was worth a lot more to him dead than alive."

Oliver said, "I know that, but I can't arrest Ivan for getting a windfall from his dead wife. What I need to know as a homicide detective is simply this: Was Roseanne Dresden on that plane or not?"

"I don't know," Rottiger said, "and that's the truth."

Oliver checked his watch. He had just enough time to clean up and make it to the restaurant. He set his wineglass down on the sleek bar and then handed his card to Rottiger. "You've been very helpful."

"If you say so."

"I know you can't talk policy, but it's my understanding that a flight attendant can hop an airline without a ticket if she's on her way to work."

"That's certainly true."

"We know that Roseanne wasn't a flight attendant on 1324. We were told that she was on her way to San Jose to work. If you happen to stumble across anything that would definitely put Roseanne Dresden on flight 1324 or any paperwork that assigned her to work in San Jose, I'd love to know about it."

Rottiger stuck the card in his jeans pocket. "I don't see how that would happen. I try to mind my own business and do my job."

"Same with me, Mr. Rottiger, but some people don't want me to do my job. For instance, take your airline. My partner, Detective Dunn, and I asked WestAir about assignment sheets. We didn't get anywhere and there was no one in the task force who could help us. We were told to fill out papers and just wait. Now, how am I to close a case if I'm being shined on like that?"

"It doesn't surprise me. But you have to understand that WestAir is in a chaos right now."

"Let me ask you one more thing."

"Sure."

"Is it possible for Roseanne to suddenly hitchhike on a plane without a job assignment and without a ticket?"

"It's not procedure, but . . . if she made a sudden decision to escape from the bastard, and she had a good friend working the flight, maybe someone would bend a rule, let her hitch a ride, and clear it up later."

Oliver nodded. "Thank you for your time, Mr. Rottiger. If I have any more questions, can I feel free to call you again?"

"Absolutely, as long as you're discreet. WestAir can't find out about our chat."

"No reason they should know."

A tear fell down Rottiger's cheek. "She was a wonderful woman and a good friend, Detective. All of them who worked flight 1324 were wonderful. We were like a family. I am happy to help in any way I can as long as my job's not jeopardized."

Oliver cleared his throat. "In that case, I do have one more favor." He pored through his notes. "Uh . . . could I have the phone number of your lap-dancer friend. I'd like to talk to her about Ivan Dresden. Maybe she didn't like him initially, but money makes strange dancing partners."

Rottiger dug out Oliver's business card. "I have your number, Detective, and I'll give it to my friend. If she's interested in talking to you, she'll know where to find you."

Oliver wasn't perturbed by his refusal to give out the lap dancer's phone number. If need be, he could always visit Leather and Lace, flash his badge, and ask for Ivan's friend. And the dive would cooperate because Oliver was a detective and that held sway. Besides, though he wasn't a regular, he wasn't unfamiliar with the establishment.

7

MARGE'S EAR WAS hot and sore from being pressed against the receiver for so long. On top of that, she'd made the mistake of wearing the new pearl studs that Will Barnes had given her, making phone work extremely uncomfortable. But they were so pretty and she was so thrilled with the gift that she couldn't help herself. The voice on the other end of the line was giving her a hard time.

"Yes, I know that Roseanne Dresden's name is on the victims list," Marge explained. "I'm asking you if she had always been on the list or was her name added later because I know that lists are revised when more information is given . . . no, don't put me on hold . . . Shit!" She slammed down the phone.

Decker happened to be passing by her desk. "Everything all right?"

"I hate being sent into the electronic void." She checked her watch. "I'm on lunch hour. I think I'll pay our illustrious paper a visit."

"How's your afternoon?"

"Not bad."

"In that case, since you'll be in the area, pay a visit to North Mission Road. It's been a while since we've talked to the recovery team. Find out how many bodies on the list they've recovered and/or identified. Also, while you're there you can ask them if they've recovered any artifacts that might have belonged to Roseanne Dresden."

Marge had been taking notes. After he stopped talking, she stowed her pad in her purse. "Not a problem. What about you?"

"I've got an appointment with Arielle Toombs, the only person other than Rottiger that returned Oliver's call. She didn't sound thrilled, but I got her to commit to a time. Nice earrings, by the way."

Marge's smile was wider than her neck. "Will got them for me."

"Will's a nice guy."

Marge picked up her bag and studied her boss and her friend. "You look tired, Pete."

"All of a sudden we've got another epidemic of burglary reports, mainly from people who had to evacuate their homes when flight 1324 went down."

"Yeah, Paul Deloren was talking to me about that. How many of those calls do you think are legit?"

"Not all of them, that's for certain. We're going through them one by one along with the insurance investigators."

"I know we've had a surge of DUIs this past week."

"That and drunk-and-disorderlies, discharging a weapon in a public place, and about twice as many assaults as normal. Bar fights, but domestic violence, too. And higher-than-normal sudden heart attacks."

"The aftermath," Marge said. "You, me, and everyone else are going crazy. At least this time, there's a reason."

THE CITY'S LARGEST and oldest newspaper had set up its headquarters in downtown L.A. over 125 years ago when the area had breathed the air of youth, with its bustling streets, its posh department stores, and the famous Angel's flight cable car. In its fourth reincarnation, the paper had settled into its current headquarters at Spring and First streets. The structure was a paean to American Art Deco and the WPA artists who fashioned the building, with its bronze bas-relief, friezes, carving, and adornments.

Once inside, Marge stood in a rotunda, the centerpiece being a rotating globe banded by the signs of the zodiac done in bronze relief. To her right was a brief history of the paper; the left side was manned by a uniformed guard; and straight ahead, through alarmed turnstiles, was a bank of elevators. She had several names and numbers from her phones calls this morning and gave them to the guard, who rang up a couple of extensions. He announced that Mr. Delgado would be with her shortly.

Twenty-six toe-tapping minutes later—after reading a self-aggrandizing history of the paper—Marge saw a stocky man lumber through the turnstiles. He had jet black hair combed straight back, Dracula style, and dark brows gave a roof over startling pale blue eyes. His skin was tan but without wrinkles, so Marge put his age in the late twenties to early thirties. He wore a white shirt, black slacks, and penny loafers. His blue-and-gray-striped tie was loosened at the neckline.

"Mr. Delgado?" Marge asked.

"Rusty is fine." He stuck out his hand. "I'm sorry. I didn't catch your name."

"Marge Dunn." She shook his hand. "Thank you very much for seeing me on no notice."

"No problem. And this is about . . ."

"It's complicated," Marge told him. "Is there somewhere we can go that's more private?"

"Uh, sure . . ." Delgado's voice edged toward the higher side of the male range. He led her into the heart of the paper. If Marge had expected an area overrun with cubs and stringers and editors barking out commands, she was sorely disappointed. The floor was filled with open cubicles and was as quiet as a library. Placards hung from the ceiling—HEALTH, REAL ESTATE, CALENDAR, METRO, HOME: section headings of the *Times*.

She tailed him down a foyer where featured photographs and prize-winning articles hung on a wall, passing a display case filled with vintage news cameras, and into a second area of open cubicles. A skeleton wearing a hula skirt and a coconut-shell bra was displayed on a pole.

"Obits," Delgado announced.

"The place is empty." Marge smiled. "People must be dying to get out."

Delgado smiled back. "How can I help you?"

Marge launched into her prepared spiel, a dodge to keep the young man from asking too many questions. "I work for Ace Insurance Company, which subcontracts for other more recognizable insurance companies. I've been assigned to find out about the original victims list from WestAir flight 1324 that was given to your paper for publication by WestAir itself, and compare it to the final list of flight 1324 victims. Originally, Tricia Woodard did the articles on the crash. I thought she might be able to help me."

"Tricia is out of town." Delgado looked baffled. "Isn't there only one list?"

Marge's smile was gentle. "That's what I'm trying to ascertain. I was told that the list was updated several times during the first couple of days after the crash, and that additional people were added."

"Excuse my ignorance, but who would be added on? Isn't there a flight list of everyone on the airplane?"

"Only those who have purchased tickets. That wouldn't include infants and toddlers—"

"Ah, yes, of course. And you're investigating the names because . . ."

"It's routine after every crash." Marge didn't know if that was true, but she suspected it was. "Before insurance pays, it wants to make sure that those who were listed as dead actually died. Sometimes, especially with small infants, well, I hate to be graphic. Let's just say it's impossible to make identification on the bodies . . . or even to find the bodies can be tricky. Even with adults. Sometimes, people commit fraud."

Delgado's curiosity was definitely piqued. He was smelling a story. "How so?"

"Well, let's put it this way. Someone calls up and says Ms. So-and-So also had an infant daughter who perished in the crash. Ninety-nine-point-nine percent of the time, that's what happened. Every once in a blue moon, you get a real psycho who made up Ms. So-and-So's daughter to collect more insurance, or the infant actually does exist, but she was mercifully tucked away with grandparents and not on the plane. We've got to check things like that out."

"People actually claim that children are dead when they're not?"

"Mr. Delgado, when it comes to insurance payment, we've seen everything."

"I'm sure you have."

"So you have the list given to you by WestAir?"

"Sure, and I could get that for you right now. But in the future, all you have to do is pull it out of the paper's archives."

"See, that's the rub. I'm not looking for the first list that the paper printed. I'm looking for the first list that was called in to you from WestAir. Just to see if there are any discrepancies."

"So why can't you get this information from WestAir?"

"I did," Marge lied. "But Ace Insurance has asked me to go directly to the paper and compare it to the WestAir list." She let go with a wide smile and a wink. "You're a newspaper person, you know how important it is to check your facts."

Delgado nodded. "If anyone had a list, it would have been Tricia, but she's on vacation."

"Dang. And there's no one else who might have had that list?"

Delgado thought a moment. "Let me see what I can do. Would you mind waiting here for a few minutes?"

"No problem. Thank you very much, Mr. Delgado. You've been an enormous help. It sure beats talking to voice mail."

"I'm glad, although I haven't done anything." Delgado smiled. "Wait right here. As I said, it may take me a few minutes."

After he left, Marge thought about Delgado, who wasn't much older than Vega. Her daughter seemed to be making unexpected headway in the social-arts department. After her first successful party experience, Vega was once again asked out by Josh, from her particle-physics course. This time it was dinner. After the requisite panic attack, she calmed down enough to accept the invitation and call Marge for more advice. When Marge suggested talking about a recent book, Vega went out and bought the top-ten books on the *New York Times* hardcover nonfiction list and polished them off in three nights.

The minutes stretched on.

Marge checked her BlackBerry. Will Barnes had called, text messaging that he was coming down to Santa Barbara for an interview. Did she want to come up? A weekend in the resort city sounded nice, and she was thinking about walks on the beach and a terrific halibut dinner when Delgado came back, holding pieces of paper in his hands. Marge stood up, but Delgado didn't hand her the sheets right away.

"The first list actually printed by the paper wasn't hard to find. That's this one." He gave it to Marge, then rattled another piece of paper in front of her eyes. "As far as I can tell—and I'm not positive about this— but I believe this is the original list given to us by WestAir, and just as you said, it has fewer names than the list the newspaper printed."

"See? I actually was sent here for a purpose." She held out her hand.

"Uh, I should have asked you this in the beginning. Could I see some ID, please?"

"Sure." Marge rifled through her purse and debated showing Delgado her police identification. Sometimes, when she showed it quickly, people barely read it. This wasn't one of those cases. Delgado wanted to verify who she was. She said, "You know, I don't have my business cards with me. I can show you my driver's license." She presented it to him. "Don't read my birth date. It's not polite."

He smiled, but studied the license. "You are indeed Marge Dunn, but you could be anyone."

The only way she was going to slip out of this unscathed was if he smelled a big scoop slipping away. "You know, maybe I should wait for

Tricia Woodard and go through proper channels. We both want to be careful, right?"

Delgado frowned. "What are you really after, Ms. Dunn?"

"Why don't you let me look at the list and I'll tell you."

The young man made a calculated decision. He handed her the slip of paper. Rusty was nothing if not efficient. At the bottom of the first list were three names that had been added to the printed list. The first two were Campbell Dennison and Zoey Benton. Marge's eyes scanned the list and found ticketed passengers to match: Scott and Lisa Dennison and Marlene Benton. These poor souls were children under the age of two. She'd verify them later.

The last name on Delgado's added list was Roseanne Dresden.

Marge pointed to the first two names. "It looks like these two were the children of ticketed passengers. This last one—Roseanne Dresden— she was a flight attendant who worked for WestAir. But she wasn't working the flight; she was on her way to San Jose. Any idea why she wasn't on the first list?"

"None whatsoever. What do you think?"

"Spoken like a true newspaper person. Any idea who called her name in as an official victim?"

"Probably WestAir."

"Probably, or do you know that for sure?"

"No, I don't know that for sure. I didn't have anything to do with compiling the list. That was Tricia's job. I'm just showing it to you, and I probably shouldn't be doing that because you suspect something is amiss. Want to tell me about it?"

"I don't think anything's wrong. I was sent to verify who called Roseanne Dresden in as a victim and who added her to the official list. It was probably WestAir, but we need to verify that, just to make sure it wasn't called in by a third party who wanted to scam insurance."

"Then the woman would be alive," Delgado said.

"Alive and scamming or she could be dead by some other means. It could have been called in by someone who had something to gain if Roseanne had died."

Delgado was definitely interested now.

Marge said, "Let me ask you something theoretically. What if it wasn't WestAir who called in her death? What if it was a third party? You wouldn't automatically add Roseanne's name to the list, would you?"

"No. Tricia would have fact-checked the call with the desk editor and with WestAir. What are you thinking? That Roseanne might have faked her own death or that she was murdered?"

"I'm not thinking anything, I'm just verifying." Marge placed a hand on his shoulder. "Could you do me a favor, Mr. Delgado? Could you find out the name of the person at WestAir who called in Roseanne's name as one of the official dead? And if it was a third party, who fact-checked her name with WestAir? If you keep me in the loop, I'll keep you in the loop."

Delgado ran his fingers through his hair. "I wouldn't want Tricia to get into trouble because of this."

"I can appreciate that, sir, but you wouldn't want your paper looking like a bunch of boobs. And you certainly wouldn't want Roseanne or anyone getting away with fraud. I don't think we have to get Tricia involved. All I want is verification that it was WestAir and not a greedy relative who phoned in Roseanne as a victim."

"I take it Roseanne Dresden's body hasn't been identified. Otherwise why would you be bothering with this?"

The guy was sharp. Marge said, "The recovery efforts are still ongoing, but no, she hasn't been officially ID'd. How about if we both keep that fact a secret? The fewer people who know what I'm doing, the better off we are."

Finally, Delgado nodded. "Give me a day to poke around and dig through some phone slips, okay?"

"Great." Marge wrote down her cell number. "Whatever you find out, I'd like to hear about it. For someone to commit fraud and profit from a death is not only pathetic, it's immoral."

"I agree, but just look at 9/11."

"Of course," Marge said. "You know, your paper should write a story about that. You know how vultures swoop within minutes of tragedy to find a profitable angle for themselves."

Delgado considered the idea and found it a good one. He spoke quietly and with a conspiratorial air. "If your investigation turns out to be fraud, I'll run the whole thing past the desk editor. I'm sure with the right pitch, I can parlay this into some kind of a feature story."

8

STUDIO CITY HAD gotten its moniker from its proximity to the major movie corporations and broadcasting systems. It was ten minutes away from Universal, a quick trip across the canyon from Paramount, CBS, and all of old Hollywood, and a speedy fifteen-minute freeway drive from NBC in Burbank. The Greenwich Village of the Valley, it was a section of boutiques, florists, clubs, and coffeehouses, and most important, it had a big bowling alley where the beautiful and young Hollywood elite were often seen spending a recreational night out, just being plain folk.

Arielle Toombs lived in a wood-sided complex that was shaded in the hot, hot summers by dozens of lacy elms and giant sycamores. Each apartment had its own private balcony, but the pools, gym, and the recreation room were communal—enjoyed by anyone with a rent check that didn't bounce.

Morning fog had given way to a tent of blue above, and as Decker climbed the stairs to Arielle's third-floor apartment, he was already planning his weekend. Cindy and Koby were coming in for a way-overdue Friday-night dinner, Saturday would be synagogue and study group in the afternoon, but Sunday would be his to plan, time unscheduled and unfettered by obligations. If Hannah had arranged something with her friends, a very frequent occurrence since she reached her teens, maybe he and Rina would take a spin out to Oxnard, to the kosher winery and restaurant. It had become one of their favorite places.

Decker's knock was answered by a woman in her thirties: brunette, tall, and lithe. Her eyes were deep green and set off by her clothes—jade-colored, cotton capri pants, and an orange T-shirt. Her hair was pinned back into a ponytail and her feet were housed in flip-flops. "Are you Lieutenant Decker?"

"Yes, I am." He showed her ID to back up his claim.

She smiled and said, "I suppose I should have asked who it was before I answered the door. But like they say, no harm, no foul. Come in. Would you like something to drink?"

"Water would be great."

"Still or sparkling?"

Only in L.A. "Either would be fine," Decker said.

"Not a problem. Take a seat anywhere. Please excuse the mess."

The mess consisted of newspapers lying on a mattress-style black sofa. It was low-slung and tufted with buttons, but surprisingly comfortable. Arielle's living space was open and she had kept the furnishings sparse. Besides the sofa, the area had two side chairs, and a coffee table made out of acrylic. When she came back, she was carrying two glasses of sparkling water. She handed one to Decker, took a sip from her glass, and then sat down. "I don't know how I can help you. It's company policy to direct all questions about 1324 to their official task force."

"I know that. And you should know, though, that the company can't take away your freedom of speech."

"It isn't that," Arielle said. "It's just that in a crisis like this, so much misinformation is circulated. WestAir is just trying to keep it to a minimum." She flipped her ponytail over her shoulder. "The guy over the phone, I forgot his name."

"Detective Oliver."

"Yeah, him. He mentioned Roseanne Dresden. That he had a couple of questions about her?"

"Actually, yes. I'd like to talk to you about Roseanne."

Tears instantly pooled in her eyes. She put down her water and wiped her eyes. "Sure."

"You knew her well?"

"Since eighth grade."

"That's a long time."

"Yes, it's a very long time."

"You're from Fresno?"

"Born and bred."

"What brought you down to L.A.?"

"A boyfriend."

"Did you come before or after Roseanne?"

"Before, I think, but I'm not sure. We weren't close in high school. We ran in totally different circles. If you would have told me we would have winded up close friends, I would have said you were nuts."

"Why's that?"

"She was one of the popular kids and I wasn't. To tell you the truth, I didn't like her much back then. I thought she was a snob. We became close when we both started working for WestAir. The crash was horrible on so many different levels, but I can't tell you how devastated I was when I found out about her. I was shocked that she had been scheduled to work San Jose."

"Really." Decker took out his notepad. "Why's that?"

"I would have thought that she had no use for . . . anyway. When I thought about it, I figured it made some sense. She was having a hard time at home and maybe she felt it would do some good to get away, and San Jose opened up."

"I've heard she had a rocky marriage."

"Her husband was cheating on her and wasn't subtle about it. Still, there must be two sides to every story."

"What would you say his side was?" Decker asked.

A deep sigh. "I loved Roseanne. I truly did. She was lively, funny, loyal, and would give you the shirt off her back. She had an open heart and time for everyone."

"But . . ."

"But every once in a while . . ." Arielle shook her head. "What can I say? That eighth-grade side of her would materialize and she could be absolutely awful. She could cut a person down with a few well-placed words."

"A person like her husband?"

Arielle looked at the ceiling. "Roseanne was usually such a sweetie, so if you'd never seen it, it would throw you off guard. But I remember this one specific time that my boyfriend and I were at a dinner party with them—Rosie and Ivan. She was *really* upset with him, and was zinging him all evening. Every once in a while, he'd try to zing her back, but he was clearly out of his league."

"Ouch."

"Yeah. Exactly! Ivan probably had it coming, but it was still pretty ugly, especially since . . ." She waved her hand in the air. "Never mind."

Decker said, "Now's not the time to play coy, Ms. Toombs. I really need to know what was going on between them."

Arielle paused. "Why?"

It should have been Decker's turn to say never mind. Instead, he fed her a little white lie. "We're investigating the crash for insurance fraud. There seems to have been some dispute as to whom she named as benefactor of her policy. If she and Ivan had been having long-standing problems, it might have some bearing on the claim and counterclaim."

"Well, if Rosie would have known what was going to happen to her, I'm sure she wouldn't have left the twit a dime. But I don't know if she had gotten around to changing her insurance policy."

"So what were you hesitant to tell me a few moments ago?"

"Oh, golly! It's just that Roseanne wasn't such an angel herself."

"Ah . . ." Decker nodded.

"But it's still Ivan's fault. She didn't start doing anything until he stepped out on her repeatedly."

Decker said, "Was she seeing anyone specific?"

"I suppose I should lay all the cards on the table. About six months ago, Rosie broke off a long-standing affair that she was having with a married man. He was in his fifties. I don't know how rich he was, but I do know he spent a lot on her. Every time we went up to San Jose for work, and we'd have to spend the night there, she'd come back the next day with something shiny on her finger or on her wrists or earlobes. One time he bought her a diamond watch—a Chopard. That's a very expensive brand."

"Yes, it is. So maybe that's why she was planning to work from San Jose."

"If this had happened six months ago, I would have said of course, that's the reason." Arielle took a long gulp of her water. "But she broke it off and was resolved never to see him again. Mr. Married Man began having ideas about the two of them running off into the sunset, and while he was good for a trinket or two, she definitely didn't want him around permanently. When she broke off the affair, Rosie told me that he was very upset with her. The whole thing ended badly. That's why I found it so odd that she was on the plane, planning to work in San Jose."

"Maybe they reconciled."

"I . . . honestly don't think so. She was trying to reconcile with Ivan. They were in counseling together, although it wasn't working, according to her."

"I'd like to talk to her ex-lover. I'll need his name."

"I can give it to you, but what relevance would it have to her insurance policy?"

"We're just checking out all kinds of avenues," Decker said. "Maybe if she was going to marry this guy, she would have changed her policy."

"No, you're on the wrong track. She had no intent of marrying Ray. Raymond Holmes. He's five ten, two-seventy, and like I said, in his fifties. He was a builder. I found him as dull as dry toast. Roseanne would never marry him."

"Why not? He could certainly give her the security that Ivan wasn't giving her."

"Roseanne never cared about security. Her father has money and she was earning a good living. Roseanne was interested in a shoulder to cry on and Ray was perfect for that . . . although I'm sure the jewelry didn't hurt."

"Tell me something, Ms. Toombs. How did Roseanne . . . with all her attributes . . . hook up with a loser like Ivan Dresden?"

"Have you ever met Ivan?"

Decker shook his head.

"He's *really* good-looking. It's his best asset. It's his *only* asset. If he would have just been a slacker, and a spendthrift, I think Roseanne would have tolerated him because he's great arm candy. It was the affairs. They made her look small. Even though she had her own fling, her heart wasn't into it. She was planning on leaving him, but like I told you before, I don't know if she got around to changing her insurance policy."

If there was ever a convenient time for Ivan to whack her, it would have been then. Yet now that Decker had found out about Roseanne's lover, her being on the flight to San Jose made a lot more sense, despite Arielle's insistence that the relationship was over. Decker said, "I'll take Raymond Holmes's phone number and address now."

"I'll give you what I have, but it may not be current."

"That's not a problem. I'm sure he's listed, at least professionally."

"Yeah, according to Roseanne, he owns a successful contracting company."

"According to Roseanne," Decker repeated.

"I believe her. Roseanne was a lot of things, but she wasn't a liar."

"She was cheating on her husband. Isn't that lying?"

Arielle thought about that. "More like lies of omission rather than lies of commission. I don't know if she ever told Ivan about the affair. And I doubt that Ivan cared enough to ever ask."

———

DECKER'S CELL PHONE displayed a new message: Marge, and there was urgency in her voice. He called her back immediately and she picked up on the third ring.

"Where are you?" Decker asked.

"On my way back to the station house from the Crypt. We can put the brakes on the Dresden mystery. A female body just showed up on a slab from recovery."

"Roseanne?"

"Nothing definitive, but who else would it be? Roseanne was the only female in the crash unaccounted for. The body is badly burned and badly decayed. The skeleton is extremely fragile. It took them almost four hours to transport it to the Crypt."

"Do they have the jaw for dental records?"

"They have the entire skeleton, Pete. The problem is that it's going to take a while to X-ray the teeth. Every time they touch something, a piece crumbles. Except for one area that was relatively unscathed."

"Which area is that?"

"Back spine."

"And the pathologist is pretty sure it's her."

There was a pause. "You don't want to let go of this, do you?"

"I guess I just don't like spinning my wheels. My fault. I made the assignments before recovery was done. I'm sure she'll be identified and that will be that. I'll call up the Lodestones and let them know the news."

Marge said, "Even if the dentals aren't perfect, we caught another break. We found some intact fabric and there was discernible writing on it . . . like a message T-shirt. Pink. We can go back and check if Roseanne owned a T-shirt like that one, maybe there's even a photograph with her in it."

"Great." Still, Decker felt oddly disappointed. Some aspect of him had bought into the Lodestones' fantasy idea that Roseanne hadn't been on the plane. "Well, we'll get some kind of identity soon enough, so it certainly doesn't pay to put any more time into the case."

"I wish I would have known about it earlier in the day. Save me a trip to the paper bullshitting with a reporter and pretending I was an insurance agent . . . although I must say I pulled it off nicely."

"I used an insurance dodge, too."

"Great minds think alike."

"Call up Oliver and tell him to put the case in storage until further notice. I'll meet you back at the station house and we'll see what other mayhem the residents of the West Valley have cooked up for us."

9

A T THE SOUND of the tentative knock, Decker lifted his head from his paperwork. It was Marissa Kornblatt, the squad room secretary, and her expression was as reluctant as her entrance. "So sorry, Lieutenant. I tried the intercom but your phone's not working."

"I unplugged it. Otherwise, I can't get anything done. What's going on?"

She handed him a thick pile of pink message slips. "These were last hour's calls, but that's not the issue. Farley Lodestone is on line three, and in typical fashion, he won't take no for an answer."

It was the seventh time the bereaved stepfather had called in two weeks. It was getting to be a morning ritual. He wasn't taking the recent news well.

Hello, Farley—they were on first-name basis now.

No, they haven't positively ID'd the body yet, but they're working on it. Yes, I'm so sorry it's taking this long, but we all want to do the best possible job. The coroner and I will call you when we've got something definite to tell you.

Decker picked up the phone. "Hello, Farley. Pete Decker, here."

"You must be sick of me calling."

"Not at all. I just wish I had something to tell you. I haven't heard from the coroner's office yet, but it's only eleven in the morning."

"I just got off the phone with them, Decker. Not with the whole office. With Cesar Darwin. You ever talk to the man?"

"Several times. He's a very competent doctor."

"Good to hear, specially 'cause he talks with an accent."

"He's originally from Cuba. Is he the one doing the identification for the recovery?"

"He's the one, and that's why I'm calling you. When I talked to him, he sounded cagey."

"Cagey?" Decker raked his fingers through his hair. "In what way, Farley?"

"Like he knew somethin' and didn't want to tell me. Call him up for me and find out what's going on. If you call me back and tell me I'm bein' paranoid, I'll believe you. But I want you to be damn straight with me, Decker, if you also think that he sounds fishy."

"Fishy?"

"I asked him if he got to Roseanne's autopsy—a straight yes-or-no question. The problem is he didn't give me a straight yes-or-no answer. What I got was doctor-talking, jumbled-up bird crap. I come to trust you, and I suppose that's a compliment of sorts 'cause I don't trust no one. So do me the favor, Decker. Call him up and see if your bullshit detector is as finely tuned as mine."

THE CALL TO Dr. Darwin was quick, but the answer wasn't at all to Decker's liking.

"I think this might be better if we meet in person," he answered.

Cesar Darwin had been in the country for twenty-five years, but his accent was still thick and he was hard to understand over the phone. Decker thought it was because Cesar had been holed up in the Crypt talking to corpses instead of seeing patients with beating hearts. He probably didn't get a lot of auditory feedback.

A face-to-face meeting was probably a good idea.

"It's complicated?" Decker asked him.

"Yes."

"What time works for you?"

"I have another autopsy. How about two? I'll be done and I'll be hungry. I know a great Cuban place not too far from here. Unless you want to meet at the Crypt."

Decker thought back to his prekosher, Floridian days. Cuban cuisine offered very little in the way of pure vegetarian entrées. Even the rice and beans were often mixed with lard. On the other hand, the Cubans made a great cup of strong coffee. Besides, anything was better than the stench of dead bodies. "Cuban sounds fine. Give me the address and we'll meet you there."

"We?"

"I'm bringing along Detectives Dunn and Oliver. I fear that I might need them."

WHILE DECKER NURSED his coffee, Oliver, Dunn, and Darwin gorged on *pastelitos*—little puff pastries of ham, chicken, pork, and a Cuban specialty, *pacadillos*, a spicy ground beef. In addition to the savory tarts, there was a pot of pork adobo. Sides included fried black beans and fluffy white rice. The day was mild, which was convenient because the East L.A. storefront restaurant had no air-conditioning. The sidewalks were humming with activity, some of it legal, some of it otherwise, but it wasn't Decker's district and he wasn't in the mood to look for trouble. Even though Decker couldn't eat the food, he could smell it and the aromas had aroused his taste buds. Thank goodness he kept kosher. It helped keep his weight down.

There must have been considerable spice in the food because Marge was sweating even after taking off her sweater and rolling up the sleeves of her white blouse.

"Really good." Oliver had shed his suit jacket and was now in the process of loosening his tie and rolling up his own long sleeves. "How's the coffee, Loo?"

"Good. And I should know. I've had four cups."

"Caffeinated?" Marge asked.

"According to my heart, yes."

Darwin summoned a local girl of about fifteen. She had chocolate, curly hair and gang insignia tattoos inked across her arms, neck, and back—everything from snakes and tigers to butterflies. The artwork was intricately done, which meant a lot of needles and a fair amount of pain. She wore a denim miniskirt and a black wife-beater T. Her toenails were painted black and her feet were shod in flip-flops. Lazily, she got up from her chair and took out a pad. The doctor had explained to them that her father owned the place and this was her employment since she dropped out of school.

"Coffee, Dr. Cesar?"

"For the table, Marta."

She turned to Decker. "I think you had enough coffee."

"You're right. I'll take water."

"You don't like Cuban food?"

"I had an enormous breakfast," he answered her in Spanish. "I'm just not hungry."

Marta wrinkled her nose. "You talk the talk, but you don't walk the walk. I bring you some dessert, okay?"

"What kind of dessert?"

"Does it matter?"

"I don't eat anything baked with lard."

She harrumphed and turned tail. A few minutes later she was back with the coffees and a plate of sizzling hot fritters. "Vegetable oil only."

Decker smiled and picked up the fried concoction. It melted in his mouth. "Oh, man, this is good. But it requires coffee."

"I'll bring you decaf."

The better part of an hour had passed, and it was time for the discussions to begin in earnest. Decker turned to Darwin. "I'm sure my fellow detectives are grateful for the meal, but that's not why we're here. What's going on, Doc?"

"Ah, yes, the reason I called you down." The doctor ate a fritter and blotted his lips on a paper napkin. "This is a very perplexing case, yes, and a most difficult autopsy. The skeleton has been thoroughly charred, everything reduced to bones and, unfortunately, ashes. We hope to make a definite identification through the teeth. We do have an intact skull, but it is very delicate. Since we don't want to damage forensic evidence, we have been treating it quite gingerly. As a result, it has been hard to get the exact angle to match the dentition in the radiographs given to us by Roseanne's dentist. The jaw is thicker in bone mass, so it is a bit sturdier and easier to position. But I must emphasize, what we are working with is very fragile." Darwin stopped talking, taking a sip of his coffee. "I've had three forensic odontologists compare and contrast the pre- and postmortem radiographs. We all agree that the skull does not belong to Roseanne Dresden."

The table fell silent. Oliver coped with the news by eating three fritters in a row.

Darwin said, "As you well know, the recovery team has accounted for all the missing females involved in the crash except Roseanne Dresden. So this unexplained female body poses a problem."

"You're sure it's female?" Marge asked.

"The pelvic bones, by the angle and appearance, are almost certainly female," the doctor answered. "But even if it was a small male or an adolescent boy, we'd still have a problem. Still unaccounted for from the crash are two male bodies: an old man in his seventies and another man in his forties. We do not have the pelvis of an old man or a man in his forties. It is most certainly a woman, and I would say probably a young woman. But an *old* young woman, meaning I think the body predated the crash. Once the mandible did not match up with Roseanne Dresden's radiograph, we began to study the bones more carefully. On the top of the skull there is a well-formed depression."

"Blunt-force trauma," Decker said. "Homicide."

"Probably that would be my ruling if the body was in better shape.

Right now I'm going with inconclusive because of all the extenuating circumstances."

"How long has the body been lying there?" Oliver was up to number five in the fritter department. Last one, he swore to himself.

"If it would have been discovered before the fire, I would have had a much better idea. Now it is almost impossible for me to say."

Decker twirled the ends of his mustache. He did that in order to prevent his hands from taking more dessert. "Can you at least tell us a race?"

"Possibly Caucasian, possibly Hispanic."

Oliver said, "Well, in L.A., that'll narrow it down to a few gazillion people."

"Was she inside the wreckage of the building or was she found in the ground under the building?" Decker inquired.

"You'll have to ask recovery, but I think there is still quite a bit of foundation left from the building. I can't imagine why anyone would dig under the foundation and discover a body."

"If she was found in the wreckage and not under the foundation, her death can't be any older than the building," Decker surmised. "So let's find out when the building went up. Then we'll go through the missing persons from that time forward. I'd like to send the skull out to a forensic reconstructionist and put a face on the bones."

"The bones are too delicate. They would break under the impression material needed to make a cast of the skull. Then you would lose any forensic evidence that the original skull might produce."

"This is a nightmare," Marge said. "We finally find a missing body, but it isn't Roseanne. Instead of one possible homicide, we now have two."

Inwardly, Decker groaned. He hated cold homicides and this one was in deep freeze. But his main concern was dealing with Farley Lodestone. "Is there anything you can do to help us pinpoint a time of murder?"

"From the skeleton, no. But I think we have tremendous good luck in one regard."

"The clothing!" Marge said.

"Yes, the clothing." Darwin ate the last fritter and called for the check. "A chunk remained remarkably intact. No label but it seems that Jane Doe was wearing a shirt with lettering on the back. It was preserved because she was buried faceup and the shirt material was synthetic and not as prone to decay. I have it enclosed in a protective plastic bag. We can go back to my office and examine it under a microscope."

Marta, the tattooed teenager, handed the bill to Darwin, but her eyes were on Decker. "Dessert okay?"

"Delicious."

"Next time you come here, Germando can fix you up real good. No problem if you're a vegetarian. We can do somethin' for you."

"I'll keep that in mind."

"Yeah, we get all kinds of requests nowadays. No this, no that, no this, no that . . . man, even the *cholos* are picky. Everyone's tryin' to cut down on the fat."

THE L.A. COUNTY Coroner's Office was on North Mission Road in the once-notorious Ramparts district, northeast of downtown L.A. The police substation was now squeaky-clean, but though the mark of Cain was fading, it wasn't entirely gone.

The morgue was two buildings separated by a walkway, offices to the right, the Crypt on the left. A perennial swarm of black flies welcomed the visitor at the front doors. After the detectives signed in and donned protective garb, including shoe covers and face masks, Darwin took them down to the Crypt, the smell in the elevator growing stronger with every inch of descent. No matter how many times Decker had dropped by, it was the stink that always got to him.

The corridor was quiet, the doors of the foyer leading to the glassed-in autopsy rooms and the refrigeration area used for the storage of the bodies. Because of the tremendous glut of corpses, there were cadavers on gurneys in the hallways, most wrapped in plastic sheeting, but others were more visible, skin gray and growing mold.

The pathologist's office was off the main hallway, set up like a galley-style kitchen with cabinets above and below, and stainless-steel countertops that spilled over with instruments of the trade—microscopes of various intensities along with scales, calipers, scalpels, tweezers, and camera equipment. There were seven jars containing body parts that floated in unnamed scientific liquids, mostly digits being rehydrated for fingerprinting. Darwin's desk was tucked into a corner and was piled high with papers. The office provided adequate space for one person, but was crowded for four adults.

The activity centered around a microscope, the doctor and the detectives taking turns as they tried to make out details on a sullied piece of cloth. The swatch was roughly a six-inch square, most of it mud-colored. With the aid of the lens, Decker could see individual threads that still carried some of the original pink dye. Darwin reduced the magnification in order to make out the lettering, the clearest section directly in the middle of the fabric. The paint was rapidly flaking off.

Decker peered into the eyepieces. "Takes a little getting used to."

"Yes, it does," Darwin agreed. "But you can make out words."

"I can make out letters."

"What letters?" Marge took out her notepad.

"*V-e-s* . . ." A pause. "It looks like *v-e-s-t-o-n.*"

Marge wrote it down. "What else?"

"Underneath the *v-e-s-t-o-n* is *d-i-a-n.* Underneath that is *a-p-o-l* and underneath that is . . ." He let out a short breath. "I think it's *p-e-k* . . ." He peered at the area with intensity. "Everything else is smudgy."

Darwin said, "Look before the *p* in the *p-e-k.* I think there is an *o.*"

"Yeah . . . yes, I see it. So it's *o-p-e-k.*"

"*Opek?*" Oliver said. "The oil cartel?"

"That's *o-p-e-c,*" Decker told him.

Darwin said, "Look in the upper-left corner. You can also see lettering."

Decker shifted the protected fabric and found the section that the pathologist was referring to. "Yes, I see it. *A-j-o-r.*"

"Exactly."

"Anything else I should be looking for?"

"That's all I could tell you at this magnification," Darwin told him. "Perhaps we can scan it into the computer and it can bring up more information."

"Good idea." Decker pulled away from the instrument and rolled his shoulders. "Anyone else want to take a look?"

"I'll take a crack at it," Oliver said. The group waited in silence as Oliver looked over the fabric. "Yeah . . . that's all I can make out as well." He lifted his eyes from the lens. "Not exactly much to go on. The letters are obviously part of bigger words."

Marge said, "We have to take the cloth in context."

"What context?" Oliver asked.

"Well, for starters, what was the shirt used for?" Marge examined the fabric. "Because of the printing on it, I'd say that the garment was originally a T-shirt, a sweatshirt, or a jacket."

Decker added, "Since the material is synthetic, my vote is with a jacket. T's and sweatshirts are usually cotton."

"I agree," the pathologist said.

Marge continued to peruse the cloth. "There's a lot of lettering on a single patch, and usually jackets don't have long messages on the back. And the way the partial words are stacked on top of one another . . ." She got up from her hunched position. "To me that suggests some kind of list."

Oliver said, "So what kind of list would be on the back of a jacket?"

Decker's brain fired up. "Margie, let me see your notes for a second." After reading her pad, he hit the paper with the back of his hand. "It's like doing a gridless crossword without any clues. Still, if you do enough crosswords, your mind fills in the blanks. *V-e-s-t-o-n.* If I say it instead of spell it, it helps. Veston. How about the city, Galveston. For *o-p-e-k,* how about Topeka. *D-i-a-n* could be lots of things, but if we're in that part of the country, I'd say Indianapolis."

"Maybe that's the *a-p-o-l,*" Marge suggested.

Decker said, "In any case, I think we're looking at a tour jacket."

"Sweet," Marge said. "Unfortunately, we don't know *whose* tour jacket. But we know that it was once pink. I'm betting it's a girl group, a group with a girl as its lead singer or a solo girl."

"Madonna?" Darwin said. "She was really popular."

"She's been around for a long time," Marge said. "I bet there's some nut out there who's an expert on Madonna's tours."

"You picture Madonna going to Galveston?" Oliver asked.

"What's wrong with Galveston?" Marge countered.

"Nothing," Oliver said. "I'm sure it's a great city except in hurricane season. Superficially, it just doesn't seem like her crowd."

"A country star," Decker said.

"With Topeka and Galveston, I'd say that's a good guess."

Decker said, "How old do you think the jacket is?"

Darwin shrugged and the small lab fell silent. So many unanswered questions.

Oliver bent over and looked into the eyepieces, adjusting the lens for stereoscopic vision. He shifted the cloth to the upper-left corner, reading the letters aloud. "*A-j-o-r.* These letters are bigger and not stacked. I don't think this word is part of the list of cities. So the question is . . ." He looked up. "What are these letters and I'm saying . . . that maybe the letters indicate the band."

"Ajor," Marge said out loud. "Maybe *major*?"

"Shit!" Oliver hit his head. "Oh man! What about Priscilla and the Major?"

"Now there's a blast from the past," Decker said.

"Who?" Marge and Darwin asked simultaneously.

"They were a singing duo in the seventies. They played soft rock, if I had to categorize it, but they were very popular with the country circuit because he was a retired army major and very patriotic."

"He played guitar, but she was the star," Oliver said. "They were big in their time."

"True," Decker said, "although I don't think I ever bought one of their albums."

"Albums," Marge said. "Now you're really dating yourself."

"They came in somewhere between acid rock and disco," Oliver told her. "They were a nostalgic group even in those times."

"You know a lot about them," Marge told Oliver.

"My ex liked them," Oliver said. "Me? I never bought any of their albums, either, but I remember Priscilla as being a fox. That's old-speak for being a hottie."

10

LET ME THINK out loud for a moment." Decker sat at his desk. Across from him were Marge and Oliver, awaiting further instructions. "Two cases: Jane Doe and Roseanne Dresden. Jane is a homicide . . . Roseanne?" He shrugged. "We're reserving judgment on her. Recovery's still digging, but it's been a while. Someone has to talk to the husband."

"And ask him what?" Oliver asked. "Did you kill your wife?"

Decker answered, "The fact is we don't know if she's even dead. We do suspect that the Dresden marriage was in trouble. David Rottiger and Arielle Toombs said that the couple was headed for divorce. Plus, Arielle told me that Roseanne had broken up with a paramour named Raymond Holmes six months prior to her death. She said he didn't take it well. For all we know, he could be involved."

A pause.

"We have to approach Ivan Dresden in a nonthreatening way. I think it's far more likely that he'll talk to us if he thinks we're investigating a missing person rather than a homicide. So far that's true."

Marge said, "If the guy is as money hungry as all say, we can tell him insurance won't settle until they find a body."

"That's probably true," Oliver said.

"Up to a point," Decker said. "Anyway, we can tell him that the police are investigating her whereabouts for insurance purposes. Since her body hasn't turned up, we're thinking that she may be alive."

Oliver said, "What are we after, Loo?"

Decker said. "First, we need to hear his story. Second, it would be helpful if we could obtain his permission to pull phone records, credit-card receipts, bank records, to see if there's been any activity since she disappeared. We can tell Ivan that it will be an important part of the insurance investigation."

"Do we bring up the old flame, Ray?" Marge asked.

"Use your discretion."

Marge said to Oliver, "You call up Ivan or should I?"

"You can do it. I'd rather call up Ivan's lap-dancer friend."

"Lap-dancer friend?" Decker asked.

"Yeah, David Rottiger told me Ivan had a thing for a lap-dancer friend of his. Ivan met her at one of Rottiger's parties."

"Interesting." Decker nodded. "Do you have name?"

"No, Rottiger wouldn't give it to me, and at the time, there was no reason to push. But I know where she works and I'd be happy to conduct a field interview with her."

"I bet." Decker smiled. "Actually, she may be a legitimate source of info later on. But first talk to Ivan. And see if you can conduct the interview in his condo because it'll give you an opportunity to see the way he's living. Get on his good side. We're trying to wrest permission from him to look at Roseanne's paperwork. Once we sort through all the credit slips, the bank statements, and the phone records, we'll get a clearer idea about her last days."

Oliver said, "Have you told Farley Lodestone about the latest developments?"

"Not yet." Decker sighed. "This is not going to improve his trust in the justice system. If he wasn't so bereaved, I'm sure he'd gloat."

Marge said, "You know, if Roseanne was on flight 1324, there could be someone who worked the gate that remembers seeing her board the plane. I'd like to go down to WestAir's airport counter next week and talk to the desk people."

"They're only going to refer you to the task force," Oliver said.

"Maybe woman-to-woman, I can get some information. Now that Roseanne's been missing for so long, I'd like to take one more crack at it."

Decker said, "I think it's a good idea. So we've got some strategies mapped out with Roseanne. Let's move on to problem number two—our skeletal Jane Doe, who was probably a homicide. We need to identify the body and we can't put a face on the bones because the bones are too delicate to mess with. So what *can* we do? We can find out when the apartment building went up. We can also locate someone involved with Priscilla and the Major to see if we can date the jacket."

"Wanda Bontemps is on the computer trying to get a bead on the singing duo," Marge said. "I did manage to Google them right before the meeting. Over five hundred thousand references, but no official Web site. How old would either of them be?"

"Sixties." *Not all that far from his age,* Decker thought. "While Wanda is tracking down the duo, somebody needs to go down to building and safety and find out when the apartment building went up. Let's go with Lee Wang and Jules Chatham. Both of them are good with bureaucracy, paper shuffling, and details."

"Chatham is on vacation," Marge said. "I think Lee is at his desk. I'll talk to him."

Oliver said, "You're talking about a twenty-five- maybe thirty-year-old building. That's a lot of tenants, Loo."

"Someone must have a record of everyone who rented there for tax purposes. Talk to the current owners and work backward. I'll draw up an assignment schedule. We can confer again tomorrow morning.

Maybe by then Wanda will have found a location for Priscilla and the Major."

"Are you going to wait until the morning to call Lodestone?" Oliver asked.

"No, I'm going to call Lodestone as soon as you leave. Then I'm going to go home and forget about all this stuff. It's Shabbos tonight and that means I get a day of rest. And even if I don't get my day of rest, I'm at least entitled to a last supper."

MUNCHING A PEANUT-BUTTER-AND-BANANA sandwich, Wanda was still at the computer when Oliver and Marge came out of Decker's office. She didn't bother to look up from the screen as she spoke. "The wonders of modern technology. Almost everyone in the universe is just a click away."

Oliver said, "What have you found out about them?"

"First off, the original duo is a thing of the past. The original Major—Huntley Barrett—has been dead for twelve years. Priscilla used to perform with another guy, Kendrick Springer, but the fans and the reviewers didn't like him at all. You should read the comments." She shook her head in dismay. "Passions ran very high about Huntley's replacement."

"Does Priscilla still perform?" Marge asked.

Bontemps shrugged. "That's an interesting question. She doesn't have an official Web site, but she does have an agent. I can't find any current concert dates for her. Last one I found was seven years ago." She looked at her notepad, tore off the top sheet of paper, and gave it to Oliver. "Her agent."

Oliver glanced at the slip of paper. Miles Marlowe with a phone number. It was after six and Marlowe was probably gone, but he'd leave a phone message. "Anything else?"

She handed him a four-inch stack of paper. "Everything I've pulled up and thought worth printing, I printed for you."

"Jeez, I feel a little guilty." Oliver hefted the pile. "Like I just nuked a forest or something."

Bontemps smiled. "Sir, don't take this wrong, but I would have never thought you to be the environmentally conscious type."

"Don't tell anyone, Wanda, but I even recycle."

PRISCILLA AND THE Major's last top-ten song had been recorded over twenty-eight years ago, but they had left behind a rich legacy of blogs, K-Right (order by toll-free number, only available through this TV offer) boxed-set CDs, and a host of sixtysomething fans wishing nostalgically for singable melodies and clean lyrics. As Oliver read through the stack of computer information, he discovered that though the couple had divorced, they had remained friendly up to the day the Major had died. Priscilla had moved to Florida specifically to minister to him during the final months of his life. As a result, the Major, the business brains behind the duo's success, had left her his very sizable estate, including a collection of sixty vintage guitars, most of which Priscilla had auctioned off. There had been a daughter and it had been big news when Priscilla had given birth, but what happened to the girl was anyone's guess.

After going through the material, Oliver stored the sheaves of paper in the newly created Jane Doe folder, and was just turning the key to his desk's lone file cabinet when his cell rang. The window displayed a number that looked familiar, although he had no idea who was on the line. Since it was his cell and not the desk phone, he answered it by the regular hello rather than "Oliver."

"I'm looking for a . . . a Detective Scott Olivier."

Pronouncing it like the great, late actor. Oliver liked that. It gave him gravitas. "This is Detective Oliver. Who am I talking to?"

"Miles Marlowe. Uh, it's says here on my message that you called regarding Priscilla Barrett?"

"I did—"

"Well, she isn't interested in taking on any partners."

"That's good because I'm not interested in being her partner." Oliver held back a laugh. "Where'd you get that idea?"

"Because you called yourself detective."

"That's because I am a detective."

"A real one?"

This time Oliver let go with a chuckle. The man sounded old and feisty. "Yes, a real one, Mr. Marlowe. I'm with Los Angeles Police Department and—"

"Well, you've got to understand what I'm dealing with," Marlowe interrupted. "All sorts of wannabes calling me to partner with Priscilla and they all got titles. I've had sergeants, I've had captains, colonels, and lieutenants. I've even had some royalty: two princes and one duke. I thought you were one of those. You know . . . remaking my lady into Priscilla and the Detective." A couple of quick, short breaths—a smoker or emphysema. "Not a bad ring, but it sounds more like a TV show than a singing duo. Anyway, what do you want with my lady?"

"I'd like to talk to her, sir."

"Why?"

"It's part of an ongoing investigation. I only need a little bit of Priscilla's time."

"Nothing grisly in the investigation, I hope. She's a delicate soul."

"Nothing grisly at all," Oliver lied. "I've been doing some homework on her. Last I checked, she was living in Vegas."

"She was in Vegas for a while. Drew really big crowds, but she decided it wasn't for her. Like I told you, she's a delicate soul."

"Understood, sir. Anyway, being an old fan as well as a detective, I thought I could talk to her—"

"I thought there was an ulterior motive. The woman still has the 'it' factor."

"I'm sure she does," Oliver said, "but I assure you I have no ulterior motive—"

"Well, this is what I'm gonna do for you. I'll give her this number. She'll call you when she's ready."

"I think I'm going to need a face-to-face, sir, and the sooner the better. If you want, I'll be happy to call her up directly."

"You want to talk to Priscilla, you go through me. For all I know, you could be an agent, trying to steal my lady. You just want to meet her, Detective Olivier. Don't deny it!"

Oliver decided to lay on the schmaltz. "Okay, Mr. Marlowe, you got me. I'd love to meet your lady."

"Now that you admitted it, we can get somewhere. So how do I know you are who you say you are?"

Oliver said, "Sir, why don't you come down to West Valley Division of LAPD and we'll go together to meet the lady. That way you'll see that I'm legitimate and you can see I actually work as a detective."

"Hmm . . ." Marlowe pondered the suggestion. "All right. I suppose I could come down and check you out in the flesh. If you're legit, you can follow me to her house. She happens to live in the West Valley . . . Porter Ranch."

"Does she, now? Well, that's certainly convenient for all of us."

"Not for me. I work in Hollywood."

"Then I appreciate your taking the time to go out of your way to introduce us. It's really not necessary, especially since I'm so close—"

"Now don't you be getting any ideas about popping in on her, Detective Olivier. It's a gated community with full-time guards."

"I wouldn't do that, sir, that would be stalking. When is it convenient to meet you?"

"It's not my convenience, Detective, it's Priscilla's. I'll call her up and call you back."

"That sounds fine, Mr. Marlowe."

The phone hung up abruptly. Ten minutes later, just as Oliver was pulling his Chrysler PT Cruiser convertible out of the police parking lot, his cell rang.

"How about Monday at three?"

It was Marlowe, no introduction necessary. Oliver said, "Sounds great. Thanks for setting it up so fast."

"I'll come out to the police station to meet you. But no monkey business or I'll have your badge."

"You're welcome to it," Oliver whispered.

"What?"

"Thank you very much, Mr. Marlowe, you've been a big help."

11

THE KINDLING OF the candles signified the onset of the holy day of rest, welcoming the Shabbat bride with song and food. Showered and shaved, Decker felt clean and renewed. Since he'd decided not to go to synagogue, he dressed casually—a pair of khaki pants, a black polo shirt, and sandals. His stomach rumbled from the aromas emanating from the kitchen, and his mouth was watering by the time he sat down at the table. Seven place settings of china and crystal: Rina had done the centerpiece herself, the arrangements courtesy of her new hobby. She had turned their backyard into an English garden. The colors and the bouquets were dizzying. Insects and birds abounded. She called it their personal Eden.

Tonight, Rina had elected to wear an emerald-green A-line dress and silver flats. Her hair had been tied up in a knot, covered by a lacy mantilla that fell gracefully down her back. Hannah had two girl-friends over for the weekend, and Cindy and Koby rounded out the guest list. Whenever she had company, Rina and her cooking gene went haywire. Dinner started out with fresh-cured gravlax with a mustard dill sauce. The fish course was followed by a puree of squash-and-carrot soup spiced with cinnamon and ginger, on its heels an arugula salad with grapefruit and orange segments. By the time the entrée was served—turkey breast stuffed with wild rice, with green beans amandine and baby carrots for sides—no one was really hungry. But that didn't stop anyone at the table from eating. Nor did it dissuade the guests from polishing off the plum cobbler and a bowl of the season's first cherries.

After they'd stuffed themselves silly, Rina tried to make everyone feel more virtuous. "It's mostly fruit except for the crumble topping."

"That's the best part," Koby told her. "I'll have another piece."

"I can always count on you, Yaakov," Rina told him, spooning another scoop of the streusel-topped concoction onto his plate.

"That's because I have no stop button when it comes to food."

"Lucky you," Decker muttered.

Rina tossed her husband a "behave yourself" look, even though she knew what he meant. At six two, one-fifty, Koby was as thin as grass. A wiry man, but deceptively strong. Like Decker, he was also handy around the house. In honor of Shabbat, he wore a white shirt and black slacks and loafers without socks. Cindy wore a black knit skirt and a turquoise sweater that set off her red hair, courtesy of her father's DNA. Hannah and Cindy had nearly identical coloring, red hair, red eyebrows and eyelids, and clear alabaster skin that freckled in the summertime. The difference was only in the eye color: Cindy's eyes were brown whereas Hannah's were green. The sisters resembled each other even though they had clearly come from different mothers.

"Are you two getting any vacation time?" Decker asked his older daughter.

Cindy said, "Nothing definite yet."

Koby said, "We're trying for a weekend in Santa Barbara."

"Do you need help clearing?" Hannah asked her mother. She and her two friends had finished dessert ten minutes ago. They were itching to leave and talk about important issues—school, poetry, alternative rock, Gossip Girl books, and boys, boys, boys.

Rina said, "Just bring in your plates and load them in the dishwasher. I'll do the rest and call you when it's time to bench."

"Are you sure?" Hannah asked. But it was clear the girl was grateful to be dismissed.

"Positive." Rina turned to Cindy. "Your father installed a new Shabbat dishwasher that has been an absolute godsend. I don't know what in the world took us so long to buy it."

"Those built-in dish drawers?" Koby asked.

"Yes, from the same company. We bought the full-size dishwasher for meat and a dish drawer for dairy. I lost a bit of cabinet space, but what we save on time spent doing dishes more than makes up for it."

"We're thinking of pushing out the kitchen," Cindy said. "That's why we're asking." When she noticed her father's face, she smiled. "No, I'm not pregnant, but we do want a family. And it would be nice to have a genuine room for our future progeny."

Koby added, "With home prices so expensive, we both think it is better to remodel."

"Who's going to do the work?" Decker asked.

"I am . . . and whoever else wants to help," Koby answered.

Three pairs of eyes focused on Decker's face. "Like I don't have enough to do?" But he knew he'd cave in. That's the way it was with children.

Cindy said, "We're a ways off from lugging around two-by-fours, Dad. We're still gathering information." She turned to Rina. "The food was delicious. I'm stuffed."

"Thank you. Can I make you a care package?"

"I was hoping you'd offer." Cindy stood up and began to clear.

"You sit," Decker told his daughter. "I'll help."

"Age before beauty," she replied. "Actually, Dad, I am so full that it feels good to move."

Decker said, "You know what? Why don't you and I clear together and let Koby and Rina relax?"

Koby said, "It is an offer I won't refuse."

Rina smiled. He was trying to get time alone with his girl. "Great. I haven't read the paper yet."

"Neither have I."

"Then we'll share," Rina said. "I'll even pour you a scotch, Yaakov."

The two of them retreated to the living room while father and daughter cleared the dining-room table of dishes and brought them into the kitchen.

"I wash and you dry?" Cindy offered.

"All you have to do is rinse them and put them in the dishwasher. Why don't you let me do that?"

"You put away the food. I don't know where it goes."

"Deal."

Cindy turned on the tap. "This is nice. Doing dishes together. Like old times but better."

"Yeah, the old times were pretty good, too." He gave her a brief smile as he scraped food into the garbage. "How's GTA?"

"Busy. You know how it is. The weather starts getting warmer, it's open season on cars."

"Crime in general. When it's wet and nasty outside, no one wants to work—even the psychos. How do you like teaming with Joe?"

Joe Papquick was her partner. "He's fine. Not exactly loquacious, but he tells me what I need to know. It's pretty routine, actually. You wind up investigating the same shops, the same junkyards, the same people. It seems the thieves rotate through twenty or so auto yards and it's just a matter of the choppers getting caught with their pants down."

"Be careful," he warned her. "Routine doesn't exclude bad surprises."

She smiled. "Joe has this saying. If you don't treat every call like it's your first, it could be your last."

"He is so right. If you're feeling too comfortable, you let your guard down."

"I'm careful. And it's not always routine. Every once in a while, you make a good guess, and because of it, you get another sleaze bucket off the streets."

"Makes you feel pretty good."

"Very good, even though most of the time it's grunt work."

"That's being what being a detective is."

"I would think homicide's *a little* more exciting."

"It is more exciting, even though you get your obvious smoking gun cases. Then you spend lots of time trying to extract a confession."

"There's an art to that."

"Absolutely. But sometimes no matter how skillful, you don't get what you want. Then you hope forensics will buttress the case. And when that doesn't work . . . that's when it's really frustrating. The 'what did I miss?' second-guessing game. First question is always Did I get the right person? You go through the file over and over, trying to find the magic bullet."

Cindy said, "How often do you actually find something you missed when you look through an old case?"

"More than you think. The key is to put it away for a while so you review it through fresh eyes. Even with that, I'd say the success rate is maybe . . . I don't know. I'd say you have a fifty percent chance that you find something that'll jump-start something dead in the water."

"Not a bad baseball percentage."

"But dismal in murder," Decker said. "It's always hard to watch a case go cold. Then there's the occasional cold case that falls in your lap." He told Cindy about the sudden appearance of a disinterred body. As he spoke, she listened carefully, adding a word or two at the right spots. If she hadn't chosen to be a cop, she would have made a hell of a shrink.

She said, "And forensics is sure that the body isn't the flight attendant?"

"I went down to the Crypt and saw the sets of radiographs myself. So now instead of a solve, I've got two open cases."

"That's a pisser, but it's really interesting. Did the apartment building have a basement?"

"No, it was a typical California building: wood-framed stucco, no basement."

"What about subterranean parking?"

"I believe it had a lot in the back . . . built in days when land was a lot cheaper. I'm remembering it as one parking space per unit and the rest was street parking."

"And how many units did the building have?"

"Fifteen. Why do you ask?"

"You said the body was found above the foundation."

"I don't think I said yes or no. Why do you ask?"

"Back then, didn't they build lots of Southern California buildings with crawl spaces between the subfloor and the foundation?"

"I would say yes. The earthquake codes were different. They don't do that anymore. Usually the subfloor is attached to the foundation."

"But in the older buildings, that's where they put the plumbing, right?"

"Yeah, they'd put the sewer lines down there, especially if the building was multistoried."

"You should find out if the building had a crawl space. It would be a perfect dump for a body since most of the tenants wouldn't be aware of its existence. Or maybe the person who killed your Jane Doe could have been someone involved with constructing the building."

"That's exactly what we're thinking. We're looking up the builders as well as the tenants. And all the tradesmen. Plumbers, phone people . . . pest control."

"But, Daddy, wouldn't those people stick out? I mean, if you see a guy walking around your house or apartment, you're going to ask who it is."

"And . . ."

"All I'm saying is that a service guy might feel intimidated dumping a body in a building. He might be scared that someone would see him poking around. I'm thinking that anyone who would dump a body into the crawl space has to feel he wouldn't attract attention."

"That's a very good point," Decker told her. "So running with your idea, maybe we're dealing with a janitor or super or maintenance guy who lived in the building. No one would think twice about seeing him getting dirty, hauling out trash, or poking around the insides of a building."

"When in doubt, look at the maintenance man," Cindy teased him. "I've watched enough of those crime-reconstruction shows to know it's always the janitor."

Decker smiled. "I'll tell someone on the team to check it out. Good thinking, Detective."

Cindy felt herself go hot and knew she was blushing. Whenever her father praised her, she felt an inordinate swell of pride. She looked down and pretended to be interested in the dishes. "Who's primary on the assignment?"

"Either Scott or Marge. I don't even know if they figured it out yet."

"Sounds like you have your hands full, Dad. But look at it this way. You're not pushing paper."

"Yeah, be careful what you wish for."

Cindy placed a Pyrex pan in the dishwasher. "Koby was offered a promotion."

"That's wonderful!" Decker told her. "When did this happen?"

"Couple of weeks ago."

"And you're first telling me now?"

"He doesn't know if he wants it. It's more money but more time on the job, more paperwork, and it takes him off the floor and primary patient care, which is what he really likes. He shouldn't be killing himself for a few extra dollars. But he's obsessed with saving money for the construction."

"Don't worry about it. I'll help you with the remodeling."

"I know and I really appreciate it. But even if we can do most of the framing ourselves, there are still skills that we're not going to attempt like electrical and plumbing. Last thing I want is a broken sewer line or a fried husband or father."

"I agree."

"Whatever we decide, it's going to take money. Mom's offered to lend us some cash, but Koby has his reservations. That's why he's considering the promotion or options that will make him more money."

"Money's important, but he should be happy."

"That's what I tell him." Cindy paused. "Alan offered to help out."

"Uh . . . fine."

Cindy gave her father a smile. "Did I detect a bit of hesitation on your part?"

"Not at all. Your stepfather keeps your mom happy and that makes everything easier." Decker gave a tepid smile. "I just never knew he was handy."

"He and Mom have been really into home improvement. I think they own stock in Lowe's or something."

"What are they doing?"

"Installing new appliances—new dishwasher, refrigerator, and microwave. Alan also built a bookcase and a table."

"How'd his handiwork come out?"

"Not too bad, actually."

"Good. We can use as much help as possible. Do you have an architect?"

"We have a neighbor who's helping us out at a reduced fee. AIA certified. Nice woman who does good work. I lucked out: a neighbor architect, a handy father and husband, a somewhat handy stepfather . . . count my blessings."

"We'll have good old barn raising."

"Thanks, Daddy, I really appreciate it." Cindy offered him a luminous smile. "And I'd like to add that I'm very proud of you."

"Me?"

"You're talking to me like a colleague instead of a daughter. To wit, we've been together for almost an hour and you have yet to give me a word of advice except to tell me that I shouldn't treat any police case as routine, and that's just what my partner says, so I can't even claim that was an overprotective daddism."

Decker started to say something, but nodded instead.

"Is it hard for you not to give me advice?" Cindy asked. "Tell me the truth."

"Well, put it this way." Decker thought a moment. "My tongue is nearly severed from biting it so hard."

12

S A SATELLITE airport, Burbank usually had manageable
crowds, which translated into shorter check-in and security lines,
and officials who were friendlier and, in general, less bureaucratic. But even a small airport had post-9/11 concerns, and the head of
security kept Marge Dunn parked on the wrong side of the metal de-
tectors since she was lacking proper authorization. Because there wasn't
any hope of getting clearance from WestAir, Marge resorted to plan B,
working her charm on the staff behind the check-in counter.

There was no scheduled WestAir flight in or out for the next two
hours and the sole person manning the counter appeared lonely and
bored. Marge put him in his late twenties, sporting a round face and a
pinched mouth. She smoothed her navy skirt, rotating the waistband
until the zipper sat against her left side. Why the contraption on this
particular skirt moved to center when she walked was one of those
unexplained mysteries of life. She sauntered up to the WestAir desk
and flashed the man her cheeriest smile. He responded in kind and displayed his own white teeth.

"Can I help you?"

"I think you can. I'm from Acona Insurance Corporation, which is a subsidiary of Livalli Corp. We're working on a specific claim in regard to flight 1324 and we need verification for the benefactor that the victim was on said flight—"

"I'm sorry," the clerk said. "All questions regarding flight 1324 need to go through the WestAir task force. I can give you the task-force phone number, if you'd like."

Marge leaned over and dropped her voice to a whisper. "Can I be frank, Mr. . . ."

"Baine."

"Mr. Baine, I'm Marge Dunn." She held out her hand and a reluctant Mr. Baine shook it. "Your task force has a problem returning telephone calls. I don't think they're very anxious to settle their claims." She watched Baine's reaction. When he didn't immediately defend the company, she depressed her brain's ad-lib button. "We suspect the company is having severe cash-flow problems. We understand that they've even withheld some payrolls checks—"

"Only once," Baine interrupted.

"I'm not here to knock the management, Mr. Baine, I just need information." She brought her face closer to his. "I'm representing one of your own flight attendants—Roseanne Dresden. I just need to verify that she was on the flight and then I can give her poor husband a little solace as well as money."

The clerk harrumphed.

"Do I detect a note of skepticism?" Marge inquired.

A shrug. "I didn't know either of them very well."

"Yet you have your opinions."

"She was well liked. He wasn't."

Marge nodded. "I'll hear anything you want to tell me."

"My opinions won't help your situation. Why do you need verification for Roseanne specifically?"

"All of the other bodies have been recovered except hers."

Baine was taken aback. "I thought they found it a couple of weeks ago."

"False alarm."

"Really." Baine pursed his little lips. "That's too bad."

"It's heartbreaking, actually. Her parents are waiting for news, but we've got nothing to tell them." Marge paused for effect. "This is the situation, Mr. Baine. Roseanne wasn't ticketed for the flight. We were told that she hopped one of the jumper seats, and was on her way to work in San Jose. But we haven't found *anything* that puts her on the plane other than the fact that no one has heard from her since the crash."

"And that's not enough?"

"Not in this century. If she boarded the flight, she had to pass through security. None of the security agents specifically remember seeing her, but that was a long time ago." A little lie, but it was harmless. "All I want to know is who worked the gate for flight 1324. Maybe someone remembers seeing Roseanne board the flight."

Baine was silent, weighing something in his brain. He picked up a phone and turned his back as he spoke into the receiver. A moment later he hung up and pointed to the exit. "Directly across the street, there's a coffee shop. She's waiting for you there. You can't miss her . . . she's in uniform."

"Thank you. And she has a name?"

"She does, but it's up to her if she wants to give it to you."

"Thank you."

"You're welcome." As Marge turned to leave, he said, "It was actually two times."

She faced him. "Pardon?"

He crooked a finger and she leaned over. Baine whispered, "WestAir held back a month of paychecks—for all their employees. We had to accept the conditions or else the company claimed it would file for Chapter Eleven. Even with that, there still may be some cutbacks."

"Wow, that's a rotten deal."

"What can I do? I need this job."

"At least the cuts affected everyone," Marge said.

"So they say," Baine answered. "Last I heard, the CEO still owned his yacht."

———

A SLIM ATTRACTIVE redhead held out her hand to Marge. "Erika Lessing."

"Marge Dunn."

Introductions done, they sat opposite each other at a corner table. The coffee shop was one of those retro cafés made to look like a fifties automat. The tables and chairs were tubular metal and the upholstery was faux leather colored oxblood red. Waitresses wore white uniforms protected by frilly aprons and had little white caps on their heads.

Erika was easy to spot in her WestAir uniform: the white shirt, black skirt, and yellow blazer made her look like a bumblebee. She seemed no older than her late twenties with her ginger hair swirling in a nest of curls. Her eyes were dark brown and tired. "You're a claims adjuster?" She focused her eyes on Marge's face. "My father was an adjuster. I worked for him for several summers. I got to know the business very well. There's good money in insurance. You want to know why I didn't pursue it?"

"Sure."

"I got tired of people lying. Idiots padding every claim, trying to suck the company dry because the morons figured that insurance is paying, so why not? The company retaliates by raising rates to exorbitant levels, or worse, by stalling legitimate claims and dragging its heels. Meanwhile, some poor jerk with a totaled car taking the bus to work for months, waiting for the check to finally materialize five years later. It deals with the worst aspects of human beings."

"Tell me how you really feel," Marge said. "Don't hold back."

Erika's smile was angry and tight. "Eliot told me you're looking for the people who worked the gate for flight 1324."

"Eliot being the Mr. Baine at the check-in counter."

"Yes, that's him. He called me because he knew I was across the street, trying to relax and read the paper before I go to work."

"I'm sorry to disturb you, but you can understand why this is important."

"I worked the gate," she admitted. "Normally I wouldn't talk to you, but if after all this time, someone is still nosing around Roseanne Dresden, I figure it's time to say my piece." A deep sigh of regret. "I feel like unloading, and tag, you're it."

"I'm open to anything you want to tell me."

"You don't know how stressful the last couple of months have been." She pointed to her chest. "*I* checked in all those people. I feel like I sent them off to die. I know it's not rational, but . . ." She shook her head. "Honestly, I'm still in shock. I'm depressed all the time. And angry and listless. And I feel so damn guilty!"

"Things sound very tough at your company and it doesn't sound like you're getting any support."

"None. They don't even like us to talk about it. Afraid we'll say something that might inspire more lawsuits. Right now that's all they're concerned about. But you didn't hear that from me."

"Of course not."

Erika's eyes moistened. "So here's my story, Ms. Dunn. In general, I made good decisions. I took the right job for me . . . well, up until the incident. I bought a condo when rates were low. I have a wonderful set of friends . . . but everyone has their downfall."

"And yours is men," Marge said automatically.

"It's that obvious?"

"I've been there. Don't fret. There's hope in the future."

"I'd like to think so." Another sigh. "I liked Roseanne, I really . . ." Her voice choked up. "I just have this thing for bad boys. I've gone to the altar three times and I'm only twenty-eight. Just when I think I'm ready to finally settle down, some wise guy with a sexy smirk winks and worms his way into my heart."

"Ivan Dresden."

"Have you ever met him?"

"I've seen a picture. He's good-looking."

"Gorgeous but a real con artist, but ultimately it was my decision to take off my clothes. I didn't care that he was married, but I should have cared that he was married to Roseanne. I considered her a friend, and for those six months, I lived in fear that she'd find out."

"Who finally called it off?"

"I did. You can't work with someone in a closed environment like the inside of a plane if there's bad blood. Your life may depend on them."

"And you're sure that Roseanne never found out?"

"I'm certain she never knew. Not that I didn't have a couple of close calls. Once when we were out to lunch she broke down and confessed that she thought Ivan was having an affair. When she muttered those words, time stood still. I almost confessed, but then it was clear that she was railing against another woman. Good thing I was slow to react. Apparently, the creep was two-timing both of us!"

"Do you remember the name of the other woman?"

"Melissa . . . Miranda . . ." She shrugged. "No one who worked for WestAir." She took another sip of coffee. "I have a reason for telling you about my sordid little escapades. What you're really looking for—if I understood Eliot correctly—is a witness who saw Roseanne board flight 1324."

Marge felt her heart jump. "You saw her board the aircraft."

"No, I didn't see her board the aircraft and that's the whole point. Since I had an affair with Roseanne's husband, I made it a point to notice Roseanne so I can prepare myself. I have to do that . . . prepare myself mentally. I'm fair and I blush easily. I didn't want her asking questions like 'What's wrong?'"

"Aha."

"If Roseanne would have passed through those gates, I would have noticed her. But I didn't see her. That means she wasn't there."

"Could she have boarded the aircraft before you got to the gate?"

"No, because I was already at the gate checking people in when the aircraft came in from an early morning flight from San Jose."

"Could Roseanne have been on the flight coming in from San Jose and not have gotten off the plane?"

Erika gave the question some thought. "It's possible. Sometimes the flight attendants don't deplane, but usually they do. We prefer to freshen up in facilities that are bigger than a bread box. Anyway, that wasn't the story, was it? The story was she boarded the plane here in Burbank and sat in a jump seat."

"But it is possible that her husband got Roseanne's flights all mixed up. He could have been listening to his wife with half an ear and jumped at the opportunity to get rid of her so he could call up one of his many girlfriends."

"Can I ask why you, as an insurance adjuster, have delved into Ivan Dresden's bad habits?" Erika narrowed her eyes. "You know you haven't shown me a lick of identification. Insurance adjusters do that routinely. So why don't you tell me who you really are since I was forthright with you?"

Marge gauged her hard eyes. Erika was hostile, but she was also in pain. There had probably been times in the heat of the affair when she had wished Roseanne dead. Now she was carrying around an irrational guilt that her wish had come true. Marge dug into her purse and pulled out her badge and ID card.

"Police?" Erika was genuinely surprised. "Why are the police involved?"

"Because Roseanne's body hasn't turned up, so officially she's a missing person. It's been over two months since anyone heard from her, so it's very likely that she's dead . . . and it's starting to look like she didn't die in the crash. That's where I come in. I'm from homicide."

"You think she was *murdered*?"

"Right now I'm trying to rule out murder. Unfortunately, I haven't been able to do that."

"You think it was Ivan?" Erika kneaded her hands. "Don't answer that. I don't want to know."

"I couldn't answer you even if I knew. But I'm being honest when I tell you that I don't even know *if* she was murdered. That's why I need to talk to everyone who was involved with the crash. So far, your company has been making things very difficult. But you have been very helpful."

"Don't make me regret it."

"You won't regret it. You're bringing justice to a friend."

"That's a nice way of putting it."

"One more question and then I'm done," Marge said. "Was anyone else working the gate with you, Ms. Lessing?"

The woman didn't answer. She stopped playing with her hands, took a final sip of her custom coffee, and stood. "Sara McKeel. But you didn't get the name from me."

THE NUMBER OF missing women who fit the physical forensics of Jane Doe's charred body was staggering. Decker had pulled up over a decade's worth of missing-persons files—from 1971 when the building went up through 1981—when Marge knocked on the door frame to his office.

"Come in, sit down, and tell me some good news," Decker said. "Because from where I'm sitting, things are sucking big-time."

"Why's that?" Marge pulled up a chair and sat across from the lieutenant.

"One hundred and seventeen women and girls went missing between '71 and '81 in the Valley alone. Some were probably custody cases, some may have resolved without our knowing it, but some have to be open files. A few of you unlucky souls are going to be assigned the nasty task of announcing heartbreak to families who may have felt they were finally moving on with their lives."

"I think we should let Wanda and Julius do the calling. Both of them have nice phone voices."

Decker handed her a bunch of stacks. "You're a sergeant. Make the assignments as you see fit."

"I love my rank." Marge took the paperwork and sat it on her lap. "I wanted to bring you up-to-date with Roseanne Dresden."

"Good or bad?"

"Illuminating. I had two interviews with the women who worked the desk for flight 1324. Neither remembers Roseanne boarding the aircraft. One of the flight attendants—Sara McKeel—wouldn't swear that Roseanne didn't board, but she didn't *recall* seeing Roseanne that morning. The other flight attendant was a woman named Erika Lessing and she told a different story." Marge recapped the conversation. "Erika swears up and down that she would have noticed if Roseanne had boarded the plane. She had an acute madar—mistress radar."

Decker nodded. "But Lessing didn't know if Roseanne was on the previous flight from San Jose and had stayed on board."

"No, she couldn't tell me that. So I guess the next thing to do would be to call up San Jose and ask them if Roseanne boarded 1324 from their location."

Scott Oliver knocked then walked into Decker's office, looking very Casual Friday. Navy crewneck sweater with a blue oxford-weave shirt underneath, and black chino pants. Sneakers on his feet. Decker said, "Who gave you the day off?"

"We're interviewing Priscilla Huntley in about forty minutes. If we're going to take a trip down memory lane, I thought I'd look the part."

Marge said, "You look way more fifties than seventies, Scott."

"First of all, I can't come to work in torn jeans and a tie-dye shirt, stinking of tobacco and weed, unless I'm doing narcotics, which—thank God—I'm not."

"You did narcotics?" Marge asked.

"About a zillion years ago when I was young, invincible, and hook-ers had diseases that could be controlled by antibiotics. But let us not digress. While my dress might not be in sync with those patronizing a Zeppelin concert, I think I would have melded very nicely with the Priscilla and the Major crowd, even back then."

"Explanation accepted," Decker said.

Oliver said, "We've got to go, Margie. Her agent is waiting for us. He absolutely refuses to let us interview her without him being there."

"Why's that?"

"He's protective of Priscilla, but more than that, he's madly in love with her. He doesn't want a stud like myself horning in on his territory."

"Uh-huh—"

"What uh-huh! Some women find me utterly charming." A pause. "Some women find me ludicrous. So what? I'm too egotistical to believe them, and even if I did, I'm too old to care."

13

USUALLY MARGE DROVE, but since they opted to take the Cruiser—Scott's Venetian-red Chrysler hot rod, not a police car—Oliver was behind the wheel. He was annoyed for several reasons. From the moment Marge sat down in the passenger seat, she started in with the cell phone, yakking to her daughter nonstop. He was also pissed because he was following Miles Marlowe—Priscilla's aged agent—who was in an old Buick, tooling along at the speed of ten miles per hour.

Marge spoke into her cell. "So go to the movies and then study for your microbiology test . . . Vega, the test is a week away. Two hours of diversion will probably clear your mind . . . okay, okay, you know yourself better than I do . . . uh-huh, uh-huh . . . So how about if Willie and I take you both out for dinner on Saturday night? That way you don't have to refuse Josh twice in a row."

Marge switched to the other ear.

"That'll work? No, honey, it's not a problem, I'm sure Willie would love to meet him—"

Oliver cleared his throat.

"Honey, I'm about to go interview someone. So we're on for Saturday, all right? Okay . . . okay . . . okay . . . okay . . . bye." She hung up her cell and spoke to Oliver. "I'm going out on a double date."

"Who gets the backseat?"

Marge punched him in the shoulder.

"Move it!" Oliver told the Buick in front of him. "Just put your foot down on the accelerator. The pistons will do the rest!"

"He can't hear you—"

"The old man belongs on the Galápagos with all the other ancient tortoises," Oliver said.

Marge leaned back and pretended not to hear.

Twenty minutes later, Miles Marlowe turned right into a gated complex, then slowed the Buick to a stop, rolled down the window, and pointed to a spot where he wanted the detectives to park. Oliver maneuvered the Cruiser into the tight space on the first try while it took Miles five minutes to ease the Buick into a space that was roomy enough for an African elephant. Finally, the old man got out and hobbled over to Marge and Oliver. He was stooped over, but even in the prime of his height, he must have been a short man. He wore thick glasses and had a gigantic nose. His eyes were milky blue and slightly rheumy. His best feature was a thick mop of snow-white hair. The agent checked his watch. "Don't worry. I already called Priss to tell her that we'd be late."

Oliver checked his watch: 3:03. "Is her place a far walk from here?"

"You're standing right in front of it." He pointed to the house. "After you."

The development was filled with luxury homes with a minimum of thirty-five-hundred square feet of interior space sitting on an acre plus lot. There were an assortment of architectural styles and Priscilla Huntley's piece of the rock was a variant on the Tudor mansion. The front lawn was emerald green, with a stone walkway lined with leafy bushes of red and pink roses, English lavender in full bloom, yellow and white daisies, and rosemary sprouting lilac-colored blossoms. Ground cover swirling around the brush included sage, mint, and thyme. A soft breeze emitted a scent somewhere between sachet and stew.

The house was fashioned from bricks and stucco that formed high peaks, and was topped by a slate roof. A massive stained-glass window ran from the top of the door's keystone to just below the dormer window that sat in the middle of the pitch of the roof. Square mullion windows sat symmetrically on either side of the entrance—a recessed set of heavily carved, walnut double doors. The old man rang the bell: it chimed low and melodious and went on for several seconds.

"'Springless Year,'" Oliver whispered to Marge. "Probably their biggest hit."

To Oliver's surprise, Priscilla Barrett answered the door.

She had aged well. In Oliver's recollection, she had never been youthful-looking, even when she was a young pop star, but that might have been due to her conservative style more than her face. Even when she had been a singing sensation, Priscilla's hair had always been coiffed, her makeup had been expertly applied, and she was always dressed fashionably. In that regard, Priscilla hadn't changed a whit. She had well-tended, shoulder-length platinum hair, wide blue eyes, and a hint of pink cream softened her lips. She wore a silk tunic over slim-fitting jeans, her feet housed in platform espadrilles. Her fingers were slender: her nails long, with white French tips.

"Miles, my love, so good of you to act as an escort." As her voice softened, it became sultry. The old man smiled at the compliment. "Can you be a love and take the children for a walk?"

"I thought I might stay here with you, Priscilla, and make sure these two don't get out of line."

"Nonsense, the boys need you more than I do." Slowly she moved her gaze over to the detectives. "The boys are my Yorkies. They adore Miles." A pause. "Besides, I think I can handle these two on my own."

Marge offered a hand and made the introductions. "I'm Detective Sergeant Dunn and this is Detective Oliver and I assure you there's nothing to handle."

"I don't know about that." Back to Miles: "They're in the kitchen. Take them off my hands. Imelda will help you with the leashes."

"I don't trust them alone with you, Priscilla."

"Oh don't be ridiculous! Go on, Miles." She threw open the doors. "I'll be fine."

Miles had no choice but to go. When he was gone, Priscilla heaved a dramatic sigh. "I love my critters, but they're unruly. I thought about calling that dog expert on TV. I don't know if he'll do the dogs any good, but the publicity wouldn't hurt."

"I was looking online at all your reviews, albums, and performances," Oliver said. "You seem to be doing just fine in the publicity department."

"One can never get too much publicity."

They were still standing outside.

Priscilla was still looking at Oliver. "How old are you?"

"Old enough to know that you haven't changed at all."

Priscilla smiled. "I bet when the Major and I used to come on the radio, you'd turn the dial to another station."

"Then you'd be wrong," Oliver lied.

Priscilla said, "Okay. Name our four number one hits."

"'Springless Year' . . . but that's a no-brainer because it's your doorbell tone. Uh, let me think . . . 'Petunia and Porky' . . . a little sappy for my taste. I did like 'Jammin'' and 'Request for Lovin'.' I don't remember if they were your number one hits or not."

Priscilla tried to hold back her delight. "I'm impressed. Either you're sincere or you've done some homework."

"A good cop comes prepared. This brings us to why we're here."

"Yes, I suppose I should let you in." She stood aside. "Come on. I hope you like pink."

———

PRISCILLA LED THEM up the grand staircase into a twenty-by-twenty square room: pink walls, pink carpet, pink ceiling, pink light fixtures, and pink furniture that included a desk and chair, and two love seats facing each other with a pink coffee table between them. The walls hosted a slew of framed vinyl records, three of them platinum, three of them gold, and a complete archival history—print and photographs—of Priscilla and the Major—with a big emphasis on Priscilla. There were hundreds of black-and-white snapshots: the duo with two presidents, with senators, governors, mayors, foreign dignitaries including royalty, and countless other celebrities. At least six major magazine covers, six covers of Sunday magazine inserts of all the major newspapers. Space not taken up by photographs was occupied by newspaper clips and reviews, everything framed in pink.

Marge felt her heart beat a little harder. The piece of nylon fabric that had been salvaged from the charred body had pink threads. She carefully looked over the room and even read a few articles. She was amazed that the duo had been *that* big. Oliver had told her that their music was a little corny, coming out in a time when political protest anthems were all the rage. Later, the folkies and acid bands had given way to sex-heated thump-a-minute disco and dance music, made even more frenetic by the frequent use of cocaine by the clubbers. Priscilla and the Major didn't fall into that genre, either, yet they spanned the late sixties through the seventies and into the early eighties before they were done in by familiarity and age.

"Wow," Marge said, "this is something else!"

"Why bother having the stalkers build me shrines when I can build my own?" Priscilla said.

"You have stalkers?"

"In my heyday, I had many, young lady. I had everything from fans that waited hours to buy Priscilla and the Major tickets to bodyguards and gigolos. I had the paparazzi and journalists hounding me all the time. I met the most important people of the decades, including several queens, a couple of kings, and a few presidents. And I thought it would never end." A wry smile. "But it did."

"This is amazing," Marge said.

"It is a constant reminder that it is better to have made it and gone downhill than to have never made it at all. And there is quite a bit of recompense even when one fades into the woodwork. I still have money and I can shop without being mauled. I don't live in my memories, but I sure as hell enjoy them. Whenever I feel blue, I come in here and feel very pink. Now sit down—both of you—and tell me why you're here."

Since Oliver was clearly on the woman's A-list, Marge decided to let him handle the details. He rooted in his briefcase and came up with the colored pictures of the scanty forensic evidence they had gathered from charred Jane Doe. "This is really going to tax your memory." He handed her the pictures. "We found this bit of fabric. We were wondering if you could possibly identify it."

She scanned through the photographs very quickly. "What am I looking at?"

"We thought maybe you could tell us."

"And why did you think I could help you?"

"Honestly, we were thinking that the fabric came from a rock band souvenir tour jacket."

"One of my souvenir tour jackets?"

"You tell us," Oliver answered.

"C'mon, handsome. My memory's good but not that good!"

Oliver came over and picked out one of the snapshots. "See up here in the left-hand corner. We were thinking that this was part of the word *major*."

"Yes, I see it . . . maybe." She handed him back the photographs. "Why do you want to know?"

"We found an unidentified body, Ms. Barrett," Marge said. "We're trying to date the bones from this piece of cloth. If it was one of your souvenir pieces of clothing, we would have a starting point."

"I couldn't possibly tell you yes or no or even maybe," Priscilla said.

Marge tried to hide her disappointment. "It's important, Ms. Barrett. Maybe you could take another look?"

"I can't help, but don't look so down, Sergeant. I've got something to show you."

THE ROOM NEXT door was identical in size and also pink.

No furniture.

Instead, the space was filled top to bottom, and right to left, with racks and shelving units stuffed with clothing and souvenir memorabilia, probably everything that had ever been sold by Priscilla and the Major. There were racks of sweatshirts, sweatpants, T-shirts, and jackets, along with cases of hats, scarves, flags, banners, pins, posters, and cases of vinyl records, eight-track tapes (that went *way* back, Scott thought), cassette tapes, and newer-cut CDs. Everything was done in shades of pink, the most prevalent hue being powder-puff.

The room was a paean to Priscilla's compulsiveness, and a blessing for the detectives. Everything was sorted by item and by year. It was going to take a while to find the right piece of cloth, but with time it was a task that was doable.

Oliver said, "This is incredible!"

"I have clones in storage. I used to have even more until I donated about half of the clothing to victims of Katrina and the Phuket tsunami. My accountant and agent were happy with the decision. I got a big write-off and some free publicity."

"How much time do we have to look?"

"Take as much time as you need, handsome. And if either of you see anything you'd like or you can use, help yourself." She turned to Marge. "How about a sweatshirt?"

Marge didn't want to seem impolite, but felt uncomfortable with freebies. "Sure."

"Take my newest one. What are you? Medium?"

"Large."

Priscilla fished out a sweatshirt and gave it to Marge. Oliver picked up a CD in the 1998 section. "I don't think I've ever seen this."

"It was my first foray into jazz. Gimme. I'll autograph it for you."

"That would be great! I really like jazz."

She signed it and handed it over to him. "This was my first solo album in over a decade. It brought me out of retirement. It also got great reviews."

Oliver noticed that it had been produced nine years ago. Good reviews but no doubt lousy sales. Marge was already comparing sweatshirts to the photographs that they had taken at the Crypt.

Priscilla said, "Let me see those pictures again, Sergeant."

Marge looked up from a rack of clothing dated 1968. She gave her the snapshots along with a piece of paper with tour-city names that might correspond to the fabric's abbreviated letters. "We were thinking it's a tour jacket and these cities might have been on the tour."

Priscilla looked at the list of the cities and then sorted through the photographs, this time studying them with a determined gaze. "Hmm . . . this narrows it down a little. We did play Galveston. Start at around 1973."

SITTING AT HIS desk, Decker looked at the jacket from *Priscilla and the Major's America the Beautiful* tour, comparing it to the forensic photographs taken off the piece of fabric. He specifically liked the way the configuration of cities had been handled, how the *s* in Galveston was over the *p* in Indianapolis, but was just slightly to the left of the *p*. If he had an overlay of the fabric—the next step—he was sure the letters would have lined up perfectly.

"So if we're correct, the body is no older than 1974. But that doesn't mean the murder was committed in 1974. Our victim could have been wearing the jacket long after the tour."

Marge said, "It still shaves a couple of years off the front end. The building was put up in 1971. As far as the back end, I give it maybe five years to own a jacket like this."

"Let's get a list of all women in the area who went missing since 1974. Our next step is to find out which ones are still missing. Of those verified as still missing, first concentrate on the women who lived near the apartment or had a boyfriend, friend, or relative who lived near the apartment. It's going to mean calling families and opening up wounds. Sorry, but it has to be done. Also, we need that list of all the tenants who have ever lived in the apartment. Did we do that yet?"

"Bontemps is working on it," Marge said.

Oliver said, "It sure would help if we could put a face on the body. Are you sure there's no way we can use the facial bones to create soft tissue?"

"You heard the pathologist," Decker said. "The facial bones are way too delicate. We're working on a computerized model, but that's going to take time also because we need measurements. All we can do is be patient."

Oliver said, "On to the other missing person in our lives."

"Roseanne Dresden," Marge said. "Did her stepfather call today?"

"Like clockwork. I've got to say that his theories are sounding a lot less loony now than they did a few months ago." Decker began to tick specific incidents off his fingers. "WestAir has not helped us substantiate that Roseanne was on flight 1324. Also, the first victims list that the paper received did not include Roseanne's name on it, and no one at the paper remembers who called in Roseanne's name as a victim. Furthermore, according to you, Margie, the desk attendant at WestAir . . . what's her name?"

"Erika Lessing."

"Right. She swears that Roseanne did not board the flight from Burbank. Now, Roseanne could have come on board from an earlier flight from San Jose, but so far no one's verified that. Then, when we add to the mix a cheating husband as well as a cheating wife who had an ex-boyfriend in San Jose, we come up with a lot of unanswered questions. We need to start retracing Roseanne's last steps. It's time to pull a warrant for her phone records and her credit cards, her ATM accounts . . . any paper that might give us ideas about her last days on the planet."

"Any specific judge in mind, Loo?"

"Try Elgin Keuletsky." Decker spelled it out loud. "Present what we have and I think he'll be simpatico."

"What about Ivan Dresden?" Oliver asked. "I thought we were going to interview him and ask for his help in locating Roseanne."

Decker said, "We will, but later. Right now let's stay clear of him. Don't even let him know we've got suspicions. After we get a better handle on Roseanne's final days, maybe we'll be lucky and something will point to Ivan as the bad guy."

"We've interviewed some of Roseanne's friends," Oliver said. "How about if I talk to a few people who know Ivan . . . discreetly, of course."

"Discreetly?" Decker answered. "Do you have someone in mind, Scott?"

"Well, we can't talk to any of his friends or coworkers without him getting wind of our poking around. But as I recall . . . there was a lap dancer that Ivan put the make on."

"You have a name?"

"No name, but I have a club—Leather and Lace."

Decker smiled. "And you're familiar with the establishment?"

"I've been there a couple of times."

"And you want to go down to the club and find this elusive lap dancer?"

"I think it would be negligent not to."

Marge said, "I might have a name. Try Melissa or Miranda."

"Where'd you get that from?" Oliver asked her.

"Erika Lessing. Apparently he was two-timing Erika and his wife with someone with a name like that."

"I'll check it out." He looked at Decker. "What do you say, Loo?"

"Okay, Scott, you win. I'm assigning you a trip down to Leather and Lace."

"So I can put in for charges like drinks and the cover?"

"As long as they're reasonable and part of the assignment."

Marge said, "You must be in hog heaven . . . or in your case pig heaven."

Oliver tried to look wounded, but in actuality he was feeling no pain. A lap dancer paid for by the LAPD. If that wasn't paradise, what was?

14

DECKER COULD SMELL the aroma from the driveway, the undeniable scent of garlic, onion, and herbs: a sure indication that something good was going on in the kitchen. Involuntarily his mouth started to water. Although he wondered why Rina was cooking midweek, he didn't question her decision. He was famished and tired and delighted that dinner or some facsimile was minutes away. When he came through the door, the background noise of conversation abruptly stopped and he found that there were several sets of eyes focused in on him—Rina, Cindy and Koby, and their elusive teenage daughter of late, Hannah Rosie.

His wife looked put together, her long black hair in a ponytail and covered with a bandanna, although there was moisture on her brow, meaning the kitchen was probably hot. Cindy and Koby had on jeans and T-shirts. Hannah was dressed in a jean skirt over leggings, a scoop-neck T-shirt, and combat boots. She had beads around her neck, her earlobes jeweled in big white hoops, and her wrists were bedecked in multiple bangles. No piercings or tattoos, but only because tattoos were forbidden by Jewish law and Hannah had a fear of needles. Thank God for small favors.

"Hi, kids," Decker began cheerfully. He kissed his wife and his daughters, and hugged his son-in-law. "To what do I owe the pleasure?"

"We've finalized the plans, Dad. I thought that maybe you could take a look at them tonight . . . if you have a moment."

"I think we can work that out. How do they look?"

"The plans are beautiful," Koby said. "The cost is not."

Decker poured his son-in-law a scotch. "Don't worry about it."

"He means that and so do I." Rina had inherited some paintings from an old lady whom she had befriended. A half-dozen of them turned out to be valuable, one of them extremely valuable. That one constituted their retirement, giving the Deckers a lot of emotional freedom and flexibility.

"You are always generous, but I do worry." Koby took a nice-size shot. "We are living in a nutshell barely big enough for the two of us. Now we have big plans for eighteen hundred square feet of living space."

"Eighteen hundred seems reasonable, especially if you're thinking about starting a family . . . hint, hint."

Cindy smiled. "Eventually, hint, hint."

"Reasonable if we had a bigger budget." Another sip. "This is good."

"Thank you," Decker said. "Another?"

"It sounds tempting, but no."

Rina clapped her hands. "Shall we sit down?"

"I'll serve with Cindy, Eema," Hannah volunteered.

"Good idea, Hannah Banana." Cindy made a face. "Does it bug you when I say that?"

"Nah, but only you can get away with it."

The meal was copious. Rotisserie chicken over rice pilaf, green beans, and, of course, the requisite salad. Hannah had also grilled some corn and red peppers. Everyone sat down at the table, dishes were passed around, and the meal began. For the first five minutes, there was little talk except to relay compliments to Rina and Hannah for cooking such a delicious feast. Halfway through his dinner, Decker made a stab at conversation.

"So tell me about the plans?"

"They are lovely and costly," Koby replied.

Cindy said, "They look terrific."

More eating.

Decker said, "Well, anytime you want me to help you get started . . . knocking out walls, just give a ring."

Koby said, "That may be sooner than later. How about this weekend?"

Cindy cleared her throat. Koby said, "I was thinking only about the kitchen."

"Koby and I have been having a little debate on this." Cindy's smile was tight. *Uh-oh,* Decker thought. "I don't want to do things piecemeal. I think we need to hire a contractor because the plans have become more complicated. Koby would rather gather up a crowd and do it all himself—like a barn raising."

No one spoke.

"I like building things," Koby said.

"Kobe, you're working a full-time job and moonlight as it is. It's a lot of weight to hold."

"I have strong shoulders."

"I'm sure you'll work it out," Rina said.

Decker snapped his fingers. "You know what? I have an idea."

Uh-oh, Rina thought. She said, "I'm sure they'll work it out, Peter."

"I'm sure they will, but just let me run this by you," Decker said. "Remember Mike Hollander?"

"From Foothill?" Rina said.

"Yeah, you know he retired about ten maybe twelve years ago from police work. He has a construction company—"

"Peter, he must be like seventy now."

"Just listen. What he does is get all these old-time construction pros—plumbers, plasterers, electricians, air-conditioning guys—who have retired, calls them up, and gets a crew together. They've done quite a few renovation projects for the elderly in their neighborhood."

"If Mike is seventy, how old are the old guys, Daddy?" Cindy asked dubiously.

"They're probably all around Mike's age."

Hannah wiped her mouth. "Uh, this is not of interest to me. Mind if I check my e-mail?"

Decker told her to go ahead. Rina said, "Do you think Mike's up to it, Peter? How long has he been at this?"

"They're experienced guys, Rina."

"Didn't Mike have bypass surgery?"

"Last time I spoke to him, he told me he never felt better."

"How much do they charge?" Koby inquired.

"I have no idea, but I'm sure he'll be reasonable," Decker told him.

Rina said, "I don't know about this, Peter. Maybe they should ask the architect for some recommendations."

"What would it hurt if I called Hollander up?"

No one answered. Koby looked at Cindy. Cindy looked at Koby. They both shrugged. Koby said, "I think it couldn't hurt to ask."

Decker got up from the table. "It'll only take a minute."

"Now?" Rina said. "We're in the middle of dinner."

"It'll only take a few minutes." Decker dashed inside the kitchen before Rina could continue to protest.

Cindy said, "Let him make the phone call, Rina. Otherwise we won't hear the end of it."

Rina said, "He means well, but sometimes he doesn't think things through."

"I think it's a good idea," Koby said. "There is wisdom in age."

Cindy said, "There's also angina and arthritis in age."

Koby said, "The food is excellent as always."

"Delicious," Cindy concurred.

Decker returned looking very pleased. "We're having lunch tomorrow." He looked at Koby. "I'll bring the plans with me as long as you brought them here. Anyone want to join me?"

"I'd love to, but I'm on shift," Koby said.

"I'm working," Cindy said. "But I'd like to meet him before we start. No offense, Daddy, but he is a little on the old side."

"None taken." Decker looked at his wife. "I thought of someone else. How about Abel Atwater?"

Rina said, "You've *got* to be kidding me!"

"The man knows his way around a toolbox."

"Peter, he's an amputee!"

"So I won't put him on a ladder." To Koby, Decker said, "He's a terrific jack-of-all-trades."

"When was the last time you talked to Abel?"

Decker shrugged. "I don't know. About six, seven years ago. Doesn't matter. We have that kind of a relationship."

"How'd he lose a limb?" Koby asked.

"War injury in Vietnam."

"So it wasn't from a construction accident."

"No, no, no," Decker said. "He's actually quite agile—"

"Peter, the man is not only an amputee, he has demons."

"Last I heard, he doesn't drink anymore."

"The last you heard as of six years ago," Rina said. "What about his chronic depression?"

"So what's better than making him feel useful?"

Cindy said, "Uh, Daddy, I appreciate your help, but I think we might need something more than an amputee and old men with heart conditions." She shrugged.

Koby said, "He already called up Mike. He might as well keep the lunch date."

Abruptly, Cindy burst into genuine laughter. "All right. There's nothing wrong with having lunch with an old friend. I do, however, have my reservations about Abel and his battle with the bottle."

"Okay. Abel's out but Mike's in," Decker said.

Cindy threw up her hands. "Deal."

Rina began to clear dishes, but Decker told her to sit down. "I'll do it."

"I'll help you," Koby said.

"Bring in dessert while you're at it," Rina told them.

When the men left the room, Cindy said, "I married my father. Mr. Do-It-Himself." She shrugged again. "What the heck. I figure when the house is torn apart, Koby will come to his senses."

"That's very smart of you."

"Sometimes, it's useless to make plans," Cindy said.

Rina smiled. "There's an old Yiddish expression: *Mann macht und Gott lacht.*"

"Which means?"

"Man makes plans and God laughs."

THE RECTANGULAR STAGE was in the center of the room, the mirrored floor lit up from underneath. Surrounding the stage were bar stools of sweaty, boisterous men shouting encouragement to sinuous, wet female forms that pirouetted from four corner poles. Beyond the stage were sets of tables and chairs. A horseshoe-shaped bar spanned three walls. It was hot and moist and dark except where the spotlights hit the supple women.

There was a three-drink minimum at fifteen bucks a pop, whether it be water or booze. The clients were served by dancers wearing high-cut, black leather thongs and sheer lace bustiers.

Scott Oliver had chosen a corner table, and nursed a beer while taking it all in. He recognized three girls so far and that surprised him. He hadn't been to Leather and Lace in over two years, and with the high turnover of dancers, he hadn't expected to see anyone familiar. The dropout rate in these establishments was higher than a midcity school, some girls leaving because they had amassed enough money, others leaving because drugs and alcohol finally got the better of them, ravaging the faces as well as the bodies. It was a hard life, made more difficult by the constant onslaught of boors the women catered to. Oliver liked to think of himself as a respite for the women. He tipped big and dispensed legal advice free of charge. Of course, it wasn't really free.

The women would often do him favors in exchange, but in his mind the barter was a fair one.

A man was approaching him—midthirties, black T-shirt, black jeans, and leather motorcycle boots. He had a round face, small lips, thick brow, and dark curly hair. Dante Michelli was the owner of Leather and Lace and five other gentleman's clubs. Oliver had heard that Michelli was a self-made man, a third-generation Italian-American from Brooklyn. As far as Scott knew, Michelli ran a clean and safe environment, the security of his patrons and girls ensured by a half-dozen bulldozer-looking men parked at strategic places about the floor. He took a seat at Oliver's table without asking permission.

"What can I get for you, Detective?"

"I'm fine with my beer, Mr. Michelli, but thanks."

"Call me Dante." He waved a finger in the air and a leggy woman with a platinum crew-cut hairstyle was there within moments. "Get the man a fresh beer, Titania."

"Not necessary, but thanks," Oliver said.

Dante said, "You look like you're here on business."

"I am, but it has nothing to do with your business."

That was exactly what the owner wanted to hear. The beer came a minute later, cold and premium quality. Oliver reached into his wallet, by Michelli put his hand over Oliver's. "Don't even think about it."

"I won't argue." Oliver put away his billfold. "It's either you pay or I have to file a forest's worth of paperwork just to get reimbursed."

The two men returned their eyes to the stage. Michelli spoke, still looking over his undulating ladies. "What do you need besides a beer?"

"I've got a problem, Mr. Michelli. I need to speak with one of your girls, only I don't know her exact name. It might be Miranda or Melissa."

Michelli shook his head. "Not familiar. What does she look like?"

"I don't know."

"So what do you know about her?"

"Only that she knows a man named Ivan Dresden." Oliver sneaked a quick peek at Dante before returning his eyes to the stage. The man's face was a blank. "I'm way more interested in Dresden than I am in the woman. Maybe you know him?"

"What does he look like?"

"Dark, good-looking, in his thirties. Some kind of finance guy."

"That describes ninety percent of the clientele."

Oliver was still looking at the stage, specifically at a blonde with size triple E hooters. She was pixieish, around five five, with a pug nose and long hair, and wide eyes. Her boobs were very nice to look at but *way* out of proportion to her body. It was a wonder that she didn't fall forward whenever she took a step. "The man I'm looking for had a wife who perished in a plane crash a couple of months ago."

Dante didn't even have to think about it. "Jell-O."

Oliver laughed. "Excuse me?"

"Sweet and jiggly in all the right places." Dante regarded Oliver and grinned, showing perfectly shaped, yellow-stained teeth. "One of Jell-O's regulars was getting too far behind in his tab. I was getting a little antsy, but he recently paid it off."

"How big was the bill?"

"Fifteen grand."

"Wow," Oliver exclaimed. "That's a lot of lap dancing."

"That's nothing," Michelli said. "We have guys that run up that kind a bill in a single evening. But there was something about this dude I didn't trust. I told Jell-O to take care of it . . . get some kind of ante into the pot. A week later, he paid it off in full."

"Credit card, check, or cash?"

"Cash. That's when Jell-O told me that the customer was always yakking about his wife dying in a plane crash. Not that he cared about the woman, just that he expected to come into lots of cash very soon, waiting for insurance to pay off." Michelli took a fistful of peanuts from the nut dish and popped them into his mouth. "That true?"

"If she did perish in the crash, yes, that would be true."

"But you think he bumped his old lady off or something."

"I'm investigating a case, Mr. Michelli. Right now all I want to do is talk to the girl."

"You're looking at her," Dante said.

"The blonde with the ginormous ones?"

"That's her. I told you she was sweet and jiggled in all the right places."

15

IN THE BACK dressing room, Oliver waded through racks of costumes, trying not to ogle the women in various stages of nudity. The back wall was a full-length mirror harshly lit with makeup bulbs, and bisected width-wise by a countertop obliterated by creams, powders, ointments, glosses, brushes, and makeup of all textures, colors, and sizes. There were several occupied bar stools, but most of the women stood as they painted their faces like warrior chiefs.

Jell-O's given name wasn't Melissa or Miranda, but it was Marina Alfonse and Oliver imagined her for a moment in a sailor's suit and hat doing a hornpipe. She was in the corner, dressed in civilian clothes, and in the process of taking off her makeup. He went over and introduced himself, producing his gold shield for validation. "Marina Alfonse?"

She gave it a steely glance. "Yeah?"

"Dante Michelli said you wouldn't mind talking to me."

That gave her a moment of pause. "Yeah?"

"I'd like to talk to you about one of your customers."

"Who?"

"Ivan Dresden."

She didn't answer, but her eyes lowered to the floor. A moment later she lifted them back to the mirror and continued to examine her reflection. Each time she removed a layer of face paint, she looked younger, until she was milkmaid fresh, with startling blue eyes and dimples in her cheeks. Dressed in a black wife-beater and jeans and low-heeled sandals, she looked sexier than she had an hour ago, gyrating for an audience.

"Why are the police interested in Ivan?" Marina's voice tried for casual but fell several notches short.

"We're just dotting our t's and crossing our i's."

"Isn't it the other way around?"

"It was a joke," Oliver said.

"Ha ha." The girl was about twenty-five, with the cynicism of an old man. "David Rottiger gave me your card. If I wanted to talk to you, I would have called you."

She was pissed and Oliver wondered why. Rottiger had claimed Marina wasn't interested in Ivan, but a good-paying customer can generate interest. "Just trying to get a little information."

"If you're interested in Ivan, ask Ivan."

Oliver took an educated guess. "Sweetheart, there's a lot of insurance money at stake. If you want to help him out, just answer my questions." That shut her up and he continued. "David Rottiger said when you first met him, you didn't like Ivan. So what changed?"

"Ivan's okay. He's a steady customer, a big tipper, and I don't want to piss him off."

"No one has to know we talked."

She shrugged.

Meaning she was going to call the guy as soon as Oliver left. Marge had already gotten the warrants for Roseanne's phone and credit card receipts, so Ivan couldn't put a monkey wrench in that. Still, it was more desirable for Ivan to be kept in the dark. Oliver needed leverage to use against her.

"Why didn't you like him when you first met him?"

"I thought he was a jerk," Marina said. "I don't care about a married man flirting with me, but not in front of his wife. That wasn't cool."

"Did you know Roseanne?"

"When I met her, she seemed cold. Ivan tells me she was frigid. 'Course he was flirting with me all evening, so it's natural that she wasn't going to like me."

"Do you date Ivan?"

"It's against the rules."

"Rules are meant to be broken."

"Mr. Michelli is a good boss and runs a clean place here. That's all I have to say."

"Look, honey, I don't care what you do on the side. I'm just trying to get some handle on Ivan Dresden. He's supposed to come into lots of money *if* his wife's body is ever recovered. Until insurance finds the corpse, Dresden is going to be looked into by insurance *and* by the police. If you have something going on, we're going to find out."

Marina addressed him with a tight mouth and hard eyes. "He buys me dinner and I hear about his problems. That's it."

"Sex?"

"You like hearing nasty details, don't you?"

Oliver rolled his eyes. "Let's talk theoretically, Marina. Say you were having an affair with Dresden when he was married. And now his wife is missing because we can't find her body. That means someone's going to come after you. Now, that someone could be me . . . *or* that someone could be my hard-ass female sergeant partner, who won't give a solitary shit if your bra size is triple J."

"As opposed to you, who does give a shit about my bra size?" She ended the sentence with a sweet smile.

"I'm taking the fifth on that one," Oliver answered. "How did Ivan pay down fifteen gees on his lap-dancing tab?"

"He's got a job. He's got stuff."

"What kind of stuff?"

"He's got the condo now that Roseanne is dead. Maybe he took out a loan on it."

"Maybe or you know for certain?"

"Look, all I know is that he paid off Mr. Michelli, so now everyone's happy. Besides, Ivan's got muscle with the banks because he has insurance money coming."

"Maybe he has money coming . . . maybe not."

She started biting her thumbnail. "He makes it sound like it's a go."

"Insurance is going to scour through Ivan's personal records before the company releases a red cent. So if the clever Mr. Dresden is counting on a windfall, he may want to rethink his position. Were you having an affair with Ivan?"

She shrugged. "None of your business."

"Marina, we've got warrants for paperwork." They did have warrants, only it was for Roseanne's paper not Ivan's. "Hotels, motels, gifts, dinners . . . everything is going to show up on credit-card receipts. I'm personally going to check them out, flashing your picture to hotel clerks and maître d's. Someone is bound to recognize you. So tell me your side of the story."

She appraised him very carefully. He wasn't going away. "Nothing to tell. Boys and girls have been doing the nasty for years. So what?"

"What I really want to know is did you fuck him before or after Roseanne died?"

Another shrug.

"I'll take that as a yes."

"She was fucking around, too, you know."

Oliver acted as if the news was a surprise. "Tell me about it."

Marina's eyes widened enthusiastically as she shunted the blame of their sordid affair onto Roseanne. "Ivan told me she had lots of one-night stands. She was a flight attendant. You know how *they* are!"

Most of the female flight attendants Oliver knew were hardworking, married women. "Uh-huh. Did Ivan ever mention any names?"

"No. Just that she was doing it with some rich old guy up in San Jose."

"Name?"

"Roy something. I think that's what Ivan said."

"Could it have been Ray?"

"Sure."

Consistent with the information given to Decker by Arielle Toombs. "Anything else you know about him?"

"Just that he and Roseanne were involved for more than just a one-night stand. Ivan said he bought her gifts. He found a diamond watch. When he asked her about it, Roseanne told him it was Christmas present from WestAir. She told him the diamonds weren't real." A sarcastic laugh escaped from her lips. "He said that the brand was Chopin and that's a very expensive watch brand. So he knew she was lying."

"Chopard?" Oliver asked.

"Maybe that was it. Anyway, I don't see WestAir giving out diamond watches as Christmas presents."

"That's true. How long have you been sleeping with him?"

"None of your business. Believe me, I'm discreet. Otherwise Ivan would stop coming here to see me." A nervous laugh. "Gotta keep them wanting more. *Please* don't tell Mr. Michelli. It's against the rules and I need this job!"

So now Oliver had the leverage he needed. He said, "I'm always interested in a fair trade. If you don't talk to Ivan, I don't see why I should say anything to Dante Michelli. And we both know that I'll find out if you talked to Ivan. Do you get my drift?"

Marina nodded slowly. "I know how to keep my mouth shut."

"And so do I." Oliver handed her a card. "Call if you think of something you'd like to tell me. Any little detail is fine. Even if you think it isn't important, it might be."

Marina swept her foot along the floor. "So when do you think the insurance company will pay out?"

"First we need a body, Marina. Nothing's going to happen until then."

"Okay." She tapped her toe on the ground. "Ivan told me they were kaput, you know. Roseanne was going to divorce him and take him to the cleaners."

"That part was probably true."

"Just lucky for him that she died before she could divorce him."

Oliver's smile was slow and wide.

Sometimes people make their own luck.

SAME MIKE HOLLANDER but older: the man looked his full seventy years, with a ruddy round face, a big, bulbous nose, and a mop of snowy hair. A thick white walrus mustache obscured the top of his lip, and now he had added a goatee. With just a little bit more facial hair, Mike was Santa Claus incarnate. He wore glasses and a hearing aid, both new since the last time they had met. Maybe hiring his crew and him wasn't one of Decker's finest moments of planning. Not that he looked feeble, but he showed his age. At least his handshake was firm.

"Great to see you, Pete."

"Likewise, Mike, you're looking good."

"I'm looking old, but that's better than looking fine in a coffin."

"C'mon, you're not ready for that."

"Not if I can help it, but God may have other plans."

"You sound like my wife."

"That's good. Rina was always wise."

They were sitting in a booth at a local coffee shop, halfway between Devonshire and Foothill. Mike had retired in the district he had served for over thirty-five years. The waitress—a fifty-plus woman with a bouffant hairdo—seemed to know Hollander by taking his order as "the usual." Decker asked for a salad and coffee.

Mike may have looked elderly, but he looked happy. Decker told him that.

"Finally doing what I want to do," Mike answered. "You know I always like working with my hands. Now I get to do that and help people out. Problem is we're getting too successful. I'm busier than I'd like to be." He sipped his coffee. "But being busy never killed anyone."

"How many people do you have working on a crew?"

"Anywhere from twenty to thirty."

Decker was taken aback. "That's a huge amount of people."

"I know lots of seniors with time on their hands . . . retired men who drive their wives crazy. You don't know how many pies I get from grateful women. We may work a little slower, but because there are so many hands, the job moves faster than traditional contractors. You've got the plans for your daughter's house?"

"I do." Decker brought them out of his briefcase and spread them across the tabletop. Hollander adjusted his glasses and studied the drawings silently. After a few minutes, he took out a pad of paper and began to make notes. He didn't speak for the next ten minutes, and when he did, he was all business.

"The architect did a good job. Thorough. The plans aren't that complicated and he specked out several options depending on how much they want to spend. I also know discount places for appliances, flooring, hardware, granite, marble . . . fit-and-finish materials. If your daughter can call me and tell me what she has in mind, I could probably price this out for you in a couple of weeks."

"Any idea of the cost?"

"You're adding about eight hundred square feet, including a new kitchen and two and a half bathrooms. Hmm . . . depending on material . . . oh, anywhere between sixty and one-twenty."

"That's quite a range."

"Depending on materials. You're not going to get lower than sixty. If you do, the guy's a crook."

Decker knew that was true. "That price is doable."

"You're paying for it?"

"I'm going to offer to help them out. My son-in-law is going to do some of the demolition himself."

"That'll save some money. You know I'll give you the best price I can, but these people gotta come away with some money in their pockets."

"Absolutely. Thanks for looking at the plans. I'll have Cindy call you as soon as she can."

"Great." Hollander slipped the prints in his briefcase. "So enough about me. Tell me what's happening in the wonderful world of detective work."

The waitress arrived with their food just as Mike had asked the question. She looked at Decker. "You're a cop?"

Hollander said, "Best detective I ever worked with. Now he's a lieutenant. If he had acted more politico, he could have made captain."

"I blush," Decker said.

"We like cops coming in here," she said. "They keep an eye on the riffraff."

The restaurant skirted the edges of Devonshire's border. Decker gave the waitress his card. "If you have problems, give me a call."

"'Preciate it. Enjoy the meal. It's on the house."

The men nodded. Hollander said, "So what's been taking up your time other than bureaucracy?"

"Actually, we've got a couple of interesting ones in homicide." Decker told him about the body in the flight's wreckage that turned out not to be the body they were looking for.

"The flight attendant is still missing," Decker told him.

"And you have no idea who the unidentified body is?"

"Not a clue. Sometimes in these kinds of crash scenarios you find extra ID. I've never heard of anyone finding an unexplained body."

"Maybe it was a stowaway hiding in the baggage."

"You know, I thought about that. Three things militate against it. First of all, there are really tough security measures now, so I don't see her slipping through. Second, she had a nice-size bash on her skull. Third, she was wearing a very old jacket that was probably manufactured around 1974. If the body was in better shape, we could have had a forensic artist slap a face onto the facial bones. But the biological material is so delicate that the D.A. refuses to let the artist make a cast of the skull and face. If the bones crumble, we lose forensic evidence."

"The bash mark on the skull."

"Exactly. We're thinking about doing some computer forensics but it's never as good as putting a face on the bones."

Hollander sat back in his chair and stroked his goatee. He looked very wise. "This is ringing a bell. It's going to take me a second or so to bring it up." He took a bite of his hamburger, ketchup dribbling onto his goatee. He dabbed it with a napkin but the hair still looked pink. "Good food for a coffee shop and they serve turkey burgers. Red meat for me nowadays is a no-no . . . ah, I got it."

He put down his sandwich.

"I confess to missing my old profession now and then. You ever watch those true detective shows on TV?"

"What ones? Like that private detective on cable?"

"No, no, like *Forensic Files* or *Cold Case Files* or *The New Detectives*?"

"Occasionally one of them will catch my interest."

"Yeah, most of the time it's just dogged detective work and the bad guy confessing, or today it's all DNA. But I saw something on one of the shows that was a similar situation to your case. The fingers had been removed or acid-washed and the skin of the face had been flayed off, leaving only the face muscles."

"No way to ID the body."

"Yep, that was the culprit's plan. And it almost worked because the forensic artist couldn't create a forensic face. She didn't have the usual bony landmarks to work with and the D.A. wouldn't let the police re-move the muscle because it was forensic evidence."

Decker was listening really carefully now. "Go on."

"What they wound up doing was reproducing the skull in three di-mensions from some kind of machine."

"What kind of machine?"

"I'm sketchy on the details, Pete. I saw the show a while back . . . couple of years. But I remembered it because it was so different. They took X-rays and used the X-rays to make the three-dimensional copy of the skull. The police took the skull to the judge and the judge allowed it to be used for forensic purposes. The forensic artist used the copy skull to put a face onto the bones."

"Did it work?"

"Yeah, someone recognized the face and they caught the guy."

"Do you remember the case?"

He thought a long time. "It was an African woman who was living in the U.S., so she didn't even have relatives that reported her missing.

I think it happened somewhere in the middle of the country. Sorry, but I don't remember names, but I'm sure there's a copy of the show somewhere. It was either *Forensic Files* or *Cold Case Files*."

Decker was writing furiously. "What is that? Court TV?"

"*Forensic Files* is on Court TV. I think *Cold Case Files* is A and E." Mike took another bite of his food and chewed it slowly. "You could call up someone at the station that works with the shows. Maybe they would remember."

"I'm sure I could order a copy of the show, if we could figure out what show you were watching and what case you saw. I'm thinking that the episodes might be listed online." He looked at Hollander. "We could check it out. Would you mind coming back to the station house?"

"I thought you'd never ask."

16

THE SQUAD ROOM was two-thirds empty, the majority of the
detectives out in the field investigating the ever-flowing tide of
felonies. Like the ocean, there was a rhythm to crime, a high
period followed by a low period that seemed to correspond with the
phases of the moon.

The open space was divided up by groupings of desks with placards
hanging from the ceiling to reveal the detail of the detectives working
below the signs. The areas encompassed the usual divisional felonies—
burglary, GTA, CAPS, juvenile and sex crimes, bunco, etc., with homicide tucked into a corner—private and rarefied. Shelving filled with
casebooks lined a good portion of the wall space with several dog-eared
district maps pinned at random spots along the drywall.

Marge Dunn had just received a packet of Roseanne Dresden's phone
records. The last call made from the missing woman's cell originated in
San Jose—12:35 A.M.—and she had connected to her house number,
the line engaged for thirty-five seconds. Roseanne's records begged the
question: what was she doing in San Jose a little after midnight when

WestAir said that she was on a flight from Burbank to San Jose the next morning at eight-fifteen?

It was possible that Roseanne flew into Burbank from San Jose on an earlier flight that morning, and never deplaned—which would explain why Erika Lessing never saw her.

Did an earlier flight even exist?

Logging on to WestAir's Web site, Marge looked up flight schedules. The former flight 1324 had been retired. Instead there was a new flight—247—with the first departure from Burbank to San Jose now leaving at eight-thirty instead of eight-fifteen: a very thin sugar coat on a bitter pill, but who could blame WestAir for trying to make the public forget. More important, there was an earlier flight—246—that flew from San Jose to Burbank, it's first departure at five o'clock in the morning. That meant that Roseanne could have come down from San Jose to Burbank and then turned around and gone back on the doomed flight 1324.

But why would Roseanne do a quick turnaround on a commuter flight unless she was working *actively* as a flight attendant? Marge circled Roseanne's last call and wrote in the margins: *Roseanne in SJ and trying to locate hubby? Did she talk to him?*

Ivan could verify that. Then Marge noticed that the call was only thirty-five seconds. She wrote on the margins of Roseanne's phone records.

Answering machine?

Did Roseanne's husband get any message about her working agenda? Was that why he put her on the flight from Burbank back to San Jose? Had she left a message on the machine that she was in San Jose and was now working the route?

But that didn't sync with WestAir's story.

Marge stared at that final call. No matter how many times she did this task—retraced the last moments of someone's life—it always gave her pause, seeing a marker that pinpointed one of a person's final acts before the trip into the great void. Marge knew that in Roseanne's case, there was a faint possibility that she wasn't dead, that she had deliberately walked away from her current life to start up again as someone else, but that was stretching credulity.

She looked up just in time to see Decker and an elderly companion walk into the squad room. She did a double take.

"Hollander!" she cried out. "Is that you?"

"Feels like me." Mike patted his chest and arms. "By God, I think it is me!"

Marge got up from her onerous task, walked over, and slapped him on the back. With a wide smile, he gave her a quick hug and regarded her at arm's length. "Dunn, you still look as good as the day you deserted Foothill for this clown. And now I find out, pouring salt on the wound, that you outrank me."

"Yeah, well, I promise I'll use my power for the good of mankind. What brings you into enemy territory?"

"Him." He crooked a finger in Decker's direction.

"By personal invitation," Decker told her. "We're going online. Hollander remembered seeing some kind of technique that could help us identify our Jane Doe from the apartment building fire. Care to join?"

"I just got Roseanne Dresden's phone records. I need to go over them, but keep me posted." To Hollander: "Great seeing you, Michael. Don't be such a stranger."

"Last thing you need is an old fogy like myself bothering you."

"It's never a bother and I might even learn something from a veteran."

He tapped his temple. "I collected a lot of stories working in the Naked City. Sometimes I remember my cases as if it were yesterday. Other times, it's like working a cold case. My memory's in deep freeze until some clue reopens the file and it all comes back to me in a rush."

"I'm like that now," Marge said. "I can only imagine what I'll be like at your age, Mike."

"Well, lucky for you that when you reach my age, you'll probably forget this conversation."

SITTING AT DECKER'S desk, both of them in front of the computer monitor, they logged on to Court TV, methodically going through the *Forensic Files* cases: over one hundred episodes, each with a thumbnail description. As Decker brought up each show, Hollander repeated the same phrase. "No, that's not the one."

An hour later they had exhausted the entire list.

Hollander got up and stretched. "I'm sure I remembered it from somewhere. I'm just not that smart or creative enough to make it up."

Decker had his doubts. With age, sometimes recollections get confused, although Mike appeared to be sharp. "Do you want to go through them again?"

"No point to it, Rabbi. It's not any of the episodes we looked at." He scratched his head and sat back down. "Maybe it was a *Cold Case File.*"

"Let's have a look." Decker logged on to A&E and then on to the Web site for *Cold Case Files*. There were over one hundred episodes for that series as well. As with *Forensic Files*, each show came with a thumbnail sketch. Unlike *Forensic Files*, a half-hour program, *Cold Case Files* was an hour, sometimes divided into two half-hour cases; sometimes one case occupied the entire hour.

Decker brought up episode number one.

"No, that's not it."

Thirteen episodes later, they struck oil.

Mike exclaimed without hesitation, "That's it."

Decker was surprised, expecting another dead end. "'Reconstructing Murder/Fire Flicks?'"

"It's the first one," Hollander said. "There's a trailer tape. Does your computer have sound?"

"I think it does." He pressed the bullhorn icon and unmuted the sound on his machine. All the computers in the squad room worked with muted sound. To hear conversation between the detectives was a must. Sometimes someone would overhear two people talking and add something very relevant. There was a reason why the detectives sat at open tables and weren't housed in cubicles.

Decker played the intro to the episode. Like all good trailers, it revealed nothing about the actual case other than that the crime originated out of Wisconsin. Decker scrolled down the Web page to an icon that said *Buy This Episode*. The price was definitely within the departmental budget, so he clicked the icon. The response told him that this particular tape was no longer for sale.

"Well, that's terrific." But then Decker thought a moment. "The case involved forensic reconstruction and was made into a TV show. I'm thinking that it must have been some kind of long-term, high-profile murder. If you describe what you saw to Wanda Bontemps, maybe you two can go online together and cull through some of Wisconsin's notorious murder cases. See if anything looks familiar."

"Good idea, although it might take up time for your detective." Hollander curled the ends of his walrus mustache. "I was just thinking to myself that somewhere this tape exists. Maybe it's in A and E archives, or if it isn't, maybe I can contact the producer. Let me do some research before we bother a detective."

"If that's what you want to do with your free time, I won't complain." Decker raised up a finger. "Let me see if I can get you on as a consultant. That way you'll get a little money for your services."

"If you do that, Pete, then I won't complain."

Decker qualified: "As long as your consulting doesn't interfere with my daughter's remodeling plans."

Hollander punched him in the shoulder. "What kind of lieutenant detective are you?"

"Blood is thicker than a paycheck."

MARGE LEANED AGAINST the wall, arms folded across her chest, waiting as Decker looked over the phone records. She said, "I'm trying to figure out the best way to approach Ivan Dresden to make him feel like he's on our side."

"With her last call coming out of San Jose, he may actually be on our side." Decker flipped through phone records. "What was Roseanne doing there?"

"Maybe working, but maybe she was visiting her old boyfriend."

"So-called old boyfriend: nothing's been verified. Is this Raymond Holmes's phone number?" Decker recited the numbers out loud.

"Yep."

"Roseanne hadn't called it for the last six months. That jibes with Arielle Toombs's account . . . that she had severed the relationship a while ago. But he did call her about three months before the crash."

"Hmmm . . . what did we find out about Holmes?"

"He lives in San Jose at 5371 Granada Avenue. No wants, no warrants, no priors."

Oliver walked into Decker's office, rubbing his eyes and rolling his shoulders. His emerald tie was slightly askew and the collar of his jacquard white shirt was wilted. Marge checked her watch. It was almost four in the afternoon. "Hot time last night at Leather and Lace, Scotty?"

"Wish it were so." Oliver yawned. "I just got out of court. Peabody homicide."

"Kerry Trima," Decker said. "The one with the inconclusive DNA. How'd it go?"

"The PD was wet behind the ears. He spent all his time attacking the DNA expert and gave our circumstantial evidence a free ride. He could have easily put a giant hole in my testimony, but luckily he didn't ask the right questions. I think the jury will be swayed despite the lack of a smoking gun. What are we dealing with now?"

"Roseanne Dresden's phone records," Marge said. "Did you get my message?"

"About the midnight San Jose call?" Oliver shrugged. "What was Roseanne doing in San Jose eight hours before she allegedly perished on a flight from Burbank to San Jose?"

"That's what we're trying to figure out," Marge said. "I think it's time to talk to Ivan the Terrible. Maybe he knows what she was doing there. And since Mr. Dresden fancies himself a ladies' man, I figured we should interview him together and you should do most of the talking. You two can talk about Fifi at Leather and Lace."

"Her name is Jell-O, not Fifi."

"Jell-O?" Decker laughed out loud. "Is that for real?"

"Her given name is Marina Alfonse," Oliver said. "By the way, I've altered my opinion of the young lady and that may have some bearing on the case. When Rottiger first talked about Marina's reaction to Ivan, he implied that Marina thought that Ivan was a jerk. Fast-forward to last night. Now I find out they've been humping in secret because it's against the rules to fuck your clients. Meanwhile, Dresden's jacked up fifteen gees' worth of lap-dance bills."

Both Decker and Marge gasped.

Oliver said, "Yeah, I had the same reaction. The owner, a no-nonsense guy named Dante Michelli, got antsy and told Marina to collect a partial payment. To everyone's surprise, Dresden paid the bill off in its entirety. Marina thinks he might have mortgaged the condo to get the cash, a condo he now owns because Roseanne is presumed dead from the crash. That spells *m-o-t-i-v-e* to me."

"How'd he get a second mortgage on the condo so fast?" Marge wondered. "Insurance and the coroner haven't declared her officially dead yet."

"First of all, it's been over two months since the crash, so the loan wasn't necessarily a fast one. Second, maybe he has an in with the loan officer at the bank. Eventually, even if we don't find the body, Roseanne's insurance policies are going to have to pay out."

"Not if we declare her disappearance a homicide," Marge said.

"And what evidence do we have for that?"

"Well, we certainly don't have any evidence that she was on the plane," Decker said. "Especially with her last phone call coming in from San Jose."

Marge said, "There is a possibility that she flew in on the five A.M. flight from San Jose going to Burbank and then flew back out on the doomed eight-fifteen flight."

"I thought WestAir didn't have a work assignment for her on that flight."

"As far as we know, they still don't," Marge said. "So how do we approach Ivan?"

"Ask Ivan why Roseanne was in San Jose. Then see if he knows anything about Raymond Holmes."

"So you *want* us to bring up her ex-lover?" Oliver asked.

Marge said, "The last call on Roseanne's phone was to her house from a tower in San Jose."

"Okay . . . so you're thinking she went up to see him."

"It's possible, although there doesn't seem to have been contact between them for a good three months before the crash."

Oliver nodded. "So with Ivan Dresden, we're, what . . . using the approach that we think Mr. Holmes was the last one to see her alive so help us make him the bad guy?"

"It may be true," Decker said.

"But we're still considering Ivan the Terrible a suspect even though we're not approaching him that way."

"Yes."

"And we're figuring that if the heat's on Raymond Holmes, Dresden may feel relaxed enough to open up."

"Especially if we appeal to his ego," Marge said.

"We need your help, Mr. Dresden," Oliver acted out. "The police are counting on you."

"Yeah, we can lay it on as thick as peanut butter," Marge said. "You never can go wrong appealing to a man's ego. Guys are basically fragile creatures. I mean, we women really don't even need to put out. A few well-placed compliments are all it takes for a movie and dinner."

17

I T WAS A condo in a neighborhood of block-long condo com-
pounds, all of them refurbished, seventy swinging-singles apartment houses, each building bleeding into the next. The exteriors
were fashioned from wood and stucco with balconies for every unit.
The sycamores and elms that had been planted three decades ago as
little sprouts were now mature trees providing shade and greenery—a
good thing because summer temperatures in West Valley often reached
one hundred degrees and beyond. Weaving in and out of courtyards
abloom with impatiens and azaleas, Dunn and Oliver passed two
swimming pools, four Jacuzzis, a glassed-in gym, a recreation room,
two resident coffeehouses, and dozens of parking lots, giving the complex the feel of a planned community with suburbia mall overtones.

The Dresden unit was on the third floor of a three-story building. Ivan answered the knock with a scowl on his face. Briefly, Marge
studied the man and decided that pictures didn't do him justice. He
had thick black hair, startling blue eyes, and a strong chin, his only
imperfection being small pits and dots that landscaped his skin. He

was slightly shorter than Marge, around five ten, but he carried himself with an air of haughtiness thanks to a good-looking face and a sculpted body. He wore a black muscle T, long black sweats, with a towel around his neck, though he didn't look as if he had just worked out. Every hair was in place, not a bead of sweat anywhere.

"Thanks for seeing us, Mr. Dresden," Marge said.

"Do I have a choice?" he snapped back. "It's not enough that I have to grieve for my wife, but you people are preventing me from getting my insurance. Money can't take the place of Roseanne, but I don't see why I should have to suffer any more than I'm doing."

They were still standing outside. Oliver said, "Maybe it would be better if we talked indoors, sir?"

Dresden snorted but moved out of the way. The detectives entered the condo and looked around. The furniture was chain store contemporary, but nicely appointed. The place wasn't a sty, by any means, but it could have used some tidying. There was a week's worth of newspapers scattered about, and a trash can filled with empty beer cans, take-out Styrofoam cartons, and dozens of torn health-bar wrappers. Plus, the room would have benefited from a woman's touch—flowers, pictures, candles—because everything was done in stark lines and in pale colors—whites, grays, and pastel blues, except for a lone black leather couch.

"As long as you're here, you might as well sit down." Dresden threw some newspapers onto the floor, revealing a sofa cushion. He waited until the detectives sat, then resumed his lament. "Maybe if I smile and say 'pretty please,' you'll let me have what's rightfully mine."

"What makes you think we're withholding anything from you?" Marge asked.

"Oh, c'mon! Do I look like a moron?" He pulled the towel off his neck and snapped it in the air. "I know that insurance companies will do anything not to pay, but it doesn't help that the police keep asking about a body. Like it's my fault that the recovery crew is a bunch of incompetent jerks?"

Oliver stepped in. "So you think that your wife died in the crash, Mr. Dresden?"

Dresden became incredulous. "Of course she died in the crash! You have another idea, I'm open to suggestions!"

"I know you're aggravated." Oliver crossed and uncrossed his legs. "Insurance hasn't helped us one iota, either. And WestAir . . ." He waved his hand. "They've been downright obstructionist. So you're our last hope. We need your help."

"And if you help us out, we might be able to help you out," Marge said.

"Mutually beneficial," Oliver told him. "We're going to have to ask you a couple of questions, but don't take it the wrong way. We're just doing our job." Dresden made a sour face, but Oliver recognized mollification when he saw it. "When was the last time you heard from Roseanne?"

Dresden scratched his cheek. "These questions . . . do I need a lawyer?"

"Why would you need a lawyer?" Marge asked.

"Look, Ivan . . . can I call you Ivan?" Oliver asked. "We're here to get help. I'm not asking these questions to trip you up. I'm asking questions because we're trying to get a time line for your wife, which, by the way, is also what insurance needs."

"We're trying to re-create her last night before the crash." Marge held up her notepad. "I got it broken down into hours. Just filling in the blanks."

"Routine stuff," Oliver said.

There was silence. Then Dresden said, "Okay. I'll help you out as long as you tell me that Roseanne's parents didn't send you."

"They didn't send us and that's the truth," Marge said. "But I'll be honest. They've been calling the station house nonstop for the past two months. They don't like you."

"They're fucking nuts!"

"They're persistent in their opinions," Marge said.

"Exactly why I didn't tell them the truth about the last time I saw Roseanne." A sigh. "Roseanne and I had a monster fight the day before the crash. She stormed out of the condo around . . . I guess it was about four in the afternoon." His expression held a faraway look. "Next morning, I heard about the crash." His eye watered. "I totally freaked . . . I . . ."

He didn't finish his sentence. Oliver said, "Did you know that she had been assigned to work flight 1324?"

He took a few moments to catch his breath. "I got this phone message from her the night before . . . that she was subbing for someone and was up in San Jose for the evening. She told me that we'd talk about what happened when she got back the next morning. But then . . ." He threw up his hands.

"Okay," Marge said. "What time did she call you?"

"I don't know really. I got in very late and didn't call her back." He shook his head. "I wish I had . . . you know, talked to her before it happened. We had our issues, but still . . . you can't imagine how guilty I feel." He slapped his hands over his face. "I just can't think about it. It's too upsetting."

Marge said, "I'm sorry to have to intrude like this, but where were you the night before the crash?"

"Not in San Jose. I can tell you that much. I was upset after the fight. I went out and got drunk. Not the smartest thing to do, but . . ."

"What was the fight about?" Marge asked.

"The usual." The detectives waited. "Money."

"Nothing about women?" Oliver didn't wait for an answer. "We've done enough homework to know that things weren't great between you two. You had your side friends and she was angry about it. But we also heard that she had some friends as well."

Dresden went silent. Oliver supposed that even though Dresden was fooling around, his wife's infidelity had wounded his pride. Gently he said, "Was the fight about her infidelity?"

"That wasn't the core issue. But when we got angry, we both threw around the dirt. We had a more . . . liberated way of thinking. Anyway, the fight, like most of our fights, was about the almighty buck."

"We heard she was pretty pissed off about your side friends," Marge said.

"And I was pissed off about her sugar daddy. But like I said, that wasn't the main issue."

"Could she have flown up to San Jose to see him?"

"Doubt it," Ivan answered too quickly. "That ended a long time ago."

"How long?" Oliver said.

Then it was clear to see that the lightbulb went off in the husband's brain.

One, Roseanne was up in San Jose.

Two, the recovery team never found her body.

Ivan became wide-eyed. "You think Roseanne went to see him and something happened to her?"

"We're investigating everything," Marge said. "The sooner we find out what happened, the sooner you can get your money."

"Specifics would help, Ivan, to make sure we're all on the same page," Oliver told him. "For the records, who is *he*?"

"You don't know?"

"How about a name?"

"Raymond Holmes. When I saw him, I couldn't believe that Roseanne would sink that low for a Chopard watch."

Marge said, "Never underestimate the power of jewelry."

Ivan snorted again. "In answer to your question, sure it's possible that Roseanne went to see him."

"But you said that Roseanne told you she was subbing for someone," Marge said.

"So what? It's still possible that while she was in San Jose, she saw the fat prick and they had a fight. Roseanne was really good at starting arguments. And she was even better at really pissing you off. I could totally see that asshole losing it."

"You knew him personally, Ivan?" Oliver asked.

"Nah . . . never met the dude. Just saw a couple of pictures. He looked like a football player gone to seed."

"So how could you know if Raymond Holmes had a temper?"

"Even if you didn't have a temper to start with, a couple months with Roseanne, you'd develop it real quickly. Look, I know that Rose-anne broke it off. I finally gave her an ultimatum—him or me. She didn't have to think too long. I was there when she made the phone call. Still, Mr. Fat Ass has some problems with the word *no*. He kept calling her. I happened to answer the phone once. I told him to lay off my wife and he got really nasty. I said if I ever saw his ugly face around Roseanne, I'd kill him. He told me that I'd better be quick, otherwise he intended to shoot first." He looked at Marge. "We never met and nothing ever happened, but even with just the one conversation, I could tell that the guy had a nasty temper."

"Sounds like you have one yourself," Marge said.

Dresden rolled his eyes and looked at Oliver for solace. "I never met the guy in person. I'm just trying to giving you opinions, that's all."

"And we're happy to hear them," Oliver said. "But we got a problem, Ivan. We think that WestAir never issued a work order for Roseanne for flight 1324. As a matter of fact, we can't find any work order for Rose-anne in San Jose, period."

The room fell silent. Dresden became irritated. "So maybe I remember the message wrong. Maybe Roseanne just said she was in San Jose and we'll talk about the fight later and I *assumed* that she had flown up on an assignment. So much has happened between then and now . . ." His anger suddenly retreated into sorrow. "So much that I want to forget. So you're just going to have to accept my lapses of memory, all right?"

"Fair enough, Ivan, because we do know that the last call on Rose-anne's phone went through a tower in San Jose to your home phone," Oliver told him. "So how'd you find out about Raymond Holmes?"

"Roseanne started showing up with things that went way beyond her salary. The last straw was her trying to make me believe that a Chopard watch was a giveaway from her airline, which was one step away from Chapter Eleven."

Oliver laughed. "Yeah, we've heard that WestAir has financial problems."

"The company was always late with its payroll, so talk about lame lies. At that point, I pressed her and she confessed." A bitter laugh. "All those times she was on my case just because I enjoyed a night out with the boys. Meanwhile, she's boffing a butt-ugly old guy for a fucking watch."

Oliver raised his eyebrows. "I guess you two really did argue a lot about money."

"I told you, all the time. Roseanne was always getting on my case because I liked an occasional good time."

Marge said, "Maybe she got on your case because your occasional good time was costing a hell of a lot more than her occasional good time."

Dresden's eyes darkened. "What's that supposed to mean?"

"It means, Ivan, that we're not idiots and that we've checked out a couple of things before we came down to see you," Marge said.

Oliver said, "Not that I'm making any value judgments, because I've been to Leather and Lace myself. But on my salary, I forgo the lap dancing that's reserved for the honchos that can afford to stick a C-note down a babe's G-string."

Dresden was silent.

"Mr. Michelli likes to maintain cordial relationships with the police," Oliver went on. "We know you paid off an enormous lap-dance bill. You certainly don't have to answer this question, Ivan, but we are a bit curious. Where'd you get that kind of money?"

"I work, you know."

"That's a lot of overtime," Marge said.

"Fucking-A right about that!"

"How'd you come up with fifteen thousand dollars in one lump payment?"

"Like you said, I don't have to answer that."

"Of course not," Oliver answered. "Although maybe you don't want to leave us in a curious state. That's when we start snooping around."

"Snoop all you want," Ivan growled. "I have nothing to hide."

How many times had Marge heard that before? She said, "We'll find out if you have a second on the condo."

"I don't even officially own the condo," he spat out. "Until she's declared legally dead, all of her assets are frozen, for your goddamn information."

Oliver held up his hands. "Peace, bro, we're just trying to figure things out."

"Well, if you want to figure things out, why don't you ask Raymond Holmes where *he* was the night she phoned me."

"Absolutely." Oliver stood up and put his hand on Dresden's muscled shoulder. "I'm not trying to take you down, bro. I'm just trying to get to the truth. In the long run, it's good for you, because once we find out what happened to Roseanne—either in the crash or up at San Jose—you can get your money."

Dresden was still fuming about his exposed personal life. Still, he blurted out, "I sold my car and I'm driving Roseanne's Beemer. I can't sell it, but I can sure as hell use it."

"See how easy that was?" Oliver said.

"I should be taking a vacation in Mexico to clear my mind. Instead I'm working harder than I ever did. I'm also doing overtime."

"Fifteen thousand dollars must constitute a lot of overtime," Oliver said.

"Three thousand worth of overtime, ten gees for my old clunker. The rest came from pawning the jewelry given to Roseanne by Mr. Fat Ass. The Chopard watch went for about twenty cents on the dollar. Some lucky babe is going to get a very sweet deal."

18

MARGE KNOCKED ON the open door to the Loo's office. "Have
a few minutes?"

"Sure, have a seat." Decker looked up from the list, noticing that Marge and Oliver were smiling. "How'd it go with Ivan Dresden?"

After relating the bulk of the conversation, Marge said, "He told us
Roseanne had left a message on the answering machine. She said she
was up in San Jose."

"And that was about the only part he got right," Oliver said.

Marge said, "The first time he told us about Roseanne's message, he
said that she was subbing for someone in San Jose. After we adroitly
pointed out that WestAir hadn't assigned Roseanne a shift in San Jose,
he changed the line and said that she was up in San Jose, but he didn't
know why she was there."

"So why *was* she there?" Decker said.

"Dresden pointed to the obvious, that she went up north to visit
Raymond Holmes."

"Yeah, he was also quick to tell us that Raymond Holmes has a temper," Oliver said.

"Dresden met Holmes?" Decker asked.

Marge said, "No, he never met him, although he claimed he talked to the guy on the phone. From what we gathered, they got into a verbal pissing contest, but that was as far as it went."

Decker said, "Do we know where Ivan Dresden was when his wife was in San Jose?"

"He was out for the evening, but didn't say where," Marge said.

"My guess is Leather and Lace," Oliver said. "I think he'd like to keep his proclivities quiet until he gets his insurance money."

Decker said, "If Roseanne was planning to come home from San Jose the next morning to talk over the fight, she probably took the five A.M. WestAir flight from San Jose to Burbank. So there's a possibility that someone on that flight might have remembered her."

"I thought about that," Marge said. "The flight attendants and pilots who worked the five A.M. WestAir flight also worked flight 1324. Ergo, those WestAir employees are no longer alive to identify her."

"The passengers from the five o'clock flight made it out alive." Decker wondered how they felt, dodging the speeding bullet. "Maybe we can hunt down a passenger list and see if any of them remembers Roseanne."

Oliver said, "Even if no one remembers her, she still could have been on the five o'clock flight."

"Of course." Decker thought a moment. "If Ivan's telling the truth about Roseanne's last words, that she said she was coming home in the *morning* to talk about the fight, why didn't she deplane from the five A.M. flight at Burbank and just go home?"

Marge said, "One: She never made it back to Burbank. Two: She made it back to Burbank, deplaned before Erika Lessing came into work, and that was the last anyone ever saw of her again. Three: She got a last-minute assignment shift and was on flight 1324. Recovery just hasn't found her body."

Oliver said, "Option one points to her being bumped off in San Jose, option two means she was bumped off in Burbank, option three, she died in the crash. Or, there is an option four—she's alive and kicking under a new identity."

Marge said, "Since the last phone call on her cell came from a tower in San Jose, we're thinking we need to talk to Raymond Holmes."

"When did you want to do this?" Decker asked.

"I've got a light schedule tomorrow," Marge said.

"Can't make it tomorrow," Oliver said. "What about Thursday?"

"Thursday, I'm jammed," Marge said. "I can do it myself, Scott."

"Someone call up Raymond Holmes and make an appointment to interview him," Decker told them. "If it's tomorrow, I'll go up with Marge. If it's Thursday, I'll go up with Scott. I want to talk to him personally. Roseanne's parents have been calling me specifically, and I feel I owe them something."

Marge said, "I'll give Holmes a ring and let you know."

"Great. By the way, before you two leave . . ." Decker handed them each a stapled packet of papers. "Here's your homework: the complete list of the tenants from the destroyed Seacrest apartment house from 1974 to the present. I've taken 1974 to 1983. Scott, you take '84 to '94, and, Marge, you've got '94 to the present."

"What do you want us to do?" Oliver said, scanning the sheaves of paper.

"Go down the list and verify that all the names in your years are accounted for—either alive or dead with a death certificate. If you find a name that you can't verify—there's bound to be some of those—check them against our burned-up Jane Doe to see if any are potential candidates."

"There're a lot of people on my list," Oliver said.

"There are a lot of people on my list as well," Decker said.

"All that phone calling . . ." Oliver shook his head. "Carpal tunnel has wreaked serious havoc these days. It's grounds for disability, you know."

Decker reached inside a desk drawer and pulled out a bandage. "Here you go."

"How's that gonna help carpal tunnel?"

"It won't. But if you put it across your mouth, it'll stifle your bitchin'."

FEELING HIS EYES close, Decker sensed the papers slipping from his fingers, and wondered if he should give into that blissful sensation of nothingness. The alternative—to snap open the lids in an attempt to squeeze out a little more work before nodding off—seemed like a colossal waste of time and energy."

"Do you want me to save you the puzzle?" Rina said.

Decker opened his eyes and took in a deep breath. "You can do it if you want."

Rina took the papers that had landed on his lap and chucked them onto the floor. "Turn off the light and let's go to sleep."

No sense arguing with logic. Decker reached over to his nightstand table lamp and turned it off. He slithered under the sheets and slapped his forearm over his brow. "What time is it?"

Rina plumped up her pillow before settling down into bed. "A little past eleven."

"You're married to an old man."

"I know. I was dying to go clubbing and you spoiled everything." She stroked his arm. "What fascinating tidbit of police-science reading had you so captivated?"

Decker smiled in the dark and took his arm off his eyes. "I was going over a list of tenants that had resided in the now-destroyed Seacrest apartment from 1974 to 1983."

"You're trying to find your Jane Doe among those names?"

"Exactly. I've verified about half the people on my roster. I was just going over the rest of the names to see if something jumped out at me."

"Like what?"

"A familiar person from an old high-profile case of long ago."

"Were you with LAPD as far back as '74?"

"Yes I was, but not homicide. Juvenile and sex crimes." Again, he smiled. "As you may recall."

"Yes, I recall something about that." She rolled next to him and snuggled against his arm. "Wow. It seems like ages ago that we met."

He put his arm around her shoulder and drew her close to his chest. "What a glorious day it was. I was doing my best Jack Webb and you didn't appreciate it."

"I did so. I thought you were very handsome and charming."

"Really?" Decker shrugged. "I couldn't tell."

"You weren't supposed to be able to tell. I would have died of embarrassment."

"Then thank God I was dense."

Rina said, "Did any names on the list ring a bell?"

"About a half-dozen names seemed vaguely familiar. I've checked those off and I'll look them up in the police files first thing in the morning. Maybe I'll get lucky, but I'm not harboring great hopes."

"And you don't have any other way of identifying the bones?"

"Did I tell you I spoke to Mike Hollander today?"

"No, you didn't." Rina propped herself up on her elbows. "How's he doing?"

"Good, actually." Decker sat up as well. "He looks the same only a bit grayer and older. I'm sure I looked the same way to him."

"You haven't aged at all," Rina said.

"Spoken like a true wife."

"Did you show him the plans?"

"Yeah, yeah, Mike was great. He told me he'll make it a priority and get some numbers back to Cindy and Koby right away. But that's not why I mentioned him. We got to talking about the Jane Doe and our inability to reconstruct a face directly on the bones because they're too fragile. Anyway, he said that he saw something on a *Cold Case File* that he thought might work."

"What?"

"Something about a computer-generated process that replicates a skull in wood or plastic. The upshot is that a forensic artist can create a face because the bony landmarks are visible in the model. I was a little confused about the process and so was he. The problem is that the tape of the episode is no longer for sale and we can't seem to locate a copy."

"Does Mike remember the case?"

"No, and that's the problem. There was a little trailer for the episode, but it just hinted at the forensics and didn't mention anything specific, except that the case took place in Wisconsin."

"I'm sure the tape exists somewhere."

"Hollander said the same thing. He's trying to hunt it down. In the meantime, I have Wanda Bontemps looking up high-profile cases in Wisconsin." Decker threw his head back and blew out air. "We're not at desperation time yet, but we're getting there."

"It'll work out."

"Sometimes it does, and sometimes it doesn't."

"Maybe you should take a breather from trying to identify the victim and instead concentrate on the apartment house."

Decker scratched his head. "Excuse me, I'm confused. There is no apartment house."

"There is an apartment house, albeit crushed and burned. Walls talk, Peter, even burned ones."

"Sure, I have long conversations with walls all the time, especially when I'm talking to idiots."

"You mock, but it's true."

"I'm not mocking." Decker turned off the sarcasm. Rina didn't offer advice that often, so it paid to listen when she did. "What do you mean?"

Rina said, "Just because concrete, ash, and wood are inanimate objects doesn't mean that they have nothing to say. In Judaism, we have a definite concept of walls being harbingers of messages."

Decker smiled. "The writing on the wall."

"That was literal. The Mene from the book of Daniel. In that case, the message was cryptic and volumes have been written on what it meant. But the messages are not always so mystical. Look at the laws of Tzarat ... leprosy ... not the bacterial kind of leprosy that we see today.

Instead, it's a spiritual leprosy. One contracts Tzarat when one does *lashon harah*—gossips against his fellowman. It is manifested by sores all over the body."

"Like when Miriam spoke against Moshe in the Bible."

"She wasn't talking badly about her baby brother. She just thought he should spend more time at home with his wife. But G-d took umbrage. In that case, she was immediately stricken by Tzarat, because Miriam was a prophetess and a holy woman should not be gossiping about her brother even if it was with good intentions. There's usually a warning system with Tzarat. First the walls of the home contract the disease as a visible sign to its inhabitants to change their ways. If these writings on the walls are ignored, the disease progresses until Tzarat is contracted corporeally by the occupants."

"Okay," Decker said. "Next time I find a Jane Doe, I'll look for sores on the walls of her living room."

Rina kissed her husband's hand. "You scoff, Lieutenant, but that's exactly what you do as a detective. You scour a crime scene to help you solve a murder."

"Good point, Rina, except in this case, the crime scene was destroyed."

"Nothing is ever fully destroyed," Rina pointed out. "Look at Jerusalem, Peter. Anytime someone excavates in the ground—like for an archaeological dig or even just to build a new foundation for a building—something is always left behind. It could be anything from modern-day trash to old coins and relics and water jugs. About ten years ago, someone discovered an ancient tomb from the Second Temple era right in the middle of the suburban area of Rahavia. Just because something was destroyed on top doesn't mean that the underneath has no story to tell."

"I'm not saying that *everything* was destroyed. Obviously recovery has unearthed hundreds of body parts and personal effects. All I'm claiming is that the original crime scene was blasted into oblivion and the ground is basically an ashtray."

"Sometimes ash is a great preserver," Rina insisted. "If you take one of those tunnel tours underneath the Western Wall, you can actually see where the Romans dismantled original stones from the Second Temple. They knocked down almost the entire structure and burned what they didn't smash into smithereens. And they're still finding a lot of stuff had been preserved."

"Jerusalem's a lot older than Canoga Park."

"But L.A. has its own relics. Look at the La Brea Tar Pits . . . and all the stuff we've unearthed from the Chumash Indians."

"So if I find a saber-toothed tiger, I'll concede defeat," Decker answered.

"Now you're being sarcastic again."

Decker smiled. "Look, sweetheart, I understand what you're saying. And I know Jerusalem is filled with history despite all the destruction. But the Second Temple area was a lot bigger than the apartment house on Seacrest. So it stands to reason that more of it would have survived."

"Okay, that's true," Rina admitted. "But it doesn't have to be a massive structure to tell a story. Look at the Burnt House in Jerusalem. In the early seventies, archaeologists unearthed a Roman house from the Second Temple that had been burned down. Much of was preserved by ash. Not just the structure, Peter, but also they dug up a lot of ancient artifacts. And that house wasn't nearly as big as the apartment building on Seacrest. So what do you have to say to that?"

Decker smoothed his mustache. "Point well taken."

And it was true. At a crime scene, he often wound up looking through piles of detritus to locate that one crucial nugget of evidence. Because of his conversation with Rina, he realized that he had neglected a very important aspect of the investigation. No one had actually gone down to the original crime scene—the place where recovery had found the Jane Doe—and checked it out for forensic material in person.

"Now what are you thinking about?" Rina asked him.

"I'm thinking that you are a very bright lady. It's time I visited a crime scene."

19

SOMETIMES L.A. SUNRISES were preceded by spectacular, awe-inspiring displays of color—brilliant oranges, royal purples, and shocking pinks. On other occasions, they consisted of an insipid, dishwater-gray light breaking through an overcast sky. Such was the case this morning. June gloom had covered the basin with a layer of lint, and it was chilly and damp: what the locals would describe as just plain yucky.

It didn't help that Decker was staring into a desolate area—a seven-foot Cyclone fence encircling a pit as if it were a zoo cage under restoration. Inside, several excavators and steel bins of biohazardous material stood inert and ominous. Yellow caution tape flapped in a wind pungent with the odor of charred blackness. He raised the zipper on his bomber jacket and sipped hot coffee from his thermos. Then he checked his watch. It was a little before seven. The crew wasn't scheduled to be out until ten, and the one person he did manage to reach—an NTSB field officer named Catalina Melendez—was a mother of two school-age children and couldn't make it down before eight.

That was okay. It gave Decker ample time to look around and absorb what he had neglected. He capped the thermos and laid it on the sidewalk. He grasped the cold metal of the makeshift fencing and peered inside the perimeter.

What had it been like . . . to have been trapped in that inferno?

Staring into bleakness, he suddenly sensed motion from the corner of his eye. "Hey," he yelled out. "Hey! Police!"

A shadowed figure pivoted and took off, scaling over the fence and dropping to the ground on the opposite side from where Decker was standing, vanishing within moments. There was no way that Decker could catch up and he let it ride. The person could have been someone homeless camping out, or more likely, it was a vulture, scavenging for coins. Disaster sites were often pilfered for valuables.

Decker scribbled down a few cursory notes, then took out a camera and began snapping pictures. By the time he had taken most of his detailed photographs, it was almost eight. Catalina Melendez showed up twenty minutes later. She was small, with mocha-colored skin, and solidly built. Wisps of curly black hair were blowing about her face and in her mouth. She pulled them from her lips with fingers topped with clipped nails. She wore black slacks, boots, and a black bomber jacket with a yellow NTSB emblazoned on back.

"Sorry I'm late." She pulled out a set of keys and began sorting through them. "My six-year-old had an accident involving a carton of orange juice. How long have you been waiting?"

"Not so long," Decker lied. "I really appreciate you coming down this early . . . it's Officer Melendez, right?"

"Yeah, but call me Cat." Again, she pulled strands of hair from her mouth. "It looks like we've got a little wind and that's not helpful. It blows the residue around. I hope you have a mask. You don't want to be breathing in this muck."

Decker pulled a face mask from his jacket and put it on.

"Here we go." Cat opened one of the five padlocks that secured the area. "It's Detective Decker, isn't it?"

"Pete is fine."

"You're from local homicide."

"Yes . . . West Valley."

"And this is regarding the Jane Doe we found about ten days ago."

"That's the story. Can you tell me where you found the body?"

"Sure can," Cat said. "Watch your step and try to stay on the pathway."

Decker looked down at a well-worn, rutted groove running through the area. He was surprised at how much powdery burned material remained and remarked upon it.

"Yeah, we're going through it really slowly, not only for the purpose of gathering corroborating evidence for the accident, but to make sure we don't overlook any biological material. Technically, body parts are the coroner's responsibility, but we're much more used to doing this than they are."

"And technically, anything revolving around Jane Doe is our department because it's pretty clear that she was a murder victim."

"Yeah, we all knew that the Jane Doe wasn't our missing body from the accident—the flight attendant."

"Roseanne Dresden."

"Yes, mysterious Roseanne."

"Any signs that she was on the plane?"

"You'd have to ask the coroner for details, but frankly . . ." Cat lowered her voice. "I think someone made a mistake . . . or worse."

Decker said, "Fraud."

Cat shrugged. "Insurance detectives are pretty much on the ball, but you can't catch every liar out there. And the more time that goes by, the harder it is."

Decker knew it wouldn't have been the first time that some scamster badass had disappeared after telling the spouse to make a death claim. Afterward, the two of them would ride into the sunset with the insurance money. It was possible that Roseanne and Ivan were in cahoots with the intent of defrauding insurance.

He and Cat walked gingerly around pits and pools of the charred material. Evidence buried under the ruins, not unlike the house in Jerusalem that Rina had been talking about. An occasional wind kicked up. Swirling cinders encircled their ankles like a swarm of bees. It was a black, barren landscape of fire and smoke, yet healthy shoots of emerald-green plant matter had surfaced and stretched toward the sunlight. Ash was a terrific fertilizer. The only other colors in the lightless painting were provided by wrappers and cups from fast-food chains. Cat bent down and picked up a McDonald's bag filled with garbage and ants.

"Ick!" She looked around for a designated garbage bag and dropped the refuse inside. "So freaking annoying. It contaminates everything. Lucky for us, we're almost finished."

A preliminary conclusion reached by at least the media was that faulty hydraulics were to blame. Decker asked her about it.

"Not for me to say," Cat answered. "We've got zillions of pieces in an airplane hangar. Engineers will sort them out and get to the bottom of it, but it takes about a year. Sometimes longer. Sometimes never."

Decker said, "You said you knew right away that the body wasn't a crash victim. How'd you know if you weren't the one who examined the body?"

"Experience. The remains were too intact. Most of what is pulled up has been scattered and pulverized."

"Still, you've identified everyone else involved in the accident."

"Yes, the coroner's office has done an amazing job. Incredible what a good team can do with a single tooth and a femur. Anyway, after you see enough accident sites, you know what belongs and what doesn't." Cat checked an electronic compass. "Okay, we found her right about there." She pointed to small white chalked spot. "I entered the coordinates in my little organizer. I figured that eventually someone from homicide might want to take a look at the spot."

The area was near the southwest corner of the apartment building. Decker gloved up and squatted down. "Can I take a look?"

Cat squatted next to him. "Sure. Just go slowly."

Using his fingers, he pushed aside ash and debris, filtering the material through his fingers, attempting to pick up anything that might have been associated with his Jane Doe. "Do you know if she was found under or above the foundation?"

"It's hard to say because the collapse of the building broke through a lot of the foundation. And when we started digging around, it was hard to separate before and after. I'll tell you this much. We always recover lots of incidentals at accident sites, especially if the integrity of the building was compromised."

"Like what?"

"Money, jewelry, drugs, guns . . . almost anything people want to hide."

Decker continued sifting. He wasn't having much luck. Things that appeared solid at first glance disintegrated through the gaps in his fingers. He scooped up more of the cinders and let them fall through his fingers, repeating the process for several minutes as he dug deeper. Abruptly, Decker touched upon something embedded in the soil. His fingers dug around the object until he loosened it from the packed ground. What he pulled up was hard and round and sooty with a hole in the middle. Despite the heat and the fire and what must have been several thousand degrees' worth of Fahrenheit temperature, the object had managed to retain its original shape.

"What is it?" Cat asked.

Decker wiped the object on his bomber jacket to remove some of the soil and gave it to her.

"A plastic ring," she said. "Looks like something you'd find in an eight-year-old's goody bag . . . or a prize that you'd find in a quarter gumball machine."

"Can I take a look at that again?"

She handed the ring to him. Even though it had been scorched with dirt, Decker could make out a blue stone or piece of glass in the center. If it had been gold and the glass had been a gem, it would have resembled a cabochon sapphire in the middle of a man's pinkie ring. He was amazed that the plastic had not melted. Perhaps it had been shielded by the body or had been buried even deeper. He held it up to the strong, midmorning sunlight. As he bathed the object in the warmth of the rays, the stone began to change from dark blue, to ice blue, to pale pink. He let out a chuckle.

"What?" Cat asked.

"I know what this is. It's a mood ring." He regarded her face. "You're too young to remember the original fad; mood rings were really popular in the sixties and seventies. This may have belonged to my Jane Doe. Can I keep it?"

"If you think it might help."

"It might. Maybe someone remembers a young woman wearing a mood ring."

Cat stood up and so did Decker. She said, "First, let me take a picture of the ring and categorize it—date, time, and place. We need to make sure it didn't belong to any of the victims of the accident."

"Yes, of course." Decker waited until she was done and then dropped the ring into a small paper evidence bag. He peeked inside. Bereft of light and heat, the stone had paled to something between cold steel and graveyard gray.

IT FELT EERIE to be taking a flight from Burbank to San Jose on WestAir, sitting in an aircraft identical to the one that had plunged into nothingness just months ago. Decker felt a palpable tension during takeoff, and relief after the plane had reached cruising altitude and a quick beverage service had begun. He checked his watch, first to measure his heartbeat, which was thumping more than normal, then to calculate the time until arrival. It was almost two and they had about forty minutes to go. He glanced at Marge, who was looking over her notes. She had her hair pulled back into a ponytail and wore a white shirt and a black skirt. Black pumps on her feet. Recently she'd started wearing reading glasses. These were small and dark framed. It gave her a sort of sexy, schoolteacher look.

Decker said, "So you found Raymond Holmes to be cooperative?"

"Very."

"Even though we're interviewing him about his mistress and he's married?"

"That was his only request . . . that we keep the family out of it. I told him I didn't see a reason to include the wife and kids, and after that, he was easy." She took her glasses off, regarded Decker, and raised her eyebrows. "Almost too easy."

"Glib?"

"I don't know, Pete. We've all been thinking along the same lines, that Roseanne wasn't on that plane. That means we could be interviewing her murderer."

"True. But first let's just find out about their relationship. If he's involved in her disappearance, at the very least we need him to admit that he saw her the night before she vanished."

"So how do you want to handle the interview?"

"I guess it depends what we find out from WestAir in San Jose. Were you able to get any cooperation from the corporate honchos or are they still being difficult and referring you to their special task force?"

"Actually, WestAir has seemed to ease up a little. Someone gave me a name—Leslie Bracco. Apparently, she manned the check-in desk for the five A.M. flight from San Jose to Burbank. I couldn't get an interview with her first thing, so we're talking to her after we talk to Holmes. I made it around five."

"That'll work. Let's handle Holmes like we handled Ivan Dresden. We're just talking to him to get a timetable of Roseanne's last movements."

"Makes total sense." She leaned to her left and looked out the window. "How long do you think the interview with the flight attendant will take?"

"I don't know. Could be twenty minutes, could be two hours. Why?"

"Just curious."

Decker chuckled. "Dinner date?"

"I told Will to make it for eight. I figured that would give me enough time."

"I would hope so. I'm scheduled to leave on an eight-forty flight back home. When are you getting home?"

She squirmed in her seat. "I'm taking the five-thirty tomorrow morning."

Decker smiled.

"What?" she protested. "I'm a natural early riser. Why fight mother nature?"

"I didn't say anything."

"You're being technical, Decker." She punched his shoulder. "One smirk said it all."

20

⚡

A S THE THIRD-LARGEST city in California and the tenth largest in the United States, San Jose didn't get much respect. Mainly
noted from the sixties Hal David and Burt Bacharach song "Do
You Know the Way to San Jose?"—a name they used because it fit the
lyrics rather than for any other specific purpose—the city wasn't the
sleepy little burg that most people assumed. It was a megalopolis of a
million people with skyscrapers, museums, parks, colleges, and lots and
lots of high-tech headquarters. San Jose and its burbs of Sunnyvale,
Cupertino, and Santa Clara made up the heart of Silicon Valley—the
core of everything electronic and technical.

There were about a dozen people who lived in the area who were *not*
associated with Apple, IBM, Intel, Adobe, Sun Microsystems, Oracle,
Cisco, Hewlett-Packard, etc., etc., and Raymond Holmes was one of
them. The man was self-described as a real-estate developer, but his
house wasn't an advertisement for his financial prowess. It was a modest one-story, wood-sided, ranch-style abode—white with green shut-
ters—and sat on a lot of around six thousand square feet. There was a

nice patch of green lawn that ended in an eclectic, multicolored flower bed that was in bloom—impatiens, begonias, daisies, rosemary bushes, azaleas, and purple statis.

Decker parked the rental curbside and killed the motor. He turned to Marge. "If he's married, why did he ask us to meet him at his house? Even if his wife and kids are out right now, she could come home with an emergency."

"Beats me," Marge said. "People do strange things."

They shrugged simultaneously, got out of the car, and walked up to the front door. Decker rang the bell and Holmes answered it a toe tap later.

He had been described as a big guy and that was no lie. His five-foot-ten-plus frame must have been carrying an extra one hundred pounds of weight, most of it gut hanging over his belt buckle like a muffin top, stretching the fabric of his black polo shirt to the limit. His hips, being much smaller, were housed in baggy khaki pants and his feet were shod in running shoes but no socks. His face was round and smooth with a slight double chin. His eyes were saucers of coal, his nose upturned, and his mouth lined by a gray-and-auburn goatee. White was taking over what had once been a full head of dark hair. Half-style reading glasses were perched on his nose. His eyes were looking over the lenses. "You're the detectives from Los Angeles?"

"Yes, sir, we are," Decker answered. "And you are Raymond Holmes, sir?"

He sidestepped the question. "Could I see some identification?"

"Of course." Decker took out his badge and ID card and Marge followed suit. The big man studied them very carefully then spoke in a reedy voice that belied his size. "Can't be too sure these days. All this terrorism and identity theft. You never know who's really who. Come in."

Marge and Decker stepped into an empty room in a half-finished state of remodeling. The space had been drywalled but not painted, and they were walking on subflooring. Punched-out holes in the walls indicated where outlets and light switches were supposed to go. The area was filled with light from generous windows. Holmes led them through what was most likely a dining room and into an area that was the kitchen, judging from the rough plumbing. The main attraction was a folding table and four chairs. The contractor indicated for them to have a seat.

"Sorry about the dust, but it was easier to meet here than at my office."

"You're in the construction business?" Decker asked.

"Real-estate development," Holmes told him. "This is one of my many projects."

Decker looked around. "This is what . . . 1940s vintage?"

Holmes parked himself on a chair, his knees spread apart to allow room for his stomach. He took out a handkerchief and wiped his forehead. It wasn't particularly hot, but it wasn't unusual for big men to sweat. "Are you interested in real estate, Detective?"

Decker smiled. "My daughter and son-in-law are about to undertake some renovation, so I guess I'm curious. How long have you been in the business?"

"All my life." He checked his watch. "Listen. I don't mean to be rude, but I chased away the crew to have some privacy because we're talking about a . . . delicate matter. They're supposed to come back in about forty minutes."

"Then we should speed things up," Decker said. "First of all, Mr. Holmes, I want to thank you for seeing us on such short notice."

"You were a little sketchy on the details," Holmes said. "Something about Roseanne Dresden. Did she leave me some money or something?"

Marge and Decker exchanged glances. Decker said, "Her estate hasn't been settled. That's why we're here. Recovery hasn't found her body at the accident site. It's been a while, so we're considering Roseanne Dresden as a missing-persons case."

Holmes pulled out another tissue and mopped his brow. "I don't want to sound callous or strange, but in these cases, do you always find the body?"

"No," Decker said, "but there's usually something that indicates that the person was on board: personal items or at the very least a ticket. For the flight attendants who don't have tickets, there's usually a work assignment. So far, we've come up empty."

Marge said, "No one remembers seeing her boarding the plane."

"Matter of fact we have the opposite," Decker said. "The desk clerk who was working the gate at Burbank swears that Roseanne didn't board the plane."

"So that's why at this point, we're considering it a missing persons," Marge said.

Decker said, "If something is recovered from the accident site that puts Roseanne on the flight, then of course this discussion is moot. But since no one has seen or heard from Roseanne, we're investigating her disappearance."

"I thought that I read that they found her body. Like a couple of weeks ago."

Decker said, "Recovery found a body, but it wasn't Roseanne."

Holmes dabbed his brow. "Who was it?"

"We don't know."

"So how do you know it's not Roseanne?"

"From our forensic odontologist. The teeth don't match."

"And that's what they're basing it on?" Holmes blinked several times in rapid succession. "Teeth?"

"Yes, sir, enamel is the hardest substance in the human body. Often teeth do survive when everything else is burned up."

"So let me tell you why we're here," Marge said. "The last phone call on Roseanne's cell went through a San Jose tower."

Holmes didn't respond.

Marge gave him the date of the call. "We're just trying to locate Roseanne's final movements before she disappeared. The call was from San Jose, you live in San Jose, you have a relationship with the deceased—"

"*Had*, Detectives," Holmes said. "Past tense. I *had* a relationship with her. We broke up about eight months ago and I haven't seen her since."

The detectives were silent. Decker counted to six before Holmes spoke.

"I'm sorry I can't help. If you would have just said something on the phone, you wouldn't have had to come up here and waste your time."

"As long as we are here, we'd like to ask you a few questions," Decker said.

"Just to get a little background on Roseanne," Marge added.

Again, the big man looked at his watch. "You got about thirty minutes."

Decker said, "Could you tell me the last time you saw Roseanne?"

"I don't remember the exact date, but I can look it up in my old calendar book. It'd be there because we went to Percivil's and I made a reservation." His jaw began to chew something imaginary. "It was her favorite spot." Chew, chew. "She got all teary-eyed and I knew it was over. She said she was going to try to work it out with that rat husband of hers. Nothing I said would change her mind."

"And you never heard from her again?"

"No."

Decker said, "So if I were to check out the date, which you said can be easily verified, and then check Roseanne's cell number, I wouldn't find any calls from you to her after your evening at Percivil's."

This time his jaw muscle froze in a gigantic bulge as if it were a solid tumor. "What I meant to say is I never *saw* her again. I think I called her a couple of times."

"What were the phone calls to her about?" Marge asked.

Holmes said, "I was trying to get her to change her mind. It didn't work. That's that and I've moved on. End of Roseanne, end of discussion."

Decker smiled. "How about giving us a few more minutes?"

Marge said, "Just indulge us, Mr. Holmes. It makes you look better."

When the big man turned quiet, Decker took that as a signal to continue. "I'm sorry to have to ask you this, Mr. Holmes, but where were you the night before the crash?" He gave him the specific date.

"I don't remember." He stared at the detectives, wiping perspiration from his face. "If you write down the date—and any other dates you want—I'll let you know if I was anywhere except home."

"The specific call was made around midnight," Decker said.

"If it was midnight, I was probably home sleeping. I get up early in the morning."

"Well, maybe you could just tell us what you did that night," Marge said.

"Or even what you did during the day," Decker said.

"Like I said, I'll check the calendar and give you a call." Holmes blinked again. "I'll even xerox you the page. Any other dates you want to know about? Get it all out. That way, you don't have to keep asking me where I was."

Marge and Decker exchanged quick glances. Decker said, "How about xeroxing that entire week?"

"Sure."

"When can we expect it to arrive?" Marge said.

Decker said, "How about tomorrow? I'll give you a FedEx number."

Holmes blinked and wiped sweat off from his brow. "If it gets you guys off my back, why not. Tomorrow by three o'clock via FedEx. What's the account?"

Decker gave him the number. "Thank you for cooperating so fully with our investigation."

"Sure. You know, I have mourned Roseanne's death for a long time even before she actually died, know what I'm saying?"

"I think so," Decker answered.

"Then we're done here?"

Marge said, "Not quite yet. And we really thank you for cooperating in such a delicate matter. If you hadn't talked to Roseanne for a while, how did you hear about her being on the doomed WestAir flight?"

Holmes gave Marge a condescending look. "The crash made front-page news because the plane was going to San Jose. Locals died, Sergeant. It was a very big deal."

"But how did you find out about Roseanne specifically?"

"From the victims list." He rocked his chair until the two front legs came up a few inches. The chair tipped, but he caught himself before he fell backward. "I was devastated! I had no idea she was still flying this route." He licked his lips. "I still had feelings for her. I didn't make it to work that morning, I was so upset." He patted his forehead dry. "I don't think I fully accepted our breakup until that day. And now you tell me she wasn't on the flight . . . God, I don't know what to think . . . what to feel."

"She *may* have been on the flight," Marge said. "We just don't know."

"Would you also xerox the week of the crash for us?" Decker asked. When he received a sour look, he said, "Might as well get it all done with."

"Okay," Holmes snorted. "Are we done?"

Marge said, "Some of the people that we talked to implied that you had a hard time accepting that the relationship was over."

"What do you mean?"

"Ivan Dresden said that you two had words," Decker said.

Holmes's jaw muscles tightened. "So?"

"He told us you threatened him."

"Not before he threatened me." The big man leaned forward. "Look, we were both talking out of anger and frustration. Roseanne could be a real frustrating woman." He threw up his hands. "Hey, it's all water under the bridge. I've moved on. I'm sure the bastard has moved on as well . . . unless, of course, he's the reason why Roseanne is missing."

"You think he murdered her?" Marge asked him outright.

"I wouldn't put it past him. He was a real asshole. Did he also happen to tell you how many women he was fucking while they were married?"

"I understand that he played around," Marge said.

"The man was a dog!" Holmes bellowed. "He was spending all of her money on lap dancers, and then he has the nerve to get outraged because Roseanne wanted a little attention."

"How'd you meet Roseanne?" Decker asked.

"I had a business meeting in Los Angeles and was coming home. She was the flight attendant. She looked a little sad and I asked her about it. She denied anything was wrong. It wouldn't have been professional for her to talk about her personal life with a passenger. Later, by sheer coincidence, I ran into her at her hotel bar. At first, I could tell that she thought I was just an old fat guy looking for a quick lay. But after we talked awhile . . . we clicked. I mean we really clicked." His face darkened. "We spent six months together before we went to bed. We had something special, although I'm sure you find that hard to believe."

"Not at all," Marge said.

Holmes checked his watch, placed his hands on his knees, and hoisted himself up. "I'm sorry, but you two really need to leave now. The crew's coming back very soon and all this talk has opened up wounds. I need a few minutes to compose myself." He was breathing hard. "I'll FedEx the calendar pages for you. Then we're done here."

Decker stood and gave him his business card. Marge gave him one as well. She said, "One last question, Mr. Holmes. Do you have any idea why Roseanne was in San Jose if she hadn't been assigned to work here?"

"I couldn't even hazard a guess," Holmes said.

"Hazard one," Decker insisted.

A big sigh. "C'mon, I'll walk you out."

Decker didn't move.

Holmes said, "It might be flattery, but maybe she finally got fed up with Ivan and was thinking about seeing me."

"But she didn't visit you."

"No, she didn't. Maybe once she got up here, she changed her mind. Or maybe she was visiting some friends. She worked the San Jose route for a while. She had some friends here, you know."

"Girlfriends or boyfriends?" Marge asked.

"I was thinking girlfriends, but maybe she had another boyfriend. I wouldn't know because like I said, we weren't in contact anymore."

Marge got out her notebook. "Can you tell me the names of some of her girlfriends?"

"Uh . . ." Another flick of the wrist to see the time. "I remember a Christie and a Janice. Or was it Janet?"

"Last names?" Marge asked.

Another sigh. "Christie . . . somethingson. Jorgenson, Ivarson, Peterson . . ."

"A Scandinavian name?"

"I think so."

"What about Janet or Janice?"

"I never knew her last name."

"What does Christie look like?" Marge persisted.

"Medium height, shoulder-length blond hair, blue eyes, button nose, anorexic with long legs and skinny calves. I think we met her around two, three times for dinner. Janice or Janet I met only once. She was a brunette, light brown eyes, good figure, and older. You've got to go now. My wife never found out about the affair, thank God, and I want to keep it that way. I been very cooperative and I expect some reciprocalness."

Reciprocity, Decker said to himself. "We'll do what we can. You have my card, Mr. Holmes. If you think of Christie's last name or anything else that could help us track Roseanne's last movements, we'd be much obliged."

"Aren't you curious about what happened to Roseanne?" Marge asked.

"Sure I'm curious, but that's as far as it's going to go. Now I'm concentrating on my marriage and my kids." Holmes smoothed his goatee. "But if you do find something, I wouldn't mind a phone call. Especially since I'm being so cooperative."

"I know, sir," Decker said. "We'll do what we can."

"Then I'll do what I can for you, Lieutenant. You know how it works. I scratch your back, you scratch mine."

21

AFTER DECKER PULLED away from the curb, Marge asked, "What do you think?"

"The verdict is still out."

"He was pretty cooperative."

"I know. He kept telling us how cooperative he was being."

"That could be his nerves talking."

"Or it could be guilt. He was sweating a lot." She thought a moment. "On the other hand, he's sending us Xeroxes for the dates we requested."

Decker shrugged. "He could be sending phony ones."

"But then once we started verifying things, we would trip him up. He's got to know that. It would be nice if we find Christie Norsewoman. If Roseanne visited her the night before the accident, she'd be Holmes's alibi."

"Maybe our next interview knows Christie Norsewoman," Decker said. "Leslie Bracco. When are we supposed to meet her?"

"Five. It's only three-thirty."

"Can you call her and see if she can meet us earlier?"

"Sure, why not?" Marge turned on her cell phone. "I've got some messages. Maybe one of them is Leslie." She listened to her answering machine and then punched in her code. "It's Vega telling me she's fine, but she's turning off her phone to study. That girl is so high-strung— oh, it's Willie . . ." She smiled as she listened. "Ah, he's so cute . . . this one's from Scott . . ."

"What going on with him?"

Marge listened for a moment. "Mike Hollander's looking for you. He's all excited. He got hold of the tape of the Wisconsin case."

"That's good."

"Call him back when you've got a chance . . . wait, this is Leslie Bracco . . . she's going to be late. 'Don't come any earlier than five-thirty.'" Marge snapped the cover back on her cell. "We've got two hours to kill. Want me to call back Oliver?"

"Absolutely. See if you can get Hollander's number. I don't have it on me."

"Sure. I'm flagging a little. How about we get a cup of coffee?"

"I wouldn't mind some food, actually. Last time I ate it was six in the morning and it was only a bowl of Cheerios. I could use something substantial."

"Rina didn't pack you a lunch?"

"She offered, but I told her not to bother. Lately it's been hard to take anything on board. Lord only knows what's next. Maybe bombs made out of roast beef."

THE CELL RANG just as Decker was paying for two tuna-fish sandwiches with coleslaw and french fries, plus two cups of coffee, all of it courtesy of LAPD. He was feeling more alert after having eaten, which made him wonder if he'd missed something crucial during the Holmes interview. He recognized the number as the one he had dialed about an hour ago and depressed the green button. "What's the good word, Mike?"

"Life is good, Pete, and getting better. The name of the technology is Rapid Prototyping and here's how it works—I think."

"Hold on a sec, Mike. Let me get inside the car so I can hear you and scribble some notes."

"Sure. Take your time."

After he was ensconced in his seat—this time Marge elected to drive—Decker took out a notepad. "I'm going to put you on speakerphone so Margie can hear you as well." He jacked up the volume, pushed the button, and laid the phone on the dashboard of the rental.

"Hi, Marge," Hollander said.

"Hey, Michael. How does it feel to be a cop again?"

"Real good."

"You have a home with us, buddy," Decker said. "We're ready. Lay it on."

"I'm reading off my notes, so bear with me. Like I said, the process is called Rapid Prototyping. It's used in industry to construct models. Let me give you the example like the tape did. Suppose Ford Motor Company designs an engine block on a computer? Now a computer image is a two-dimensional representation of something three-dimensional. But the company needs a three-dimensional object to work with. Say, for instance, using Ford Motor again, the company wants to place it in the hood of the car to see how much room it's going to take up. That's where Rapid Prototyping comes in. It's a technology that makes a three-dimensional model off of the two-dimensional computer image."

"Got it," Marge said.

"This is how Wisconsin solved the problem. The first thing they did was to run the skull through a CT scan. I called up the coroner's office. They don't have a machine, but all hospitals do. Maybe we can ask county to borrow one. It's not far from the Crypt. Anyway, once you have the machine, you'll also need a technician to take serial cross-section X-rays of the entire skull. Are you two with me?"

"We are," Marge said. "Go on."

"Okay. Now each X-ray image from the CT scan is a one-millimeter cross section of the skull."

There was a long pause. Marge said, "Mike, are you there?"

"Yeah, wait a sec . . . okay, here we go. Once you have the X-rays, you need someone to feed the shots into a computer that interfaces with this prototype machine. The computer tells the machine to laser-cut a piece of paper for every CT-scan X-ray you have. So each piece of paper represents a millimeter cross-sectional outline of skull. Not the inside part, obviously, just the perimeter. Am I making myself understandable? 'Cause it's much easier once you see the tape."

"I think I got what you're saying," Decker said. "You have a cross-sectional paper silhouette that's one millimeter thick."

"Exactly, except that each paper silhouette is only around one one-thousandth of an inch because the computer interpolates between the X-rays to make the model smoother."

"Okay," Decker said. "Go on."

"So . . . where was I? Oh, here I am. The machine cuts out a paper silhouette about one-one-thousandth-inch thick and stacks it onto the previous paper silhouette. So in the end, you have a huge stack of paper silhouettes that represents the skull. Then another part of the machine squeezes the stack of paper silhouettes together until you have a three-dimensional representation of the original skull."

Decker said, "Let me recap. The original skull is fed through a CT scan that takes cross sections of the skull about one millimeter thick. Then the CT-scan images are fed into a computer that's attached to the prototyping machine. The prototyping machine cuts paper silhouettes of the computer model based on the CT-scan images. Each silhouette is about one-one-thousandth-inch thick. The paper silhouettes are stacked upon one another in order. Then another part of the machine compresses the paper so that the skull is basically reconstituted out of paper."

"Exactly." Hollander paused. "You're pretty quick at this."

"I've done some carpentry in my day," Decker said. "Gluing layers of thin laminate on top of one another to get an odd shape. What you end up with is a skull that is in essence made out of wood."

"Perfect!"

"And the forensic artist uses the wooden skull to construct a clay face onto."

"One hundred percent. And here's the best part, Deck. There's legal precedent for doing this. The Wisconsin court ruled that the replica skull could be used for forensic purposes since the model was accurate with all its bony landmarks."

"So let me get this straight," Decker said. "We need to transport a very delicate skull to a CAT-scan machine. Once I do that, I need a CAT-scan technician to take a bunch of serial X-rays. Then I need to find a company who has access to a machine that does Rapid Prototyping. After we find the machine, we still need to find a programmer who can program the X-rays into the computer, and lastly, we need a technician to run the machine that produces the three-dimensional object."

"It sounds like a lot, but I bet getting your hands on the machines isn't as hard as it appears," Hollander said. "We've got some automobile plants in the Valley."

"You're right. I'm not worried about finding the machinery. I am worried about finding the funding."

There was a brief silence over the phone. Then Hollander said, "You see, that's why I'm glad I retired. I liked the detective part of the job. It was the red tape that was always a bitch."

THE RANCH HOUSE was in the same area as Raymond Holmes's renovation project, similar in style but tired. The paint job was cracking in spots and the landscaping was patchy. There was a porch with several lawn chairs, and that's where Marge and Decker waited for Leslie Bracco to make her appearance.

As the time crept toward six o'clock, Marge called up Will and asked him to push the dinner reservation off until nine. In a gallant act of chivalry, Will told her that he was off early and that he'd be happy to drive down south, saving her some time and aggravation. There were a number of great restaurants in San Jose and several of them were open late.

Leslie showed up at six-ten, a set of keys in her hand. She was small and compact, square in the shoulders, a woman in her late forties, with helmet-clipped black hair streaked with silver. Green eyes and thick lips sat in a round face with big, apple cheeks. She wore a dark brown pantsuit, the jacket hugging a dusty-rose-colored wool sweater. Her shoes were simple brown flats. "I'm so sorry I'm late. The meeting just went on forever. We've been doing a rock-bottom savings promotion to try to woo back customers and it's been very successful. WestAir has agreed to keep it going." She opened the front door. "Have you been waiting long?"

"Not too bad," Decker said.

"You're just being nice." She walked into the house and began opening drapes and turning on lights. The detectives followed.

"It gave us a little time to catch up on our work." Decker smiled and she smiled back with bleached white teeth. "I'm Detective Lieutenant Decker and I believe you've spoken to Detective Sergeant Dunn."

"Hi." Leslie shifted her purse from one arm to the other and held out her right hand. First to Marge then to Decker. "Sit anywhere you'd like. Sorry for the mess."

The mess was a newspaper folded neatly on the coffee table. Other than that, the place was immaculate. The decor could have been lifted from a furniture ad—a traditional rose-patterned upholstered couch, matching love seat and armchair-with-ottoman arrangement. Sitting in the corner was a piano, the top obscured by family pictures. More photographs were hanging on the walls. The beige carpeting was thick ply and spotless.

Leslie threw her purse on the sofa. Then she looked at it and placed it upright on a walnut end table. "Can I get either of you coffee? I'm making decaf for myself, so it's no bother."

"That sounds fine." Marge looked at the wall snapshots; most of them displayed Leslie, a husband, and three kids in the usual vacation backdrops. A more recent photograph appeared to be a skiing vacation—six young adults with four babies and toddlers. There was no husband in that picture, but there was a picture of a pale bald man holding a baby. He was wearing an old terry robe and had an ear-to-ear smile.

Leslie was a widow and her husband had probably succumbed to cancer.

The flight attendant caught Marge staring at the photograph. Her eyes welled up with tears. "That was Jack." A forced smile. "It's been three years and I still miss the hell out of him."

"Boy, was he proud," Marge told her.

"Yes, he was." She wiped her eyes. "Our first grandchild. How do you take your coffee?"

"Black," Decker said.

"Same," Marge answered.

"You two are easy." She disappeared and came back a few minutes later with a tray and three mugs of coffee. She placed it on the sofa table and handed out the mugs, then sat down on the love seat, taking off her shoes and placing them neatly under the end table. Finally she curled her toes under her legs and picked up her mug. "Wow! That tastes good!"

"It does indeed," Decker said. "You don't look old enough to have four grandchildren."

"Five, actually. That picture is old. And thank you for the compliment. People tell me I wear my age well. I think it's because I had a good marriage. Jack was an airline pilot. We both loved to travel. Even when the kids were little, we'd schlep them everywhere. One of my sons inherited the wanderlust. My daughters are much more rooted."

"Do they live near you?" Marge asked.

"The girls both married computer guys and live in nice houses in a great school district. My son and his wife live outside of Sitka, Alaska, and work for the Fish and Game Department."

"There's a switch," Decker said.

"He definitely followed his own muse." Leslie took a sip of coffee. "I understand from my boss that you wanted to talk to me about Rose-anne Dresden. How can I help you?"

"So WestAir knows you're talking to us?" Marge said.

"Oh yes. They've asked me to cooperate fully, which I would do without their orders, but it seems important to them that I appear helpful . . . beyond making coffee."

Decker smiled. "Hey, sometimes that's enough. Anyway let me give you some details. Roseanne Dresden has not been seen or heard since the accident. So, at first, it seemed logical that Roseanne had jumped the plane without a ticket and had perished along with everyone else. Our problem is we can't find any verification of that. No body, no personal effects, no ticket, no work order . . . absolutely nothing."

"We're treating it as a missing-persons case," Marge said. "We're trying now to retrace Roseanne's last movements before she disappeared. We found a phone call on her cell, around midnight on the night before the accident. It came from a San Jose tower. Would you know anything about that?"

"No, nothing." Leslie shook her head. "But I think I can help you in a big way. I saw Roseanne the morning of the accident." Again, pools formed in her eyes. "I was working the ticket counter." She smacked her lips shut. "I knew the entire crew. It's everyone's worst nightmare . . . oh my, here come the faucets again." Tears erupted and trailed down her cheeks. She pulled a tissue and dabbed her eyes. "Every time I think about it, I just can't stop crying."

"I'm sure it's still raw for you," Decker said.

"That's a good word . . . raw. That's exactly it."

Decker waited a few minutes for her to get the emotion out and for his racing heart to slow. Then he said, "You saw Roseanne the morning of the accident?"

"I saw her and I talked to her."

Marge tried to appear calm. She flipped the cover on her notepad. "And when was this?"

"Very early in the morning . . . around four-fifteen maybe. She was hitching a ride to Burbank."

"Was she in uniform?" Marge asked.

Leslie shook her head. "No, she was in civilian clothing. I was surprised to see her. She hadn't worked San Jose for a while. She said she had come up from Burbank the day before to talk to management about being transferred . . . specifically to be based in San Jose." She looked down. "She was very frank. She was unhappy in her marriage and she wanted to move and be closer to her parents."

"She came into San Jose the *day* before the accident?" Decker asked.

"That's what she said."

"Did she say what time she arrived in San Jose?" Decker said.

"No, but that wouldn't be too hard to find out. She probably came in on a WestAir flight. And I imagine that if she wanted to speak to management, it would have to be before five. That's when the offices close."

Marge's brain took note. When she and Oliver interviewed Ivan Dresden, the stockbroker had said that his wife had stormed out of the condo around *four* in the afternoon. That would make it very hard to meet with management before the company closed.

Someone was fibbing.

The look on Pete's face told her that he was thinking the same thing.

Decker said, "Okay . . . so we have you seeing her the morning of the crash, around four-fifteen A.M. Are you positive that she took the early flight back to Burbank? Is it possible that she changed her mind?"

"I can't answer that because I don't know, but I wouldn't think so."

"Did you actually see her board the aircraft?"

"Oh, boy." Leslie thought for a moment. "I can't swear to that, either, but I can't imagine her not being on the flight since she told me she was on her way back home." She took another sip of coffee. "I suppose it's possible that she got a call from management . . . but at that hour of the morning?"

"Nothing on her cell," Marge told her.

Decker said, "If Roseanne was in civilian clothing, does that mean she wasn't working on the early-morning flight to Burbank . . . what was the flight number?"

"That would have been 1325, but we changed the numbers . . . obviously."

"Okay, so say Roseanne boarded 1325 in civilian clothing. Does that mean she wasn't working the flight?"

"I would say yes to that."

"So if she wasn't working 1325, do you have any idea why she would have jumped back onto flight 1324?"

"Maybe she was substituting at the last minute," Leslie said. "Or by that time, maybe someone from management had called and asked her to come back up for another interview."

"Nothing on her phone records indicated that," Marge said.

"Maybe she called management on an office phone to save long-distance minutes," Leslie said.

"Do you think she did that?" Decker asked.

"I don't know, Lieutenant, I'm just throwing out possibilities."

"We appreciate that," Decker answered. "So she told you she had come up to San Jose to try to get a job based in the city."

"Yes."

"Any idea where she stayed?"

Leslie shrugged and averted her eyes. Marge said, "We've talked to Raymond Holmes, Ms. Bracco."

"Please call me Leslie." She smiled. "So you know about him."

"Yes, we do," Marge said. "Did Roseanne mention Mr. Holmes to you?"

She thought for several moments. "Not specifically to me, but it was common knowledge that they knew each other."

"Do you know Raymond Holmes?" Decker asked.

"Oh yes. He used to travel WestAir quite a bit . . . not lately, though. Maybe Roseanne soured him on the airline."

"And you know they had an affair."

"He'd occasionally talk about Roseanne . . . where they went, what they did. I thought it was very tacky, but Roseanne was open, so I suppose he figured why not be open as well. Ray isn't the most . . . modest of men. He used to brag about his financial prowess . . . trying to impress. It never impressed me."

Marge said, "Mr. Holmes told us that he hadn't seen Roseanne for about six months prior to the accident."

Leslie said, "I wouldn't know."

"He also mentioned a girlfriend of Roseanne's in San Jose . . . two of them actually." Marge checked her notes, not because she forgot the names but to look official. "Christie and Janet or Janice."

"Christie Peterson and Janice Valley. They're both working as flight attendants for WestAir. Janice is based in Reno now . . . has been for the last four months, I believe. Christie lives in the area."

"So it's possible that Roseanne could have stayed with Christie?" Decker said.

"Certainly. Would you like me to call her for you? I feel better about that than my giving you her home phone number."

"That would be great," Decker said.

Leslie got up from the love seat and went behind closed doors. Ten minutes later, she emerged with several slips of paper. "Here's her address and her telephone number. She said she could see you in about a half hour."

"That would be perfect," Decker said. "Did you ask her if Roseanne had stayed with her?"

"No, that's not my business, that's your business. I only told her that two detectives from L.A. are here and would like to speak to her about Roseanne. Christie was quite emotional. Please tread lightly."

"That's what we try to do," Decker answered.

"I know. You're only doing your job." A sigh. "Since it's going to be dark, I drew you a little map."

"That'll help," Marge said. "Thanks so much."

"Here's my card if you think of anything else you want to ask me."

Decker took it and reached inside his pocket. "And if *you* think of something germane to the case, here's my card."

Leslie took it, reached down from her purse, and pulled out a Side-kick. She entered the number with professional efficiency. "Done."

Decker smiled. "You're very thorough, ma'am. You'd be a terrific asset to any company."

"Thank you." Her smile was tinged with sadness. "I was always a compulsive person. I think it's because of my background—alcoholic, abusive parents. If you're unlucky, you fall into their same bad habits. If you're lucky and you meet a man like Jack, you develop more benign habits as a way of coping with anxiety."

22

WITH A DECENT eye for detail, Holmes had described Christie
Peterson accurately, down to her long legs and svelte calves. She
topped out around five six and was very, very thin, her sweatpants ballooning around her like bellows. Since she was wearing a short-
sleeve top, her twig arms were visible, elbows jutting out like nunchakus.

The flight attendant lived alone in a two-bedroom boxy condo near
the heart of the city. Her furniture was functional and nondescript, sitting on wall-to-wall off-white Berber carpeting. She had prepared for
the detectives' visit by setting out a pitcher of water along with a bowl
of mixed nuts. Sipping white wine, Christie had offered to pour Char-
donnay for the detectives, but both of them had declined.

Decker explained why they had come for a visit and Christie had
confirmed what both detectives had suspected. Roseanne had stayed
the night with her. When they asked her about Roseanne's state of
mind, the flight attendant did not hesitate.

"She was upset with Ivan," Christie told them.

"Did she tell you why?" Marge asked her.

"She sure did. It was that lap dancer he was seeing—Marissa or Melissa, something with an 'M.' Roseanne knew that they had a thing going, but what really infuriated her was that Ivan was still going to the club and spending money on her." A soft laugh. "Roseanne felt that if he was screwing her, he should be getting it for free!"

"When did she contact you about staying at your place for the evening?"

"Hmm . . . I have to think." Christie took another sip of wine. "Maybe around ten or eleven in the morning, I'd say."

Marge pulled out Roseanne's cell-phone records. "I have a call to a San Jose number at ten thirty-three A.M." She gave her the date and read the digits out loud.

"That's me," Christie said.

"And do you remember what was said in that conversation?"

"Just that she was coming up and needed a place to crash for the evening. I heard the tension in her voice and asked if everything was okay. She told me she'd tell me all about it when we met. I didn't push it."

"When did you two get together?" Decker asked her.

"Around . . . sixish." She licked her top lip and put down the wineglass. "We went out for a bite to eat. She was still upset. She did mention something about a fight, but she was clearly was more interested in the future. She had come up to interview for a transfer back to San Jose. She was seriously considering divorce and wanted to be closer to her parents."

"Did she tell you what time she was interviewed?"

"No." The flight attendant shook her head. "Nothing about the time."

"How'd the interview go?" Marge asked her.

"Well. She said they had a position for her. She was happy. I remember her saying something like . . . 'at least something in my life is working out.'"

"How long did dinner last?" Marge inquired.

Christie shrugged. "I don't remember." She brightened. "I can tell you that we were back in my place before nine because I went out that evening. I invited Roseanne along, but she declined. She was calling it an evening."

"Where'd you go?"

"Mostly likely I went to one of the local clubs."

"What time did you get home?" Decker asked.

"I can't honestly say, but Roseanne was still up. We talked a little bit. She seemed calmer and I remember saying: you look better or refreshed or something like that. That's when she told me that she had finally decided to leave Ivan."

"Did she seem happy about her decision?"

"*Happy* isn't the right word. More like . . . at peace. I think she felt that this was the only way to move her life forward. I just gave her support. I went to bed late that night: that much I remember. She was gone when I woke up. I suspect she never even went to bed. She left the key and a real sweet note on my dining room table."

At last! Marge thought. Maybe they'd have something concrete from Roseanne. "Do you have the note?"

"Sorry, no. I threw it away." Tears formed in the flight attendant's eyes. "Maybe it's better that I threw it away. It's so painful when I think about her."

DECKER PUT THE car key in the ignition and glanced at the clock in the dash. It was almost eight. He still had time before his flight took off, but not as much time as he thought he'd have. "Are you sure I can't drop you off somewhere?"

Marge said, "No. Will seems perfectly okay with meeting me at the airport."

"He's a good guy." Decker started the car.

"That he is." She sank against the passenger headrest and closed her eyes. She really needed a good dinner and a fine bottle of wine. Marge furrowed her brow. "What's that noise, Pete?"

Decker heard it just as soon as she asked the question. A loud *thump, thump, thump* as the car wiggled and wobbled. "Not good."

"No, it's not."

Decker braked carefully, slowing to a crawl and pulling over to the curb at his first opportunity. They both got out of the car to inspect the damage.

There was not one, but two flat tires—passenger front and rear.

"Holy moly," Marge said. "This is serious stuff."

"Shit!" Decker stamped his foot. He looked at his watch.

Marge placed a hand on his shoulder. "I'll take care of it, Pete. You call a taxi and catch your plane."

Decker was still staring at the drooping car frame. "I can't believe it!" He bent down to further examine the flats. "Son of a bitch!" He got up from a crouch. "Some motherfucker cut the tires!"

Marge was stoic as she dialed Will Barnes's cell. "It happens. Go call a cab and get out of here."

"No friggin' way I'm leaving you to take care of this mess alone!"

"I won't be alone. I'll have Will."

Decker ignored her and dialed information for the toll-free phone number of WestAir.

"Hey there, it's me," Marge said into the receiver. "We have a setback here. Someone slashed the tires of our rental . . . No idea, only that it had to have happened while we were at our last interview because the tires didn't go flat until we drove . . . Yeah, we didn't even notice it until we were several blocks away. Where are we? That's a very good question. Hold on and I'll get my GPS . . ." She pushed several buttons on her phone. "Hi, Willy, are you still there? . . . Okay, it looks like we're on Bradford Street." She hunted around for the nearest address. "We're parked in front of 13455 Bradford. It's a residential area . . . No, you don't have to come down. I'll cab myself to you, but I want to wait until the police . . . Thanks, honey. If you insist, then I'll see you in about fifteen."

She hung up and regarded Decker, who was on the phone. "I'm on hold."

"Will's coming down."

Decker said, "Are you going back on the five-thirty A.M. WestAir?"

"Yep, but you really don't have to stick around."

Decker held up his hand and spoke into the phone. "That sounds fine. Yes, I'd like the confirmation number. Can you hold a minute while I get a pen?" Immediately Marge handed him a pencil and her notepad. Decker whispered thank you. "All right, I'm ready now." He wrote down the number and hung up. The next call was to Rina. By the time he was done explaining the situation to his wife, Marge had called the police and the car rental company.

Ten minutes later, Will Barnes pulled up behind the deflated rental. He got out, thumbs locked under a thick leather belt that held up a pair of faded jeans. A white shirt with a bolo tie completed the image. Barnes was tall and muscular, in good shape for a man in his late fifties. He shook hands with Decker and gave Marge a peck on the cheek. Barnes's round ruddy face had been treated to a very smooth shave. His dark eyes grew smokier as he assessed the situation. "Damn, that's a pisser!"

"Do you know if there's a vandalism problem in this area?" Decker asked him.

"Can't say for sure, Pete. The local police would know that better than me. But I do know that this is Silicon Valley. There are lots of teens here with too much money and too little supervision."

"Looks like kids to me, too," Marge said. "Some ass riding by in a convertible, slashing passenger tires as he goes."

A squad car pulled up behind Barnes's car. Five minutes later, a tow truck from the rental car service joined the festivities. After introductions were made all around, the cops assessed the wanton vandalism and began writing their reports. Neighbors began peeking through windows and opening front doors. Suddenly people began to walk their dogs, asking questions, looking woefully at the sorry rental. A few had had minor incidents—a smashed window and occasional graffiti. Most were quick to say that the neighborhood was safe.

It took a little under an hour for the police to finish up. By the time order was restored, it was almost ten and Marge was famished. She looked at Will. "I'm still up for dinner, although I have no idea what's open."

"The place I originally wanted to go to closes at eleven," Barnes said, "but I managed a reservation for three at Sarni's. Great, basic Italian food and it's open until midnight."

Marge slipped her arm around Will's waist. "My hero." She smiled at Decker. "I take it that's okay with you."

Decker said, "Thanks for the invitation, but I'm beat. If it isn't too far out of the way, just drop me off at my motel."

"You've got to eat, boss," Marge said.

"I'm fine, really. You two go have a good time."

Barnes didn't try to talk him out of it. "Where's your motel?"

"The Airport Foundation Inn."

"It's right on the way."

The three of them piled into Barnes's Honda Accord. Twenty minutes later, Decker found a nearby coffee shop and ordered an egg-salad sandwich on rye toast and decaf coffee. He doodled on his notepad as he thought about what had become of Roseanne.

He made a chart entitled "The Last Day of Roseanne Dresden's Life" and summed it up in the following steps.

1. Sometime before 10:33 in the morning, she has a fight with her husband, and calls up Christie Peterson to crash at her pad for the night.

2. Then she calls up WestAir in San Jose and asks for an interview. According to Christie, Roseanne wants to transfer to San Jose to be closer to her parents. She goes for an interview. There's a position available.

3. She goes out to dinner with Christie around six in the evening.

4. Christie goes out at nine and returns late. Roseanne is still up. She tells Christie that she has decided to file for divorce.

5. Roseanne meets Leslie Bracco at four-fifteen in the morning on the day of the crash. She basically tells Bracco the same thing she told Christie. As far as Leslie knows, Roseanne has boarded the five A.M. from San Jose to Burbank.

From this point on, there were loads of possibilities for Roseanne.

1. She could have died in 1324—a strong possibility.
2. Once again, she could have waged war with her husband, Ivan, when she returned. This time with deadly results.
3. She could have gone back home, packed up her belongings, and walked off the face of the earth. But then why would she bother with an interview in San Jose?
4. There is a slight chance that she didn't hop the return flight to Burbank. Maybe she changed her mind and remained in San Jose, and something bad happened to her here—either with Raymond Holmes or maybe some other unknown factor.

Decker scratched his head and doodled as he finished the last of his sandwich. He took out his cell and called up a number he had written on his notepad earlier in the afternoon. The line was answered after three rings. A gruff voice growled out a hello.

"Mr. Holmes, this is Lieutenant Peter Decker . . ."

"Hold on a minute." Decker heard muffled conversation behind the receiver. Several minutes later a whispered voice shot venom over the line. "Do you have any idea what time it is?"

Decker looked at his watch and spoke calmly. "I have eleven-oh-six. I know you get up early, but I thought I might catch you before you went to bed. If this is a bad time, I'll call you tomorrow—"

"First you disrupt me at work, now you bother me at my home. This is harassment!"

"Not harassment, Mr. Holmes, just a few simple questions."

"You can ask them through my lawyer."

"Not a problem, but are you sure you want to get into that? I know you want to keep your wife out of police business and I have no problem with that. But if you go the lawyer route, she's going to find out—"

"What do you *want* from me? I haven't seen Roseanne in over eight months. What can I do to make you believe me? Take a lie-detector test?"

That was exactly what Decker wanted. What luck! "That's an idea. It sure would take the heat off. When's the next time you're coming down to L.A.?"

"I don't come to L.A. anymore!" he spat out. "The real estate is way too expensive. Besides, why should I make it easy for you when you're the one who's harassing me? If you want my cooperation, you *come* to me. Set it up in San Jose, and if it's convenient for me, I'll show up!"

"All right . . . I'll get back to you and give you a choice of dates so you can pick—"

"And you'd better call during business hours—nine to five. If you call after five again, I will file a complaint. Then you *will* be dealing with my lawyer!"

"I hear you, Mr. Holmes. Again, thanks so much for all your help. Trust me, sir; I get no satisfaction out of being a pest. I'm just doing my job. And I assure you, once you pass the test and we rule you out, we can both move on."

There was a long pause. When Holmes's voice came back on the line, it had lost most of the poison. "I certainly hope you mean that. I'm sorry that Roseanne is dead or missing or whatever, but frankly, that doesn't concern me anymore. She left me high and dry and I don't owe her or her memory a damn thing. I've got bills to pay and a family to support and I don't need the police breathing down my back."

"I understand—"

"No, you don't understand." He sighed heavily. "I want to get this over with. How about tomorrow at noon? I think I can probably get away for a couple of hours."

"*Tomorrow?*"

"Yes, *tomorrow*. Is that a problem?"

"It's a little short notice—"

"Look, buddy, I'm doing you the favor. You're already up here, so set up the damn test with someone local . . . shit, my wife is calling me. Call me tomorrow at ten and tell me when and where."

Holmes hung up.

Decker had taken several cards from the uniformed officers who had investigated the slashed-tires incident. They seemed like nice enough guys. Just maybe San Jose would be courteous enough to help him out and set him up with an experienced polygraph examiner. It was useless to call the station house right now.

He finished up his sandwich, wondering whether he should phone Marge to let her know of his plans, to give her the option of staying on as well. He didn't want to interrupt anything, but he did want to keep her in the loop.

He caught her just as she and Will were leaving the restaurant, explaining the situation as succinctly as he could.

"He offered to take a polygraph?" she said.

"If I can set it up tomorrow around noon, he said he'd be there. You don't have to stay on, but I figured I'd give you the option."

"Of course I'll stay. I'm as curious as you are. I'll have to do a little rearranging, but I'm there, boss."

"Okay. I'll call you tomorrow morning around eight."

"I suppose that's better than waking up at five in the morning. Speaking of which, do you want to take care of the airline tickets or should I do it?"

"That's right. We have to change the reservation. I'll do it, Margie. I've got nothing else to do, and at this point, I know the eight-hundred number by heart."

23

A T EIGHT O'CLOCK in the morning, Decker started making phone calls. By the time he had managed to find and secure a reputable polygraph examiner—now known as a forensic psychophysiologist or FP—schedule an exam, and obtain financing, his right ear was hot and his throat was scratchy from talking for almost two hours sans break.

The best that he could arrange under such short notice was a three P.M. test situation at the local D.A.'s office, the cost of the exam to be split between the West Valley substation and Roseanne's parents. The Lodestones had no idea that their Rosie had done a little mischief on the side, but it didn't matter to them. They were possessed—and rightly so—with finding Roseanne's body. If there was evidence of foul play, the Lodestones were keen on finding Roseanne's murderer. Ivan was still the Lodestones' first choice for bad guy, but Raymond Holmes would make a decent runner-up should the facts and data point in his direction.

The scheduled time was much later than Holmes had anticipated.

He balked, he screamed, and he cursed, but in the end, he showed up on time and without a lawyer. It took about twenty minutes for the FP—an innocuous-looking, gray-haired woman of sixty named Sheila Aronowitz—to set up the exam. After all the electrodes, cuffs, and straps were cinched across Holmes's body—causing the contractor to remark that if he was going to be electrocuted, he wanted a last meal— Sheila insisted on talking to him before actually asking the questions. She needed to be sure that Holmes understood the mechanics of the machine, and what all the paraphernalia was about. She also insisted that Holmes have something to eat because she felt that a steady blood sugar level was necessary for optimal results.

The rapport building and snack time took a little over an hour.

When she felt they were both ready to take the plunge, she asked ten questions.

1. Is your name Raymond Holmes?
2. Are you married with three children?
3. Do you live in San Jose?
4. Do you work in San Jose?
5. Are you fifty-eight years old?
6. Did you know Roseanne Dresden?
7. Have you seen Roseanne within the last year?
8. Have you seen Roseanne Dresden within the last four months?
9. Did you have anything to do with Roseanne Dresden's disappearance?
10. Did you murder Roseanne Dresden?

Decker, Marge, and a right-out-of-law-school deputy PD named Grant Begosian sat behind a one-way mirror watching Holmes pouring out a flood's worth of sweat as he slugged through the ten simply stated questions. Decker knew that one of the measurements of a polygraph test was galvanic skin resistance, mainly the wetness off one's fingertips.

Holmes's score on that indicator must have been off the scale even against a baseline question like Is your name Raymond Holmes?

It had been a while since Decker had witnessed a polygraph. Gone were the days of paper-loading, needle-dancing analog machines. These days polygraphs were digital, and as Sheila asked her questions, she regarded a laptop monitor, clicking on the keyboard at various intervals. The actual test didn't take long. When it was over, she unhooked Holmes from the straps and the cuffs and the galvanometers. Meticulously, she gathered up her equipment as Holmes eyed her silently, dabbing his face with a sodden handkerchief. When she was a step out of the doorway, the contractor couldn't contain himself. He blurted out the obvious question.

"How'd I do?"

Sheila smiled beatifically and said that she'd be back in a moment and asked if she could get him anything. Holmes opted for a cup of coffee and a croissant.

DECKER, MARGE, AND PD Grant Begosian were still staring at Holmes behind the one-way mirror, marveling at the production of the man's sweat glands, when Sheila stepped into the interview room. The three of them raised their eyes in unison, directing their expectant gazes at the FP. Decker said, "How'd he do?"

She said, "You'll just have to wait a moment. I don't want to be precipitous in my conclusions."

They waited as Sheila booted up her laptop and zeroed in on the polygraph. Her facial expressions were unreadable as she examined her data. She seemed to be perfectly comfortable working in silence as three people scrutinized her every movement. Eventually she sat back in her chair and looked up from the monitor.

"It is my opinion that Mr. Holmes was not being deceitful."

Marge made a face. "He passed?"

"It is not a graded examination, Sergeant; it is a measurement of four involuntary physiological processes. I can't vouch for the man's credibility. All I can say is that from the measurements of his blood pressure, his heart rate, his respiratory rate, and his GSR, Mr. Holmes seems to have answered my questions in a nondeceitful manner."

"On all ten questions," Decker said.

Sheila smiled. "On nine questions actually. The only question that indicated a hint of deception—I'd have to rank it as inconclusive—was when I asked him if his name was Raymond Holmes. That's not unusual. The first question, being as it is the first question, sometimes produces a surge of anxiety as measured by the physiological indicators no matter how much we try to put the examinee at ease."

"Thank you very much, Mrs. Aronowitz." Decker tried out a smile. "If Holmes is telling the truth, that's good to know. We'll direct our energies elsewhere."

Deputy PD Begosian said, "Thank you for coming on such short notice." The lawyer turned to Marge and Decker.

"My pleasure." Sheila took out a piece of paper. "Who do I bill?"

Decker took the invoice and handed her his card. "I'll take care of it. Call me if you have a problem and thank you."

"In case you should need my services again." She handed everyone a business card. As soon as Sheila left, the PD said, "Do you want to tell him the news or should I?"

Decker regarded Begosian, who looked way younger than his own daughter. He was too thin, too fresh, and too boyish for legal gravitas, but they all look that way in the beginning. If he stuck around long enough, he'd grow into the position. "I'd like to tell Mr. Holmes the good news, if that's okay with you. I want to make sure there are no hard feelings. I may need him later on."

"Be my guest."

The two detectives entered the interview room, where Holmes was pacing nervously. "You can relax, sir," Decker said. "I think we're finally done."

The contractor stopped treading the concrete. "Done as in done with the interview or done as in done harassing me."

"The polygraph indicates that you haven't been deceitful." Decker held out his hand. "I really appreciate your total cooperation and I thank you again for your time."

Holmes gave the gesture some thought, then wiped his right palm against his pants and shook hands. "I suppose you were only doing your job."

"Yes, sir, that is the truth." Marge offered her hand as well.

Holmes shook hands with her as well. "Then we're done."

"Absolutely," Decker said. "You're free to go and I promise not to call you unless I have a specific question in mind."

"What does that mean?"

"You did know the woman," Decker said. "Maybe I could call you for some help . . . some insight."

"As far as I'm concerned, I've helped you as much as I can," Holmes told him.

"I'm sure you're right. Good-bye and good luck."

Holmes looked at Decker with agitated eyes. "What does that mean? Good luck?"

"Take it easy, sir." Decker smiled. "I was referring to your house. Good luck with your construction."

"Oh . . . okay. Thanks." Holmes tried to return the smile but failed. "And good luck to you with Roseanne and the case. I mean that." He dabbed his forehead with a tissue. "But don't bother me again. I mean that, too."

With that, Holmes left the room; he elected to slam the door shut.

THE EXTRA DAY in San Jose gave Marge and Will Barnes another night together. Although the two lovebirds extended a dinner invitation to him, Decker politely declined, anxious to get home. He wanted to take a taxi to the airport, to be alone and think, but Barnes insisted on acting as chauffeur. As he drove to San Jose International, the two lovebirds spent the majority of the ride talking about what restaurant they wanted to go to. Decker zoned out, emptying his mind, which wasn't hard. In his present state of maximum fatigue, it seemed impossible for him to will up a conscious thought. He fought sleep, deciding to succumb on the plane ride back to L.A.

When they pulled up to the curb of passenger loading and unloading, Marge got out with him. "What now, Loo?"

"For me, a hot dinner and a hot shower sound like a plan."

"What's our next step with Roseanne?"

"I haven't gotten that far."

"I should talk to Ivan again," Marge told him. "We know he lied about the time of the fight. He said it was in the afternoon and we know that Roseanne left L.A. in the late morning. I say we ask him about it, using the approach that we're just trying to button down a couple of details and there's been a little inconsistency, blah, blah."

"Great."

"I'll have Oliver call him tonight to set something up."

"Do you want to bring him into the station house for questioning?"

"I think we'd get more information if we came to him."

"Set it up and let me know." Decker rubbed his eyes. "Have you finished checking off the names of your tenant list for the Seacrest apartment?"

"I've done a little over half."

"I've done about sixty to seventy percent. Let's all finish up with that within the next couple of days."

"I'll make it a priority."

Decker gave her a thumbs-up sign. "Have a great time."

Marge smiled. "He's taking the position . . . Will is."

"In Santa Barbara?"

"Yes. I'm excited. It takes everything to another level."

"Yes, it does."

Spontaneously, she gave Decker a big hug. "Regards to Rina."

As Decker watched her slide into Will's car, the two of them zooming off, he realized he had a big smile on his face.

"DO YOU THINK they'll get married?" Rina asked him.

Decker pulled back the covers and nestled into bed. "Not right away. They're still about ninety miles away from one another. But now it's a car trip instead of an airplane ride, so it's moving in a more committed direction."

"How old is Marge?"

"Past forty."

"And he's in his fifties?"

"Yes."

"Good age for both of them," Rina said. "I hope Will likes the flute."

Decker smiled. Marge played the instrument, but only when she was alone. For her, it was personal expression, like singing in the shower. "They really do seem to have a lot in common."

"That's nice." Rina moved over to be closer and Decker put his arm around her shoulders. "I wish them happiness and lots of luck." She faced her husband. "You look exhausted."

"I am."

"Fruitful trip?"

"In some ways. Roseanne's ex-lover passed a polygraph and a flight attendant was pretty sure that Roseanne took the five o'clock flight from San Jose back to Burbank the following morning. It still seems that she disappeared once she reached Burbank."

"You're still thinking about the husband?"

"Yes, that's the logical choice. I'm sure he has some secrets." Decker shrugged. "All the people who died in the accident, I bet they died with a lot of secrets as well."

"Secrets from man, but not from G-d."

"That's a humbling thought." Decker frowned. "I don't know if I really believe in that personal of a God. I, for one, feel that God has better things to do than to get involved in the trivialities of our petty lives."

"Sometimes I think that's true, too. I mean, why would Hashem care if I wore a blue or pink dress? Although that isn't the Jewish way. We really do have the precept of Hashgacha Pratite—that G-d watches over our every moment and our every movement."

"To each his own."

"Then there are other times where I'm positive that Hashem is involved with our petty lives. So many important things happen serendipitously that I just can't chalk them all up to coincidence."

"I suppose if you're an atheist, that's exactly what you do . . . chalk it up to coincidence."

"I'd rather believe in divine intervention. It's much more romantic and much more poetic."

"That's because you have romance and poetry in your soul. Me? I believe in God but for an entirely different reason. I need God. Who else is there to curse when things go poorly?"

24

I T WAS ONE of those rare moments when he took time out to
smell the roses. Looking down at his sleeping daughter, her carrot-
colored hair flowing over her face and the pillow, he realized that
although life was passing too rapidly, he hadn't gone through his days
on earth without producing miracles. Two of them to be exact, but
this time around he had been more fortunate. Cindy, although full-
time in his heart, had been only part-time in his life. With Hannah,
he was fully experiencing her teenage years with all their trials and
tribulations. Sometimes it felt as if the drama would never end, but
the flip side told him that he was lucky to be there when she needed
him.

He tapped his daughter's shoulder. "Wake up, Rosie O'Dee. It's a
beautiful morning and I love you."

Hannah inhaled deeply and opened her eyes. "Love you, too."

He kissed her forehead. "I'll be waiting in the kitchen for you."

"Five more minutes?"

"Not today. I'm taking you to school."

She rolled over and pulled the covers over her head. "Can't Eema do it?"

"You don't want my scintillating company?"

"I love your company, Abba, I just want to sleep."

"I realize that you have an unlimited capacity for slumber. Unfortunately, it's time to face the music."

"Can you feed my fish and take my backpack?"

Decker glanced at his daughter's aquarium. Going to the tropical fish store used to be a weekly outing. Lately Hannah had better things to do on weekends, and the tank was down to two angelfish, and two enormous bottom-feeders—an upside-down catfish and a clown loach. The good news was that the remaining stalwarts were healthy. He dropped flakes into the water and picked up Hannah's book bag, which weighed no less that fifteen tons. "Do you have any preference for breakfast?"

"No."

"How about cereal and juice?"

"I'm not hungry."

"You have to eat something."

"Just juice. I'll have a glass of milk at school."

"I see we're on the liquid diet today."

"With all this conversation we're having, I could have had my extra five minutes of sleep."

"And missed out on talking to me?"

"*Arg!*" She sat up and pushed her hair from her eyes. "I have to get dressed now."

He saluted and left. In the kitchen, he put on a pot of coffee and poured his daughter a big glass of orange juice, knowing that she'd drink about a third of it. Hannah was tall for her age, no surprise there, and being a typical teenage girl, she hated her body, which consisted of gangly limbs emanating from a thick middle. Actually, her middle wasn't thick, it was just that the rest of her body hadn't caught up to it. She was in the throes of puberty, which included the adjectives *moody, secretive,* and *sarcastic.* Then there were those other times when she was vulnerable and unbelievably loving.

His cell rang. The familiar voice on the other end said, "I didn't wake you, did I?"

It was Koby. "Not at all," Decker answered. "I'm assigned chauffeur duty this morning. What's up, big guy?"

"After considerable effort, I not only managed to secure a machine but a technician as well. It has to be promptly at five this afternoon or else we lose our technician to happy hour."

"Wait a minute, I'm confused." Decker poured himself a cup of coffee and took a swallow. "What are you talking about?"

"The computerized tomography machine and technician for your skull."

Decker's brain was awhirl in confusion. "Are you telling me that you've got a machine and a technician to do the CT scan on the Jane Doe skull that I'm trying so desperately to identify?"

"Yes, that is exactly what I am saying."

"First of all, thank you very much. I'll call the morgue and get on it right away. Second of all, this is the first time I'm hearing about the plan. Who called you to set this up?"

"Our favorite detective, Scott Oliver. I do him a favor because deep down inside, I know he is still pining for my wife. Anyway, I am starting my shift in ten minutes. Cindy tells me that you can come on Sunday to help with the house."

"Yes, that's true. What time?"

"Cindy is making brunch, so maybe eleven? Rina is doing a landscape design for us. Hannah, of course, is invited as well, but I suspect she'll have better things to do."

"Eleven sounds great, Yaakov, and thanks again. I'm sure you had to jump through hoops to get permission for us."

"That is true, but at least the hoops were not on fire."

BY THE TIME that Decker had checked off every name on the Seacrest tenants' list, it was a little past two in the afternoon. Not that he had succeeded in locating everyone. Still unaccounted for were seven women between the ages of twenty-four and fifty who had lived in the apartment building sometime between 1974 and 1983. Adding his seven to the other detectives' lists of missing females, the total number was a daunting twenty-six. That meant further investigation with the avenues of exploration closing in on them.

It was imperative to add a face to Jane Doe.

Thank God for Koby. As the head nurse in neonatology, he had access to everything medical. But it was his persuasive powers that really sealed the deal. The man was the epitome of charm. And it didn't hurt that the radiation tech was one of his good friends.

Coincidence or Hashgacha Pratit?

Right now Decker was too tired to ponder philosophy. He had a caffeine headache and an empty stomach. It was time to satisfy more primal needs. He picked up his jacket and met up with Marge and Oliver in the police parking lot.

"Welcome back," he said to Marge.

"Thank you, thank you. We've got a scheduling conflict."

"What's that?"

"We got hold of Ivan the Terrible," Oliver said.

"He wasn't happy to hear from us," Marge added.

"I can imagine. What's going on with that?"

"After much cajoling, we got him to agree to meet us at his condo at around six, after he gets off work."

"But we found out that he usually leaves around four-thirty, five," Oliver said.

Decker said, "He's going to show up at his condo early and claim you weren't there on time and he couldn't wait."

"That's exactly why we'd like to be at his place no later than four," Oliver said. "Just in case he's intent on pulling some kind of stunt."

"If we're there by four," Marge said, "there's no way we'll be able to take the skull over to the hospital."

"The skull's still at the morgue?" Decker asked.

"It was as of four hours ago."

"Okay," Decker said. "I'll grab some lunch, go over to the Crypt, and handle the transportation myself."

"If you're in the mood to be a nice guy, you might want to give Mike Hollander a call," Oliver told him. "I'm sure he'd like a piece of this."

"Yeah, Mike's been working hard, calling up factories all morning long to find that Rapid Prototyping machine." Marge laughed. "He's working harder than I ever saw him work when he was at Foothill."

"Back then he was talking about retirement," Decker said. "Be careful what you wish for."

"The old guy's definitely got the fire in his eyes."

"I'll give him a ring," Decker said. "Actually I wouldn't mind some company over the hill." He turned to Oliver. "Thanks for setting things up with Koby, Scott, but how about clueing me in next time?"

"I was going to tell you this morning, Loo. I had no idea that the kid could pull strings so fast."

"Fair enough," Decker said. "Koby moves fast when he's motivated."

Oliver smiled wistfully. "That is a fact that I'm well aware of."

AT 4:10 IN the afternoon, a black Beemer zipped by the unmarked and pulled into the underground parking lot, bass-thumping rap booming from a fortified stereo. As Dresden blithely drove by, Marge sat up in her seat and rolled her shoulders, exchanging glances with Oliver. "How many minutes should we give him before we meet up with him?"

"If we move now, we'll probably get to the door around the same time he does."

"Let's do it."

They got out of the unmarked and arrived at the condo just as Dresden was inserting the key into the lock. The broker looked confused as his eyes skittered from Oliver's to Marge's face. Addled and nervous, Marge thought, like a trapped rat.

Ivan glanced at his watch. "Wasn't our appointment at six?"

"We were in the area and thought we'd take a chance." Oliver inched sideways until Marge and he were flanking Dresden. "We just have a few questions. You might as well get it over with."

"Do you mind if I open my door first?"

Neither Marge nor Oliver answered the rhetorical question. They continued to crowd him, leaving him little elbow room to open the door. He almost had to sidle in to cross his own threshold. Once he was inside, the two detectives entered without being invited in.

Ivan threw his briefcase and black suit jacket on the couch and left his car keys on the kitchen countertop. Unknotting his red tie, he let it droop around his neck like a scarf and opened the top button of his blue dress shirt. He opened a cabinet and took out a bottle of Johnnie Walker Blue. After pouring himself a few fingers' worth in a cut-crystal glass and adding the merest hint of water, he took a sip, smacked his lips, and smiled. "So . . . what do you want?"

Oliver said, "Mind if we sit down?"

"Why bother if you're only going to ask a few questions."

"You've got a point."

"A good one. What do you want?"

Neither detective answered right away. Marge's focus drifted from the stockbroker's face to the walls of the condo. Evidence spoke volumes. It said that Roseanne had flown back to Burbank from San Jose. However, it was silent about Roseanne being in the plane crash. Meaning if she made it back to Burbank and she wasn't on flight 1324, she had to have made it home.

Somewhere in the condo was her story.

Where were you, Roseanne?

She lowered her eyes to the floor, scanning for bits of blood spray still clinging to the baseboard or stain in the grout between the tiles. Her eyes also swept over the pristine white carpet hoping to find something—a little blob of biological matter that didn't quite clean out. Doing it as fast and as naturally as she could while Oliver occupied Dresden with conversation.

"The thing is, Mr. Dresden, that there are a few inconsistencies with the story you told us—"

"It wasn't a *story*," Dresden protested. "A story is fiction. What I told you was the truth, so let's get that straight, okay?"

"Sorry, sir," Oliver apologized. "I don't mean to belittle your honesty or anything like that. I'm just trying to get the facts straight."

"I don't know how I could be any clearer." Dresden took another sip of scotch. "I'm not trying to make myself look good. Otherwise I wouldn't admit to a fight."

Out of the corner of his eyes, Oliver saw Marge walking around, scrutinizing the place. He needed to keep Dresden's attention off of her. "The thing is, sir, we don't think that your wife died in the airplane crash."

"So you've told me before. Just because they haven't found her doesn't mean she wasn't there."

"Mr. Dresden, we know that Roseanne came back from San Jose to Burbank the morning of the accident. We know that because we have gone up to San Jose and we have talked to people who put her on the flight back to Bob Hope Airport. We also know that she wasn't working the early-morning flight. We know that because we've talked to people who worked for WestAir who said she wasn't assigned that route and she had been dressed in civilian clothes. Are you with me so far?"

Dresden was silent, nursing his drink. Oliver realized his hands were shaking.

He said, "What we're all wondering is why Roseanne would go *back* to San Jose when she just arrived from there if she wasn't working the route?"

"How would I know?" Dresden's eyes darkened. "Maybe she got a call from her boyfriend."

"Who are we talking about? Holmes?"

"Who else? Maybe the rich bastard made her an offer that she couldn't refuse. Ever think of that?"

Marge spoke from across the room. "As a matter of fact, sir, we did. We interviewed Holmes. He hadn't spoken to her for the last three months of her life."

Dresden sneered. "And you *believed* him?"

"No, we didn't believe him. That's why we asked if he would take a polygraph test for us."

"That's a lie-detector test—"

"I goddamn know what a polygraph is!"

"So we were kind of wondering," Oliver said. "Maybe you would do the same thing."

"Take a polygraph?" Dresden tried to sound incredulous. "For what reason?"

"Just to clear yourself."

"Of what? First of all, those stupid tests are notoriously unreliable. You know they can't be used in court."

Oliver smiled benignly. "Of course. But when a person passes them, well . . . we like that."

"I told you before and I'll tell you again. Roseanne and I had a terrible fight. She stormed out of the house and that was the last time I saw her."

"Yeah, what time did you and she fight again?" Oliver asked.

"What?" Dresden asked.

"When did the terrible fight take place?"

"Around eight in the morning."

"Eight in the morning?" Oliver questioned him.

"Yeah, something like that. I already told you that. Don't you guys take notes?"

"As a matter of fact we do. That's why I'm puzzled. The first time we spoke to you, you told us that you two had fought around four in the afternoon."

"I did?"

"Yes, you did."

"No, you must have made a mistake," Dresden insisted. "It was the morning. We fought right before I went to work. Roseanne just woke up on the wrong side of the bed. She started in on me, blasting me without any provocation. I was stupid, I was lazy, I wasn't any good . . . just insulting the shit out of me. I couldn't figure out what I did other than say 'good morning.' Maybe I didn't say it with enough *feel-*

ing. Maybe she had her period. Maybe she was just in the mood to be a bitch. As long as I live, I will never understand women."

Welcome to the club, Oliver thought. "Why did you initially tell us that you fought around four in the afternoon?"

"I don't remember telling you that, Detective." Dresden shrugged. "I mean, if you say I did, I believe you, but I don't know why I would tell you we fought in the afternoon when it was the morning. What would be the purpose of that?"

Oliver noticed that his hands were no longer shaking. Either the booze was making him relax or he felt more comfortable with the questioning. "Well, then that clears up one inconsistency we had. But we still have a problem and it's a biggie. Where did Roseanne go once she landed in Burbank?"

"I have no idea," Dresden said. "Everyone has been telling me that Roseanne died in the accident. You two are the only ones who seem to think that she didn't die in the accident . . ." He turned his attention to Marge, who was writing furiously in her notepad. "What are you doing?"

"Just making some observations . . . trying to get a feel for your wife's life."

"Yeah, well, I think I've answered enough of your questions. You can leave now."

Marge dropped her pen. "Oops." She fell to her knees and looked under the rim of the couch. "Where did that sucker go?"

Her hand slipped underneath. One spot of the carpet felt stiff, indicating that it had once been covered with something sticky. It could have been blood, but that wasn't what she was after. Something small and metallic pink had winked at her. She reeled the object in with her fingers: rectangular and flat and about the size of a packet of cigarettes.

A cell phone—a metallic pink that abounded with small daisies. She flipped it over. On the back were the block letters R.D. She held it up for Ivan to see. "What's this?"

"That's mine." Ivan leaped across the room to wrest it from Marge's grip. His skin had turned sunburn red. "You can go now!"

"Yours?" Marge asked. "You have a pink cell phone with the initials R.D. on the back?"

"Get out!"

Dresden's cell started to chime. Without thinking, he reached into his pocket and abruptly stopped. Too late: he'd given himself away.

Oliver held up his mobile. "I just called your cell, Mr. Dresden." He pointed to the pink case. "That baby isn't ringing, but your pocket is."

"So what the fuck does that prove? I lost my phone months ago. You found it for me. Thanks. Now get the hell out of here or I'm not only calling my lawyer, I'm calling the cops!"

Oliver held up his hands. "Peace, bro. We're going."

Dresden jerked the door open and screamed, "Don't come back unless you have a warrant!" He was flushed, with shaking hands that rattled the ice in his scotch.

Marge and Oliver crossed over the living room carpet as they made their way to the open door.

They took their sweet time.

25

DECKER SHIFTED THE phone from one ear to the other. "Run that by me again."

"I dropped a pen in Dresden's apartment," Marge said. "When I bent down to retrieve it under the couch, by accident, I pulled out a pink cell phone. Dresden claimed it was his, but when Oliver called Dresden's cell-phone number, his pocket rang . . . not the phone that I found."

"Okay."

"Then he claimed that this pink cell phone—with daisies all over it and the initials R.D. on the back—was his lost cell phone."

"Okay. So what are we trying to do—hold on a sec." Hollander had emerged from the bowels of the Crypt. Decker checked his watch. "What's going on?"

"They'll be packed up and ready to roll in ten minutes."

"It's almost five."

"I called Koby. The tech agreed to wait, but I think it's going to cost the LAPD a gourmet dinner."

"We can manage that. So we're still okay with the hospital to use the machine?"

"That I haven't asked because I don't want to know the answer."

Decker raked his hands through his hair and exhaled. "How long does it take to pack up a friggin' skull?"

"Patience, Loo." Hollander smiled and played with the curled ends of his mustache. "You don't want to lose evidence, do you?"

Decker rolled his eyes and returned to his phone conversation. "Sorry, Marge, I'm back. So what's going on here?"

Marge said, "In short, both Oliver and I are convinced that I found Roseanne Dresden's phone. If she died on the plane crash, what was her phone doing under the couch?"

"You just happened to find her phone?"

"Yep," Marge fibbed. "I dropped my pen and found the phone. Simple as that."

"You weren't hunting around for anything."

"I was taking notes around the condo, but I wasn't hunting for anything other than my dropped pen."

"No opening drawers or closets or—"

"No, nothing like that. I dropped my pen and I found the phone."

"And now Dresden's claiming that it's his phone?"

"No, he's claiming that it's a phone that he lost months ago."

"And how are we going to disprove that?"

"It was in a pink case with daisies and has the initials R.D. on the back."

"It still could be his phone."

"I know." She thought a moment. "The easiest thing is to find out where Roseanne purchased the phone and see if it matches the invoice. Then we could find out if Dresden ever purchased a phone like that."

"Even if we found out where Roseanne bought the phone, which I don't see how we can do that, it won't prove anything. Dresden could say she bought it for him. Or he could just deny that you even found her phone. How would you prove otherwise?"

Marge said, "It's a distinctive phone, Pete. How could I describe it that clearly if I had never met Roseanne?"

"Dresden could still claim she bought it for him."

"With the initials R.D. on the back?"

"She used it and then gave it to him."

"Then how about if I interview some of Roseanne's friends? I'll have them describe Roseanne's phone to me."

"To counter that, Dresden could say that you found out what it looks like by talking to her friends and then framed him."

Marge tried again. "How about if I wrote out a statement about what happened this afternoon? Oliver and I could sign and date it, and then we'd have proof that our observations about the phone predated all the interviews with Roseanne's friends."

Decker thought about her suggestions. "I think one of our secretaries is a notary. Get her to witness the signing. That way Dresden can't claim that you postdated the documents."

"Great."

"That takes care of the honesty issue for you and Oliver, but it doesn't take care of the witnesses. Dresden can always claim that you coached Roseanne's friends to say what you wanted and they cooperated because they hated him. He'd have a point. Roseanne's friends did hate him."

"What if we take the notary with us? Have the witnesses sign a piece of paper that this was the first time we asked them questions about Roseanne's phone."

"That could work," Decker conceded. "Okay, let's do this. Keep the interviews really clean. Call up Roseanne's friends and request a brief face-to-face. We'll ask each of them two questions. One: Did Roseanne own a cell phone? Two: If she did, describe it for me using as much detail as you can. We'll have statements for them to sign, saying that the witnesses answered these two questions without prompting or any kind of interference from LAPD. We can have their signature notarized. That will legitimize the statements against corruption."

Decker shifted gears again.

"Okay, round two. Where are we going with all these nice, notarized statements?"

"If Roseanne died in the crash, her cell phone should have been found at the accident site or it should have been obliterated. Instead, we find it under her couch. We're claiming that Roseanne wasn't in the crash, but went home to her condo after taking the five A.M. flight down from San Jose into Burbank. And that was the last we ever heard from her."

"The cell could be an old phone."

"Or it could be her most recent phone. We know she had it with her in San Jose because she made a call from it. So we have to assume that it returned with her. So what was it doing in the condo if she died in the crash?"

"Maybe she sped home after she reached Burbank, lost the phone in the condo, and didn't have time to look for it because she raced back to the airport."

"The condo's in the West Valley. No way she could make that trip and get to the airport on time to make the flight even if there was *no* traffic on the freeway. We all know what kind of traffic is on the 101 at seven, seven-thirty in the morning."

"I just thought of something," Decker said. "Where was her car at the time of the crash? Wasn't it parked at the airport?"

"I have no idea, but I do know that Dresden is driving the Beemer now. My guess is that he's planning on keeping it because he already sold his car to pay down the lap-dancing debts. Ivan was quick to remind us that although her assets are frozen, there's no law that prohibits him from using her car."

"There probably is a law against it, but who's going to take him to court?"

"Pete, even if Roseanne's Beemer was parked at the airport, it doesn't mean that she drove it there. It could have been planted after the fact."

Hollander tapped Decker's shoulder and gave him a thumbs-up sign. "We're ready."

"Marge, I have to go in thirty seconds. I'm assuming you're going through all this hassle with finding witnesses to identify Roseanne's phone in order to convince a judge that Roseanne's phone had no business being in her condo if she had died in the crash. Therefore, if she didn't die in the crash, the phone under the couch means that Roseanne was in her condo the morning of the crash, and disappeared right after that. We suspect Ivan, and Roseanne's phone being under the couch is a good reason for us to get a search warrant."

"I couldn't have said it better."

"On a lucky day, it might work. First, get the witnesses to describe the phone. And even if we find witnesses that swear that the phone was Roseanne's, there's nothing to stop Ivan from claiming that he bought a phone exactly like it."

"Pink with daisies and an R.D. on the back?"

"Maybe Ivan was getting in touch with his feminine side."

THE GROUP CONSISTED of Decker, Hollander, Koby, two coroner's investigators—Gloria and Fred—and a computerized tomography (CT) technician named Jordon Shakman. The tech was six five and black and went by the nickname Shak. He and Koby had known each other for over seven years, drawn to each other by work and by how well their names meshed. Back when Koby was single, the two of them used to party together, always making dinner reservations as Koby and Shak, which perked up ears especially when Shaquille O'Neal used to play center for the Big L Unit. Needless to say, they got star treatment even *after* they showed up. People realized that they weren't the real deal, but they were big enough to look mean, and no one questioned their identity.

"Record time," Koby told the tech when they were done.

Shak said, "It goes faster when we're working with a skull instead of some little freaked-out kid."

"It would freak me out," Decker said, looking at the CT tube.

"At least the CT is open," Shak said. "You should see the reaction to an MRI tube. I've seen grown men reduced to tears when we start to slide them in."

"What's our next move?" Decker asked.

Shak turned to the coroner's investigators. "Do you have a release order on where to send the images?"

Gloria answered. She was a woman in her late thirties with dark, inquisitive eyes. "I have all the paperwork right here." She handed Shak the folder. "The forensic pathologist will contact you in the morning to tell you where to send the images. You can send them directly to her computer, but we'll also need the hard-copy prints as well since the Crypt doesn't have the facilities to develop any images."

"We can do it for it, but it may take a couple of days."

Gloria looked at Decker. "How does that fit in with your time frame, Lieutenant?"

"Sooner is always better, but we still need to secure a prototyping machine. That could take a while."

"I've got my feelers out," Hollander answered.

"If anyone can do it, Mike, it's you." Decker turned to the technician. "Do you have any observations that you think might be important to us?"

"I'm just a tech," Shak said. "All the interpretation is done by a radiologist."

"I think we're done." Decker turned to the investigators. "Are you two all right packing up the skull?"

"We're just fine, Lieutenant," Fred answered.

Gloria said, "You can go, gentlemen."

Decker held out his hand to Shak. "Thanks for all your help."

Koby cleared his throat. "It's close to six, Peter. Cindy's shift ends at eleven, so Shak and I were going to get some dinner. Would you and Michael like to join us?"

"Great! I'm famished!" Hollander cried out. "Uh . . . if it's okay with the boss. He drove me over the hill."

It wasn't okay with the boss. All Decker wanted to do was go home, take a hot shower, and spend some time with his family. But Hollander, Koby, and Shak had all been doing him favors—big ones, and without complaint. It was time for payback. "Let me check with Rina. If she's all right with it, I'm in."

Shak eyed Gloria, trying not to be obvious. "You're welcome to come . . . both of you."

Gloria broke into a radiant smile. "I've got to get Ms. Doe back home." She handed Shak her business card. "Maybe another time."

"Great . . ." Shak's smile was oddly shy. "Great."

Decker hung up his cell. "It's fine with Rina."

Koby beamed. "Fantastic. In anticipation of your yes, I made reservations. I think you'll like the place. It has wonderful Italian food. Who doesn't like Italian?"

"This is just like the good old days." Hollander patted his stomach. "I'm having so much fun I'll even pick up the tab."

"Nonsense," Decker said. "The academy has gotten more than its money's worth today. LAPD will gladly pick up the tab."

THE VOICE OVER the squawk box announced that Farley Lodestone was on line three. Decker didn't bother to check his watch. If Farley was calling, it was nine in the morning. The man was more consistent than an alarm clock. Decker counted to three, depressed the button, and picked up the phone. "Hello, Farley. How are you today?"

"The same like every day. What's going on?"

"Actually, things are going on." Decker spoke with confidence. "We're tracking down an interesting lead, but you know I can't tell you what it is."

"Why not? I can keep a secret."

Decker smiled. "I know you can, Farley; it's just not the way we operate. I'm just saying that we haven't forgotten about Roseanne. How could we when you call us every day to remind us?"

Lodestone grumped. "And I'll continue to call until we find out something."

"I don't blame you. As a father, I'd do the same thing. I think Shareen and you have exhibited enormous patience. I want to thank you for trusting my handling of the case."

"Who said I trust you?"

Decker smiled. "Maybe I was flattering myself. You have every reason to be skeptical, Farley, but I'm out there doing what I can."

There was a pause. "Shareen says I'm being a pain in the butt. I don't care. I'm gonna call every day and keep calling every day. That's just the person I am. It's nothing personal. You understand me, right?"

"Completely."

"To show you how serious I am, I put your cell number and the station's number on my buddy-list phone program. So I can call you up anytime for six ninety-nine a month and talk as long as I want. If I'm gonna call you, might as well be economical about it."

"We're on it, Farley. Thanks for calling."

"Right now, Lieutenant, I gotta say to you thanks for nothing. But don't take that personal, either. One day, I hope to say thanks for everything."

HOLLANDER WAS ELATED over the phone. "After much finagling, pleading, and cajoling, I managed to get hold of a prototype machine at Katumi Motors. No need for thanks. Money would do just fine."

Decker's smile was wide and genuine. "Mike, you've been a godsend."

"There is a small snag. We can't use it during working hours. I had originally set up the process for next Saturday. Then I remembered, you don't work on Saturday, so I changed it to Sunday. It'll be late morning or early afternoon."

"Great. I'll coordinate with the Crypt to make sure we have the CT-scan images."

"No one likes to work on Sunday, Rabbi. You may need to pay for a round of beer."

"That can be done." Marge knocked on the frame of his open door. She and Oliver were waiting for his time. "Thanks for everything, Mike. I'll be there. I gotta go."

"No prob, Pete, and thanks for the business. Koby and Cindy are a great couple. You did good."

Decker was all smiles when he hung up. "What's up?"

"Those are the notarized statements from our visit with Ivan Dresden," Marge told him. "We've got appointments in the afternoon with Arielle Toombs and David Rottiger. They know we want to talk to them about Roseanne, but they don't know it's specifically about her cell phone."

Oliver said, "We thought that was the most unbiased way to handle it. Not to tell them anything without the notary being there."

Decker spoke as he sorted through the official paperwork. "I agree." He handed the papers to Marge. "Good work, people. Let me know what you find out."

"What's going on with the X-rays?" Oliver asked.

"That's all done. The Crypt has hard copy of the images. I've also put in a money request for the captain to get a duplicate set for our records. Best of all, Hollander's found a machine. The prototyping is set up for this Sunday."

Oliver said, "The guy pulled it off. Good for him."

"This has been his baby. He really came through."

Marge said, "Yeah, he certainly caught the homicide flu big-time."

"I'll get the paperwork from Strapp to let it rip," Decker said. "Then, once we have a facsimile of the skull, the PD's all set to take it to a judge to make sure he or she gives the okay for us to use it forensically. Hollander told me that there is legal precedence for using a prototype. So maybe we'll all get lucky and it won't get bogged down in the court system."

Oliver said, "Once we get all our material together, we'll apply for a search warrant. I think you should be with us when we present the case, Loo. Our grounds are a little shaky and I think your title will help."

"What judge were you thinking about, Oliver?"

"I set up something with Carla Puhl. I've always gotten along with her."

Decker smiled. "I'm sure you have."

Oliver winked and left.

"What are we going to do with him?"

Marge laughed. "Scott's okay. Behind that facade of a pig is a pig, but more Vietnamese potbelly than wild boar. Oliver's dirty and messy, but he's also cute and potty trained."

HER HONOR, JUDGE Carla Puhl, appeared more interested in her long red hook nails than in Decker's defense of their petition for a search warrant. With her robe hanging on a coatrack, Judge Puhl was dressed in a red tank top and a denim miniskirt. She held up a finger, cutting him off midsentence, and pointed to a chair.

"Sit down, Lieutenant."

Decker complied. Marge and Oliver were trying to fade into the background, standing near the back wall of the wood-paneled chambers, electing to let the boss handle a dicey affair.

Judge Puhl sorted through the notarized statements and shook her head. "You're telling me that the only thing you have on this poor schmuck is a pink cell phone?"

"Your Honor, his wife has been missing for over two months. She was about to divorce her husband and clean him out. The condo was in her name, the credit was in her name, she paid most of the bills. Plus, her husband has girlfriends including a lap dancer. He had run up over fifteen thousand dollars' worth of lap-dancing fees, which he conveniently paid off by selling off his car and Roseanne's jewelry after she disappeared. Ivan is currently driving Roseanne's BMW."

"So what does this have to do with a pink cell phone?"

"Dresden admitted that he and Roseanne had a big fight a day before she vanished. As Sergeant Dunn was questioning him about the fight, she dropped her pen and happened to find a pink cell phone—"

Again the judge cut him off with a wave of her hand. "What do you want to do with this cell phone, Lieutenant?"

"Ivan Dresden first claimed it was his phone. When it was clear it wasn't his current phone, he said it was a phone that he'd lost a long time ago."

"He owned a pink phone with daisies?"

"We felt that was dubious as well."

"You didn't answer my question. What do you want to do with it?"

"For one thing, I'd like to see if it was Roseanne's most recent phone. We can do that really easily. Just charge it up and see the dates of her last outgoing call. It's a very simple thing to do . . . to check whether or not the man is lying. And if it was Roseanne's most recent phone, it puts her in the apartment on the morning of the accident."

"It puts her phone there. Not Roseanne."

Decker was silent.

Puhl said, "Even if Roseanne was there, it doesn't mean that she still didn't die in the crash. She could have gone home, lost the phone, and returned to the airport."

"We timed the round trip, Your Honor," Decker said. "Rushing and driving at fifty miles an hour, she could have made it with about five minutes to spare if there wasn't traffic and if she only spent five minutes at home. But she would have been traveling between the hours of seven and eight in the morning. We all know what morning freeway traffic is like."

"Hmm . . ." Judge Puhl tapped her fingernails on her desk. "Okay, Lieutenant, this is what I'm going to do. I'm going to give you a warrant to seize the phone that Sergeant Dunn and Detective Oliver describe in these notarized papers. That way you can test your hypothesis on the spot. If it wasn't her most recent phone—if it was an old phone—then the search ends there. If it was her most recent phone, then I'll allow you to continue on with a search."

"Your Honor, there is a very likely chance that Mr. Dresden may have destroyed or misplaced the evidence."

"Then shame on him! He lives in the twenty-first century, he knows better than to tamper with something like that. If that's the case, then I'll also allow your team to search the condo, but I'm putting limits on it, Lieutenant. Don't even bother with printing, fibers, hairs, or even minor blood seepage. The woman lived there; you're going to find all of the above. What I'll allow you to search for is evidence of blood loss and spatter patterns that is beyond and/or defies a reasonable amount of blood loss typical for a household injury. I have no problem with your bringing out your blood-spatter experts. Just don't make too big of a mess, all right?"

"We'll do our best. Thank you, Your Honor."

She spoke as she wrote out the warrant. "One word of caveat. If you or your experts find a large amount of blood loss on a cushion of a couch or a chair, or on the bed, without any concomitant spatter to go with it, please proceed with caution. Men tend to forget that we women sometimes leak during our periods. You don't want to arrest the man because Roseanne wore a faulty Tampex."

26

A STRONG SERIES OF raps on the front door produced the wanted voice on the other side. Decker said, "Police, Mr. Dresden, open up." When no immediate response was forthcoming, he said, "We have a warrant, sir. Open the door now!"

A couple of seconds later Decker heard the dead bolt sliding, but the door remained shut.

The voice said, "I need to see the warrant!"

"I can show it to you as soon as you open the door."

"And if I don't, what are you going to do? Break down the door?"

"There's no need for drama, Mr. Dresden. We have . . ." Decker rolled his eyes at Marge and Oliver. "We're here to seize the phone that Detective Sergeant Marge Dunn found by accident a few days ago. That phone is described very specifically in the papers."

The door flew open. Dresden caught it before the doorknob punched a hole in his interior wall. He narrowed his eyes when he saw Decker. "Who're you?"

Out came the identification. Dresden studied the credentials as

Decker studied the stockbroker. Ivan was a good-looking man in that dark, brooding, Gothic fashion. He wore a muscle shirt and a pair of gym shorts and had a towel around his neck. His face was dry, without a hint of flushing: the workout had yet to occur, or it had occurred a long time ago, or it never occurred at all. He certainly spent more time than necessary on confirming that Decker was who he said he was.

"You have nothing better to do than harass me after I just got home from work?"

"Serving a warrant works out better when you're home, Mr. Dresden."

The stockbroker scowled. "Let me see that warrant."

Handing him the paperwork, Decker was stone-faced as Dresden slowly made his way through the legalese. It wasn't that complicated.

Dresden slapped the warrant into an open palm. "I told your two *lackeys* over there, it was an old phone. It's gone. I threw it away. You wasted your time, but I suppose that being on the government dole, that doesn't matter much to you."

Decker's face was flat. "The warrant states that we can look for it."

"And mess up my apartment?" Dresden's chuckle was sarcastic. "No thank you, I'll pass."

At this point, Decker had had enough. He bullied his way past Dresden, careful not to knock him on the shoulder. "You don't have any choice, Mr. Dresden. We're here to do a job and that's what we're going to do." He stood in the center of the condo's living room and began to glove up.

Marge and Oliver followed. She said, "If you have the phone, Ivan, make it easier on all of us and just fork it over."

"Didn't you hear what I just told you?" Dresden screamed out. "I threw the phone away!"

Decker spoke to his detectives. "Dunn, you take the kitchen; Oliver, you handle the bedrooms; and I'll do the living room." His eyes returned to Dresden. "We're not going away. This warrant says that if we don't find the phone, then we're allowed to bring in our blood experts and start looking for evidence of a crime. And that'll take up even more time. So make yourself comfortable and let us do our job."

"This is totally absurd—"

"If you have the phone, now's the time to make your move."

"I don't have the *fucking* phone!" Dresden growled. "I threw it away . . . what's the fucking use! I'm calling my lawyer!"

"Whatever you need to do, sir." Decker took out his cell and connected to the techs. "It's Lieutenant Decker from West Valley, I'm looking for Mike Fagen . . . sure I'll hold."

"Who's your captain?" Dresden shouted.

Decker said, "Are you talking to me?"

"Yes, I'm talking to—"

"Hold on a minute," Decker said to Dresden. "Mike, it's Lieutenant Decker. It looks like we're going to need you because Mr. Dresden has admitted throwing the phone away. When do you think you'll start spraying?"

"Spraying?" Dresden was aghast. "Spraying for what!"

"Hold on a sec, Mike, I can't have two conversations at once and Dresden's antsy." Decker threw a hand over the mouthpiece of the mobile. "My superior is Captain Strapp. If we don't find the phone, we're going to spray for blood and blood spatter. Don't worry about your carpet. It only glows bright blue if there's blood protein. Otherwise nothing will show up." He spoke into the mobile. "Sorry, Mike. When can you make it over here?"

"I don't believe this!" Dresden ranted as he paced back and forth. "I'm still grieving for my wife and you have the nerve to barge in and accuse me of mur—"

Dresden stopped himself and turned away. His face hadn't been flushed before, but it certainly was now—fire-engine red and bathed in sweat. He now looked as if he had completed that strenuous workout. Decker often wondered about the exact purpose of exercise. If it was just to elevate the heart rate, there were lots of other ways to do that without spending mind-numbing hours killing one's feet on a treadmill: sex, stress, and caffeine instantly came to mind.

"If you break or ruin anything in my home, I'll sue your ass off!" Dresden cried out. "You have no right to . . . what the fuck is that!"

Dresden was responding to noises emanating from one of the bedrooms. He stomped down the hallway and Decker could hear him venting his spleen at Oliver.

After completing his phone call to the tech, Decker took a few moments to get the layout of the room and decide how he wanted to organize the search. Dresden was probably telling the truth when he'd said he threw the phone away. If there was something incriminating on it, he'd dump it without thinking. Yet there were those occasional perpetrators of violent crime who retained damning evidence. Some of the criminals were too arrogant or too lazy to bother chucking the offending article, but others kept indicting evidence as a memento; something that allowed their warped minds to visit and revisit the crime over and over.

The component that occupied the most space in the living room was a stark white entertainment unit complete with drawers, cabinets, and shelving—almost a quaint nod to yesterday's technology because nowadays so many families were buying flat-screens. It appeared that Ivan hadn't moved up yet. Maybe that was the first thing on his agenda as soon as he got the insurance money.

Dresden's white elephant unit contained a big bulky TV behind pocket doors and lots of shelves on either side of the screen. One side was taken up by DVDs, CDs, and stereo components; the other side held a row of books, another row of CDs, and a lone shelf devoted to curios and pictures: six silver-framed photographs, all of them showing Ivan in various poses of physical prowess. The only hint that a woman had once lived there were several scattered scented candles and a small collection of porcelain cats.

Decker started by carefully taking out the books, the CDs, and the DVDs and searching behind them. When nothing materialized, he checked behind the audio/video equipment. Satisfied that the phone wasn't stashed anywhere in the entertainment unit, he began looking under couches and chairs. Since the condo's living room, dining room, and kitchen were open space divided by a breakfast bar, he could hear Marge opening and closing doors in the kitchen.

"Any luck?" Decker asked her.

"Not so far. What about you?"

"Zilch."

The three detectives searched through the late afternoon until the sunlight dimmed and early evening set in. They rooted through drawers and cupboards, peered under couches and chairs, snooped inside medicine cabinets, and turned over the master bedroom's mattress to see if anything had been squirreled away. Ninety minutes had elapsed before the blood-spatter experts arrived. By that time, Ivan had all but barricaded himself inside his home office.

Once the techs arrived, it took another hour to focus in on the areas to test. They decided to concentrate on spraying the carpet under the couch where Marge had found the pen and felt something sticky. Then they moved on to the walls, the floorboards, and the baseboard molding in the kitchen. They also sprayed the walls in the living room, office, the guest bedroom, and the master bedroom. Last, they applied luminol to the marital mattress. By then night had fallen. They drew the drapes and turned off the lights, shrouding the condo in inky darkness.

To say there was no blood-protein luminescence at all would have been a lie. A very careful eye could pick up random specks of blue in the kitchen (accidental cuts made in food preparation), a decent amount of glow around both bathroom toilets (urine as well as blood glows blue under luminol), and as Judge Puhl had predicted, there were several splotches of blue on the master bedroom's mattress (old menstrual leakage). But there was nothing indicating a bloodletting had taken place anywhere inside the condo.

The lights were turned back on. Decker then asked if the techs would luminol the corners of the dining-room and the coffee tables as well as the breakfast bar. His logic was that maybe a physical altercation had taken place and perhaps Ivan pushed Roseanne, causing the phone to fly from her hand and under the couch. Just maybe she fell and hit her head on the table, and the blow knocked her unconscious or dead.

The breakfast bar and the corners of the tables were tested and came up clean. The breakfast bar did glow slightly, but that could have been caused by raw chicken or ground beef spilling juices. Luminol did not distinguish between animal or human sera. The techs took a slide scraping, hoping to have enough material to test for presence of human blood.

And that sticky area that Marge had felt under the couch—Decker had felt it as well—showed no luminescence. The matted carpet nap had probably come from some other source, most likely a food accident.

Four hours later, Decker was thanking Dresden for his time and for his cooperation. Dresden was magnanimous in his forgiveness, shaking Decker's hand with a firm grip. "I hope that this finally puts to bed some very evil rumors about my love for my wife. It was hard enough grieving the first time, Lieutenant. By these hideous innuendos, I've felt like I've had to grieve all over again."

Decker said, "We're sorry for any inconvenience, Mr. Dresden, but your wife's body hasn't turned up. We're doing our job and I'm sure you can appreciate that."

"I realize you're public servants, but it's still a terrible thing . . . to lose your wife and then be a suspect in her disappearance. Now if you don't mind, I'd like you to leave. I could use a little privacy . . . not to mention the cleanup."

"Of course." Decker granted Dresden a slow smile. "By the way, I didn't see your lawyer anywhere."

"I decided not to call him. Why bother wasting bucks when all he'd do was twiddle his thumbs and watch you work. I knew I didn't need him. I had nothing to hide."

THEY PILED INTO the unmarked, Oliver driving them back to the station house to pick up their respective cars, Marge sitting shotgun. Oliver said, "Could it be that the sleaze had nothing to do with his wife's disappearance? Lots of guys cheat. Most of them don't kill their wives."

"Yeah, that part's true. But of the guys who kill their wives, almost all of them have girlfriends." No one spoke for a second. Marge looked over her shoulder at Decker in the backseat. "What do you think, Loo?"

"I don't know. He seems sleazy enough. Maybe Roseanne did die in the crash. Just as likely, she was murdered elsewhere."

Marge said, "Even if she was murdered elsewhere, it doesn't mean that Dresden didn't do it."

"Or he could be innocent," Oliver insisted. "Maybe the phone we saw was Roseanne's old, lost phone. Maybe she bought another one exactly like it."

"Then why didn't Ivan just tell us that?"

"Because he knew that our finding Roseanne's phone would make him look bad."

"Not as bad as throwing it away," Marge said. "That's an immediate sign of guilt."

Decker said, "If Ivan did it and the condo wasn't the murder scene, where else could he have done it?"

Marge shrugged. "Maybe he did it in his car. Maybe that's why he sold it."

"Who'd he sell it to?" When the question was met with silence, Decker said, "Maybe we should find out?"

IN THE HEART of the north Valley sat the major parts manufacturing plant for Katumi Motors, the factory housed in a white, cinderblock rectangle, and fronted by a green lawn sporting a flower bed that spelled out KATUMI in white petunias. The commercial area held industries of all types, along with granite, brick, lumber, and marble yards. Decker often came here for wholesale prices whenever he embarked upon a home-improvement project, and each year it seemed to get uglier and uglier. Today the Sunday skies held rain clouds and the smoggy, foggy air was infused with gloom. The bad weather plus the lack of anything green made the vicinity feel like an old, depressed company town.

Once inside Katumi headquarters, he was led to the third floor and introduced to Brian Alderweiss, a lab-coated, thirtysomething tech who was the undisputed leader of Katumi's Rapid Prototyping. The monolithic machine took up a nice portion of its dedicated room with computers, monitors, and other unidentifiable equipment occupying most of the wall space. It took some time for Brian and his assistants to load the CT images and then to calibrate them to the laser arm of the apparatus. He spoke as he worked. "The most important transmitted data is for us to tell the beam what portion of the image to cut out. If you mess this up, you're not going to get the model you want."

"Take your time," Decker said generously. Hours later the techs were still calibrating and Decker rued the casual comment he had made, even though there was damn little he could do about it. Besides, this entire day wasn't about him. It was about trying to give an anonymous set of grieving parents a body to bury.

When the programming was finally put into action, a precision laser beam did as told, happily cut through paper-thin laminates of wood, one sheet stacked atop another.

Alderweiss said, "Our machines take our virtual designs off our computers and transform them into cross-sectional computer images. In our specific case, we use the technology in anything that involves innovative or major design reconfigurations that will affect hood mechanics—things like engine blocks and radiators. It helps to be holding a physical model to see if it actually does fit the space it was designed to fit."

"So the technology is basically a CT scan for machines," Decker said.

The technician gave Decker's off-the-cuff words more consideration than they deserved. "In a way, yes, but we keep pushing the technology further and further. From the virtual cross sections, we use computer-aided design software to re-create the model in the physical. And with today's accurate technology, we not only fabricate models, we also can now fabricate small car parts with a very high degree of accuracy."

Hollander piped up. "Who'da thunk we'd be using all this fancy robotic technology for police work?"

"Isn't it amazing?" Alderweiss gushed over his baby. "In the five short years that I've worked with Rapid Prototyping, I've seen advances in the technology that have gone way beyond my imagination. For instance, traditionally the fabrication of a model was made by laying successive layers of liquid or powdered material. That allowed us to create almost any geometry, but it didn't help us with negative volume, which is all the stuff inside the perimeter model. Now we can actually make quality machine parts—inside and outside—using specific computer directions. You can go almost anywhere with that."

Decker nodded, although he wasn't quite sure what Alderweiss was talking about. The man was certainly enthusiastic about his topic. His wide hazel eyes sparked fire every time he spoke. Decker was also learning that the *rapid* part in Rapid Prototyping was a loosely defined term. For something the size of a human skull, the machine had to produce dozens upon dozens of successive layers of paper silhouettes. The process would take hours. Eventually all the cut-out silhouettes would be fused together to form a nearly exact replica of Jane Doe's skull.

Alderweiss said, "Imagine what this kind of high-resolution technology could do for you?"

"Probably a lot," Decker said, trying to match the tech's enthusiasm.

"Take, for instance, things like stab wounds. Someone could do a CT scan of the depression, and our laser machine could trace the outline, image by image. Eventually, you'd have a replica of the knife with tool marks and all."

"Except that flesh isn't bone," Decker pointed out. "The wound closes once the knife is pulled out, so the dimensions would be off."

Alderweiss didn't comment.

"But the applications are limitless," Decker added.

The tech nodded but kept future conversation with Decker to a minimum. Hollander, on the other hand, had bonded with Alderweiss and the two of them continued to marvel at the wondrous fusion of science and machine.

It was around six in the evening and it looked to be a very long night. It had taken the mighty laser hours just to reproduce about a quarter of the skull, meaning that the final prototype wouldn't be ready until the wee hours of tomorrow morning. Decker was more than willing to put up with the wait and the monotony to assure a judge that the forensic chain of evidence had not been broken, but he felt terrible about crapping out on Cindy and Koby with the house. And to add even further to Decker's guilt, he had canceled on his daughter and son-in-law *after* Koby had put in extra hours and extra effort to help Decker with the CT scans.

He made a show of stretching. "If I'm not needed right now, I think I'll take a little walk . . . loosen up the old bones."

"We'll still be here," Alderweiss said.

Hollander said, "I'm getting hungry. How about a little takeout, Brian?"

"Sounds good to me, but we'll have to do delivery."

"Around my parts, pizza is a staple."

"Okay, I'll order in. Cheese and what?"

"Whatever you want." Hollander turned to Decker "Loo?"

"Maybe later."

"Hey, if you want to go out and meet someone for dinner, I'll stick around. You know me and machines. Never met one I didn't like."

"Thanks, Mike, I just may take you up on it." Decker excused himself, walked outside into the setting sun. He dialed Cindy's number and she picked up on the third ring. "How's it going?"

"Well . . . let me put it this way. We now have a gigantic hole in the back wall. I suppose that's progress . . . sort of."

"I'm so sorry I couldn't—"

"Dad, I'm a cop; I understand, and it's absolutely fine. You absolutely had to do this . . . to replicate that skull. Because until you put a face on your Jane Doe, there's no way you're going to solve her murder. And I know how obsessive you are with open cases. I'm excusing you for the betterment of society."

"You're very sweet and understanding, but I still feel bad about taking Mike away from the job."

"You know, Loo, the more work that piles up, the more that Koby will see that we need outside help. Right now we've got a huge pile of drywall that's about to avalanche over his beloved rose garden. I think he's finally beginning to see that we can't do this all by our little lonesomes, no matter how well Koby wields a nail gun."

"I'd like to make it up to you two," Decker told her. "What are your plans for dinner?"

"We haven't gotten that far yet," Cindy said. "We're still in the 'tarping the giant hole' stage."

"Rina's visiting her parents in the city. I've got to stick around the area until the skull is complete. That doesn't mean I have to be glued to the machine. Hollander can watch it in my absence, but I can't go too far. If you can meet me, I'd love to take you both out."

"Where are you?"

"Approximately Roscoe and Sepulveda."

"There's nowhere to eat around there."

"Unless you're interested in consuming marble or brick, that's true. But if you're willing to drive out to the Valley, I'm sure I could find something a little more south."

"I'm afraid I'm going to have to pass, Daddy. I've got a mess to clean up. Can I take a rain check?"

Decker was disappointed but tried to keep his voice even. "Anytime."

"How's the skull coming?"

"Slow, but like you said, it's our best shot for finding out the identity of our Jane Doe. The technology is impressive, even for a Luddite like me."

"It's really too bad I can't get away. It sounds really fascinating. Are you also having a forensic computer artist come up with a face?"

"Yes, ma'am, we are doing that as well."

"Be interesting to see how well they match."

"Yes, it will be interesting. Please thank Koby again for helping us out so quickly."

"You can call him and thank him yourself. He's on my naughty list right now. There are about a thousand things I'd rather be doing than sledgehammering a kitchen. On the other hand, he and Mike Hollander get along famously. I think Mike's a father figure for him. He was a great choice, Daddy. Thanks."

Decker smiled. "Sometimes I get it right."

"Sometimes," Cindy admitted, "but don't let it go to your head."

27

LOOKING AT THE replica skull made out of fused paper and perched on a stand, Lauren Decanter turned the base slowly, studying Jane Doe inch by inch as the skull completed a 360-degree revolution. "Absolutely amazing!" She looked up at Decker in awe. "This is the real deal. You can see all the necessary anatomical landmarks and then some."

"The wonders of modern technology," Decker said. "Although she didn't die by modern technology."

Lauren's hands touched the cranium. "An old-fashioned bop on the head." She returned her eyes to Decker's face. "What can you tell me about the case, Lieutenant?"

"I thought a lot about it on the way over. This is what we have so far. By the teeth remaining in upper and lower mandibles, both the coroner and the forensic odontologist think she was in her early twenties at the time of her demise. We also know that she died during or after 1974 because she was wearing a band sweatshirt that was produced in 1974."

"Which band?"

"Priscilla and the Major."

Lauren thought for several deliberate moments. "No, I don't think I ever heard of them."

"They were a duo. The Major was originally from the military and I think he actually served in Vietnam. But Priscilla was the main attraction. She sang and wrote the songs. They were a little on the sappy side: a throwback to an earlier era compared with all the acid and psychedelic rock that was going on at that time."

"Hmm . . ." She started to take notes. "Priscilla and the Major. I would think that the duo would have attracted a more conservative crowd with the man being in the military."

"Certainly the army was not a popular institution at the time, so yes, they did attract a more conservative element. But they had their share of Top 40 hits. Their songs were played on major radio stations and they had a sizable following. If I had to compare them to anyone at that time, I would say the Carpenters. Do you know about the Carpenters?"

"He played the guitar, she played the drums. And she died of anorexia, right?"

"Yes, but back then, no one realized that she had problems. Instead, they were touted as the clean-cut alternatives to the unwashed, restless youth. Nixon invited them to the White House. If I remember correctly, I think Priscilla and the Major also entertained Mr. Pres. She's still alive, living in Porter Ranch, if you want to talk to her. Apparently, she loves the color pink."

"Very feminine. So a fan of Priscilla would probably be a more conservative person although not ultraconservative if she was listening to the Top 40 stations."

"That about sums up my assessment."

Lauren took more notes. "So, being as she was dressed in a sweatshirt and liked a conservative band, you don't see your Jane Doe as a pickup or hooker gone bad?"

"Why do you ask?"

"Because a bash in the head . . . to me it seems impulsive and unplanned. Something that a john might do to a hooker or a drunk might do to a pickup if she said no."

"I agree that it was up close and personal, but I'm thinking it was done by the woman's significant other—a boyfriend or a husband. I have a feeling that the girl, if in her early twenties, might have been a bit innocent for her age."

"Why's that?"

"Next to the body I found a mood ring. Do you know what that is?"

"Refresh my memory."

"A mood ring has a stone that changes colors to reflect your mood. If it shines red or in the warm-color spectrum, you're happy, and if it shines blue or in the cold-color end, you're sad. The stone obviously adjusts to skin temperature."

"So it was blue when you found it?"

"Almost black." Decker shook his head. "I'm sure it's been black for a very long time. The point is mood rings were a fad that was geared to adolescent girls. That's why I'm thinking that our Jane Doe was a little innocent. Someone who's into peace, love, and alternative spirits." A pause. "Sometimes young women are swept off their feet by the wrong type of boyfriend."

"I see," Lauren said. "Are you talking to the forensic computer artist as well?"

"If he wants to talk, I'll be happy to chat with him. It would be interesting to see how well you two match in your interpretations of the face."

"Most of the time we're pretty close." She smiled. "You've given me a good start. Thanks for your insights."

"When do you think you'll have something for me?"

Lauren turned on her laptop. "I think I'd like to do a little research into the period."

"What kind of research? Maybe I can help you out?"

"You already have. What I need now is visual input, because re-creating a face is a visual thing. I want to look up Priscilla and the Major . . . I'd like to see what kind of fans they had and if there are pictures of their fans. I also would like to read old articles and fashion magazines. For this case, I think *Seventeen* magazine might give me more hints than *Ladies' Homes Journal* or *Vogue*."

"She definitely doesn't seem like the *Vogue* type."

"No, but her mother might have been. Rereading the material kind of brings a visual life to the era for me." She studied Decker's face. "You are a Vietnam vet, right?"

"Indeed I am. A lot of detectives my age are 'Nam vets."

She stared at him further. "But there's something in your face . . . you definitely had your wild side."

"It's all wrinkles, huh?" Decker held back a smirk. "My rebellion was pretty tame and it was a long time ago."

"You're also an oldest child."

Decker nodded. "But that's also no surprise. Oldest children like bossing people around, so the police academy fits that primal need pretty well."

Lauren studied him for just a moment longer. "There's something playful going on inside your head right now. As I look at your eyes, they're teasing me without being flirtatious. I bet you have daughters."

"I have daughters and I have sons." He paused. "Stepsons, but for all intents and purposes, they're my sons. I've been their only father since they were six and eight and now they're in their twenties."

"But your daughters are yours biologically."

"Yes."

"Hmm . . . you just seem like you've had recent experience with children."

Decker laughed. "Okay, I confess. My older daughter is almost thirty, but my younger daughter is only fourteen."

"Aha!" Lauren said triumphantly. "I knew it. I have a nose for this kind of thing. When I do reconstruction, it's as if the person is talking to me, directing my fingers. It's like a sixth sense."

"How are you on the stock market?"

"Sorry, Lieutenant, I've never been any good at numbers."

DECKER THOUGHT HE was getting an early jump by arriving at the Crypt by nine the next morning. Lauren was already at her station and had immersed herself in the 1970s—photographs, articles from *Time* and *Newsweek,* magazine spreads from *Fashion Weekly, Seventeen,* and *Vogue,* several vintage pieces of seventies clothing. She was still studying the skull, but she had put eraser tips on the anatomical landmarks. On the left side of the tabletop sat several rectangular loaves of adobe-colored clay. Her carving tools were neatly laid out on her right. Priscilla and the Major whispered from a CD player.

"I wish I could play their songs on a phonograph," she told Decker. "That would really get me in the spirit."

The forensic artist wore a white chef's apron over her jeans and black cotton top. Her chestnut-colored hair was tied back in a ponytail, and she wore no makeup. When she finally put the first slab of clay onto the replica skull, Decker wanted to sing "glory hallelujah."

"Are you going to watch me the entire time?" Lauren asked him.

"I'm making you nervous?"

"No," Lauren told him. "But you are changing the energy of the room. This process is instinctual. The skull talks to me and she may not want to say what's on her mind if you're around."

"Okay, then . . ." Decker paused. "How about if I come back in a couple of hours?"

"She and I will be talked out by the end of the day. Why don't you stop by then?"

A glance at his wrist told him it was 9:20. "Around three?"

"That would be great."

AT 3:18, SHE had made a lot of progress, but she was far from done. The face was shaped but the features were blurry, like staring at a likeness without corrective glasses. The work area was covered with reddish clay shavings. She stepped back from the head and rolled her shoulders.

She laced her mud-covered fingers together, stretched out her arms, and cracked her back. "I'm glad you came in. Sometimes my posture is terrible."

"Can I get you a cup of coffee?"

"You know . . . I think I forgot to eat my lunch." She walked over to an industrial sink and washed her hands. It took her quite a while to get all the clay off her fingers and out of her nails. When her hands were spotless, she dug inside a brown paper bag and pulled out a baloney sandwich with lettuce on white bread. "Wow, I'm hungry."

"Can I get you something to drink?"

"No. I have my soda." She pulled out a can of Coke and a bag of potato chips.

Decker said, "I do believe that you are the first woman I've met who drinks regular soda."

She took another bite of her sandwich, opened the bag, and daintily pulled out a chip. "I'm not into food so much. I don't have a very good palate. My friends all say I eat like I'm a ten-year-old." She opened her soda and drank it with a straw. "They have a point."

"Hey, what you're eating looks pretty good to me."

"You want a bite?"

"No, no." Decker smiled. "I'm good, thank you."

"No palate, but God more than made up for it in the visual department. This job is really a calling." She ate another chip. "It's not enough just to be artistic. You also have to be acutely tactile, to feel the face taking shape under your fingers and let it guide you rather than the other way around." She finished her sandwich and ate a few more chips. Then she wiped her hands and face with a napkin and patted her stomach. "I feel much better. Well, back to work."

"How much longer are you going to work?"

"I really don't know. If you want, you can come back in a couple of hours. There might be more to show you."

"Around six?"

She picked up a scalpel. "That seems perfect."

AT 6:10, JANE had emerged from a fuzzy clump of mud into something distinct. She had a wide nose, a pointed chin, a wide mouth, a hint of cheekbones, and a prominent brow. Without taking her eyes off the bust, Lauren said, "What do you think?"

"I think you're amazing."

"Thank you. Do you have a moment to talk?"

"Of course." He took a seat next to the artist. "What's up?"

"Well, I'm having a conversation with her and we haven't reached a conclusion. I thought that maybe we could brainstorm."

"Sure, if you think it will help."

"First thing is that Jane has a broad forehead and pronounced cheekbones. I think she has Latina or Native American ancestry. Maybe Alaskan."

"Interesting. The pathologist thought she might be Hispanic."

"I have to agree. Secondly, in the seventies, there weren't as many anorexic women as there are now. Plus, her being so young . . . I gave her a little more cheek fat. What do you think?"

"I think that's fine."

"Okay." Lauren smiled. "So let's move on. You're thinking that she was murdered in the midseventies."

"During or after 1974. That was the date of the sweatshirt."

"Okay, so I was doing a little research. In that era, disco was pretty big. I've listened to a little Barry White and Donna Summer. Priscilla and the Major were not considered disco, right?"

Decker smiled. "Correct. Think of disco as John Travolta in *Saturday Night Fever.*"

Lauren nodded but her expression was a blank.

"White suit, big hair, big crystal globe ball in the center of the dance floor."

"It sounds like a bar mitzvah."

"Uh . . . yeah, kinda. Disco was the ultimate dance music. Priscilla and the Major were soft rock."

"Yes, they sound like soft rock. So that modifies the hairstyle from something more extreme to something more conservative. I've been looking at some fan magazines around that time. *Charlie's Angels* was a really big TV hit."

"Indeed it was."

"If you think the young woman was a little bit innocent and maybe fad oriented, I'd consider the three stars of the TV series. What we have is three really different types of hairstyles—we have Jaclyn Smith, who had the classical long wavy brown hair. We have Kate Jackson, who had dark, blunt cut hair parted in the middle, side bangs . . . kind of perky and Ivy League college student. And then there was Farrah Fawcett-Majors, who wore her hair . . . well, I don't know what you'd call it. It was like hair all over the place. There were bangs and side wings and layers and flips. I would think that would be a very hard hairdo for the average girl to manage."

Decker smiled. "Man, this is a quick hop down memory lane. I will tell you this. Farrah Fawcett-Majors's hairdo inspired a very popular look. There were lots of women with major-league side flips."

"Like Jennifer Aniston's layers in the early 2000s." Lauren thought a moment. "If she is Latina and conservative, I don't see her as the blond, blue-eyed Farrah Fawcett-Majors type. I was thinking that maybe she'd have the long brown hair of Jaclyn Smith."

"Honestly, Lauren, at that time, everyone was trying to look like Farrah Fawcett-Majors, regardless of hair or eye color. She was the big one."

"So why don't I do this?" Lauren suggested. "I can put all three Charlie's Angels hairdos on Jane—the blond Farrah with all the flips, poker straight like Kate Jackson, and long and wavy like Smith. That way we can take pictures of Jane with all three hairstyles and it might increase our chances of finding who Jane really is."

"Good idea. You can also modify the hair and eye color. She may be a natural brunette, but there are a slew of blondes from a bottle."

"Okay. If we do Farrah Fawcett, we'll give Jane blondish hair and blue eyes. For Jaclyn, let's try out darker blue eyes but dark hair. Kate will be brown eyes and brown hair. I have one final comment, Lieutenant. We might try a few pictures with Jane wearing glasses. Contacts were expensive back then. Even though the bigger glasses were coming into vogue, I think large rims would have overpowered her face. I'm voting for small granny glasses."

"Whatever you think."

Lauren pulled out a box of pastels and began to sketch. Twenty minutes later she had concocted a sketch of a young woman with dark eyes, dark hair, but a modified Farrah Fawcett hairdo. An oval-shaped face with a broad forehead; rimmed granny glasses sat on the bridge of her nose. Her lips were stretched into a wide smile that showed teeth. But it was her eyes that gave Decker pause; not the color, but the expression. They connoted someone who was chronically cheerful, an individual who couldn't possibly conceive of anything ever going wrong.

The forensic artist regarded her finished product. "Let me try to reproduce this look on our Jane Doe clay model."

"How long will that take?"

"Another half day at least. I'd like to sleep on it overnight. Why don't you come back tomorrow in the late afternoon?"

"That sounds like a plan. Let me recap just to get it straight in my head. What you're going to do is set out all sorts of possibilities for Jane . . . all kinds of wigs of seventies hairstyles, different eye color, different hair color, different glasses, no glasses, but all the models will be wearing the same pink jacket and the mood ring. Then we'll take photographs of all the different permutations. Hopefully, we get a couple of them right enough to jolt someone's memory back into a time warp."

Lauren nodded. "What I think everyone wants is for somebody to lift a finger and say, 'Aha! I know her!'"

"Exactly," Decker said. "Someone who'll finally give Jane the recognition she deserves."

28

S HE HAS A face." Marge spread the photographs on her desk and
sorted them by hairstyle. "Several of them, actually."

"Several looks, but the same face." Decker was standing behind
Marge's back, peering over her shoulder. His jacket was open and he
had strapped his gun harness to his chest, but he wasn't armed. He
usually didn't bother wearing his piece when he was doing desk work.
"Lauren did an excellent job."

Marge looked back and forth between Lauren's interpretation of the
bones and the computerized face. "Amazing how close the two faces are."

"I think the final product was by mutual agreement," Decker said.

"Nice detail. One thing that's for certain: this is not Roseanne Dresden." Marge looked up from one of the pictures of Jane. This particular
one had the brunette Kate Jackson preppy shoulder-length haircut with
medium-brown eyes. Wire-rimmed glasses sat on the bridge of a nose.
"We need to compare these pictures to women around the same age
who went missing thirty years ago. That's a lot of women, considering
we don't even know the year this gal disappeared."

"It's the one thing that we have control over. Every detective in the squad room has his or her own set of Jane Doe photographs. I'm working on getting a copy for every police officer. Sometimes the craziest things happen on a routine stop."

Marge said, "Bontemps and Wang were originally doing MP files. If they're not in the field, I can assign them to take up where they left off. At least now they have a photograph to check against the missing women."

"Perfect," Decker said. "Next use the power of the post. Have Oliver take his copies of the pictures and run off a bunch of 'Have You Seen This Person?' mailers."

"How many initial copies?"

"As many as the department will allow us to print. I'd like to bump this up to a high-profile case. Who did you speak with at the *Times*?"

"It was Rusty something. His name's in the file."

"Give him a call and ask to meet with him. See if you can get someone to write a story about Jane. Use the angle that the police were looking for one woman and found another. Convince him that it's a perfect human-interest piece for the front page. Use your natural and abundant charm and sweep this poor unsuspecting male off his feet."

Marge laughed. "Actually, in this case, I won't even need charm. They have to make amends for erroneously listing Roseanne Dresden's name in the crash list. I'm sure once I remind the paper of its screwup, someone will be happy to cooperate with L.A.'s Finest."

THEY ARRANGED A meeting at one of the ubiquitous Star$, this particular one just west of downtown L.A., not more than fifteen minutes away from the skyscrapers and the paper. Since she arrived early, Marge was nursing some kind of sweet concoction that involved hot milk, chocolate, whipped cream, and a hint of peppermint. It wasn't coffee by anyone's definition, but it was sweet, hot, and frothy, and why not splurge with the pocketbook and the calories every blue moon?

She wore a lightweight navy-blue suit over a cream-colored top, with simple black flats on her feet. Her hair was now long enough to be pulled into a ponytail, although she elected to wear it loose. She had given her cheeks a stroke of blush, had lined the bottom of her eyes with the stub of a makeup pencil. A single pearl stud rested in each earlobe. She could have been the poster girl for middle management—bank clerk, paralegal, bookkeeper, insurance agent: anyone with a white-collar job who had a title but was grossly underpaid.

Her table had a beeline view of the doorway, and when the young man stepped across the threshold, Marge checked her watch. He was five minutes early; the boy would go far. Marge stood and waved and Rusty Delgado waved back. He wore a pair of khaki pants, a blue chambray shirt, and an ill-fitting double-breasted jacket that was way too low for his short, stocky frame. They shook hands and she handed him a five-dollar bill. "Not a bribe, just a friendly gesture to get yourself some poison."

"I thought coffee was good for you in moderation."

"Coffee isn't the culprit. It's all the other stuff that you put in the coffee."

Delgado smiled. "I'll be right back."

Marge sat back down. She had learned that Delgado's boss was still Tricia Woodard, but because Tricia had never bothered to call back and talk about the WestAir list, Marge didn't feel the need to talk with her. Delgado, on the other hand, had been cooperative. It made more sense to deal with a known subordinate than an unknown boss. Delgado came back with a large steaming cup of something frothy and sat down, staring at her with eager blue eyes.

She said, "I've got a good story for you to pitch to your boss."

"WestAir fraud?"

"Fraud possibly, but something even better. Murder."

"The missing flight attendant?" Immediately Rusty took out his notebook, but Marge put her hand over the pad.

"Hear me out first, then take your notes. First of all, Rusty, I'm not an insurance agent."

"You're an undercover cop."

"No, I'm a plainclothes detective sergeant, but I mostly work homicide. Originally we were looking for confirmation that Roseanne Dresden perished in flight 1324, but then things got very complicated. Another body was found at the crash site." She gave him as succinct a summary as she could. Toward the end of her recitation, Marge extracted the pictures of Jane Doe from her purse and laid them down on the table for Delgado to look at.

"This is the forensic artist's interpretation of our unidentified body that has been rotting underneath the apartment building for the last thirty years. It took us forever just to get a usable skull because the original one was in terrible condition. How we managed to get a replica to use forensically is an article in and of itself."

"Why do you think she died thirty years ago?"

"We dated the sweatshirt she was wearing." Marge pointed to a photograph. "This one is the Farrah Fawcett look. As you can see, we have others."

"I've seen pictures of my aunts . . . they wore their hair exactly like this. Amazing that such a white-bread girl made fashion inroads into the Latino community."

"Celebrity trumps all." Marge took a sip of her coffee. "Rusty, someone got away with murder. You can tell we are anxious to bring a killer to a long overdue justice. We need the public's help and you're the perfect person to spread the word."

"What happened to the flight attendant?"

"Roseanne Dresden is still officially missing."

"And you don't think that this woman could be Roseanne?"

"No. The forensic artist's rendition looks nothing like Roseanne Dresden. More importantly the dental records don't match." She leaned forward and looked earnestly into Delgado's eyes. "Your paper messed up by printing Roseanne Dresden on the deceased list. You didn't do it, but your boss did."

"But you're still not one hundred percent certain that Roseanne didn't perish in the crash."

"No, not one hundred percent. But the more days that pass without

Roseanne's body, the more it looks like foul play. When her name was printed the investigation took a step backward and we lost days that could have been spent looking for Roseanne instead of digging around."

Delgado said nothing.

"Not that this has anything to do with you. You've been helpful, Rusty, and I appreciate that. That's why I came to you first. You, Rusty, and not your boss."

"I appreciate your confidence in me." He looked worried. "But . . . either I tell my boss about you or I go over her head. Neither one is a good option."

"Handle it however you want. We all have our crosses to bear. At this moment, Rusty, you've got a great story." Marge swept her hand across the air to imitate a headline banner. "'The Search for a Missing Flight Attendant's Body Leads Homicide Detectives into a Baffling, Thirty-Year-Old Murder.' It's complicated, it's got twists, it's got pathos, and it's got mystery. All we're asking for is that the paper print these photographs and solicit the public's help in identifying her."

"It's a thirty-year-old case. The guy responsible for her murder could be dead."

"More likely he's in his fifties and is feeling very smug," Marge told him. "Look into the future, Delgado. If we find the killer, think of the arrest and the trial. Who else is going to give you such a big opportunity?"

"It is absolutely the big break everyone in my position hopes for." The young man licked his lips. "Of course I'm going to pitch it. I just hope that Tricia doesn't screw it up for me."

"You tell whoever you have to that I talk to you, not to Tricia."

Delgado shook his head. "Why are you doing this for me?"

"Because you were there when I needed you. So here's your chance, Delgado; don't blow it."

He threw up his hands. "Of course I'm in. Can we go over the case again more slowly? I want to figure out exactly how to present this to the feature editor."

"I'm happy to give you a little more time just as long as you run the photographs of our Jane Doe."

"Absolutely, Sergeant. Our readers love pictures. Sometimes I think that the captions are the only thing they're reading. The Internet wouldn't survive without illustrations and videos. No one has the patience to sift through a detailed article."

"We're a short-attention-span society."

"We were raised on *Sesame Street,* computers, and instantaneous communication, Sergeant. We did it to ourselves."

29

IMMEDIATELY AFTER THE article was published, the tips started pouring in, requiring someone to manage the phones full-time. The calls were vast and varied. It was someone's long-lost daughter, it was someone's long-lost sister, it was a friend of a friend who moved to France and disappeared, it was Aunt Janice or Cousin Ellie. The names were duly written down and checked out. Sometimes Aunt Janice was alive and well. Just as many times, Cousin Ellie could not be located and was put on a checklist.

Do you have a picture of her?

A photograph was sent via e-mail. Receiving the image, the detective in charge would immediately notice that the two people looked nothing alike and that there was a thirty-year age difference.

I don't think this is your cousin Ellie, but we'll certainly keep it in mind.

Then there were the kooks. Jane Doe was actually Gamma-Globulin Moonbeam, an alien from outer space who was sent from Alpha Centauri to infiltrate Earth. The best one that Wanda got was that Jane Doe was a reincarnation of Gucci, a woman's beloved pet Maltese who had met her untimely demise by running across the street just as a Porsche Boxster turned the corner and ran a stop sign.

All the press attention focused on Jane Doe did a fine job riling up Farley Lodestone.

"You got a woman who's been dead for thirty years getting more paper space than my daughter, who's only been missing for a few months," he yelled at Decker.

"Farley, no one has forgotten about Roseanne—"

"That's damn well only because I call you all the time!"

"No, it's because we're committed to the investigation of your daughter," Decker said. "We're not just sitting with our hands under our butts, we've gone through her phone and credit-card records at least a half-dozen times. We've called everyone she's called up in the last year. We went up to San Jose and talked to people she knew up there—"

"San Jose is a total waste of time. You know that bastard did it."

"Farley, we pulled a search warrant and inspected every wall, floor, and fiber in your daughter's condo. If something happened to Roseanne, it didn't happen there. We spent days tracking down Ivan's old car and went over that forensically inside and out and we didn't find anything. We're reinterviewing people at the condo to see if they suddenly remember something. We're going over our notes. So far, we don't have the smoking gun, we don't have circumstantial evidence, we don't even have a crime scene. Even so, we're not giving up."

Lodestone didn't answer.

"Are you still there?" Decker asked.

"Yeah, I'm here. It just pisses me off that you're spending all your time looking into a corpse instead of looking for my daughter."

Roseanne wasn't Decker's only case. Neither was Jane Doe. At the moment, he was juggling thirty detectives and hundreds of cases. What could Decker say to convince the man that he doing the best he could?

The answer was nothing.

And if he, God forbid, was in the same situation as Farley Lodestone, he'd probably feel the same way.

"Farley, all I can tell you is I'm doing whatever I can."

"Well, it ain't enough!"

"I hear you, Farley. I know you're frustrated—"

"I'm pissed!"

"I can't say that I blame you. I wish I had more news to tell you—"

Lodestone hung up on him.

Decker rolled his eyes and slammed the phone back into the cradle. He was doing all he could, but Farley was right. It wasn't enough.

Failure sucked.

DAY SEVEN AFTER Rusty Delgado's article was published, Marge took a phone call regarding Jane Doe that sounded like something more than hope. She snapped her fingers and got Scott Oliver's attention, mouthing, "Get Decker." A minute later the lieutenant was on the line. He introduced himself and Marge told the caller to repeat her story.

"Like I told the sergeant, my name is Cathie Alvarez and I'm calling about the Jane Doe in the paper."

Decker said, "Thanks for calling, Ms. Alvarez. What would you like to tell me?"

"Well, now, this is a long time ago. But I have to tell you that it looks pretty much like my older cousin Beth."

"Okay. How so?"

"The picture in the paper, the one with the granny glasses and the Farrah Fawcett-Majors hairdo. Beth used to wear her hair like that except it was dark, but so did everyone else. Beth had glasses just like that, but so did everyone else. Mostly, it was the mood ring. Beth always wore a mood ring. Not that she needed it. Beth was such a positive person. She was always smiling."

Decker became very excited and pulled out his notepad. Lauren had thought that the Jane Doe might be Latina and Alvarez fit that category. "Would you have a picture of Beth?"

"No, I'm sorry, I don't have one on me. But I mailed the article to my mother—Beth's aunt. Mom and I talked about the picture for over an hour. She agrees with me. We both think it's Beth, but neither one of us has told my aunt or uncle. If it isn't Beth, well, you can imagine how terrible we'd feel, stirring up such heartbreak."

"And may I ask who your aunt and uncle are?"

"Sandra and Peter Devargas. They're in their seventies, but still strong. They have five other children, and lots of grandchildren, but that doesn't take the place of Beth."

"Of course not."

"I'm sure they'd like to know . . . give her a proper burial if it is . . ."

The voice on the other end choked up.

"I'm sorry. I'm sure you've had dozens of calls, all of them thinking that the picture is a loved one."

"We have, but we take each phone call seriously. What happened to your cousin?"

"She and her husband vanished into thin air thirty-two years ago."

"Do you have the date, month, or year?"

"June of 1976."

Finally something concrete. Hallelujah. "Where were they living at the time, Mrs. Alvarez?"

"Please call me Cathie. They were living in Los Angeles . . . somewhere in the San Fernando Valley, but I don't know the exact address. I've lived in Long Beach for the last fifteen years. My family is from Santa Fe, New Mexico."

Again Decker felt as if he were talking to the right person. Santa Fe had lots of Native Americans. "And you say Beth's parents are Peter and Sandra Devargas?"

"Yes. They live in Santa Fe right near the Plaza. Do you know Santa Fe?"

"Uh . . . Sergeant Dunn, are you still on the extension?"

"I am."

"Sergeant, do you know where the Plaza is in Santa Fe?"

"It's the center of town."

"Exactly," Cathie answered.

Decker said, "Do you have the Devargases' address and phone number?"

"Of course, but I feel funny having you call them up just like that."

Quickly, Decker moved on. He'd come back to the parents. "How did Beth and her husband come to live in L.A.?"

"Beth married her high school sweetheart. Manny Hernandez—the BMOC. Star quarterback, just dynamite in the looks department. Every girl in the school had a crush on him, including me. But being as I was only ten at the time, I was happy that Beth got him . . . we kept him in the family. Anyway, they moved to L.A. probably for a variety of reasons. I remember my mother telling me that Beth wasn't happy at first, that she missed her family. But then she adjusted. As they tell it, she didn't call for a week and when they tried to reach her, the number was disconnected. My aunt and uncle flew out to L.A. a week later, but Beth and Manny had moved out of their apartment. From that point on, no one ever saw or heard from them again. They simply vanished."

"And this was June of '76?"

"June tenth, I think. I think their disappearance even made the evening news."

"Dunn, you want to see if you can pull up the case on the computer. I'm going to do the same."

"I've already logged on," Marge said. "Oliver's on it as well."

"Bring up any kind of photographs you can." Decker returned his attention to Cathie Alvarez. "Okay, I'm inputting the data into my computer as we speak. I just need you to stay on the line a little longer until I can . . ." Decker typed the information into the data bank. "We've been diligently looking at missing-persons files in that time frame, but we've been looking for women only. Maybe this was filed . . . okay, okay. Here we go . . . I have a missing-persons case: Ramon and Isabela Hernandez, dated June thirteenth, 1976—"

"That's the one, Lieutenant. They anglicized their names, which we all did to be more American. Ramon and Isabela became Beth and Manny."

"Let's see if I can find a picture . . ."

Marge burst into the room and shoved a printout of a photograph under his nose. Oliver followed on her heels. He said, "We've got a hit!"

Two separate pictures. One appeared to be a high-school-graduation picture of Beth—more formally, Isabela—a sweet-faced brunette with a wide smile. The second snapshot was a wedding photograph: the same fresh-faced girl in a white dress and veil posed next to a somber but handsome, strapping lad with pouting lips and dark brooding eyes.

The boy was trouble in a tux.

"You say Beth wore glasses?" Decker asked Cathie.

"Yes."

"The two photos I have show her without glasses. But it's a wedding picture and what looks like a high-school-graduation picture. Most girls in that situation would pose with their glasses off."

"That's certainly true. So you have a picture of Manny as well?"

"His wedding picture. And he is or was a good-looking guy." Decker's heart was doing a drag race. "I think the Jane Doe we found does look like your cousin Isabela."

"Did you only find Beth . . . or a Jane Doe?"

"Yes, ma'am."

"You didn't find Manny."

"Not where we found Jane Doe, no."

The line went silent.

Decker said, "Cathie, I really need to speak to your aunt."

"All right . . ."

"You sound hesitant. What are your concerns? Is your aunt ill or very fragile?"

"No, she's very strong . . ." A sigh. "It's a cultural thing, Lieutenant. Not that there is a good way to tell my aunt this news, but I think you'd get much more cooperation if you visited her personally."

"Thank you for telling me. I had every intention of going out to Santa Fe, but I thought it might be less shocking if I called her first."

"I understand, but I really think . . ." She cleared her throat. "You know, I visit my parents all the time. The trip is not a hard one. Southwest goes into Albuquerque and it's an hour's drive from the airport to Santa Fe."

"We'll pay for your ticket and your expenses—"

"I wasn't asking for a free ride."

"You're helping us with official business, you're certainly entitled to one. Can you hold on while I bring up the Southwest Web site?" He inputted the data. "Here we go. It's ten-thirty right now. There is a four-forty nonstop from LAX to Albuquerque. Is that a possibility for you?"

"You mean you want to go out *today*?"

"Yes, ma'am. The sooner the better."

"Oh my . . ." Again her voice was clogged with emotion. "I have to c ll my husband and let him know. I should be able to make the trip. It sounds fine."

"Thank you, thank you. Are there any expenses that we're going to need to reimburse you for? Like child care maybe?"

"I suppose that must mean I sound young. Thank you for the compliment. My kids are out of the house."

"You do sound young."

"I'm forty-nine."

"To me, you not only sound young, you are young. I'm going to bring along two other detectives who've been working the case—Sergeant Marge Dunn, who was on the phone, and Detective Scott Oliver. Can you make it outside Terminal One by three in the afternoon? The Southwest lines are always long."

"I'll be there."

"You should be able to recognize us," Decker told her. "Scope out the three people that look like cops."

"Wow, this is so sudden."

"I'm sure it must feel that way. I can't tell you how glad I am that you called. One thing before I let you go. Is Ramon Hernandez's family from Santa Fe as well?"

"Yes, they were from the area. Manny's mother died about ten years ago. He had a brother, but I don't know what happened to him. His father, if he's still alive, would probably be in prison. He killed two people while robbing a convenience store. I heard he got fifty years or something like that. At first, my aunt was positive that Manny had something to do with Beth's disappearance. But the private detective that she hired never found Beth or Manny."

"So as far as you know, Manny is still missing."

"As far as I know, but I don't know everything."

"Meaning?"

"Manny had the reputation of being a bad boy. It didn't bother Beth—she was in love—but it did bother my aunt and uncle. Years later I found out that my aunt suspected that Beth had been pregnant when she and Manny got married. Knowing who Manny was, I can't believe that he wanted a baby. When I became an adult, it was always my theory that they moved to California so that Beth could get an abortion and the families wouldn't know about it. I have no proof, but that's what I think."

"I see."

"Growing up, I used to go to church with my family. I distinctly remember Aunt Sandy lighting two candles at the end of every service. As a kid, I thought one was for Beth and the other was for Manny. After all, they did disappear together. But now, as an adult, I see that there was no love lost between the families even when Manny's mother was alive. The second candle wasn't for Manny at all. It was for her lost grandchild."

"Tragic," Decker said.

"It is tragic." Cathie's voice dropped to a whisper. "It's so very, very sad!"

30

A S THE PLANE descended into Albuquerque, the winds buffeted the fuselage, producing a hard landing. The jet hit the ground with a thump that traveled up Decker's spine, but he was whole and safe and that was all that mattered. Just that little bit of turbulence and discomfort had unnerved him, propelling his thoughts to the last moments of flight 1324. It was a dark space that left him momentarily terrified. He forced his concentration back to the onerous task ahead.

They had come in before dusk, and by the time that they had secured the rental SUV and hooked onto the I-25 North toward Santa Fe, it was dark. Marge drove and Cathie kept her company in front. The boys sat in back. Dunn had been to New Mexico's capital a half-dozen times in the last three years and she seemed at ease on the highway. Within fifteen minutes, the lights of Albuquerque had faded, an infinite sky blanketing the desert terrain with a myriad of pinpoint lights. There wasn't anything to see except a few lit billboards and highway signs stating that they were traveling in and out of Indian territories.

"The area was dominated by the twelve northern tribes," Cathie explained. "They settled the land thousands of years ago. The northern tribes weren't decimated like the Cherokee and the Sioux, although the Spanish didn't treat them as equals, that's for certain. My mother is from the Santa Clara tribe; my father's family, originally from Mexico, has been in Santa Fe for five generations."

The woman measured a little over five four, her weight tipping the scales at 125. She had gleaming black hair that fell past her shoulders, and when she turned her head to talk to the boys in back, the tresses were like a wave of inky silk that swirled about her head. She had light green eyes, a broad nose, and a full face. She had dressed simply, in jeans and a cotton sweater, stating that no matter how hot Santa Fe was during the day, there was always a chill at night due to the seven-thousand-foot elevation.

When the car finally crossed the Santa Fe County line, Decker didn't see much of anything that constituted a town. It took another ten minutes before Marge got off the interstate and onto a three-lane boulevard. Not much traffic interfered with their schedule. It was hard to see in the dark, but Decker could tell that the Western capital was low-rise and almost all the buildings were adobe or stucco and colored in various shades of brown. Many of the structures appeared to be fluid masses without corners and sharp edges, as if fashioned by whimsy. Others were just square boxes. Still, the uniformity of the color and material gave the town a distinct, Old West character.

The hotel where Marge had made reservations was in the center of town, right off the Plaza. It wouldn't have taken more than twenty minutes to check in, but the detectives had elected not to waste any time on triviality. They drove straight to the Ruiz house, pushed not only by a crushing sense of urgency, but also by the very real fact that they were dealing with anxious, elderly people and it was already close to nine.

The house was located in a residential area called South Capital. The streets were narrow, some without sidewalks, and many of the dwellings without clear address numbers, and it took some maneuvering on Marge's part to drive the dowager SUV through the dark alleyways.

Cathie pointed out a dirt driveway and Marge hung a left. The rut in the road dead-ended at a garage.

Two women were waiting outside, the headlights illuminating their bony frames and colorful shawls. Marge killed the motor and turned off the headlights, and instantly the environs went black except for a yellow small-wattage bulb placed over the garage. Cathie opened the car door and dusted her jeans. She went over to the wizened women and wordlessly gave each of them a small hug. The trio made their way through the darkness and opened a back door.

The detectives followed, Oliver closing the door as the last one to cross the threshold. They walked through a toasty-warm kitchen, smelling of yeast and sugar, and down a couple of steps until they stood in a low-ceilinged living room crammed with knickknacks and doodads. Crosses, candles, pottery, tapestries, woven baskets, and folk-art icons graced every shelf and sat on every table. The furniture was rustic and heavy, blending nicely with the thick-beamed ceiling and a broad-planked wooden floor worn smooth by thousands of footsteps. Although it wasn't cold inside, gentle flames were licking the insides of a beehive-shaped fireplace.

The two old ladies had taken off their shawls and wore similar outfits: loose-fitting blouses tucked into flowing, floor-length skirts. Their feet were housed in sandals. Cathie Alvarez made the necessary introductions. Lucy Ruiz, Cathy's mother, had knotted her salt-and-pepper locks into a bun. Sandra Devargas—Tía Sandy, who was Beth's mother—had tied up her gray hair into a ponytail that hung halfway down her back.

Up to this point, Cathie had spoken to Decker with animation and anxiety. But as she spoke to her mother and aunt, her voice was almost emotionless. The two women nodded and graced the detectives with tentative smiles. Then Lucy invited everyone to sit down at a round dining-room table that had been set with multicolored stoneware. As soon as the detectives were in the chairs, the old women started bringing in the food.

First came the warm corn tortillas wrapped in a towel, and served with bowls of red salsa, green salsa, chunky tomatoes, chili, cured mixed olives, roasted vegetables, and grilled chicken. When the food was on the table, Lucy came back from the kitchen with a pot of hot, spicy tea, which she poured into animal-shaped mugs.

Cathie took a tortilla and filled it with the proffered accoutrements. "Wow, Mama, how did you know and Tía Sandy know I'd be so hungry?"

The ladies' smiles were dainty. Sandy picked up the plate of tortillas and offered them to the detectives. "Please help yourself."

Lucy said, "Don't be shy. There's no sense being hungry."

Marge and Oliver each took a steaming tortilla. "Everything looks terrific."

Decker explained that he was a vegetarian, asking which, if any, of the dishes contained lard.

"Vegetable oil only," Lucy responded. "Besides, corn tortillas are not made with any kind of fat. Only flour tortillas, and even with them, I now use vegetable oil."

"It's not quite the same taste as lard," Sandy remarked.

"Yes, lard is better, but it is not good for the arteries," Lucy said.

Sandy said, "I still use lard for piecrust."

Lucy gave her a nod. "Yes, you cannot make good piecrust with oil. It is a choice between what's good for the heart and what's good for the taste."

"It isn't just taste. To get the flaky texture, you need lard."

"That is true," Lucy concurred, "that is true." She took a tortilla and filled it with meat. "Still, I've developed a decent piecrust without lard."

"Yes, it is very decent," Sandy told her. "You make very good pies."

"None of them are as good as your pumpkin pie."

Sandy blushed. "Oh, I don't think that's true."

Lucy said, "She makes the best pumpkin pie, but will only use fresh pumpkin. It's not the season right now."

Marge smiled and said, "Then we'll have to come back in the fall."

"Oh yes," Sandy said. "Please do."

Decker had finished off one tortilla and was working on a second one. He was starved and the food was delicious in the way that only homemade could be. It was a shame that Rina wasn't here. She would have dazzled the two women with her natural ability to converse on any topic. But his wife's favorite subject revolved around anything to do with the kitchen. Rina had an affinity for anyone elderly and into ethnic food.

The women got up and went into the kitchen. The savory food was followed by several plates of dried fruits, nuts, and assorted cookies. They managed lots of small talk. They asked about the detectives without being intrusive. When the polite questions thinned, Decker managed to get the women talking about their childhood. They spoke about how small and rural Santa Fe had been when they were growing up, describing it as a small pueblo town with several naturalist health spas for those who'd been stricken with rheumatic fever and had damaged lungs and hearts. Then they segued into their tumultuous adolescence during World War II, and how everyone gossiped about the secret scientists living in a makeshift, clandestine housing project in Los Alamos.

They spoke briefly about their husbands. The men were out bowling tonight and they'd be back in about an hour. Nothing about children, for obvious reasons.

By the time they had finished with dinner, it was almost eleven. Marge had told the desk at the hotel that they would be a late check-in. Even so, she excused herself and called up again just to confirm that the reservations would be honored.

No problem, the clerk told her.

That was good.

It was going to be a very long evening.

THE MEN CAME into the house fifteen minutes later and ate the leftovers, even though dinner had been included in boys' night out. Peter Devargas was thin and wiry, with light blue eyes and a beak nose. He was bald except for snow-white hair fringing his skull from the back of one ear to the other. Tom Ruiz was squat and round, with a full head of silver hair. He had a broad nose and green eyes and Cathie looked just like him. The resemblance was especially remarkable when the two were side to side.

By the time the men had finished and the dishes were cleared, it was midnight. Marge was fighting to stay awake, Oliver had turned quiet, and Decker kept going by drinking the caffeinated tea. The four old-sters were making them look bad, awake and alert and ready.

Peter Devargas said, "Well, I guess we put it off long enough." He looked at his wife. "My niece says you got a picture of Isabela?"

"Not exactly." Decker tried to explain what they had found and the process of forensic reconstruction. He talked slowly and methodically and no one interrupted him, although they nodded at the appropriate pauses. "It appears that the bones were placed there around thirty-plus years ago. From some specific bony landmarks, the forensic artist re-constructed a face with soft tissue. Your niece thought it looked a lot like her cousin."

"So what you have is some artist's interpretation of a face based on bones?" Devargas asked.

"Yes. Exactly."

"Well, let's see it."

Decker glanced at Sandy. One hand was covering her mouth, the other one was held by her sister. Cathie had taken her father's arm and was leaning against his shoulder. He took out the photograph of the reconstruction and handed it to Devargas.

The old man glanced at the snapshot and closed his eyes. When he reopened them, he was handing the picture back to Decker. "It's her."

Tía Sandy gasped, both hands flying onto her face. Lucy said, "Kata-rina, get Tía Sandy some water please."

Cathie stifled a sob. "Of course."

Tom Ruiz patted his brother-in-law on the back. Devargas's eyes filled with water, but he blinked and it was gone. "When can we get my baby back so we can give her a religious burial?"

"We'll work on that right away," Decker told him. "It would be help-ful if we had scientific corroboration that it is Isabela."

"Dental X-rays," Marge explained.

Devargas looked at his wife. Tía Sandy crossed herself, then slowly dropped her hands to her lap, the interlaced fingers clutched so hard her knuckles were white. Her voice was clear when she spoke. "She saw Dr. Bradley and Dr. Chipley."

Tom Ruiz said, "Dr. Chipley passed away a long time ago, but Fred Bradley's still around. I just saw him at the Plaza's spring pancake breakfast . . . when was that?"

"About a month ago," Lucy said.

"Do you know if he still has his old files?" Oliver asked the old man.

"I'll call him up." Devargas picked up the telephone.

Tía Sandy said, "Peter, it's after midnight."

"He'll make an exception. I know I would. You know where he lives, Tom?"

"I think he lives in Quail Run. He's a big golfer."

Devargas called up information and had the number within a few minutes, waiting several rings for someone to pick up the phone. He said, "Fred, it's Peter Devargas here. I'm sorry to wake you up so late, but we have an emergency situation. You know my daughter went missing a long time . . . yeah, Isabela. Do you still have her dental X-rays? They found some bones in Los Angeles and . . ." Devargas momentarily choked up. He gave the phone to Decker and stormed into the bathroom. Decker introduced himself to the retired dentist on the line and explained the situation.

"Oh . . . okay," Bradley said. "Now I got it." A pause. "I sold my practice years ago to Jerome Rosen, a very nice young man who moved here from New York with his family. Done very well. 'Course I sold him a very busy practice."

"So if anyone would have the X-rays, it would be Dr. Rosen."

"Hold on, young man. It's late, I'm old, and you're moving too fast. I didn't say that Dr. Rosen would have the X-rays, although he does have all my old patient files. But I kept Beth's file . . . that's what everyone used to call Isabela . . . Beth. I kept her files and her X-rays because of the special circumstances, I thought . . . well, at least, I was hoping someday that someone would make this phone call. I didn't want her X-rays getting lost when the practice was shifted from me to Dr. Rosen."

Decker gave Marge and Oliver a thumbs-up sign. Normally, they would have slapped one another a high five, but the mood was too somber to celebrate anything. "That was very smart of you to keep her X-rays."

"Well, any thinking person in my field might consider doing the same thing. Like I said, I was hoping for the phone call. Well, actually, we were all hoping for better news than this, but after all these years, how likely was that? Anyway, if the poor girl was dead, the least I could do is make sure that she was identified. God knows the parents deserve to give her a decent burial."

"When can we come over to collect the X-rays?"

"It'll have to wait until tomorrow. I got to find them first. How about one in the afternoon tomorrow?"

"That would be fine."

"Okay." Bradley gave them the address. "I'll see you then. Good night now."

"Good night." Decker hung up the phone and regarded the men. Peter Devargas had returned, his eyes as flat as his expression. "He specifically kept the X-rays. That should speed things up."

The parents nodded. They were mute and shell-shocked. Thirty-two years had just melted away. The wound had opened up and the pain was unbearable.

Decker said, "I know this is an incredibly rough time, but we're going to need to talk to you about your daughter's life. As you might have suspected, it appears that she was murdered."

"The only bones you found were Isabela?" Devargas asked.

"Yes. Just one person. We didn't find any indication that her husband had died with her, if that's what you're asking."

"It's exactly what I'm getting at," Devargas answered. "'Course you wouldn't find his bones. That's because the bastard did it."

Devargas's voice and accusation could have come from Farley Lodestone's mouth.

"I'd like to find out more about him . . . Manny."

The room fell silent except for Peter Devargas muttering under his breath. "I never liked that son of a bitch. He was bad news from the minute she brought him home!"

"We need to talk about him in detail. As far as we know, he's still missing as well. How about if we come back tomorrow and talk about what happened?"

"What happened is he killed her, son of a bitch!"

"Of course that could be a very real possibility," Decker said. "We'll need as many details as you can give us."

Sandra Devargas stepped in. "I can tell you details."

"When?" Decker asked. "You mean now?"

The old woman slapped her head. "How inconsiderate! You all must be so tired."

"I'm fine, but I know I could concentrate better in the morning. Would you mind if we came back around eight or nine tomorrow?"

"That would be fine. I'll make some breakfast."

"Thank you very much, Mrs. Devargas, I'm sure we'll all be hungry."

Cathie nodded approvingly. It would have been rude not to accept the invitation.

"Come as early as you want," Devargas told them. "I'm sure as hell not going to sleep tonight."

"No we will not sleep tonight," Sandy reaffirmed. "The truth is I have not really slept in thirty-two years."

31

DAYBREAK BROUGHT A crystalline sky against a backdrop of deep violet mountains, a scene so crisp and infused with pure colors that it almost looked artificial. Decker took an early-morning walk around the Plaza, a green square in the center of town. All around were one-of-a-kind boutiques that specialized in regional arts, crafts, and clothing. He saw the Indians setting up their wares on the sidewalk under the portico fronting the old courthouse, placing handmade silver jewelry, pottery, and sand art on worn, wool blankets. By the time he got back to the hotel, Marge and Oliver were waiting in the lobby. Peter Devargas had called about twenty minutes ago. He was ready whenever they were ready.

Breakfast with the grieving couple was a somber affair, but that didn't stop anyone from eating. The meal included scrambled eggs, trout hash served with salsa, beans, rice, and the ever-present corn tortillas served steaming hot. Fresh grapefruit juice and piping-hot coffee were the beverages of choice. When there was nothing edible left to consume, Sandra got up to clear. Everyone did their share and the dishwasher was loaded in record time.

The group adjourned to the living room, the detectives sitting three across on the couch while Sandra curled up in a chair opposite the sofa. She was dressed in a caftan, her gray hair long and loose. Devargas was in jeans and a work shirt. He leaned against the wall, staring out at a large cottonwood tree that dominated the front of his house. Cathie and her parents, Tom and Lucy Ruiz, would come by later in the afternoon.

Marge started out by addressing Sandra Devargas. "Thank you for talking to us at such a difficult time. It would be helpful if we had pictures of Beth and Manny."

"As many photographs as you can give us," Oliver added.

Peter spoke. "We got lots of Beth. I'll want them back."

"Of course," Marge said. "Pictures of Manny would be helpful as well."

"That's too bad because I burned them all," Devargas answered.

"Why do you think he was responsible for Beth's death?"

Peter turned around and faced the detectives. "The boy was a snake in the grass."

Decker turned to Sandra. "What did you think about Manny?"

She didn't speak right away, assessing her thoughts. "He was charismatic, good-looking, the star of the football team."

"He was a running back." Devargas addressed the men. "Fast on his feet and quick with a line or a comeback. Girls fell for it and for him."

"He did have his share of dates," Sandra said.

"All the attention made him cocky." Devargas spoke with bitterness. "Here, he was a big fish in a tiny pond. When he got to Los Angeles, he wasn't so special anymore. To me, he was only special in his own mind."

"Tell the truth, Peter. He had a lot of local fans."

"Well, I wasn't one of them."

"That may be, but you weren't a young girl with a free heart." She sighed. "I think L.A. took him down a notch. In the beginning, they were both miserable. I thought that it would give them motivation to move back to Santa Fe, where they were loved."

"*She* was loved," Devargas corrected.

He was sounding more and more like Farley Lodestone, Decker thought. "Did they ever consider moving back to Santa Fe?"

Sandra shrugged. "If they did, they never told me. Then, of course, they disappeared . . ."

"*She* disappeared, he cut out." Devargas glared at the detectives. "That boy is somewhere out there. If you people are worth a tenth of your salary, you'll go out and find him!"

"If he's out there, that's exactly what we'll do," Oliver said. He turned to Sandra. "Do you think that Manny was responsible for Beth's death?"

"Sometimes yes, but sometimes no," Sandra answered. "I try to give everyone the benefit of the doubt."

"How did they support themselves?"

"Beth worked as a waitress and Manny took on odd jobs."

"The boy was a damn janitor."

"There is nothing disreputable about honest labor, Peter." She looked at the detectives. "He worked as a janitor, but he also took on odd jobs—carpentry mostly. He was good with his hands."

"They were fighting all the time," Devargas said. "There was never enough money."

"At first, there was tension," Sandra agreed. "Later on they got along much better."

"How so?" Marge asked.

"Well, maybe they just adjusted. She and Manny had steady jobs, but I think what really helped was joining the church. It gave them friends with common interests and spiritual guidance."

"It wasn't like a church," Devargas snorted. "It was more like a whacky cult."

"She was raised Catholic." Sandra stepped in. "But over here, Catholicism is often mixed with our tribal customs. I'm Santa Clara Indian, so our children were always taught several ways of honoring the Holy Spirit. We're more tolerant of unconventional worship. So it was natural that Beth would be comfortable in a service that might be a little different."

"This wasn't just unconventional worship, this was a damn cult," Devargas kept insisting. "They were all gonna live together in a commune, probably get stoned on pot and have orgies."

"Peter, you don't know that at all."

"I know that Manny smoked pot all the time."

"Not *all* the time."

"Every time I saw him, I smelled it on his breath. We tried to warn Beth about him, but she wasn't having any of it."

Sandra had no comment to his pronouncement. Decker was writing notes as fast as he could. "Why do you think the church was a cult?"

"Because it was the seventies," Devargas said. "That's what the young rebellious kids did. They got together, smoked pot, and had orgies—"

"Peter, that's just not fair. There were lots of wonderful young people back then. They just had something to say."

Devargas snorted. His eyes shifted between Decker and Oliver. "You two would be about Beth's age. I bet you remember the wild times."

"I do indeed, but I wasn't part of it," Decker said. "I was in 'Nam, then I joined the police force."

"Times two," Oliver said.

Devargas gave them a begrudging nod of respect. "Then you know that these communes were excuses to take drugs and have lots of sex. Beth wasn't that type of girl, but she was smitten by that boy."

Decker asked, "Did this church have a name?"

"Church of the Land . . . some crap like that," Devargas spat out.

"The Church of the *Sun*land," Sandra corrected. "After all, it was California."

"Did you ever attend church services with your daughter?" Marge asked.

"No, we didn't," Devargas said. "We weren't interested."

"I did once," Sandra admitted. "It *was* an alternative service, but I thought it was very nice. The church rented a storefront and there were about thirty congregants."

"Do you know specifically where they rented space?"

"It was in San Fernando," Sandra told them.

Decker said, "There's the San Fernando Valley and the city of San Fernando, which is surrounded by the San Fernando Valley. You wouldn't happen to remember a street name."

Sandra thought long and hard. "I believe it was Becker Street."

Marge said, "Becker Street's in Foothill Division."

"What a memory," Decker said. "You said things got better between them. Did Beth tell you that things were getting better?"

"Yes, she did," Sandra answered. "I remember that about a month or so after my visit, Beth called me up very excited—it sounded like my old cheery daughter. The church had a small plot of land in the back of the rented space and the plants were thriving. That gave her an idea. What if they pooled their money to buy acreage in central California, and tried their hand at organic farming? She thought a collective farm would be a wonderful way to serve God and make a living. I was happy because it seemed to me that the kids were finally developing some much-needed focus."

"The scheme was phony as a three-dollar bill," Devargas said. "And if you didn't know already, guess who was in charge of the money?"

Decker asked, "Who elected Manny to be in charge of the money?"

"He probably elected himself."

"Then the kids disappeared . . ." Sandra crossed herself and looked at her lap. When she looked up again, she was dry-eyed. "We tried to track down some of the church members and talk to them. We thought that the disappearance might be related to the money that Manny was keeping for the church."

"Of course it had something to do with the money!" Devargas said. "When Manny and Beth disappeared, so did the money. We tried to meet with the church members, but they were mad and wouldn't take our phone calls. The few that would talk to us accused the kids of stealing."

"We were getting nowhere over the phone, so we finally decided to visit in person. By the time we got there, the church storefront had been locked and cleaned out."

"When you arrived in L.A., how long had the kids been missing?" Decker asked.

"Two weeks at the most," Sandra said. "The first few days that Beth didn't call, I thought that maybe she was just busy. We didn't speak every day. By the end of the first week, I was worried. That's when we started calling the people in the church."

"I read the missing-persons file," Marge told them. "It was thinner than I would have expected, so it may not be complete. But I sure don't remember reading anything about the Church of the Sunland and any cash that Manny was holding for the group."

"I read the file also," Oliver said. "There was *nothing* in there about that church or any church."

Marge said, "Did you tell the police your suspicions about the church?"

"'Course we did," Devargas said. "I told them about the church and the money and everything. I even gave them the name of that friend of Beth's."

"She was the one person who returned our phone calls," Sandra said. "When it became clear that the kids went missing, she was distraught."

"More like distraught over the missing money," Devargas said.

Marge got excited. "Do you remember the friend's name?"

"She had three names," Devargas said.

"Alyssa Bright Mapplethorpe," Sandra told them. "I remember her saying that she was a distant relative of Robert Mapplethorpe, the artist."

"Do you know what happened to Alyssa?" Oliver said.

"No, I'm sorry I don't know," Sandra said. "I might have her old phone number."

"That's a good place to start," Marge told her.

Oliver said, "Do you remember *anyone* else from the church?"

The elderly couple thought a moment and both shook their heads no.

"I'll tell you what I do remember," Devargas said. "That the police didn't consider it a crime if two grown people pack up their belongings and move somewhere else. People do that all the time, they told me. I told them, 'Well, maybe people do it, but my daughter wouldn't do it . . . worry her mother like that.' That's when I told them about Manny and him being in charge of the church money."

"It's coming back to me," Sandra said. "I remember the detective saying that if Manny stole money from the church, then the church needed to file a complaint and then they could investigate a crime."

"I knew that the church would never file a complaint," Devargas said. "First off, the church didn't exist anymore. Second off, with all the drugs and sex that was going on, I knew they wouldn't get the police involved. For all I know, they were buying the land to grow marijuana."

'Peter, you're making things up."

"I'm not saying it's true, but you can't say it wasn't."

"We hired a private detective to find Beth," Devargas said. "What a waste. He found some of the old church members, but they were no help at all. They just accused Beth and Manny of stealing and cutting out."

"I was hoping he'd find Alyssa," Sandra said. "But that didn't happen. I called her number up a month after the disappearance but the line had been disconnected."

"Who was the private detective that you hired?"

"Caleb Forsythe," Devargas told him. "He died about eight years ago. He didn't do much. Just poked around a little here and there and then asked us for a check."

"In fairness to Forsythe, by the time we contacted him, the case was months old."

"We wasted a damn lot of a time waiting for the police to do something."

"Eventually, they did look for them," Sandra said. "The case was on the evening news. They asked the public for their help. It did jump-start the investigation. The police got many phone calls, but nothing ever worked out."

"This must have been a month or two after they disappeared. I'm sure my baby had been long gone by then." Devargas suddenly turned away and went back to his window, his eyes fixed on the front yard's sprawling cottonwood. Sandra crossed herself and sighed.

Oliver asked, "Do you know how much money Manny was responsible for?"

"Around five thousand, maybe more," Devargas said. "Five thousand's a lot of money to me right now. Back then, it was a *lot* of money."

"Yes, it was," Decker agreed, "but even in the seventies, it wasn't a fortune."

"Crack addicts rob little old ladies for their fifty-dollar Social Security checks." Devargas sneered. "If Manny developed a bad habit while he was out in L.A., five thousand to him might look like he hit the jackpot."

Decker said, "Cathie told me that Manny's mother died a while back and his father was incarcerated."

Devargas spoke in hushed tones. "The acorn doesn't fall far from the tree."

"Martin Hernandez murdered two men in a robbery," Sandra said. "It was a terrible, terrible thing. Still, when Beth started dating Manny, I tried not to let it influence my opinion of the boy."

"Christian charity." Devargas snorted. "Our big mistake!"

"You don't blame the sons for the sins of the fathers. Besides, his mother, Clara, was a gentle soul. Even you have to admit that, Peter."

"That's because she was drunk most of the time."

"She started drinking *after* the kids disappeared, Peter. Different people cope in different ways."

Devargas was silent. He wasn't about to give ground to anyone.

Sandra said, "Clara and I didn't have much to say to one another, although we did bond in grief. She had a hard life. Her husband and her other son, Belize, ended up in prison. Manny was her last hope. After he disappeared, she did become a drunk and a recluse. Five years after the disappearance, she passed on. She probably died of a broken heart."

Decker said, "Would either of you know where Martin Hernandez was incarcerated?"

Sandra said, "He's in Santa Fe Correctional. The prison is a fifteen-minute drive from Santa Fe on the highway."

"Maximum security?" Decker asked.

Sandra nodded. "He's serving out a forty-five-year sentence."

Devargas said, "Parole was denied four times. Somebody has some good sense."

Sandra said, "If he lives long enough, he'll walk out in three years a free man."

"Tragedy of our justice system," Devargas growled out.

It was a pity that Decker couldn't introduce Farley Lodestone to Peter Devargas without engendering conflict of interest. They'd have an instant friendship forged in loss and cynicism. "What happened to Manny's brother, Belize?"

Both of them shrugged ignorance.

"Do you know what he was in prison for?"

"Robbery," Devargas said.

"How old would he be now?"

"He was two years older than Manny," Sandra said. "In his fifties."

"And how old would Martin Hernandez be now?"

"Our age . . . in his seventies or maybe even in his eighties," Sandra said.

"You said that Martin will walk out a free man, if he lives long enough," Decker said. "Is he ill?"

"No, but you know how it is in a small community." Sandra cocked her head in her husband's direction. "People don't forget."

"No, they sure as hell don't forget," Devargas said. "If Martin knows what's good for him, he'll live the rest of his life out behind bars!"

DECKER STILL HAD dozens of questions for the Devargases, but the queries would have to wait. Checking his watch, he was shocked to see it was almost one. In eight minutes, they had a scheduled meeting with Fred Bradley, the retired dentist who claimed he still had Isabela Devargas's X-rays. Lucky for them, Santa Fe was a small town and tourist season with its accompanying slog of traffic had yet to materialize.

Dressed in white slacks, a blue shirt, and white boating shoes, Bradley appeared to be in his eighties: a stooped-shouldered man with thin translucent skin, a gin-blossom nose, and watery blue eyes. He was the friendly sort, living the good life and playing lots of golf. He invited the detectives into his condo, whose living-room window framed a view of a small lake in a nine-hole course. After the detectives were seated, he offered them an array of afternoon refreshments. Soft drinks in hand—Bradley had opted for something harder—Decker thanked the retired dentist not only for his time but for his foresight in saving Isabela Devargas Hernandez's X-rays.

Then Bradley started talking. At first he spoke about Isabela, but then his conversation meandered into all sorts of unrelated topics. Decker suspected that the man would have gone on for hours about "how it was back then" if Oliver hadn't tapped his watch and reminded the loquacious Bradley that they had a plane to catch. They thanked him for the X-rays and headed back on I-25 South to Albuquerque.

The hour ride back to New Mexico's most populated city turned into a two-hour, bumper-to-bumper affair as they hit the rush-hour jam. It was a mad dash to catch the flight, and once they were seated— with Marge in the notorious middle seat—all three detectives let out a uniform sigh of relief. Cathie Alvarez had decided not to go back with them, opting to stay a few extra days to comfort her aunt and uncle.

Beth's X-rays in hand: mission accomplished although the trip wound up producing more questions than it answered.

"We didn't even touch on any relative of Hernandez's family," Marge commented once they were airborne. "Surely there are some of them still among the living."

"What good would talking to them do?" Oliver said.

"It would be interesting to get another point of view."

Decker said, "I have a thought. If Manny Hernandez is still alive, do you think he might have visited his father in prison?"

"Under an assumed name, it's possible," Marge said.

"Maybe even under his own name. Beth and Manny's disappearance was all but forgotten except by a few people. I don't think the current prison officials at Santa Fe Correctional would necessarily know that Martin's son Manny went missing in L.A. in the seventies."

Oliver said, "Santa Fe's a small town. I'm betting that there are still some old-time guards who remember that Manny and Beth disappeared. He'd have to have rocks for brains to sign the log in his own name."

Decker said, "We're still going to have to check the prison logs to see who visited Martin Hernandez. It may lead us to Manny. Most of the current logs are computerized, but they weren't back in the 1970s and '80s." He thought a moment. "The first thing we should do is contact the authorities at the prison, and see if Martin had any recent visitors."

Marge said, "Who visits seventy-year-old men? His wife? Well, she's gone. How about children? One was in prison himself, we don't know what happened to him. And the other one is supposedly missing."

Decker said, "Which means, in my mind, that if Martin has had any visitors, it's either the jailbird son or Manny or both."

"That's assuming that one or the other or both are still alive," Oliver said. "We have no idea what happened to Belize Hernandez."

"He isn't in Santa Fe Correctional," Marge said. "I've already checked that out."

Decker said, "Is Manny's wedding picture the only photograph we have of him?"

"So far," Marge said. "When we get back, I'll call up the local high school and ask for his yearbooks."

"You know what we could use? A current picture of Belize Hernandez. Forensics is going to artificially age Manny Hernandez's wedding picture on the computer. It's helpful to know what Manny looked like back then. But if the son of a bitch is still walking the earth, he'd be in his fifties. We need to know what he'd look like now."

32

R INA SLIPPED A silver bracelet with turquoise stone inserts onto her wrist. "It's beautiful." She kissed her husband's cheek. "Thank you so much."

"You're welcome."

"Where'd you buy it?"

"I took an early-morning walk around the Plaza. There's this strip under the old governor's palace where the Indians sell their jewelry. The particular artist is from the tribe of Santo Domingo. I'm glad I bought it when I did. Once the interviews started, I didn't have a chance to breathe. Too bad. Santa Fe seems like a lovely town. I'd like to go back with you under better circumstances. I think they have a Chabad there."

"Chabad is everywhere. When the pods sent pictures back from Mars, I think I saw a replica of the famous 666 brick building." Rina held out her arm to admire the bracelet. "You have very good taste."

"Thank you." Decker plopped into bed and threw the covers over his weary body. "Man, it was a long day. I am beat!"

"At least it wasn't for nothing."

"That's certainly true. But we're not out of the water yet. We still have to match Beth's X-rays to our Jane Doe."

"You have doubts?"

"The retired dentist, who in his infinite wisdom kept X-rays, is not only over eighty, but a pack rat. It doesn't take a big leap to imagine something getting misplaced."

He took her hand.

"Sorry if I'm jumpy. I get like this when I'm on the *brink* of a breakthrough."

"I know. By tomorrow I'm sure you will have made a lot of progress."

"I certainly hope so. It pisses me off that a murderer has eluded justice."

"He'll eventually have to account for his actions. Maybe it won't be to you or to the criminal justice system, but certainly to a higher authority. What goes around comes around: *Middah keneged middah.*"

"I wish I believed that."

"Sometimes I don't even know if I believe that. But that's the basis of faith, and I'm a woman of faith." Rina put down her book. "These cold cases must be frustrating."

"Most of the time, it's obvious who pulled the trigger. The rest of the time, we stumble and grope in darkness."

"You've made remarkable progress on a thirty-two-year-old cold case." She leaned over, kissed his cheek, and turned off the light. "Now get some sleep."

Decker dry-washed his face in the dark with his two meaty hands. "I'm tired, but I don't know if I can sleep." He threw his head back and looked at the ceiling. Shadows danced above him. "Sometimes I understand an addict's need for drugs."

"I know it upsets you that someone got away with murder, but eventually we all die, and that's when everyone sees that, ultimately, someone else is in control."

"But just suppose you die and that's it?" Decker said. "I mean that's really it! You're nothing but maggot food."

"Maybe that's the case," Rina said. "Since no one really knows, I choose to believe otherwise. Even if it turns out that I was sold a false bill of goods, I think believing in God is a healthier way to live. Faith is for the living, Akiva, not the dead."

"I love it when you call me Akiva. You sound so earnest!" He paused. "So you honestly believe that what goes around comes around, that it isn't just a silly little platitude to make you feel better?"

"I'm sure that's a part of it, but not the entire picture. Don't fret. I have a good feeling about the case. You've identified Beth Hernandez and that's the first step in bringing a killer to justice. And don't think just because he hasn't been incarcerated all these years that he's gotten off scot-free. Maybe he's had to deal with remorse. But even if he is a stone-cold psycho, as you call them, he's had to live, looking over his shoulder, for the last thirty years. Even psychos have a sense of preservation."

Decker smiled. "All right. You did it. You put me in a better mood."

"Good. Now do you think you can fall asleep?"

"I don't know." Peter stretched in bed. "I'm still a little wired. Maybe you can talk about gardening. That always puts me to sleep."

She gave him a gentle slug.

He closed his eyes, but instead of sleep, he was looking at Beth Hernandez in his head. The silence was immediately filled by Farley Lodestone's voice. Whenever he got this way, he tried to conjure up a relaxing image . . . riding horses, taking a long hike in the woods during autumn, making love . . .

He felt a stirring down below.

Maybe he could do more than just imagine making love.

His eyes swept over the clock. It was late and he wasn't in the best of moods and Rina was probably too tired, but he reached out for her anyway. She curled up in the fold of his arm, snuggling into his chest. Her eyes were closed and she showed no indication of arousal. Decker closed his eyes and felt his heartbeat slow. His limbs unfurled and his head got fuzzy. No sex, but all was good.

MARGE WAS WAITING outside the Loo's office when Decker arrived. She handed him a cup of coffee, took the keys in his hand, and opened the locked door. She said, "Did you make an appointment with Lauren, the forensic artist?"

"Yes, I did, and it's not just with Lauren." Decker turned on the lights and sat down at his desk. "We're meeting with someone who specializes in computerized age progression. I've set it for two in the afternoon at the Crypt. And thanks for the coffee."

"Someone brought in bran muffins today from Coffee Bean. Are you interested?"

Coffee Bean was equivalent to the bigger, more ubiquitous Star$s, only it was a California chain. More important, it was kosher. Even Rina bought bakery goods from the local franchise. "A muffin sounds good."

"I'll get them." Marge placed a manila envelope on his desktop. "Jails and schools open early. Look at the pictures and tell me what you think. Be right back."

Sipping coffee, Decker took a moment to settle in. Then he unwound the string that secured the flap to the envelope. There were three pictures. The first was a mug shot—front and two sides—of a man looking anywhere from twenty to forty. Stubble studded a lean face that held wild eyes and a sneering upper lip. He had thick black hair and a keloid scar that zigzagged across a protruding forehead. Not a lot of loose skin there; stitching that mother up must have hurt. The vitals put Martin Hernandez at five six and a weight of around 140 pounds. He was thirty-seven at the time of his arrest. Decker placed the picture faceup on his desk.

There were other facsimiles from the prison: Martin but at a much older age judging by the amount of white hair, scar marks, and wrinkles. There was a particular group that must have been taken on a day when Hernandez had been attacked. The camera had captured a bruised face with two swollen eyes and a split lip. His arms, shown in separate photographs, had been slashed with a knife.

The last series of photocopies highlighted a stooped elderly man in several poses with a golden retriever. With a little bit of shuffling, Decker found a newspaper article that went along with the images. Martin Hernandez and several other prisoners had been involved in a dog-training program called Last Chance. Lifers or near lifers, chosen for good behavior, had been given pound dogs, unclaimed and about to be euthanized. Local rescue agencies had picked up the best of the pups and had worked out a special program with the prison. The selected inmates had trained the dogs in very specific behaviors that would benefit those who were wheelchair bound. Included were jobs such as stopping and starting on command, fetching objects, turning lights off and on, and emergency rescue. Hernandez's pooch had been rated the top of the top, and Hernandez had been voted the number one prison dog trainer.

The old man was beaming with pride. His completely round face had swallowed up his eyes, and his lower jaw was sunken in, the usual by-product of lack of dentition. Still, gumming his way through meals hadn't seemed to depress Martin's appetite. He'd put on a lot of weight since his first mug shot.

Marge came back with bran muffins. "They're vicious out there. It was near-riot conditions. I had to use all my wiles to grab the last two muffins, and in the process, one of them lost its top, which is, of course, the best part."

"You take the one with the top. I'll take the beheaded guy."

"No, I'll take the beheaded guy. I'm on a diet anyway."

"You look great. Why do you need to diet?"

"Dieting is a chronic condition, Pete. Some days are better than others, but you're always living with it." She took a nibble of her muffin. "Ah, now that's good eats. What did you think of the pictures?"

"Manny doesn't resemble his father very much. The mug shots that show Martin at thirty-seven depict a lean, thin, short guy. The wedding picture of Manny Hernandez at twenty presents a stockier, taller man with more rounded features. I don't know how helpful these photographs will be when the computer tech ages Manny."

"I agree," Marge said. "Still, there's something familiar about Martin. I think Manny has his eyes."

Oliver knocked on the doorjamb, then came into the room. He was looking natty in a navy suit, yellow shirt, and white tie. "Sometimes life bites you in the ass, sometimes you take a chunk out of life. I looked up Alyssa Bright Mapplethorpe in the phone book. The woman was listed. Then, when I called up the number, she answered. When I told her why I was calling, she was cooperative. More than cooperative. She was anxious to help. I set us up an interview at ten."

"I'm in," Marge said.

Oliver looked at Decker, who said, "You two go. In my two-day absence, paperwork has multiplied tenfold and has threatened to take over my desk. Not to mention that I do have other detectives who have other cases. I'll see you both at two down at the Crypt."

"What's going on at the Crypt?" Oliver asked.

"We're doing a computerized age progression on Manny Hernandez." Marge brought Oliver up-to-date and showed him the facsimiles of Martin Hernandez. "It would be nice to have a bead on the brother, Belize Hernandez. He's about the same age as Manny and the two brothers might look alike."

Oliver said, "Does that even matter? I thought computerized age progression was done by a canned software program."

"It starts with the canned program, then the forensic artist steps it," Decker said. "There's still a lot of intuition involved."

"That's good to hear," Marge said. "A computer is a wonderful thing. It can render, it can reproduce, but last I heard, it can't create."

DECKER TOOK A deep breath in and out and punched the blinking light. "Hello, Farley, how are you doing?"

"I'm the same, Lieutenant. Just making my daily call to remind you that I'm still around and Roseanne ain't."

"And I'm still working on the case. Right now we're going door-to-door at the condo complex for a third time, trying, once again, to ferret out any possible witnesses who saw or even heard anything coming from your daughter's condo. The complex is a big place, Farley. People mind their own business. Still, one can hope."

"I don't know why you're bothering with witnesses," Farley said. "Just bring in the bastard and beat a confession out of him."

"You know it doesn't work that way."

"Then coax a confession from the sumbitch."

"I wish it were that simple. But we both know it isn't." Farley grumbled. In the recesses of his mind, Decker again wished he could introduce Farley to Peter Devargas. Let the two of them curse the world together. "Farley, the official flight 1324 recovery effort is scheduled to conclude in about a week. If Roseanne's remains don't turn up—"

"You know they're not going to turn up."

"The point is, Farley, once the effort is concluded, we can then make a plea to the public for help. Maybe someone will come forward and tell us something we don't know."

"Like what?"

"I don't know, Farley. Sometimes people who commit murder confess it to a friend or a lover. Sometimes they even brag about it."

"Let me ask you this, then, Lieutenant. Who would Ivan confess to?"

"We're speaking theoretically, because we have no proof of Ivan's involvement. But I could see him perhaps telling a close friend or relative. Maybe even his girlfriend."

"You mean the stripper? So bring in the wench and see if she knows anything."

"Farley, we've already talked to her. She's not saying much, and she isn't at all anxious to get involved."

"So maybe she knows something."

"Maybe she does, but right now I can't squeeze it out of her. Besides, I don't want her to go running to Ivan, saying that we're still suspicious of him."

"He knows that already."

"Yes, he does, but we haven't bothered him in a while. If we get something on him, it would be nice to have the element of surprise."

"Yeah, I agree with you there. I'm still surprised that the weasel hasn't taken off."

"I'm sure he will just as soon as he gets the insurance money. Right now that's the one hold we have over him. I'm hoping that after the recovery is concluded, a televised plea will spur someone to do the right thing."

"I doubt it, Lieutenant."

"You can never tell, Farley. A conscience is an unpredictable thing."

"The bastard doesn't have a conscience," Farley said. "God's an ironic bastard. He only gives a conscience to the good people who don't need 'em."

33

THE HOUSE SAT on the edge of the Venice Canals—Abbot Kinney's dream to bring a bit of the Old World into the subtropics of Southern California. The area was six blocks of interlocking waterways that emptied into the Pacific Ocean. Once the channels had cut through land tracts that held small bungalows and shacks. Thirty years ago, the custom-built houses started to replace the sheds and cabins, and current lot value was well over a million dollars.

From the dream of owning a communal organic farm to a three-story, architectural statement: Alyssa Bright Mapplethorpe had done a sharp U-turn somewhere. Yet, if the woman still harbored any utopian ideals, Venice, California, was the place to live. The area still hosted scores of socialists, communists, iconoclasts, vagrants, and lots of original hippies.

Marge parked in a driveway off an alley, and she and Oliver walked around to the front side. The place was a modern stack of cubes, with oversize picture windows that faced the water. Before they knocked, they stood on a porch containing two rocking chairs with a set of table and chairs, and looked outward. Beyond was a dock that secured two rowboats. Sitting under gray skies, the waters were calm, the surface split by gliding ducks shaking tail feathers, their paddling feet leaving behind a silvery wake. The air was misty and tasted of brine.

Oliver rapped on the door and the woman who answered introduced herself as Alyssa Bright Mapplethorpe. She was slim bordering on scrawny, and in her fifties, with shoulder-length gray hair, a wrinkled face adorned by a tinge of makeup—blush and lip gloss. She was dressed in jeans that emphasized her bowed legs, and a soft, cashmere pink sweater. Her feet were set into running shoes. Alyssa invited the detectives in.

The interior was as contemporary as the exterior, the floor plan essentially loft space filled with chrome and glass. The house had been built to show off the views of the Pacific. Public quarters made up the first level, with ceilings that soared upward of twenty feet, the upper levels reached by climbing a steel spiral staircase. The off-white furniture was simple in design and spare in quantity and contrasted dramatically with black ebony floors.

"Please have a seat and be comfortable," Alyssa told them. "Can I get either one of you anything to drink? How about some water?" She didn't wait for an answer. She walked to the kitchen section, took out three handblown-glass tumblers, filled them with ice, and returned with several bottles of springwater and lemon slices. "I'm always thirsty. I've been checked out for both kinds of diabetes and the tests always come back normal. I guess I'm just one of those people who dehydrate easily."

She distributed the glasses, downed her portion, and poured herself another round.

"I was in shock when you called this morning, Detective Oliver." Her eyes became shiny with tears. "This interview is long overdue."

"We appreciate you meeting with us," Oliver answered. "I also talked to the original lead detective on the Manny and Beth Hernandez case last night. George Kasabian. He's now retired, but he remembered that the church members did a good job avoiding the police."

Tears spilled down her cheeks. "It was the times. After our shock at Beth and Manny's disappearance, we were faced with the conclusion that they fled with the money. As angry as we were, no one ever suggested calling the police. The 'fuzz' was the enemy."

"Especially when the members were heavily involved in drugs," Marge suggested.

"It definitely tilted our decision not to cooperate. At the time it never dawned on me or anyone else that something bad happened to Manny and Beth until Beth's mother called a week or two later. She was distraught. She wanted my help in hunting them down. I told Mrs. Devargas to go to the police. She told me that she and her husband had been to the police and no one from the church was giving them any help."

A big sigh.

"I told her I'd look into it for her. When she called a second time, I got scared. I packed my bags and said good-bye to California without leaving any forwarding number or address. The group could tolerate the possibility that Manny and Beth stole from us. But if something bad had happened to them, we didn't want any part of it. We broke apart. We went separate ways."

"Where'd you go?" Marge asked.

"Back home to Boston . . . to college actually. I threw myself into my studies and didn't participate in any more protests, love-ins, or sit-ins. And definitely no more drugs. That side of me just died. I became an architect, got married, had a daughter, lived a quiet suburban life until my daughter grew up, the empty nest set in, and my ex and I discovered we had nothing in common. The divorce was ten years ago. He stayed in the East, I moved back to California. I had had enough of eastern winters." She took a paper napkin and dabbed her eyes. "I suppose I realized I was coming back to face my demons. My sudden split from L.A. and no forwarding information was so cowardly. It must have been so hurtful to the Devargases. They must hate me."

"Mrs. Devargas spoke very highly of you," Marge told her.

"Ill-deserved." Alyssa spoke through a cracked voice. "Not that I could have told her anything. I have no idea what had happened to them."

"We think we found Beth's body," Oliver said. "Confirmation is being done today using dental records. We're almost certain that Beth was murdered."

This time, the woman sobbed openly. Marge offered her a Kleenex from her purse and they both waited until Alyssa had calmed down enough to talk. "The poor girl. I hope it was quick and she didn't suffer."

"We told you what we know," Marge said. "What we don't know is *who* did it."

Oliver added, "We also don't know what happened to Manny Hernandez. We're open to any ideas you might have." He regarded her intently. She threw up her arms, wiped her tears, but didn't speak. "How was their relationship?"

"You mean Beth and Manny?"

Oliver and Marge nodded.

"Gosh, we were very young and idealistic and frankly addled by weed, so my memories may be clouded. But I seem to remember it as being very good."

Marge and Oliver looked at each other. "Did they fight?"

"I'm sure they did, but nothing that I can recall as openly hostile. She adored him. He was not as effusive: he's a man. From what I recall, he was nice to her. I remember he used to compliment her cooking a lot. Beth was an excellent cook. They were from Santa Fe, New Mexico . . . I guess you know that already."

"We do," Marge said. "Go on. You're a wealth of needed information."

Alyssa smiled. "You're being so nice. And I know deep inside you must think I'm a horrid bitch."

Oliver said, "Tell us about Beth's cooking."

"Oh . . . well, she made wonderful traditional dishes. Manny loved to eat and he always said that Beth should be promoted to a chef instead of a waitress . . . gosh, it's all coming back to me. Beth worked as a waitress. I suppose you know that as well."

Marge did, but confirmation was always good. "Manny was a janitor from what I understand."

"Yes, he cleaned apartment houses and offices. But he was also a talented carpenter. He designed the layout of the church—the chapel, the offices. He built the pews and the altar. Manny was a good guy. That's why we trusted him with the money for the farm . . . do you know about that?"

Oliver said, "From what we were told, all the members pooled their money and bought an organic farm up north."

"Actually, we were going to buy land and turn it into an organic farm. Manny was busy working on plans for communal living quarters. He and Beth were the last people we thought would steal."

Marge said, "We've heard that Manny could be abrasive."

"Abrasive?" Alyssa shook her head. "I wouldn't say that. If you want to find his weak spot, I'd say he was prone to grandiose thinking. He had drawn up plans for an entire industry—a farm, a barn, a corral, a livestock grazing area, and a gigantic house and guesthouses. We had to tell him to scale it back. First of all, we could never raise that much money. Second, none of us knew anything about farming. We wanted to start off small."

"How did he react to your criticism?" Marge wanted to know.

"It wasn't criticism." She poured herself another glass of water and drank it quickly. "It was . . ." A sigh. "From what I remember, he just modified the plans into something more manageable. Our goal was to save twenty thousand dollars for a down payment. We had about seven thousand in the bank, and that was pretty good considering we were living on a wing and prayer."

"A lot of money back then," Oliver said. "Certainly a good haul if you were a thief."

"Manny wasn't the only one on the signature card. As I recall, he insisted that someone else besides Beth and him be allowed access to the money. If something happened to them, he didn't want the group not to be able to withdraw the money."

Marge's ears perked up. "Who else was on the card?"

"Christian Woodhouse."

"Do you know what happened to him?"

"Sort of. I tracked him down and called him up after my divorce. I heard he was divorced as well. Currently he's the headmaster of a prep school in Vermont."

"You dated?"

"For about a month. It didn't work out, but we left on good terms. I have his number, but I'm sure he can't tell you anything about Beth and Manny, either."

"Why's that?" Oliver asked.

Alyssa rattled the ice cubes in her tumbler and drank up whatever water was left. "When Mrs. Devargas called me and asked if I had heard from Beth, the first thing I did was go over to the apartment. When they didn't answer, I had the manager open the door. It was cleaned out. At that point, my first thoughts were about the money. I called up Christian and we went over to the bank and checked on the cash. I was there when the teller told him the account had been closed."

"It doesn't mean that Beth and Manny had closed it," Oliver told her.

Alyssa looked confused, but then she understood what they were saying. "You think Christian killed them and cleaned out their apartment and the bank account?" She laughed. "No, no, no. Christian asked for a copy of the withdrawal statement. A copy was sent to him a few days later and Manny's signature was on it. I suppose I shouldn't have been surprised, but I was. A few guys from the church went looking for them."

She shook her head.

"That was a bust. Finally, I phoned Mrs. Devargas and told her that they had left—I left out the stolen money because I didn't want to make her feel bad—and I suspected that maybe they were on their way back home."

"Why did you suspect that?" Oliver inquired.

"Where else would they go?"

No one spoke.

Alyssa said, "Anyway, we agreed that we'd call each other if either one of us heard from Beth and Manny. Well, you know how that went. Your call this morning was the first I've heard about either of them in years."

"Do you think Manny murdered Beth?"

"Anything's possible, but I don't think so," Alyssa said. "There was never any indication that they were anything else but happily married. How should I put this?"

A pause.

"It was the times. We had an open community, if you know what I'm getting at."

"Free love," Oliver said.

"It's been a while since I've heard that term." Alyssa gave a sad smile. "As far as I know, when things got . . . passionate." She cleared her throat. "Neither Beth nor Manny participated except with each other. I had been a close friend of Beth's. If she was doing someone on the side, she would have told me."

Marge was trying to develop a motive for Manny wanting Beth dead. She said, "Maybe Manny wanted get into the action and maybe Beth said no. Maybe he got angry with her and struck her. Is that possible?"

Again, Alyssa just shook her head. "If Manny had wanted to participate, Beth would have gone along with it. Manny was more about food and drugs than about sex. He loved his pot, he loved his frijoles and carne. I don't remember anyone in the group having a violent temper. We were all about love and peace, Detectives. To be honest, most of the time we were stoned on weed or flying on acid. Whenever we held a private church service, we smoked weed."

"What was the difference between your private and public service?"

"Well, every Sunday we tried to do a more traditional service to attract new people. It was a mixture of Christianity, Judaism, Unitarianism, and some Indian tribal customs that we learned from Beth and Manny. The public service was conducted without drugs. If we felt that the members would fit into our lifestyle, we'd invite them to our private session. We'd meet like twice a week and that's when the drugs, booze, and sex began to flow."

Marge replayed Peter Devargas's summations about the Church of the Sunland. He had been pretty much on target. "Did Beth and Manny go to these meetings?"

"Oh, sure. They got drunk or stoned with us."

"What about the sex part?"

"I told you, I don't think so. I do remember Manny being wasted a lot. Beth always had to drive home."

Oliver said, "This is all very illuminating. But it doesn't explain why we found Beth's body and not Manny's."

"So you do suspect him despite what I've told you."

"He's still an unknown as far as we're concerned," Marge said.

"Do you think he's alive?"

"It's possible," Marge said. "Do you have any old pictures of him?"

"No. When I went back to Boston, I really finished with that stage of my life. I chucked everything and threw myself into my family and my career. The name Mapplethorpe opened doors."

"Are you related to Robert Mapplethorpe?"

"Third cousins," Alyssa said. "I met the man once or twice, but we were hardly close. Being an architect, I was way too bourgeois to be considered acceptable by his crowd. Anyway, that's immaterial. The answer is no, I don't have pictures of either Beth or Manny."

"You don't have any old group pictures perhaps?"

"I saved a couple of pictures of Christian Woodhouse. I'm sure you figured out that we had a thing going on. Maybe Christian has some old pictures. I'll give you the number I have if you want, but it's ten years old."

"It's a start," Oliver told her.

She got up and told them she'd be right back. When she was out of earshot, Oliver asked Marge what she thought.

"Her account doesn't match what Peter Devargas had to say about Manny."

"So you think she's more credible about Manny Hernandez than the old man?"

"Peter Devargas is hurting. He's looking for a scapegoat. But there are the facts. We found Beth's bones but not Manny's. The guy is still missing and now we have a witness who says that she saw the withdrawal slip with Manny's signature on it, proof that he did abscond with the cash. Peter Devargas's conclusion is a logical one."

Alyssa returned with a slip of paper. "Christian's phone number, his cell number, and his address. Don't call him at work. It's a real snooty prep school and I don't think the board would approve of his past."

"We'll keep that in mind," Oliver said. "Anything else you'd like to tell us?"

"If you talk to Sandra Devargas, send her my best. Tell her I'm very, very sorry."

"You know I have her phone number," Marge said. "You can call her yourself."

Alyssa nodded and blinked tears. "Yes, that would be the honorable thing to do. Do you have the number on you?"

"No, but she's listed in the Santa Fe directory." Marge gave her the street number.

Alyssa wrote it down. "No gain without pain, right?"

Marge nodded, although that was a warm crock of shit. There were some people who fell into mucho gain just by being born to filthy-rich parents. And there were others—like Sandra and Peter Devargas—who had very little gain but tons of pain.

34

B ECAUSE THE COMPUTER lab was on the second floor of the morgue, Decker could digest his lunch without interference from the charnel-house smell that emanated from the bottom of the Crypt. Not knowing what traffic would be like, he had allowed himself plenty of travel time, arriving at the coroner's complex fifteen minutes early, just as Marge and Oliver were pulling into the lot. The trio met outside and swapped notes. Oliver was finishing the last of a peanut-butter-and-jelly sandwich while Marge gave Decker the abridged saga of the Church of the Sunland.

"We need to talk to Christian Woodhouse, more for the sake of completeness than anything else."

"You don't think he was involved?" Decker asked. "He had access to the money."

Oliver swallowed with difficulty. The sandwich was more peanut butter than jelly. "We both came away thinking that Alyssa Bright Mapplethorpe was credible. She was there when Christian tried to take out the cash and they both saw Manny's signature on the withdrawal slip. We found her story believable."

Decker looked at Marge. "And you also believe Alyssa's assessment of Manny being a nice guy?"

Marge popped a mint into her mouth. "The verdict's still out on that one."

Oliver said, "Look, Loo. I could buy Woodhouse as a suspect if there had been remains belonging to Beth *and* Manny. But because we only found Beth, Marge and I feel that the main focus of the investigation should be on what happened to Manny Hernandez."

"Agreed," Decker said. "But give a call to Woodhouse anyway and just sound him out." He addressed Marge. "Did you round up a picture of Belize Hernandez?"

"I did," she said proudly. "Hold on for just a moment . . ." She rummaged through her purse and pulled out several black-and-white facsimiles. "Currently, Belize isn't in the New Mexico prison system, so I don't have any recent photographs of him." She handed him a sheet of paper. "I did get Belize's mug shot from 1973. He was arrested for breaking and entering and did a little time in a prison in southern New Mexico."

Decker regarded the badly printed copy. The boy had been just a smidge over eighteen when he had been arrested for the felony. He was stocky, with round eyes and a soft round face. His hair was cut marine short but with the long sideburns that were fashionable in the seventies.

Marge noticed the intense look on Decker's face. "What is it, Pete?"

"He looks really familiar, but I can't place him."

"He looks familiar because he looks a lot like Manny Hernandez." Marge handed him the other copies. "These are high-school yearbook photos of both boys."

Decker compared the high-school pictures. They did look similar, but Decker couldn't shake the feeling that he had met this guy before. He gave the copies back to Marge. "I got a call from forensics about an hour ago. We have a positive ID on Beth Hernandez from her dental records. God bless Fred Bradley."

"The forensic computer tech is in the process of buttressing up the

ID by superimposing the Jane Doe skeleton onto Beth's wedding picture, but the dental is a sure thing."

Marge said, "Did you call the parents yet?"

"Yes, I did. You can imagine how pleasant that was. Right now they're focusing their attention on getting the remains back for a proper burial." His emotions seeped in for just a moment, then he went back to work, skimming through the faxes. "These pictures will help us in the age progression of Manny. Let's go see what the wonders of modern technology can do for the science of criminology."

NORTON SALVO WAS in his late twenties, a soft and pinkish-white man with small, hooded eyes, resembling a Darwinian creature that had lost its sense of sight by living in perpetual darkness. He blinked often and Decker surmised that Norton either had dry eyes or a nervous tic. He wore a white shirt—no pocket pencil liner—black pants, and sneakers with white socks. The computer tech was congenial, though, offering a firm, dry handshake to each of the detectives. He spoke with the eagerness of an 1849 prospector, delighted to share his understanding of the newest in forensic software.

The computer lab was compact, but since it was almost devoid of furniture, it could hold the group of five just as long as everyone didn't mind the closeness of a crowded elevator. The space had two desks and two chairs and nothing else. Perched on a desktop were four computer monitors as well as other machinery that Decker couldn't identify. Norton used the scanner to input the facsimiles given to him by Marge Dunn. When he had finished, he gave the faxes to Lauren Decanter. The forensic artist was excited to be part of the group and studied the photographs with great intensity.

Salvo said, "The first thing the program needs to do is measure the cranial and facial dimensions from the photographs. While that's booting up, you want to see the superimposition of Beth Hernandez with the skull?" He didn't wait for an answer. He clicked his mouse, and within a few seconds Beth's high-school photograph appeared on the biggest of the monitors. "Okay, here we have Beth Hernandez. And over here . . ."

Another click of the mouse produced a split screen—Beth on one side, the skeleton on the other.

"Here is an angle match radiograph of your Jane Doe. Now, if we superimpose one on top of the other . . ."

The matches of the landmarks said it all, from the orbits of the eyes to the deteriorated bridge of the nose. These images together with the dental X-rays were proof enough for even the biggest skeptics.

"If there's a trial, I'm sure you'll be asked to testify," Decker said.

"Not a problem. The only thing that doesn't line up nearly perfectly is the indentation around the periphery of the skull where her head was bashed in."

A beep sounded. "All right, here we go," Salvo said. "We've got our two-dimensional faces and the computer is adding an underlying skeleton. In age progression, the computer essentially does the same thing that Lauren does. It pinpoints anatomical landmarks and then goes from there. The computer doesn't take into consideration anything intuitive. That's why Lauren's input is so valuable."

"You make me blush," Lauren said.

Norton smiled. It was shy and boyish. "So I'm going to ask the program to age the soft tissue for thirty years."

"Adding in the wrinkles and the bags and the lines," Lauren said. "As you get older, the collagen breaks down."

"Here we go." Salvo clicked the mouse and the computer spat back an image. Manny was now fifty-five with a full face that had been incised with wrinkles. His nose had broadened, his eyes were underlined with bags, and his mouth had widened, his lips thin, the corners of his mouth turned down. His once-dark hair was streaked with gray.

Lauren asked. "What did this guy do for a living before he disappeared?"

"He was a janitor," Decker said.

Marge said, "Alyssa Bright Mapplethorpe told us that he was a very talented carpenter."

Lauren said, "Do you think this guy would have had a desk job?"

"With a father and a brother in prison, not too likely," Marge said. "I'm still wondering if he's in the prison system somewhere."

"So if he were alive today, what would he do to support himself?"

"Probably what all the cons do," Oliver said. "A roofer."

"Maybe a framer, since he has carpentry experience," Decker said.

Salvo said, "In either case, that's sun exposure."

Lauren said, "And viewing the occupation and family history, he probably also smokes."

"A good bet," Decker said. "From the two pictures, his eyes look brown, but his brother has dark blue eyes. So he could be fairer than he looks."

"That would mean lots of liver and sun spots," Salvo made some modifications and the face returned, but this time leaner, older, and more desiccated. His hairline had receded, exposing a lined forehead and sparse tresses. "What about the teeth? If he smokes and drinks, chances are he's lost a couple of teeth in the process." Another click and the front part of his mouth caved in. "What do you think?"

Decker stared at the image. With his eyes still on the monitor, he said, "What do you think, Lauren?"

She regarded the computer image. "You're not happy with it."

"How can you tell?"

"I'm a professional face reader. What don't you like, Lieutenant?"

Decker finally took his eyes off the screen. "Let me see the faxes again."

Lauren handed them to him. "I know what's probably bothering you. Both Manny and his brother have round faces. Your image of Manny doesn't conform to the computer image because it looks way too lean."

"You nailed it," Decker told her. "If Manny were alive today, I think he'd be heavier."

"A football player gone to seed," Lauren remarked.

"You've got it," Decker said. "Even Manny's father, who started out being thin and wiry, put on weight."

"Prison food is high in fat, sugar, and carbohydrates," Marge said.

"Aren't meals supposed to be nutritionally balanced?" Lauren asked.

"I'm sure there's protein somewhere on the menu," Marge said, "but you don't keep the groundlings quiet by feeding them salad."

Salvo said, "If I plump up the face, I'm going to have to take away some of the wrinkles."

"Fat is a great filler," Lauren said. "Cosmetic surgeons use it all the time to smooth out wrinkles."

Salvo clicked some buttons on the computer and the next face that appeared was fuller and less wrinkled.

But Decker still wasn't satisfied.

"The old man gained a *lot* of weight in prison. This guy started out stockier. To me, he still looks too thin."

Oliver said, "Loo, if he worked construction, maybe he did more exercise and was thinner than his old man, who has been sitting on his ass in prison for the last fifty years."

Decker shook his head. "Logically, you're right, Oliver, but I just have an image of this guy as someone I've seen before. Indulge me. Put some more fat on his face."

Salvo complied. The next image showed a clearly rotund man with a smooth face.

Lauren said, "You know, heavier older men, more often than not, have more head hair than lean men their age. I don't know why that is, but it's true. Maybe it has to do with hormone levels. In any case, give him a little more hair, Norton."

"Will do." Again he played with the mouse. "What do you think?"

Again, Decker looked at the picture of Manny's father, Martin. "Cave in his chin a little . . . like his dad has."

Salvo complied and the five of them stared at the image. Marge scratched her head and turned to Decker. "You're right about one thing, Pete. This guy looks familiar."

"He does?" Oliver said.

"Yes, he does . . ." Decker's heart started racing, but he shook his head in disbelief. There were coincidences and there were *coincidences*.

Rina's words: *What goes around comes around.* Middah keneged middah.

The aphorism was nothing more than a cliché, but sometimes adages became clichés because they were true.

"Give the guy some half-glasses."

"Why?"

"A gut feeling. Please?"

"Sure." A minute later the revised image appeared on the monitor.

"Holy shit!" Marge slapped her forehead. "That's Raymond Holmes!"

Decker said, "I.e., Manny Hernandez, whose given name was *Ramon Hernandez.*"

Oliver was confused. "Are you talking about the Raymond Holmes as in *Roseanne Dresden's boyfriend*?"

"Lightning does strike twice," Decker said. "Two missing women and one guy. Of course Marge and I could be wrong and the Raymond Holmes that we interviewed in San Jose could just be a guy who owns a *construction* business who happens to be a twin for that computer image."

"Do you have a picture of Raymond Holmes?" Salvo said. "We could superimpose one image on top of another."

"No, I don't," Decker said.

Lauren said, "Norton, why don't you go on Google-face and see if the site has a picture of him."

"An excellent idea, Lauren." Clicks of the keyboard combined with clicks of the mouse. Within a minute, they were looking at a tiny group picture from four years ago that included Raymond Holmes. He had been one of five recipients of the Golden Heart Award for builders who had participated in low-income housing construction.

Marge said, "You can barely see his face, let alone get any idea of his bone structure."

"I have to agree with you on that one," Salvo concurred. "Let me Google him and see if he's been mentioned in any other capacity." The site pulled up eight hundred references to Raymond Holmes, including a doctor, a minister, a poet, an educator, a writer, and loads of other occupations. "It's going to take up a lot of time to go through each of these references. Why don't you fly up to San Jose and take a picture of the guy with a zoom lens."

"This is the guy that passed the lie-detector test," Oliver said.

Marge said, "The very one."

"If I were Manny Hernandez, as soon as that plane crashed into that apartment and I knew I'd hidden a body there, I would have rabbited."

"Well, he didn't rabbit then, but I'm sure he's rabbited by now," Decker said. "When we talked to him, I, being an idiot, told him that the body we found in the apartment wasn't Roseanne Dresden. I think in the back of his mind, Raymond Holmes was hoping that we'd mistake Beth's body for Roseanne."

Oliver made a face. "You would think that he's seen enough bad TV to know how identifications are made."

Marge said, "Since the body was badly burned, I'm sure he thought it wouldn't be so easy to identify, that we didn't have enough biological material to identify the remains as Beth Hernandez. And after passing the lie-detector test, he was feeling secure."

"Can someone fill me in, just because I'm here?" Salvo asked.

Marge said, "Raymond Holmes was Roseanne Dresden's lover. She supposedly died in the crash of 1324, but we never found her body. We went up north and gave Raymond a lie-detector test about murdering Roseanne Dresden. He passed. Either he's a stone-cold psycho or he didn't murder her."

Decker held up a finger. "Even if Holmes was feeling secure about Roseanne, once we put a face on the Jane Doe, he has to feel nervous."

"What if he didn't know that we put a face on Jane Doe?" Salvo asked.

Marge said, "It was on the front page of the L.A. *Times*."

"He doesn't live in L.A.," Salvo said. "Maybe he doesn't read the L.A. *Times*. I don't."

"What do you read?" Marge asked.

"I'm a computer guy," Salvo said. "I get all my news online. If you had a good, current photograph of him, I could maybe superimpose the two images."

Marge said, "We could go up to San Jose with a camera and hope for the best."

Decker said, "Let me regroup for a moment." He tapped his toe. "Okay. Looks can be deceiving, so let's go back to basic police work. We need to find out everything we can about Raymond Holmes. And that means another trip back up to San Jose. We go to the hall of records and pull everything we can on this guy. In the meantime, he sells renovated houses for a living. Oliver, he doesn't know you. If Holmes is still around, you figure out how to approach the guy and take pictures of him."

"Cakewalk. I'll be a prospective buyer."

Decker said, "We should check the visitation logs of Santa Fe Correctional and find out if Raymond Holmes has ever visited Martin Hernandez. Maybe we'll get lucky."

"Where does that leave Roseanne Dresden?" Oliver asked. "Do you think this guy killed both women?"

Marge said, "Roseanne made it back into Burbank."

"Maybe Holmes came down on the same flight as her and killed her in L.A."

"Scott, we checked the passengers list coming down. Holmes wasn't on it."

"Maybe he used a pseudonym."

Decker rubbed his temples. "I don't want to think about that possibility yet. First let's find out if Raymond Holmes is Ramon Hernandez. Right now I can only deal with one headache at a time."

35

IF RAYMOND HOLMES was worried about his cover being blown, it wasn't apparent from his daily actions. The contractor remained in San Jose, posing as a solid citizen. Perhaps he was, although the big man was a near perfect double for the age-progressed image of Manny Hernandez. Oliver also found him vaguely disreputable. Not that Holmes was a hard sell. His pitch was the opposite—feigned apathy. *His* homes were the best, and the market was *heating up* and the house that Oliver was interested in already had *multiple* offers, so if he was serious, he'd better get his offer in there or he'd just be plain out of luck! Throughout the interview and inspection, Oliver managed to get several good pictures of Holmes under the guise of snapping photos of the house for sale.

While Scott was occupied with Holmes, Marge was sorting through his paper trail on file with the hall of records. Holmes had filed his first income-tax return in San Jose twenty-two years ago, his occupation listed as an independent contractor. That was as much as Marge could get out of the bureaucrats. She'd need a subpoena to see the actual

return. Through a stroke of good luck—a simpatico government employee—she was able to pull his contractor's license, which, as far as
Marge could tell, was up-to-date and legitimate. From his contractor's
license number, she obtained his original application for a contractor's
license in San Jose. From that form, she was fortunate enough to get his
date of birth and his Social Security number.

After an hour on the phone with records in Santa Fe, Marge was told
that there was on file a marriage certificate for Ramon Hernandez and
Isabel Devargas. Unfortunately, Holmes's DOB and SSN didn't match
Manny's DOB or his SSN. Ramon Hernandez did have a birth certificate from Santa Fe County. Not surprisingly, that date of birth matched
the one on the Hernandez's marriage license. Maybe Raymond Holmes
had taken on someone else's identity. Maybe Raymond Holmes was just
some poor schnook named Raymond Holmes.

When Marge and Oliver returned from San Jose, they were no closer
to proving a connection than they had been before they left. As much
as they wanted to, the detectives couldn't bring in Holmes just because
he looked like a computerized age progression of a guy who might or
might not be dead.

The next day, Marge and Oliver handed Decker their meager reports
and the digital camera with a few nice close-ups of Holmes. Decker
read over their writings, then said, "He's lived in San Jose for the last
twenty-two years. Where was he before that?"

"No idea," Marge said.

"Any idea where he filed his taxes *before* he lived in San Jose?"

"I can't get that information without a warrant. And we can't get a
warrant without some evidence."

"What about Holmes's birth certificate?"

"Holmes's date of birth doesn't match Hernandez's DOB."

"I didn't ask that," Decker said testily. "I asked if you could get a
copy of Raymond Holmes's birth certificate."

"How? I don't even know where Raymond Holmes was born."

"But you have his DOB and his SSN."

"I'm not computer savvy, Pete." Marge was holding in her own frustration. "How do I use a date of birth and a Social Security number to locate his birth certificate?"

"What about the Social Security Administration? They have to have had a birth certificate to generate a number."

"Loo, you know as well as I do that they're not going to give me the information unless I have the subpoenas or an executed warrant. If you can think of a judge that'll give me the paperwork with what we have, then I'm willing to go to bat."

She was right. Something would have to break or they were at a complete standstill. "At least find out what paperwork you need to get the information. Also, you can talk to someone in computers upstairs and find out if a birth certificate is accessible from somewhere other than SSA."

"Sure, I can do that."

"I think I speak for Marge when I say I hope we're not spinning our wheels," Oliver said. "We don't have anything on this guy, Loo. I mean, we might have been able to bring him in for Roseanne Dresden, but since he's already passed a polygraph, we've even lost that excuse."

"Too bad we don't have Manny's old toothbrush," Marge said. "It would be easier to get DNA off of Raymond Holmes from an old discarded coffee cup than it would be to crack some of these bureaucracies."

Oliver said, "You know, that's not a half-bad idea. If you want, I could call up the Devargases and find out if they've saved anything from Manny."

"They threw away his pictures, Oliver, I doubt if they saved his toothbrush." Decker thought a moment. "But sure, go ahead. If that doesn't work, how about rounding up a witness who can positively identify Raymond Holmes as Manny Hernandez."

"Like who?"

"My first thought is the Devargases, but even if they did pick out Holmes as Manny, their opinions wouldn't likely hold up in court unless we have corroborating witnesses. How about Alyssa Bright Mapplethorpe or Christian Woodhouse?"

Marge said, "She hasn't seen Manny in thirty years."

"Ditto for Woodhouse," Oliver said.

"Well, they're all we've got right now that wouldn't be considered prejudicial. Make up a six-pack of pictures, and show it to Alyssa. If you can't get any satisfaction with her, we'll work on getting an interview with Christian Woodhouse. Being as he's out of town, let's go with Alyssa first."

"You're the boss," Marge said. "If you're looking for witnesses, you could also go to Santa Fe Correctional Center and show Martin Hernandez a photo array. Maybe he'd be able to identify Raymond Holmes as his son. I know he's an old man and has been in prison for the last fifty years, but it's worth a shot, no?"

Decker hit his head. "Maybe Martin Hernandez wouldn't be able to identify Holmes as his son, but his DNA wouldn't lie. I'm sure his DNA is on file with Santa Fe Correctional. Next, we'd need Holmes's DNA." He looked at Oliver. "Scotty, go back to Raymond Holmes and tell him you're *very* interested in the house. Go buy him a cup of coffee and bag the discarded container. Get any bit of trash that might contain DNA. If we get a fifty percent indicating that Martin Hernandez is Holmes's father, it might be compelling enough evidence for a judge to issue a warrant for his ID. I should've thought about it yesterday. Now I have to justify the expense of another visit."

Decker put the reports on his desk and handed the camera back to Oliver.

"Go download and print the pictures of Raymond Holmes today. Make copies for your records, give copies to Norton Salvo for forensic comparisons, and give me copies as well. Tomorrow, when I'm in Santa Fe, I want to show the photographs of Raymond Holmes to the prison guards and see if he looks familiar to anyone who works there. Lastly, I also want to check the prison logs and see who Martin Hernandez's visitors have been for the last forty years."

Oliver said, "You think if Raymond Holmes is Manny Hernandez and he was visiting his dad, he'd be stupid enough to sign in under his own name?"

Decker said, "If Holmes is Hernandez, the guy's arrogance is over-the-top. Somewhere in the recesses of his mind, he must know that we're eventually going to identify the bones as his late wife, Beth. Yet he's going about his business, selling houses."

"So maybe it's not him," Marge said. "Because if he is Manny, he's got to know that once we identify Beth, he's not only going to be our number one suspect in his wife's death, but now he moved up with a bullet to the one spot in Roseanne Dresden's disappearance."

"Maybe he thinks he's clear because he passed the polygraph," Oliver said.

"We're assuming that this guy knows he might be indicted for murders and yet he sticks around and goes about his business selling houses." Marge shook her head. "It doesn't make sense."

"Crazy," Decker said, "but never underestimate the power of complacency."

A SEVEN A.M. flight was early even for a stalwart like Decker, but he needed a full day's worth of time. Even losing an hour because of the time change, if all went well, he'd make it to Santa Fe by eleven. As he tooled down Interstate 25 North, the traffic was light and the sky was the biggest and bluest expanse that Decker had ever seen. It was sunny and gorgeous: a shame to waste such lovely weather on a visit to a penitentiary.

Santa Fe Correctional was fifteen minutes out of the city, a maximum-security institution that housed a minimum-restrict facility as well. It was a one-story complex on flat ground, the terrain composed in the main of purple sage, stunted piñon pines, juniper, wild sumac, and lots of tumbleweed. The guard tower looked like a mile-high skyscraper against the empty ethers. The air was a pleasant temperature, but as dry as a bone. Decker could feel his lips and sinuses crack by the second.

After presenting his ID at the window and signing in, he passed through a sally port and was met on the other side by a guard named

Curtis Kruse—a man in his sixties with a beer gut that strained the shirt of his khaki uniform. His arms were short but stretched with muscle, his legs were as solid as oak trunks. He had a round face, a double chin, thick white hair, and steel-gray eyes as reflective as mirrors. His hand-shake was firm but not obnoxiously strong.

"Welcome to the Land of Enchantment." Kruse led Decker into a tiny room that held a steel table and two chairs, all the furniture bolted to the floor. Nothing on the walls except a one-way mirror and two video cameras nestled in the ceiling corners. The guard shut the door. "Hope you get a chance to see more than a penitentiary."

"I don't think it's in the cards today, but I told my wife I'd bring her back for a vacation."

"Can't get better weather than this unless you got allergies. The wind's a killer."

"It's as still as stone today," Decker told him.

"Just wait until the afternoon, sir, and you'll find out why Albu-querque's the capital of hot-air ballooning. Anyway, I've been told that you're here for Martin Hernandez. Marty's been a good boy lately . . . lately, as in the last ten years."

"I heard his time is almost up."

"Two years, three months, and some-odd days. He can probably tell you the time down to the minute."

"I'm sure he could. You weren't here when he was originally sen-tenced, were you?"

"Now, that's a polite way of asking how long I've been working at SFC." Kruse smiled. "I've been here for twenty-two years. Before that I was in Casper, Wyoming, in the police department. The missus and I moved out to Santa Fe because the winters are a lot milder. She don't like the cold except if she's skiing. When I came in, Martin was already a veteran."

"Was he ever problematic?"

"He had his moments like most of the fellas here," Kruse said. "I know he was in solitary more than once, but he didn't make it a habit like some of the others. As he got older, you know how it is. The testosterone goes down and so does the aggression. Lately, Martin has reinvented himself as a hotshot animal trainer."

"Yeah, I read something about that in the papers."

"He has a way with the beasts. He should know 'em by this time. He's been living with them for the last forty years."

"How did he get into the dog program?"

"Good behavior and seniority."

"How old is Martin?"

"Seventies. I can get you the exact date if you need it."

"Sure. So you've been here in Santa Fe Correctional for twenty-two years?"

"I said it, so it must be true."

"If it's okay with you, I'd like to show you some photographs. Just want to know if you've seen any of these guys before."

"Sure, I'll have a look."

Decker took out two sets of six-packs with only one array containing a black-and-white close-up of Raymond Holmes. Forensics had tried to make it look as official as possible, but it clearly wasn't a mug shot. To counterbalance the odd photo, forensics had also interspersed six other photographs of similar-looking people, all the snapshots taken with the same camera.

Kruse peered at all the images carefully. He knew implicitly that he was being asked to make an official identification and he didn't want to make a mistake. A minute later he pointed to Raymond Holmes. "This is the guy you're looking for, right?"

"You've seen him before?"

"He's been coming around twice a year for the last, hmm . . . maybe fifteen years to visit Martin Hernandez. What'd he do?"

"You're sure about him?"

"My eyesight is still twenty/twenty. Besides, Martin doesn't get any other visitors. His wife used to come, but she died, I think, years ago. If it would help you out, you can ask some of the other guys. They'll pick him out without a problem."

"It would help tremendously."

"What'd he do?"

"We're not sure yet and that's the God's honest truth. Right now we're trying to identify him. He's going under the name Raymond Holmes, but we think he might be Martin Hernandez's son."

"That would make sense. He comes on Martin's birthday and usually sometime between Christmas and New Year's. And like I said, he's easy to remember because the old guys don't get many visitors and not one who comes so regular."

"He would have to show ID to get in here, right?"

"You want to know what name he uses when he comes to visit Hernandez."

"Exactly." Decker nodded.

"That shouldn't be too hard to find out, Lieutenant. Like I said, he comes every year on Hernandez's birthday and during Christmas and New Year's. Hold on and I'll check the logbooks."

"Thank you. I appreciate your help." Decker laughed. "You have no idea how much I appreciate it. We've been hitting a lot of walls."

"I know the feeling. While you're waiting for me to come back, I'll send in Curly and Doug." Kruse smiled, showing teeth the color of egg yolks. "I betcha a Franklin they'll pick him out first try."

"I'll pass on the bet."

Kruse's laughter was between a snort and a cackle. Decker could hear it even after the man left. Curly came in ten minutes later and picked out Holmes straightaway. He matched Kruse's words about Holmes's visits to Hernandez almost verbatim. When Doug came in, he played the same tape loop as Curly and Kruse. For good measure, a third man named Jimbo rounded out the quartet of identifiers. None of the four remembered Holmes by name, but they all remembered his face and the man he visited. The three guards were swapping Martin Hernandez stories when Kruse returned. He had made a copy of the logbook page dated December 27. The signature was bold, loopy, and very clear.

Raymond Holmes

It would be appealing to confront Holmes right now, but it would be more profitable to get a partial DNA match. Then they could challenge Holmes with the indisputable forensic information and see how he'd react.

Of course the DNA identification was predicated on Martin Hernandez being Manny Hernandez's biological father.

Decker's thoughts pounced upon another idea. He wondered if Holmes had ever been fingerprinted as Ramon Hernandez. If Holmes had been in the prison system in the last fifteen years under any name, his fingerprints would be in AFIS. But since he'd been a model citizen in San Jose for twenty-two years, it was unlikely.

Decker pondered other alternatives. If Holmes had ever been in the military, even under a different name, his prints would be on file with the army. His mind was sprinting past a panoply of ideas when Kruse's voice interrupted him. "I suppose you'll be wanting to talk to Martin Hernandez?"

"That would be terrific."

"You stay right here, sir. I'll bring in the Dog Whisperer."

36

L ED BY CURLY on one side and Kruse on the other, Martin
Hernandez, in his jail jumpsuit, looked like a walking orange.
His girth appeared to measure half his height and his face was
grizzled and gray. His gait was a slow shuffle due to age and leg chains.
They placed him down on one of the bolted chairs and cuffed an ankle
to a table leg. He sat back, crossing his arms in front, his buttocks
spread over the seat.

Kruse said, "You gonna behave, Martin, or do I have to put on the
handcuffs?"

"I'm gonna be a free man, sir." His voice was high and raspy. When
he smiled, there wasn't much tooth matter left—a couple of pegs in
front and a couple of molars in back. "I'm not gonna do nothing to
stop that from happening."

"Now, that's thinking smart."

"Can I trouble you for a smoke, sir?"

Kruse looked at Decker. "Do you mind?"

"Not at all."

"Thanks," Hernandez said to Kruse.

"Thank him," Kruse said of Decker. "Now, I'm gonna take you at your word, Martin. I'm gonna figure you to behave properly. Am I wrong for thinking that?"

"Not wrong at all, Officer Kruse."

"This man wants to ask you a few questions. You answer them honestly and to the best of your ability, okay?"

"Okay, I can do that." When Hernandez spoke, he forced out sound from his throat. "A smoke will help. Maybe a cup of coffee, too. My throat." He cleared phlegm. "It gets dry when I talk."

"So why are you smoking, Martin?"

"Man's gotta have something to do here, sir."

Kruse laughed again. "That's true. Okay, I'll be back with your smoke and coffee."

Decker regarded the con. A multilane highway of scars ran across the man's neck, all of them keloid bumpy and shiny white. It didn't take a genius to figure out what had gone wrong with the man's vocal cords.

Curly told Kruse, "I'm going to get back to my beat. Call me when you need me to take him back."

The two men walked out together, leaving Decker alone with Hernandez. The man's face, though speckled with liver spots, had few wrinkles. Several small open sores had rooted at his left temple, looking nasty enough to be the big C. His hands were worn and callused, his nails were yellow and thick and cut way below the tips of his fingers. He was missing part of his right thumb.

"When are you getting out?" Decker asked him.

"Two years, three months, eighteen days, and about sixteen hours. I served my time. I deserve to be a free man. That's what the law says."

"Are you going to continue with your work with the dogs?"

"Zactly right." Hernandez's head bobbed up and down. "We understand each other. Those dogs that we got . . . they were one step from the green room, if you know what I mean."

The green room was the gas chamber. "You saved them from death."

"Zactly right. The program over here . . . it was their last chance. We train them so they can be adopted out."

"That's nice."

"It was their last chance . . . I was."

"You identify with the dogs?"

"Zactly right. Everybody deserves a second chance. They're not bad dogs. No one understands them. That's the problem. They bite 'cause they're scared. They bite 'cause they're lonely. They bite 'cause they don't got anyone who loves them."

"They also bite because they're not trained and disciplined."

Hernandez smacked his lips together. "But there's discipline and then there's just plain meanness. Yeah, you gotta be sure of yourself if you work with untrained dogs, but you don't crack a stick over the dog's head to just get him to listen."

"But the animals have to be taught to respect your authority."

"Zactly right. It's a good lesson in life . . . to learn to respect authority. It took me a while 'cause I didn't have anyone to teach me properly."

"You had the stick cracked over your head, Mr. Hernandez?"

"Zactly right. My daddy was a mean drunk and he didn't raise me right. If he'd showed a little mercy and a little less stick cracking, I would have been a better person."

"Do you have children, Mr. Hernandez?"

"I do."

"Boys? Girls? Both?"

"Boys."

"And you raised them with a little mercy?"

"I raised them not to be fools."

"Were you a stick cracker?"

"I wasn't much of anything because I've been incarcerated for a long time. It's going on forty-three years. Most of the raising went to my wife, God rest her soul. I miss that woman. She did good, considering what she had."

Kruse returned with two cups of coffee. He placed a cigarette between his lips. After he lit it, he gave it to Hernandez.

The con took a deep drag. "Ah, this is living."

"You smoke it slow, Martin, you're only gonna get one."

"I will, Officer Kruse, I'll do just that."

Kruse said to Decker, "There's someone monitoring the cameras twenty-four/seven, so you shouldn't have any problems. Just look up at the videos and call when you need us to take him back."

"Thanks for all your help."

"No problem." Kruse smiled. "Be good, Martin, you don't have that much longer to go."

"I know that, sir, I think about that every day." After Kruse left, he said, "That's the truth. I do think about it every day."

"I'm sure you do." Decker sipped the coffee: as thick as mud and bitter.

"It ain't easy for an old man to be here," Martin complained. "The cold in the winter goes right through to the bones. My lungs aren't too good. I always worry about pneumonia, you know. Then sometimes, I'm glad to be sick because the infirmary is better than the cell block, know what I'm saying?"

"I get it," Decker answered. "Where are you going to live when you get out?"

"Can't go back to Santa Fe." He took another puff on his cigarette. "I'll get skinned alive. I dropped two people in a robbery. I suppose you know that."

Decker nodded.

"That wasn't supposed to happen. But you get all junked up on drugs and adrenaline and someone moves when they ain't supposed. I had nothing against those two boys, but things just happen when you're junked up, know what I'm saying?"

"So where are you going to go live when you get out?"

"I'll go down south—Las Cruces, Silver City, Carlsbad. Places are hotter in the summer but not so cold in the winter."

"Do you know anyone in those cities?"

He shook his head. "Nope. Don't know a soul." He finished off his coffee. "That's okay. All I need is a good place for the dogs to run around and a nearby watering hole. I'm a friendly sort. I can make friends."

"You seem like a friendly sort." Decker watched the old man smile at the compliment. "Have you kept in contact with anyone on the outside?"

"I know a few people, sure."

Decker saw his eyes narrow slightly, and switched topics. "Your wife used to visit you a lot?"

"Three, four times a week. I told you. She was a good woman."

"Did she bring the boys in to visit?"

"Sometimes."

"Are you still in contact with your sons, Martin? Do they ever visit you?"

The old man shrugged and smoked. "Once or twice, mebbe."

The man was a smooth liar, not that Decker expected anything different. But even cons have different capacities for prevarication. Decker waited until Hernandez's cigarette was down to the butt. Then he looked up at the camera and asked for another smoke.

"That's kind of you, sir," Hernandez said.

"I can be a kind person."

A few minutes later a uniformed guard came in with a lit cigarette. Decker took the smoke and when Hernandez reached over to grab it, Decker pulled his arm back, out of the old man's reach.

"Your boys ever come visit you?" Hernandez was silent, his eyes on the trail of nicotine smoke. Decker smiled and took a puff on the cigarette. "Your boys ever come visit you?"

Hernandez shrugged. "Guess you checked the logbook."

"Guess I did."

"Then you know. So why are you asking me?"

"Because Raymond Holmes isn't your son's baptized name."

"Nope, he changed it."

"Why did he change it?"

"I don't know. Why don't you ask him?"

"I just might do that. When did he change it?"

"A long time ago. You can ask him that, too."

"Give me a rough idea when. Twenty years ago? Thirty years ago?"

"I think he changed it 'bout thirty years ago . . . right after it happened."

"After what happened?"

Hernandez stared into space. Decker took another puff. "You're
wasting precious tobacco."

"Well, I don't know zactly what happened, sir. I wasn't there."

"What happened according to Raymond Holmes, your son?"

"Yeah, Ray's my son."

"You might as well tell me what happened, Martin. You can tell me
Ray's side of the story."

"What do you need with my side? Just ask Ray."

"Ray won't be as . . . credible. You're more credible, Martin. You tell
me what he told you." The old man reached for the cigarette. Decker
said, "First you tell me what happened."

"He didn't tell me much, sir, and that's the honest truth. All he said
is that it wasn't supposed to happen. But you know how it is. When you
get junked up on drugs and adrenaline, things just happen that weren't
supposed to happen."

Decker nodded. "I see." He gave the con the cigarette. "Tell me what
he told you. I can't use what you tell me at a trial because it's hearsay.
Do you know what that is?"

Hernandez took a deep drag on the smoke and didn't answer.

"I heard what happened from you, Martin, not from Ray. It's hearsay. That means whatever you tell me, I can't use it directly against Ray
because I didn't hear it directly from Ray. So *you* tell me what he told
you, okay?"

"You're confusing me. I don't want to get him into trouble."

"Martin, the boy is already in trouble. Big trouble. If it wasn't supposed to happen, tell me what went down."

"They were arguing."

"Who are they?"

"Y'know . . . Beth and Ray were arguing."

"About what?"

"What do people always argue about?"

"Money?"

"Zactly right. Ray kept telling Beth that it was just a loan and that he was gonna give it back. But she was real mad. She wouldn't listen. She said if he didn't pay it back, she was gonna tell on him."

"Where did Ray get the money from?"

For the first time, Hernandez looked genuinely confused. "I don't know. All I know is Ray said he borrowed some money and he was gonna pay it back but that damn girl wouldn't listen."

"All right. They were arguing. Then what happened?"

"It was all her fault. He was gonna pay it back."

"So what happened next?"

"I don't know zactly what happened next, sir. All I know is that Ray said it was an accident. That it wasn't supposed to happen. But once it did, he knew he was in deep shit." Hernandez furrowed his brow, conjuring up the memory. "He was planning on paying it back, but Beth was gonna rat him out. It was that damn girl's fault."

Decker said, "She was yelling and screaming at Ray, wasn't she?"

"She was. He didn't mean to hurt her. He just wanted to shut her up."

"He did more than just *hurt* her, did he?"

"It wasn't supposed to happen."

"I know that, but it happened anyway."

Hernandez sighed. "He was gonna pay it back. She just wasn't giving him a chance."

"What happened after he hurt her . . . or should we say after he killed her?"

"I'm not talking to you anymore," Martin said defiantly. "I'm getting out in a little over two years whether I cooperate or not. You can't stop me. That's the law!"

"You're absolutely right, Martin, I can't stop you. It is the law." Decker took in the con's eyes. "But you know if I put in a good word for you, there is that chance that maybe you can get out sooner."

That gave Hernandez pause—for about two seconds. He shrugged. "Well, the damn boy's in trouble anyway. I suppose what I have to say ain't gonna help him. But it probably won't hurt him much, either."

"Exactly right," Decker said.

Hernandez leaned over, his breath strong with tobacco, his voice an annoying scratch. "It weren't supposed to happen. It just did."

"I realize that."

"The boy was trying to make a clean start! He was trying to do good, to erase the slate and start from the beginning. That's why he needed tʰe money. To get himself back on his feet. He told me he really was gonna pay it back. The girl was just too damn impatient. She fucked everything up."

Decker's head started spinning. Make a clean start? Get himself back on his feet? "Was Manny in jail?"

"No, no." Now Hernandez was very confused. "No, Manny was never in jail."

And then he realized what Hernandez was saying.

Manny Hernandez was never in jail.

Belize Hernandez was a different story.

37

OVER THE PHONE, Decker said, "Yes, I still want DNA, but right now we need his fingerprints."

Over the phone, Oliver replied, "I got to find a surface then. Any suggestions?"

"He's a contractor. He works with grease and mud. What's the problem?"

"The problem is getting him to touch something. He has a recycling bin for scrap metal, a recycling bin for wood, and a final bin for broken glass. I'd love to take something, but it's clear that Ray has no intention of throwing the stuff away. I can't take a sliver from the ground without asking him. And once I ask, there's a chance that he'll get suspicious."

"No, don't do that."

"We can just wait for the DNA," Oliver said. "I have his discarded coffee cup bagged."

"Trouble is we don't have Belize's DNA on file, just his prints. Surely there's some kind of garbage over there that you can pocket that might pick up something."

"Nothing with a clear print, Loo, and that's a sad fact."

"What's he doing now, Scott?"

"I don't know. I left the house about twenty minutes ago."

"No, I mean what specific work is he doing on the house?"

"Oh . . . I think they're tiling . . ." Oliver hit his forehead. "I'm an idiot. I'll go back and ask him for a sample of the kitchen tile to show to my wife."

"See how easy that was?" Decker said. "Is the tile surface polished or rough?"

"It's polished. We couldn't ask for a better surface for latents, except maybe mirror. I wonder if I can ask him if I can bring back a sample of the mirror or do you think that might tweak his antenna?"

"Let's start with the tile. Like you said, it's a great surface. When are you coming back to L.A.?"

"I'll be in the station house between five or six, depending on traffic. What about you?"

"I should be back by then. Right now I'm working with the D.A.'s office, trying to shave some time off the old man's sentence if he testifies against his son."

"That's going to make you real popular with the locals."

"The old man is going to be released in a couple of years regardless of what anyone does. It's worth it for me to let Martin go a couple of years early if I can put Beth Devargas's killer behind bars." Decker adjusted the headset on his phone. In New Mexico, it was illegal to drive and talk unless it was hands-free. With a seventy-five-mile-per-hour speed limit on some of the interstates, the law made sense. "I'm on my way to the courthouse to talk to some of the people. What's Marge doing?"

"Trying to figure out where Raymond Holmes lived before coming to San Jose. We got an eight-year gap to fill in."

"Once we get a fingerprint match, we won't have any trouble pulling warrants for his paper trail. Hopefully, that'll bust this case wide, wide open."

IT WAS AFTER six by the time Decker pulled in to the station house's parking lot. He was tired and would be famished as soon as his stomach settled down from the roller-coaster air ride over the Rockies. There were a few souls still doing paperwork in the squad room, but Marge and Oliver were nowhere in sight. He inserted the key into the lock on his office door, when he heard a voice behind him.

"Lieutenant?"

Since Decker was hungry and grumpy and made no attempt to hide it, he figured the brave soul approaching him must have had some breaking news. Anything less would incur his wrath. He turned around and managed a tight smile. "Detective Bontemps. I take it you need to talk to me?"

"I do, sir, and it's important. I really think you'll want to hear this."

"Not a problem at all." Opening the door, Decker took the key out and turned on the lights. On his desk were a brown bag, a huge plate of chocolate-chip cookies, and a note from Rina.

Dear Peter,
The cookies are from Hannah and they're pareve.
Much love from your long-suffering but culinary-conscious wife,
Rina.

He peered inside the bag—a roast-beef sandwich with coleslaw and an apple. He brightened considerably as soon as he unwrapped the sandwich. "Sorry to eat in front of you, but I'm starved."

"Oh, go right ahead, sir."

"Have a cookie. My daughter baked them."

"I'll eat anything home baked. Can I get you some coffee? I'm getting one for myself. Gotta have coffee with cookies."

"Actually, coffee would be great." He'd finished half the sandwich when she came back. "Thank you, Wanda, have a seat. What's up?"

Bontemps's face was flushed with the excitement that came from discovery. Her hair had been recently cut, exposing a full face softened by natural-looking makeup. Her skin was mocha cream, her lips accentuated by pink lip gloss. She wore a blue blouse, a glen-plaid jacket over chocolate slacks, and oxfords covered her feet. "Lee Wang and I must have canvassed that condo complex three different times. Today the good old Lord was with us. We found someone—someone we interviewed before—but we asked our questions a little different and we got different answers."

Decker's head had been so immersed in the Hernandez boys that he had to think a moment about the assignment. Condo-complex canvassing: the Roseanne Dresden case. They had been looking and looking for any witnesses who might have seen Roseanne coming in or going out on the morning of the plane crash. He put his sandwich down and took out his notepad. "Good. Go on."

Wanda checked her own notes. Her hands were shaking. "The woman's name is Hermione Cutlass and she's a nurse. This time we phrased the question differently. We asked, 'Do you remember where you were the morning of the crash?' instead of 'Do you remember seeing Roseanne the morning of the crash?' We figured if anyone had seen Roseanne that morning, we would have heard about it by now."

"Okay."

"So this is what we got." Wanda cleared her throat. "On the morning of the crash, Hermione Cutlass was scheduled to work the seven A.M.-to-three-P.M. shift at St. Luke's in Simi Valley, but she was running late. Her daughter was home sick with the flu, and Hermione had to wait until a babysitter came so she could go off to work. By the time the sitter came, she was real late."

"What time was that?"

"She thinks it was around seven, when she shoulda been at work already. She remembered running to her car, running through the parking area, not really paying too much attention to what was going on other than getting to her car, when all of a sudden a black Beemer pulled out in front of her and almost crashed into her. She said she had to jump back to avoid getting hit. She was screaming nasty words at the driver, but she was talking to the air. The car just bolted the hell out of the lot. She was so angry that she wrote down the license plate . . ."

"She has the *license* number?"

"She said she planned to report it to the condo board when she got back home."

Decker's heart started whacking in his chest. "So tell me it was Roseanne's BMW."

"Yes, it was, but she didn't know it at the time."

"Good Lord!" He smiled genuinely. "And she's just remembering the car *now*?"

"Y'see, the first time we asked her questions, we asked if she *saw* Roseanne that morning. The answer to that question was no. *This* time we asked her what she *did* that morning."

"Recalling her morning of the crash jogged her memory about the car."

"Yes, but she didn't know it was Roseanne's car. She just wrote down the license number, worked a long day, and then forgot about the whole thing, especially once she *heard* about the airplane crash. That kinda took the wind out of her sails to be mad at anyone. All she could think about was poor Roseanne."

"Okay, okay, give me a minute to digest this." He closed his eyes and opened them. "Does she remember what time the Beemer almost crashed into her?"

"Sometime after seven but before eight."

"Before flight 1324 crashed."

"Definitely before the crash, because she heard about the accident at the hospital." Wanda took in a deep breath and let it out. "When she got home that night, it was all over the condo that Roseanne had died. Everyone felt absolutely sick about it."

"Did she know Roseanne?"

"Casual acquaintance. You know, they saw each other in the Jacuzzi or the gym or the laundry room. It's always awful when someone you know dies unnaturally."

"Yes, it is."

"I asked her, 'Are you sure you're remembering the correct day?' And she said, 'Absolutely, positively.' And then she told me the story. When she got to the part about the car being a BMW, I was holding my breath. I asked her to describe the car and that's when she remembered she wrote down the license plate."

"And she still had the number?"

"In the glove compartment, right where she left it. When I asked to see it, she asked me why. I told her I'd tell her as soon as I got off the phone with DMV. When the license plate matched, I told her that Roseanne drove a black BMW. The poor girl just about fainted. She started crying and carrying on, because she told me that it was probably Roseanne rushing to make her flight. And she said some real nasty things to the driver. In some respects, she said she wished the car would have crashed into her because then Roseanne would have stopped and missed the plane."

Decker nodded. "If it was closer to seven, maybe it was Roseanne rushing off to work. If it was closer to eight, there is no way Roseanne could have made the doomed flight. Can she narrow down the time a little more?"

"No, sir, I tried that. She doesn't remember beyond sometime between seven and eight." Wanda raised her eyebrows and licked her pink glossy lips. "And we got one other major problem. It was Roseanne's car; that is definite because the number she wrote down matched Roseanne's plates."

"But she couldn't see who was driving the car."

Wanda nodded. "It happened real fast. She was in a rush and she was flustered. And the Beemer was in a rush."

"Could she tell you *something* about the driver?"

"She said it happened so fast, she couldn't even see if it was a man or a woman. She thinks there was only one person in the car, but she won't even swear to that."

EVEN WITH JUST a skeleton crew in the squad room, Hannah's batch of forty-eight cookies was gone. Decker had resorted to picking the crumbs left behind.

"Those were good," Wanda Bontemps said. "Ask your daughter for the recipe."

"I think I'm in sugar narcosis," Marge said. "Can I adopt your daughter?"

"You've never seen her before a trig test."

"I've seen my own daughter before a particle-physics test. She can't be any worse." Marge's cell phone rang. She looked at her watch. "Speaking of which . . . It's eight o'clock, it must be Vega. Excuse me for a moment."

Oliver said, "I'm making more coffee. Any takers?"

Four hands went up. Marge covered the cell's mouthpiece and shouted, "Count me in." She talked to her daughter for a moment longer then rejoined the group. They had decided to talk in the squad room because the common tables provided more space than Decker's office. "What did I miss?"

"As it stands right now, the Loo was just saying that it's unlikely that a judge is going to issue a warrant for the Beemer unless we can implicate the car in a crime."

"We're out of luck." Oliver had returned, balancing coffee cups, cream, and sweetener. "There are no outstanding wants or warrants on the car. Ivan may be a murderer, but he obeys traffic signs."

Wanda helped him with the coffee. "Are we still thinking about Ivan as his wife's murderer?"

"What do you mean?"

The newest detective said, "If we get a match for Raymond Holmes as Belize Hernandez, isn't it likely that Hernandez was Roseanne's killer? He did it once to his sister-in-law. Why couldn't he do it again?"

Oliver said, "He could, but something's still not making sense with that."

Marge broke in. "Scott and I were talking about this. Why is the man we call Raymond Holmes hanging around, knowing full well that we found his sister-in-law's body?"

Wang sipped coffee. "Maybe he thinks we can't identify the body."

"Maybe, but I know what Scott and Marge are getting at," Decker said. "There's something out there that we're missing and it has something to do with Manny Hernandez. The old man told me that as far as he knows, Manny's still missing. According to him, Raymond Holmes is Belize, but Martin's eighty and a con, so everything is suspect until we have evidence to back it up. Until we have a positive on the prints, we don't know if Ray is Belize or if Ray is Manny."

"Who's doing the print comparison?"

"I asked for Zach Spector," Decker said. "He'll be in tomorrow at ten. I've already contacted Roswell Correctional. A copy of his prints on file should be arriving here by ten-thirty in the morning, providing that FedEx is on time. In the meantime, if we want to speculate, let's go back to the Roseanne Dresden case. What are we thinking? That her husband stashed her in the trunk while still alive—because she didn't die in the condo—then carted her off and killed and buried her somewhere?"

"That crossed my mind when Hermione told me the story," Wanda said. "But why would he do it in daylight? Why not just wait for the cover of night?"

"Ivan is not a cool cookie," Marge said. "Suppose they got into an argument. Ivan admits that they fought the day before. Maybe she came home early in the morning and they fought again. This time, he got really mad and pushed her. We found her cell under the couch. Maybe she fell backward and hit her head. She gets knocked out cold and he just panicked."

Wang said, "People fall and hit their head, but usually they don't die right away. Do you honestly see the guy throwing her in the trunk and then killing her and burying her?"

"Like I said, maybe he panicked. Ivan accidentally or on purpose knocks her out. He wraps her in a blanket, takes her out to her car, and stuffs her in the trunk. He goes out and gets rid of the body. Then, on the way back, he hears about the plane crash and figures he'll blame her disappearance on the accident. But then people might ask why her car is parked in the condo parking complex and not at the airport. So Ivan drives the Beemer to the airport, leaves it there, takes a cab back to the condo, drives to work, then turns on the faucet, and tells everyone that Roseanne died in the crash."

The group nodded. Decker was the first one to speak. "It's logical, but wasn't Ivan at work by eight-thirty or nine? If the man was racing out at seven in the morning, he doesn't have enough time to find a spot, bury her, take her car to the airport, then find a ride back to his condo so he can pick up his own car and be at work by nine."

Wang said, "Maybe the witness got her times mixed up."

Decker said, "Killing someone in a car in broad daylight is very chancy. So is dragging a body and shoving it into the trunk. There's also a real possibility that her car was speeding because she was rushing to make the doomed flight."

Marge said, "Erika Lessing, the flight attendant who worked the counter for WestAir, distinctly remembers *not* seeing Roseanne."

"A positive witness is better than a negative one," Decker said. "Roseanne could have slipped in without Erika noticing her."

"Of course," Marge answered, "but the bigger issue is that Roseanne's remains haven't been found at the crash sight."

Decker said, "That, together with a witness who saw the car speeding off, is what we're going to use to get a warrant to search the car. If Roseanne was violently murdered inside her vehicle or in the trunk, we would probably find more blood than would be expected, a reasonable amount even if Ivan cleaned the car."

"Assuming he didn't change the carpets," Wanda said. "What if he did?"

"Then that would be suspicious," Marge said.

"Exactly," Decker said. "So before we even bother a judge with a warrant, let's investigate to see if Ivan did anything with the car that would arouse suspicions."

"Like changing the carpets?" Oliver said. "What do you want? For us to start checking BMW dealers?"

Wanda said, "If he was hiding bloody carpets, do you think he'd use a dealer?"

Decker said, "Even so, start with the dealerships. Best place to order new carpets, and there aren't that many of them in this area. If that doesn't work, canvass the independent car-repair shops. Ivan's not a genius but he wouldn't drive around in a car with blood-soaked carpets."

"Yeah, but he seemed really excited about driving Roseanne's Beemer," Oliver said. "Nothing as sweet as driving a car you didn't pay for."

AT ELEVEN TWENTY-SIX A.M., a grinning Decker announced that Raymond Holmes's right finger- and right thumbprints matched the fingerprints on file at Roswell Correctional for Belize Hernandez. Upon hearing the first bit of definite news, the squad room broke into cheers. His matching prints together with the old man's story made the contractor a prime candidate in Beth Devargas's murder, and jumped Holmes to the top of the list in regard to the disappearance of Roseanne Dresden, speeding Beemer and lie-detector test notwithstanding.

With the matching prints, Raymond Holmes's visits to Santa Fe Correctional, and Martin Hernandez's assurance that he would testify against his son in exchange for his immediate freedom, Decker had no problem getting a warrant for Holmes's arrest for Beth's murder. It was signed and sealed by two in the afternoon, and at six in the evening, Decker, Oliver, and Marge were sitting in row 13, seats A, B, and C on a Southwest flight from Burbank a.k.a. Bob Hope Airport to San Jose International. Holmes would be brought in for voluntary questioning the next morning at San Jose PD and proper personnel at the police station had been informed of the mission, ready to assist the trio in whatever they needed.

To everyone's relief, Holmes agreed to come in without the necessity of announcing the purpose of the visit. But this time, he was wary enough to ask for a lawyer. Three hours later Holmes and a gray-suited man named Taz Dudley waited for Decker in an interview room at San Jose PD in a western-area precinct.

The party was about to begin.

38

REMEMBERING HOW MUCH Holmes sweated, Decker brought in a box of tissues and made sure that there was plenty of water available. Immediately, the big man poured himself a glass, drained it, and poured another one. The interview would probably be interrupted by frequent bathroom visits, which would affect the rhythm of the questioning but such is life. Holmes had dressed comfortably—sweatpants and a black T-shirt that tented over his belly like a parachute. He had socks and sneakers on his feet. His mouthpiece, Taz Dudley, was garbed in a navy shadow-stripe suit, cream-colored shirt, and a red tie.

Some minutes were taken up by introductions. Then Decker started the conversation.

"Are you comfortable, Mr. Holmes?"

"How comfortable can I be when I'm dragged away from my house and continue to be treated like a common criminal?"

Taz Dudley placed a manicured hand on his shoulder. "Let me talk, Ray. That's why you're paying me. You just settle down, okay?" The lawyer was an austere-looking man, with a portly build and a decent head of salt-and-pepper hair. He had deep brown eyes, a square chin, and a tan that either came from many Caribbean vacations or hours in a salon. "Do you want to tell us why you brought my client in for questioning?"

Decker's words addressed the lawyer but he looked at Holmes. He threw out a false start. "Your client was having an affair with a woman who is now missing."

"God, I don't believe this!" Holmes shouted.

"Ray, please—"

"No, you let me handle this, Mr. Dudley. I want to have my say. Then you can take over." He glared at Decker. "You asked me to take a polygraph test, I took a polygraph test *without* a lawyer. And I passed. Now here it is, what . . . like four weeks later, and you're back again. This isn't questioning, this is harassment. I cooperated. Yet you continue to prevent me from working, so I'm losing money there. Plus, you're costing me money to retain a lawyer. I'll tell you what I'm going to do if this continues, I'm going to sue San Jose, I'm going to sue LAPD, and I'm going to personally sue you!"

Holmes grabbed the glass of water, but knocked it down instead. Decker dabbed up the mess with some tissues and gave Holmes a wad to dab his face.

"This is just ridiculous!" The big man mopped up his wet face. "Look, I am truly sorry that the woman is missing—"

"Ray, you've said enough," Dudley interrupted.

"Okay, okay." He sat back in his chair and crossed his arms. "Just get me out of here, okay?"

"Is it your intention to arrest my client?"

"It might be."

"What the *fuck* do you want from me?" Holmes cried out.

"Ray—"

"No, I want to know why you're harassing me after I cooperated with every request you made. This is what I get from being a good citizen?"

Decker said, "If you would just hold your outrage for a few minutes, maybe I can ask you a few questions and straighten this mess out. Then we can all go home, happy campers."

"That's what you said the last time I was here!"

"Mr. Holmes, I understand your frustration. We are just doing our job."

"Have you been talking to that scumbag husband of hers?"

"Ray—"

He stood up abruptly. So did Decker. "Relax," Holmes said. "I have to go to the bathroom."

Decker nodded. "I'll take you."

"You're not going with me. For all I know, while I'm in there with you, you'll zap me with a taser."

"Your lawyer can come as well."

"This is just plain embarrassing!" He looked at his lawyer. "Make sure he stays away from my dick."

The excursion took up another ten minutes. After they were re-seated, Holmes appeared as if he had lost a little of his steam. Decker said, "I'd just like to ask your client a few questions, all right?"

"Go ahead," Dudley said.

"Thank you." Decker looked at Holmes. "The night before Roseanne Dresden disappeared, you told me that you were home with your wife all evening."

"Yes," Holmes answered.

"I really think it would be in your best interest to have your wife come in and sign a statement backing up your claim."

"You know that's just a form of intimidation, Lieutenant," Dudley said. "Mr. Holmes has admitted to an affair with Roseanne Dresden. He has also told you that he had not seen the woman in six months prior to her disappearance."

"We've been through this already," Holmes broke in. "I swear to God, I don't know what happened to Roseanne. I don't know if she died in the crash, I don't know if that scumbag husband did her in, or I don't know if she hooked up with some loser with a nasty temper. *I don't know, okay?*"

"Okay," Decker said.

Holmes wiped his wet face. "Okay." Sensing that the heat had been lifted, he sat back in his chair and took another glass of water. "Can I go home now?"

"Not quite yet," Decker said. "I have a good reason for asking your wife to sign a statement, sir. It would just be one less charge to deal with."

Holmes sat up. "What are you talking about?"

"Let me handle this," Dudley said. "Are you going to explain or is it your intention to keep us holed up for nothing?"

"Mr. Dudley, your client has an identity problem." He looked at Holmes and then reached in his suitcase and pulled out a legal document dated twenty-three years ago. "You weren't always Raymond Holmes, were you?"

Dudley picked up the paper, but Holmes grabbed it from his hand. The big man looked at the paper and a new wave of sweat washed over his face. "This is what you're asking me about?" He shook it in front of Decker. "This is what you're in an uproar about? So what? So I changed my name. I didn't think Tomas Martinez would go over too well in the Silicon Valley. You think I'm an upstart spic, is that what you think?"

The best offense . . .

Dudley took the paper from Holmes's hand. "This is a legal name change." He stared at Decker and then at his client. "What's the prob—" He stopped himself.

"What's the problem?" Decker finished the sentence. "Yes, Mr. Dudley, we do have a problem. Tomas Martinez was born in Madrid, New Mexico, and died of pneumonia when he was eight years old."

"Oh, for God's sakes!" Holmes bellowed. "Do you know how many Tomas Martinezes there are in New Mexico? It's a very common name."

"I'm sure it is, but there's only one Tomas Martinez that matches your Social Security number and date of birth." Holmes was struck silent; his lawyer as well. "You want to tell us how you came to take Tomas Martinez's identity?"

Dudley moved in. "I'd like a few minutes alone with my client."

"Of course," Decker said. "Just look up at those cameras when you're ready to talk to me."

"OKAY," HOLMES SAID after Decker returned. "This is the story and it's the God's honest truth. Are you ready to listen?"

"I'm ready to listen."

"Okay. I'm going to tell you what's going on with that and we can all go home." The big man let out a big sigh. "I got into trouble when I was younger. I had a hard life, I had an old man who beat the crap out of me. I had an old lady who was a junkie. I was the oldest, so everyone gave me shit. I'm not asking for sympathy. I'm just giving you some background as to why I did what I did, okay?"

"Sure," Decker said.

"I grew up in New Mexico, which, if you've ever been there, is a sparsely populated state with lots of wide-open space. Like I said, my old man was a con and my old lady was a junkie. I became a wild kid and there was no one around to stop me. Just me and a bunch of bums and the open road."

"Go on."

"No discipline, no nothing. I did some things that I'd like to forget."

"Like?"

"Ah, c'mon! Do I have to spell it out?"

"It would be nice."

"Jesus! Okay. Auto theft, B-and-Es, assaults. I got into a lot of fights. I was an angry, wild kid with no discipline. It finally caught up with me when I was eighteen. I did a few years in Roswell Correctional Center, and then they paroled me for good behavior. I came out a changed man, Lieutenant. This is the key. I became a completely changed man."

"A stay in prison can change a man."

"You better fucking believe it! I wasn't ever going back inside again. Never ever! All I wanted was a fresh start and a couple of breaks. I moved to Madrid, which is only about ten miles south of Santa Fe. I only stayed there for a little while because it was too close to Santa Fe for me to be comfortable. Lots of bad memories. Tomas Martinez was dead. Tomas Martinez didn't have a record. I figured what's the harm? He was my fresh start." Holmes's shirt was sodden. "I worked construction in southern New Mex and all the way up in the Four Corners. I worked hard and kept my mouth shut. I had natural talent for woodworking. I learned all I could until I felt good enough to branch out on my own. I searched for good places to live, and at that time, Silicon Valley was the up-and-coming place. The men here . . ."

Holmes laughed derisively and waved his hand.

"They've got brainpower, I'm not going to deny that. They can do amazing things with chips, motherboards, and computers, but they don't know a hammer from a screwdriver. It's Nerd City. I figured it was a good place to make a kill—to do well in the construction trade. People were coming in all over the place, and housing was sprouting up like weeds. After my visit, I said to myself, 'Buddy, you hit gold.' So I changed my name to something more white-collar and set up shop. You look at my records and you'll see I'm telling the truth."

"So I have your permission to look at your records?" Decker asked.

"No, you don't," Dudley answered. "He was speaking metaphorically."

"There's nothing to see even if I gave you permission," Holmes said.

Decker was quiet for a moment. Like all good tall tales, this one had snippets of truth. "What was your given name?"

Holmes's eyes darted from side to side. If the guy had any smarts, he had to figure that this was going to be Decker's next question.

"Is that really necessary?" Holmes stalled. "I want to put that part of my life behind me."

"Yes, it is really necessary."

"Why?" Dudley asked. "Unless it has direct impact on the so-called charges that you're going to present us with, it is irrelevant."

"It has to do with the truthfulness of your client, sir." Decker faced Holmes. "What's your given name?"

Holmes was silent. Dudley filled in the silence. "If you want to know the answer to that question, come back with a warrant."

Decker held up the palm of his hand. "It's rhetorical, Counselor. Because Mr. Holmes has to know that if he was in the prison system, his fingerprints would be on file."

Holmes reached for more tissues but had used them all up. Decker looked at the mounted video camera and asked for another box of Kleenex. "You know that sample tile that you gave prospective home buyer Oliver Scott day before yesterday? Well, it contained two beautiful right thumb- and index fingerprints."

Holmes looked green. "He was a cop?"

"He was a cop and he's looking at you as we speak. Now, when you were incarcerated way back when, we didn't have the luxury of Automated Fingerprint Identification System, but your prints, of course, were filed even if they weren't inputted into AFIS. The key is to know who you're looking for. And we damn well knew who we were looking for. So all we had to do was call up Roswell, and bingo, we had a match. Now, do you want to tell me your given name?"

"You don't have to answer that, Ray," Dudley told him. "Either charge him, Lieutenant, or we're going home."

Decker regarded Holmes. "If I book you for murder, there's no turning back. You're in the system once again, Mr. Holmes. That means you're going to spend the night in jail while your lawyer sleeps in his bed—"

Holmes held up his hand. His face had become defiant. "If you know who I am, you tell me."

"Does the name Isabela Devargas ring a bell?"

Holmes blanched and a downpour of water cascaded over his face.

"That's a woman's name," Dudley said.

"That's a dead woman's name," Decker answered.

39

DUDLEY SAID, "I need time alone with my client."

Decker ignored him. "We found her body, Mr. Holmes. She's right there where you left her. If there were intervening circumstances, now's the time to tell me."

"I told you, I need time alone with my client," the lawyer insisted.

"You can have as much time as you want once I book him for murder."

"Lieutenant, even if he talked to you now, you can't use what he says."

"I can if he allows it."

"I didn't kill her," Holmes protested. "I did *not* kill her!"

"So tell your lawyer that you want to tell me about it."

"Ray, shut up!" Dudley said.

"You shut the fuck up," Holmes snapped back. "It's not your ass on the line. He's right about one thing. You're going to sleep in a bed tonight."

"You're paying me to advise you, let me advise you. First, let me talk to you so I know what's going on!" Dudley turned to Decker. "I repeat. I need to talk to my client in private."

"I'm trying to help you, Mr. Holmes." Decker pulled out his coup de grâce and handed it to Dudley. "I've got a warrant for your arrest for the murder of Isabela Hernandez." He turned to Dudley. "The woman was once Mr. Holmes's sister-in-law." Back to Holmes. "I haven't executed the warrant yet. So if you want to talk to me, now's the time."

"Don't say a word!"

"I didn't touch the bitch," Holmes said.

"Then tell your lawyer that you want to tell me who did the murder. Tell your lawyer that you want to talk to me to clear things up."

"*Don't* say another word, Ray. He's lying to you!"

"He doesn't have a warrant for my arrest?"

Dudley stammered, "Well, yes, but if you talk to him, it'll only get you into trouble. That's the game they use, Ray. They pretend to be sympathetic, but they're not. Just let them go through the motions of booking you and I'll have you out of here by tonight."

"Or maybe tomorrow morning, depending how the docket goes," Decker added.

"So that's your advice? To let the bastard arrest me?"

"He's going to arrest you, Ray, whether you talk to him or not!"

"But maybe not for murder," Decker said.

"He's lying through his teeth," Dudley said.

Decker was lying through his teeth. The lawyer was absolutely right. But Holmes's aversion to prison was stronger than logic. He crossed his arms. "I'm not going to talk to you, Lieutenant. But if you tell me what *you* know, I'll correct your mistakes."

Holmes thought he was being very clever, but Dudley wasn't going to give up without a fight. "If you correct him in front of me, he can take those words and twist them against you, Ray."

"I'll take that chance." Holmes sat back in his chair. "Go on. Tell me what you've heard."

"Okay, let's give it a shot," Decker said. "Thirty years ago, Beth and Manny Hernandez disappeared off the face of the earth. And I know that you, my friend, were christened Belize Hernandez. You are Manny's brother and Beth's brother-in-law. And just like you admitted, you've had a long history of trouble with the law."

"And the point is . . . ?"

"You were paroled thirty-two years ago for good behavior, about six months before your brother and sister-in-law disappeared. You moved to Madrid, New Mexico, and lived there for about three months, and eventually, you moved to Arizona, using the name Tomas Martinez. You hopped around the state for a while. You lived in Mesa, Yuma, Tucson, Phoenix."

"I don't deny that, either. I worked construction. I was building up my skills. I was still that Latino from New Mexico and Arizona felt familiar to me."

"You were in Arizona for around five years—"

"I was learning my trade. So what?"

"Then we lost track of you," Decker continued on. "Three years later you take the contractor's licensing examination in San Jose using the name Raymond Holmes."

"I told you, I changed my name to Raymond Holmes to make me sound less Latino. And I did that legally. So far, all you have on me is stealing the name Tomas Martinez. And I told you I stole his name because I wanted to make a fresh start. Adios to Belize and hello to Tomas. So what? "

"No problem, Belize, but here is where we have conflicting information. Before you made that move to Arizona, we have some unaccounted time for your whereabouts and that period happens to coincide with the disappearance of your brother and sister-in-law."

"You expect me to remember every minute for the last thirty-two years?" Holmes sneered. "I bet you can't even remember what you had for dinner last Thursday."

"You're right. I don't remember what I had for dinner last Thursday. But I definitely would remember killing my sister-in-law."

"I already told you, I did *not* kill her!"

"Well, other people and this warrant say you did."

Holmes bolted up and started to pace. "Who says I killed her?"

"Sit down, Ray," Dudley told his client.

"Who says I killed Beth? I want to know a name!"

"I can't continue with the interview unless you're seated," Decker told him.

Angrily, Holmes plopped himself back down. "Give me a name."

"The D.A. will give you all the exculpatory evidence that we have, but I can't do that until you're booked for murder—"

"I didn't kill her! What do you *want* from me!"

"I want to know where you were from the time you moved from Madrid until you moved to Arizona."

"I don't remember!"

"We're going around in circles," Dudley said.

"Would you like me to execute the warrant as is?" Decker said.

Dudley said, "You're going to do it anyway."

"Taz, let me handle this *my* way!" Holmes said. "I don't remember where I was because I was too busy trying to survive. I drifted here and there."

"Did you drift here and there and visit your brother in L.A.?"

Holmes clamped his mouth shut, his eyes moving from side to side. Dudley piped in, "Don't answer anything you're uncomfortable answering, Ray."

"Doesn't matter," Decker lied. "We already know the answer to that one because we have witnesses."

"Who?" Holmes asked.

"C'mon, Mr. Holmes. Did you really think that you could live with Beth and Manny and belong to their church and have them disappear and not have people remember you?"

"I never belonged to their church!" Holmes replied.

"Everyone knew you were staying with Beth and Manny." Decker leaned in close. "Look, sir, I understand the fix you were in. You were an ex-con. No one would hire you because of your background. You couldn't go back to Santa Fe to get some help from your old lady because there were scores of people mad at you for boosting their cars or stealing their TVs. Plus your old man had dropped a couple of innocent lives. So you went to visit your brother and sister-in-law in L.A. You figured they'd be good for something. You're not going to deny, right?"

Holmes said, "I got to go to the bathroom."

"No problem," Decker said. "

Again, they took a break just as Decker was on a roll. Still, it was good to get up and stretch one's legs. When they returned to the interrogation room, Dudley was still trying to convince Holmes not to talk. But the big man was insisting that he could take good care of himself. He sat down, poured himself another glass of water, and said, "So I visited my brother. So what?"

"So what?" Decker repeated. "The first 'so what' is that your brother and sister-in-law have been missing for over thirty years. The second 'so what' is that we've recovered Beth Hernandez's murdered body, and the final 'so what' is that you're our prime suspect in her murder."

"I didn't do it!" Holmes blurted out. "*Manny* did it!"

Dudley slapped his face. "Can I please talk to you alone for a minute, Ray?"

"Absolutely, you can talk to him right after I book him for murder—"

"I swear on my mother's grave, I didn't kill her!" Holmes shouted. "Manny killed her in a fit of rage. I was there! I saw it! That's the fuck why I moved to Arizona. I needed to get far, far away."

Decker imagined the high fives Scott and Marge were exchanging after hearing Holmes's admission to being at the scene of Beth's death. But Decker was still far away from the full confession. He said, "Tell me what happened, Ray. It may bring the charges down from murder to accessory after the fact."

"Or it may not," Dudley said. "I know I'm sounding like a broken record, but he's lying, Ray. You fell into his leg trap. Don't keep pulling on it or you'll wind up an amputee."

"Taz, I swear I didn't kill her. Why should I take the fall for my stupid brother's mistake?"

"You're right, Mr. Holmes," Decker soothed. "If Manny killed his wife, you shouldn't take the fall. So tell me what happened."

Holmes held up his hand to silence his lawyer. "They got into an argument. He pushed her hard. She fell backward and hit her head. I wasn't even in the room when it happened. I was chilling in the living room and they were going at it in the bedroom. She was a freak, man. She was screaming at my poor brother and I think he just cracked."

"What were they arguing about?"

"I told you already. I don't know!"

"Take a guess."

Holmes looked away. "Probably money."

"Maybe they were arguing about the money that Manny had taken from the church funds to get you back on your feet?"

"I don't know what you're talking about."

"Sure you do, Ray," Decker said. "We've talked to people who were there. Alyssa Bright Mapplethorpe, Christian Woodhouse . . . members of the church. They remember you and your brother and Beth very well."

Holmes said, "I did not take any money and I did not kill Beth! Period!"

"I didn't say you took it, Ray. I said that your brother took it."

"Jesus!" Holmes gnashed his teeth and mopped up his brow. "First of all, Manny borrowed it. Second of all, if he borrows money and doesn't pay it back, how is that my fault?"

"It isn't," Decker said. "So tell me your side of the story. Because I have lots of others who are telling me their side and it doesn't look good for you."

"Okay, okay." Holmes wiped his face, though he wasn't sweating nearly as much as before. Dealing with the truth, even partial truths, seemed to calm him down. "This is what happened in a nutshell. I needed a place to crash. My baby brother invited me to L.A., but his bitch wife wasn't at all happy about it. Even though I never did anything to her, even though I stayed out of their way, even though I minded my own fucking business, that bitch just had it in for me. Finally, Manny couldn't take it anymore. He said he loved me, but it just wasn't working out and I'd have to leave. I told him it was okay. I told him I had a buddy in Arizona and he could probably give me a crash pad for a couple of weeks until I could find construction work there. I didn't want to work construction in L.A. Too many damn greasers. I am not a fucking Mexican. I am an American citizen from New Mexico and I'll be damned if I'd work side by side with a bunch of illegals."

"I got it," Decker said. "Go on."

"Manny felt real bad about kicking me out. I was his big brother after all. So Manny offered . . . I repeat, he offered to give me money. I said okay. I didn't ask questions. I was in a bad way and I needed help. I didn't know where it came from. I didn't ask how he got it. I only found out later, when Beth was yelling at him, that he was the treasurer of his church and that he borrowed the money from the church funds."

"When was this?"

"The night it happened. Beth was yelling at him, demanding that Manny get the money back. I felt bad that I was the reason they were fighting, so I finally knocked on the bedroom door and explained to the bitch that I didn't have a penny in my pocket. I was trying to tell her that I'd pay the loan back as soon as I got on my feet again. I even offered her interest."

"How much did he give you?"

"Around a thousand bucks."

"Try again, Mr. Holmes."

"It was a thousand dollars."

"The account was looted completely."

"You want to know what happened, you got to let me finish, okay?"

Decker said, "Go on. So Manny loaned you a thousand dollars and Beth wanted you to give the money back."

"Exactly." Holmes drank another glass of water. "Now this is the part that gets a little fuzzy. At that point, all I'm doing is trying to leave the goddamn apartment, but by then, Beth is in overdrive. Screaming at him, screaming at me, insisting that I give the money back right now! 'Fuck her,' I say to myself. 'Manny gave me the money, not her. I don't have to listen to her.' So like I said, I start to walk away, then Beth screams that she's going to call the cops on me and report that I stole the money."

He exhaled with a snort.

"She picks up the phone and starts to dial the police or the operator or information, someone. So that's when Manny goes over to her and grabs the phone from her hand. He says to her, 'Beth, you can't do that.' Then she says, 'I'll do what I please and you can't stop me!' Then, I guess that was too much for Manny. He finally decides to be a man. So he says, 'You let my brother alone and let me worry about the money. I'm the treasurer and you're nothing but a mousy piece of shit without me.' And to emphasize the point, he pushes her, not meaning to hurt her, just meaning to get her out of the way."

Holmes swallowed, his eyes as blank as the wall he was looking at.

"He pushes her a little too hard and she cracks her head against the wall and drops to the floor."

Dudley was about to say something, but just shook his head instead. He continued to stare as if the scene were taking place in front of his eyes. It was certainly replaying itself in Holmes's brain. But Decker knew that the evidence didn't match the story that Holmes was recounting. The bash on Beth's skull was caused by a blunt object striking her in the forehead region and was probably delivered face-to-face. It was not an injury that could have been caused by the back of Beth's head hitting the wall.

Decker didn't say anything. All of that would come out later.

Holmes continued to speak. "As soon as it happened, I knew we were in big trouble. I did time for burglary in a medium-security place and that was bad enough. I wasn't about to go to Santa Fe Correctional and do real hard time. My old man was there. We both knew what Santa Fe Correctional was from visiting him. No fucking way that we were going down because some little bitch couldn't control her mouth!"

Decker nodded encouragingly. "About what time of the day did it happen?"

"Not late, but it was after dark. I don't know. Maybe around six. I don't remember."

"Okay. So what happened after you realized she wasn't moving?"

"I remember feeling paralyzed. I didn't know what the fuck to do. I was in a strange city and I had no friends and here I was with a dead bitch and *I* didn't even kill her. I told Manny that we'd better just get the hell out. My baby brother's reaction was funny. He was calm and collected. Maybe he even felt good about it. She'd been getting on his case for a long, long time and he had enough I guess. He was the smooth one. He told me to help him wrap up the body and he'd take care of it. So that's what I did. I helped him wrap the body. I helped him load it into Manny's pickup. Then Manny took it from there. I don't know what he did with it. I never asked and he didn't say."

"How long was he away?"

"I don't know. A couple of hours maybe. I was cleaning up the mess while he was gone."

"And you don't remember when Manny returned to the apartment?"

"I remember it was late. We spent the night packing up the truck, and the next day, Manny took out the rest of the church money from the bank. We needed everything we could get our hands on." Holmes took in a breath and let it out. "Manny wanted us to go together, but I wanted *o-u-t*, out, know what I mean?" He pointed to his chest. "I didn't kill her; he did. Let him figure it out. Besides, I could tell he was scared. The adrenaline had worn off and I didn't want him to freak out while I was around. I told him to take the truck and go, that I'd take care of myself. I told him to look me up in Arizona in about six months after everything had calmed down. He never did call me. I never saw or heard from him again. I don't know what happened to him, if he's alive or dead or what."

Sure you don't, Decker thought. "Where'd you go after the two of you split up?"

"I hitched a ride to Las Vegas. I played the tables and turned my measly grand into five big ones. I lived it up for about a week—booze, drugs, hookers, you name it. I was the happiest that I've ever been in my life."

"What happened after that week?"

"What do you think?" Holmes laughed. "Booze, drugs, and hookers cost money. I left glitter city with about three hundred in my pocket, and thumbed a ride to Arizona. I rolled up my sleeves, learned the construction business, and became a working stiff. I started paying taxes, and I've been a solid citizen ever since then."

"And you never heard from Manny again?" Decker asked.

"Not a whisper. Maybe I should have reported my brother . . . let Beth's parents know what happened. Maybe I shouldn't have helped him wrap the body or clean up the mess. But fuck, he was my baby brother and he was in trouble and he got into trouble trying to help me out. I felt responsible, but not responsible enough to take the fall for something I *didn't* do."

Decker nodded. There was a lot about his story that rang true. Maybe Beth and Manny were arguing about the money. And it made sense that, during the argument, someone got pissed and bashed Beth over the head. Maybe it was Raymond/Belize, or maybe it was Manny. The one thing that was certain in Decker's mind was that one of the brothers killed Beth.

It also made sense to Decker that Manny had buried Beth and didn't tell his brother where. Why else would Holmes stick around after Decker and Marge had paid him an initial visit? They had told him that an old body had been discovered under the debris of the ruined apartment building. That meant nothing to Holmes because he had no idea where Beth had been buried. The contractor didn't know L.A. all that well. It would have taken quite a stretch for Holmes to assume that the body they had found had been his dead sister-in-law. At the time of the interview, he had stated that he thought the discovered body was Roseanne Dresden.

That had probably been the truth.

Still, Holmes's spiel was distinctly different from the recitation given to Decker by Holmes's father, Martin Hernandez. The old man had stated that Belize had confessed to murdering Beth even though he didn't mean to kill her. Hernandez also kept reiterating that Manny was dead.

Now, how would Hernandez know that Manny was dead unless he knew the person who had killed him? The old man had stopped short of implicating his older son in the death of his younger one, but by insisting that Manny was long dead, he pointed the arrow in that direction.

Decker wasn't positive which one killed Beth, but he was pretty damn sure that Belize had killed Manny. In Decker's mind, Belize's formal name change to Raymond Holmes was Holmes's odd way of honoring his dead brother, Ramon Hernandez.

Decker said, "You want to tell me about Roseanne Dresden now?"

"Oh God!" Holmes slapped his face. "I don't *know* what happened to Roseanne! Before she disappeared, I hadn't seen her in six fucking months!"

"I don't know if I believe you, Ray."

"Why not? I have been perfectly honest with you about everything else. I told you what happened with my brother, I told you about the money, I told you that I helped wrap the body, I told you I cleaned up the mess. I told you everything I know." Holmes mopped up his face. "I have nothing more to say."

"It's too late," Dudley told him. "He's going to arrest you for murder now."

Decker said, "You probably should have listened to your lawyer, Mr. Holmes."

"Why?" Holmes started sweating again, pools of sweat shooting out from his overworked pores. "C'mon. I was honest with you. I told you everything. I even took a fucking lie-detector test about Roseanne. How can you arrest me for *murder* after all that?"

"I just figure I'll serve the warrant and let the D.A. sort it out."

"You fucking bastard! You don't have a leg to stand on because I didn't do it!"

"I told you not to talk, Ray," Dudley said.

"You're a fucking bastard, too," Holmes shouted. "You're fired."

"Fine," Dudley told him. "You go convince some rookie PD to set your bail."

"Wait! You're not fired!" Holmes looked desperate. "Please, Taz, I'm sorry. Don't leave me alone!"

Dudley said, "I will represent you, but now, it's not so simple. I'll need a fifteen-thousand-dollar retainer, and another fifteen in two weeks. If you're short on cash, I'll take the deed to the house on Chase as collateral."

"You two gentlemen can continue this conversation a little later in the quiet of a jail room. Right now Holmes has a date with Ms. Miranda."

40

HELLO, STRANGER."

Rina had met Decker in the driveway of their home, greeting him with a smile and a huge terry-cloth robe cinched around her small waist, slippers on her feet. Stars blinked above, and the moon served as a spotlight. Although spring was fast becoming summer, there was a chill in the air as fog began to roll into the valley basin.

Decker spoke softly. "Don't tell me. In my absence, Cindy's and Koby's house is done, Sam married Rachel, Jake has a serious girlfriend, and Hannah is in college."

"Now, how did you know all that?" Rina looped her arm around his and they walked arm in arm into the house.

Decker pulled her into a hug. "Man, it's great to be back. Is the princess home?"

"It's one in the morning on a school night. Princess is home and sleeping. Where is your low-down, dirty scoundrel?"

"We're working on the papers to bring him to Los Angeles. If all goes well, he'll be gracing our jails in a few days."

"How about something to eat?"

"Actually, I'm starving. But I need to shower first."

"No problem. How about a corned-beef sandwich? Or is that too much at one in the morning?"

"My internal clock is haywire. A sandwich sounds great. Slather one with lots of mustard and mayo. Mustard for Akiva the Jew, mayo for Peter the goy."

She laughed. "Coleslaw? Or will that put you over the top?"

"Just pile it high and deep. I'll meet you at the dining-room table."

A half hour later Decker was wiping his mouth, his stomach not quite sure if it wanted to be pleasantly full or gluttonous. The matter was decided when Decker found out that there was no more corned beef or rye bread.

"I saved the last bits just for you." Rina sipped chamomile tea. "It's not easy defending corned beef against a horde of hungry teenagers."

"'Hungry teenagers' means boys."

"Specifically Hannah's gruesome twosome."

"Tzvika and Michael?"

"Who else?"

"What's up with that?" Decker asked. "The boys are best friends and they both like her?"

"But she's not interested in either of them."

"So why does she hang around them all the time?"

"I think she likes the attention."

Decker rolled his eyes. "We're going to have to watch that one. She's swatting them away like flies."

"It's when she stops swatting them away that we have to worry."

"Now that's true." Decker took in a deep breath and let it out slowly. "I think I'm going to Santa Fe *again*."

"Ah . . . you want to break the news to Beth's parents in person."

"No, I already phoned them up as soon as we booked Raymond Holmes."

"What was their reaction?"

"They were low-key." Decker drained his water glass. "Peter thanked me. Sandra invited us out to Santa Clara Feast Day as their guests. It's in August."

"By then you'll know the town pretty well."

"I'll know Santa Fe Correctional, if you want a tour. I'll need to go back there and go over the old man's testimony with him."

"Belize's father?"

"Yes. Martin Hernandez. He's our main witness against Holmes and I don't have a good feeling about him. The kind of man who'd sell his son down the river is not going to be a likable or credible witness. He's also old. A lot of questions confuse him."

Decker sat back and looked at the ceiling. "The murder charge depends on the old man's testimony and he's got a believability issue. Also, the jury is going to find out that the old man is getting early release in exchange for his testimony. That's going to take away the last little bits of whatever integrity the man had."

"Well, Belize is locked up and that's a start. Just like I said, 'What goes around comes around.'"

"It doesn't bring Beth back."

"We all die, Peter. If you're religious like I am, you believe that G-d metes out true justice." She took his hand. "You gave a definitive answer to a question that has been plaguing a family for over thirty horrible years. Furthermore, Belize will get some kind of punishment. You made sure of that. You did your part for G-d and country."

"Thanks." Decker picked up Rina's teacup and took a sip. "I appreciate the nice words. The big question mark right now is Manny; is he dead or alive?"

"And what do you think?"

"I think he's dead. I don't know who killed Beth, but I'm pretty sure that Belize killed Manny. Belize had no intention of going back to prison and his brother was just too much of a liability. When I talk to the parents, I'm going to imply that Belize killed Manny and Beth. Like

I said, it won't bring Beth back, but it might make them feel better to know that her own husband didn't kill her. And as you said, Belize is guilty of something."

Rina pushed her teacup in front of Decker. "Are you going to try to implicate Holmes in Roseanne Dresden's disappearance?"

"I'd love to do it, but I don't see how I can." Decker sipped the herbal mixture, feeling warmth penetrate his achy body as the hot liquid slid down his throat. "All I have is Holmes's last call to Roseanne three months before her disappearance."

"Not enough for a warrant?"

"Not nearly. Besides, I'm not sure he had anything to do with Roseanne. Right before I left for San Jose, Wanda found a witness who saw Roseanne's Beemer speeding out of the condo's parking facilities on the morning of the crash."

Rina nodded. "Do you think it was Roseanne speeding off to make the flight?"

"That's one theory. The other is that someone else was speeding off in her car to dump her body. We're trying to gather enough evidence for a warrant to search the car. If someone stashed her body in the backseat or the trunk, we might be able to pull up some forensic evidence."

"But even if you dredge up something forensic, how would you know it wasn't Roseanne's hair from before?"

"We're looking for large amounts of her blood. That's the only thing that's going to give us a warrant. If she bled out in the car, we'd have blood evidence in the crevices of the seats, not to mention all the carpets. If the hubby did some redecorating of the Beemer right after Roseanne died—things like reupholstered the seats or changed the carpets—then maybe, just maybe, it would look suspicious enough for a judge to give us a warrant to get into the car."

"Any evidence that it happened?"

"We've got zilch so far." Decker checked his watch. "But I've got six and a half hours before I show up at my desk. Who knows what the night will bring?"

FARLEY LODESTONE WAS livid over the phone. "You got this guy who was stalking my daughter in custody for killing some other lady thirty years ago, and you're saying that you're *not* charging him with my daughter's murder?"

Decker said, "I would love to charge him in conjunction with your daughter's disappearance, Farley, but I don't have any evidence—"

"For Christ sakes, Decker, he already admitted to killing a lady. Ain't that enough evidence?"

Raymond Holmes hadn't admitted to killing anyone. He was still blaming Beth's death on his missing brother, Manny. Holmes was keeping his story as consistent as a metronome. The subtle difference between being booked on murder and tampering with evidence was lost on the old man.

"Farley, I am committed to your daughter's case. I will not rest until I have answers. And if Holmes is the answer, he'll be charged. Right now we've got a classic catch-22. I have to have evidence to get a warrant to get evidence."

"Well, then change the goddamn system!"

"I wish I could—"

"So this monster is gonna walk?"

"You mean Holmes?"

"Yes, I mean Holmes. Who the hell else would I be talking about? This bastard murdered my daughter and you're sitting on your hands!"

Just a few days ago, Lodestone had been insistent that Ivan had murdered Roseanne. Of course Holmes's arrest had changed all that. Although Farley still detested Ivan, he was now aiming his considerable wrath at the contractor. Ivan Dresden was also venting about Holmes to Decker. At last the two men had something in common. It seemed that everyone *loved* Ray Holmes as Roseanne's killer.

Decker said, "Farley, no one has been ruled out."

"And no one has been arrested, either."

"That's correct. We're being very careful because we don't want any of our hard work thrown out because of procedural errors." Decker could hear grousing over the phone. "Look, Farley. The case that we're working on now—the one that involves Raymond Holmes—is over thirty years old. We're tenacious buggers. We don't give up just because things are hard."

Silence.

Decker said, "I'm making every effort I can to find out what happened to Roseanne. And I have no reason to think that we won't solve the case."

More silence.

"Are you there, Farley?"

"Yeah, I'm still here."

Decker groaned inwardly. "I'm doing the best I can. I understand that my best isn't always enough. I'm sorry about that. But I promise you, I'll keep at it."

Maybe we'll get lucky, he thought to himself.

Lodestone finally spoke. "The parents of the dead girl that you found. Are they still alive?"

"Yes, they're still alive."

"How old are they?"

"In their seventies."

"Nice people?"

"Lovely."

"And they've been in the dark about their daughter for over thirty years?"

"Yes."

"My, my, my. Now, that is humbling." The old man's voice had turned soft. "You gonna talk to them again? The parents?"

"Yes. I'm sure I'll be talking to them quite a bit in the days to come."

Lodestone was uncharacteristically quiet for a moment. When he finally found his voice, it cracked. "When you see 'em, send 'em my best."

"I'll do that, Farley." Decker felt his throat swell. "I know they'll appreciate your good wishes."

The line disconnected. Decker rubbed his moist eyes and took a moment to simply breathe. Inhale, exhale, inhale, exhale. The conversation had left his voice dry and he slugged down a bottle of water. Then he rolled up his shirtsleeves and went to work.

41

THE OLD MAN'S memory was suddenly steeped in senility.
Decker supposed that it was one thing to theoretically talk about
screwing up one's only living son. It was quite another thing for
Martin Hernandez to face his own flesh and blood in a courtroom and
condemn him to death.

"I didn't say that Ray did anything," Hernandez emphasized. "I just
told you that Ray and Beth were arguing."

"Actually, I have your exact words in front of me," Decker countered.
They were once again sitting in steel chairs, holed up in the luxurious
interview room at Santa Fe Correctional. "You signed your statement,
Martin. You specifically said that Ray told you that he pushed Beth,
although you do say that it was an accident and that Ray said he didn't
mean for her to die."

"I'm almost eighty, for Christ sakes! Maybe Ray told me that Manny
pushed her."

"Where is Manny?"

"How the hell should I know that?"

"I think you'd be curious about your own son."

"Being curious is not a good thing in a penitentiary. You learn real quick how to mind your own business."

Decker had no comeback to that. "I'm trying to help you get out of here early. I'm trying to help you with your dream of raising your dogs in all that beautiful, empty land in southern New Mexico. I've seen you work your animal magic and you have a lot to offer once you get out. There are lots of rescued dogs out there that can use rehabilitation." Decker snapped his fingers. "Hey, maybe you can even get yourself a TV show like that Dog Whisperer guy."

Hernandez rolled his eyes. "Lieutenant, I'm old, I'm forgetful, but I'm not stupid. Don't be playing me for a fool."

Decker nodded. "Scratch the TV show. But the rest is reality and that's totally up to you. If you start forgetting things that you said, Martin, I can still use your statement for the grand jury. That'll mean that you're back to square one and you'll serve out your sentence. All this talk will be for nothing. But that's up to you."

"I ain't gonna lie for you."

"God forbid," Decker said. "Martin, all I want is for you to tell the truth. Tell a grand jury what Ray told you. That's it. The rest is up to a court of law."

"He never ever tol' me he killed her, Lieutenant. I want to make that clear."

Decker said, "But he did tell you he pushed her . . ."

"He pushed her, Manny pushed her. All he kept saying is that he didn't mean for it to happen."

"In your signed statement, you state that Belize told you that he pushed her."

"Maybe I made a mistake. He tol' me someone pushed her. Maybe him, maybe Manny."

"Maybe Manny . . ." Decker sat back in the chair. "Do you remember the last time you saw Manny?"

"When he was a kid and the missus used to bring them in. After he married Beth, he didn't come see me no more."

"He moved to California."

"He coulda wrote."

"And Belize never told you what happened to Manny?"

The old man shook his head no.

"Did you ever wonder if Belize murdered your son?"

"No, sir." Hernandez shook his head. "I never did wonder that. I fig-ure if Manny never visited me before the Beth incident, why would he visit me after? Like I tol' you, being too curious ain't a good thing."

"What would you say if I gave you proof that Belize murdered Manny?"

"Maybe I'd care, and then maybe I wouldn't. Manny was always a mama's boy. Belize was mine, for better or worse. I mighta been rough on him, but that was because he could take it." Hernandez leaned across the table. "The deal was that I'd say what Belize told me. The deal was not that I'd lie just because you want me to. And where I come from, a deal is a deal."

"No one is asking you to lie."

"A deal is a deal."

"Ray pushed Beth. You have that in your statement to me."

"Well, maybe Ray pushed her and maybe it was Manny. You can read your statement and I can say I don't remember. I'm an old man. Ray made his confession to me a long time ago and I don't remember who did what. I'll tell your grand jury that Ray was there and you can ask me all the questions you want. But I won't lie for you." Hernandez folded his thick arms across his barrel chest. "Now, are you gonna keep your end of the bargain?"

With the old man backtracking, his statement virtually matched the statement that Ray Holmes had given him in San Jose. The D.A. could put Raymond Holmes at the scene of the murder, but now it looked like it was going to be nearly impossible to prove beyond a reasonable doubt that he killed Beth. Decker still had the old man's signed and sworn statement, when the taste of freedom had meant more to Martin than blood ties. The capital murder case would most likely move past the grand jury. "We're working on a deal, Martin, but you have to keep *your* end of the bargain."

"What can you do for me?"

"If you agree that you'll cooperate with us, you'll get *parole*. Parole means a parole officer and reporting in once a week. Parole means you can't move out of state. And most important, this parole also means you'll have to wear an ID ankle bracelet. Once you've made your statement to the grand jury, you'll be off the hook. The bracelet comes off and you're free as a bird. If you don't make a statement, you're back in Santa Fe Correctional and you'll have to make up the free time that you had in prison."

"I thought I was going to get early release period."

"I tried, Martin, but I couldn't swing it. First parole and then early release."

"When is this grand jury?"

"In about six months."

"If I agree, when do I get out of here?"

"Just as soon as the deal is inked with the DA here and in Los Angeles."

"And when will that be?"

"Hopefully in a couple of weeks. Do we have a deal?"

Hernandez sighed. "As of right now, I'm in. But don't wait too long, Lieutenant. I could change my mind. Or I could die."

AFTER TWO WEEKS of hunting down BMW dealerships, car washes, and custom shops, Marge got a break. Jim's Hot Rods, Dragsters, and Funny Cars took up residence on a side street off Roscoe in the industrial section of the San Fernando Valley. Sitting behind a wall of chain link topped with barbed wire, the shop included a warehouse whose windows and doors were protected by iron bars and a concrete yard littered with the exoskeletal remains of automobiles, trucks, and motorcycles. Jim's did everything—from little jobs like custom upholstery to converting lowly soccer-mom vans into drivable pleasure palaces.

Dunn found herself surrounded by more mullets than inside an ocean and lots and lots of ponytails as well. But she gave the guys an A for their work ethic. The place absolutely roared with activity, the noise level deafening even without the three barking pit bulls chained up in front of the main office.

Jim Franco—better known as Jumbo Jimbo, due to his height more than his girth—was cooperative and articulate. He wore a gray T-shirt (probably once white) and denim overalls, grease rags sticking out of every pocket. His hands were big and callused, his nails short and surprisingly cared for. Not that they didn't have dirt under them, but Marge could tell that the man took pains to make a decent appearance when he put on street clothes. He stood around six five and was packed with muscle. He turned to the dogs and they withered under his scowl.

"Yeah, I remember Dresden." He looked down at Marge and made her feel short. He spoke with a voice that was foghorn low. "The guy was not only an idiot, but a tool."

"Why do you say that?" Marge had to scream to be heard over the noise.

Jimbo clapped his hands and shouted, "Hey!" The din took a breather. "Five-minute break. I need to talk to this lady."

The mullets and the ponytails headed inside the warehouse. Marge waited a moment, then looked way up. "I said what did Dresden do for you to call him an idiot and a tool?"

"First off, any man who forgets to put the top up on a convertible in the pouring rain is an idiot. Second, he's a tool because that's what he is—a middle-management dick who was trying to be one of the boys. If he's a pretentious asshole, he should just be one." Jim waved a disgusted hand in the air. "No big whop. We get 'em all the time. Anyway he brought in a black 330 ci that reeked of mold. I told the guys in the shop to wear face masks and to pop antihistamines. Man, it was bad!"

"What did you do?"

"Took everything down to the metal."

"Including the seat upholstery?"

"I probably could have cleaned it up on the outside—it was leather—but I wouldn't take responsibility for what was growing inside the upholstery. It would have always smelled and who would want to breathe that shit in. Didn't matter. He wanted it stripped to the metal anyway. He said insurance would pay for it, but I didn't trust the guy. I told him I'd help him collect from insurance, but if he wanted me to do the job, it would be cash and cash only. I asked for sixty percent up front hoping to scare him off, but he agreed."

"Why did you want to scare him off? Did he give you any problems?"

"No, he didn't," Jimbo admitted. "Paid whenever I asked him to."

"Did you also replace the carpeting in the trunk?"

"Everything. Dresden wanted everything to match."

Marge winced. "That's too bad. Nothing was salvageable?"

"Why?" Jimbo gave her a look. "Something funny happen inside the car?"

"I don't know, but it looks like we're never going to find out."

The jumbo man gave her an oversize smile, exposing tobacco-stained teeth. "You know, ma'am, today *might* be your lucky day. The carpet in the trunk didn't need to be replaced, but as long as we were redoing the interior carpeting, I knew we'd probably have enough square feet left over to do the trunk, too. So it wouldn't cost Dresden extra to replace it. The car mats were a different story."

Marge's ears perked up. "Car mats?"

"Yeah, the car mats that go on top of the carpet. New car mats with the BMW logo would cost Dresden money. I told him that I could probably steam-clean the old ones as good as new, but he insisted on ordering fresh. What the hell? Didn't make any difference to me except that there was a six-week wait and it took a little extra time. Shipment got mixed up or something. Anyway, I asked Dresden what he wanted me to do with the old ones. He told me to chuck them."

"Tell me you didn't do it."

"Why throw away perfectly good mats?"

"Tell me you have them."

"No, I don't. That's why I said it *might* be your lucky day. I cleaned them up and sold them on e-Bay. I got a few bucks and the customer got a bargain."

"Do you remember who you sold them to?"

"Got it all down in my computer. She may not be happy giving back the mats. She got a good deal."

"Either she'll get them back or we'll get her new ones." Marge was writing as fast as she could. "So let me get this straight. You offered to clean the old mats and put them back in the car, but Dresden told you to throw them away."

"Yep."

"And you're positive that he told you to chuck them?"

"Are you asking if I'd swear to it in court? The answer is yes. Matter of fact, I asked him specifically if he wanted me to clean them so he could keep the mats for a backup set and he told me no. He said he wanted brand-new and that I should just chuck 'em in the garbage."

"Those were his words? 'Chuck 'em in the garbage'?"

"Yes. That's when I thought if they're going in the garbage, why not clean 'em and see how they turn out?"

"And you have the woman's name and address?"

"I do."

"What about her phone number?"

"No phone number, Sergeant. It was a business transaction, not a date."

DECKER FELT A strange buzzing sensation in his chest. For a split second he wondered about his heart, but then he realized that he had placed his cell in his interior coat pocket and the ringer was on vibrate. He looked at the cell's window: Marge. "Are we happy today?"

"We are very happy." Marge explained the situation in detail. When she got to floor mats, Decker pumped his fist and shouted "yes." "I put Oliver on contacting the woman from e-Bay. She was out and he left a message on the machine, but we both think we shouldn't take any chances. We'd like to drive down tonight."

"I agree. Take along a tech to luminol. I want this as professional as possible." Decker paused. "I hope we get something. Usually some proteins remain in the bleed-out area, but in this case, the carpets were professionally cleaned. Even if we get a little fluorescence, defense could always say it was her car, maybe she scraped her ankle and bled into the carpet."

"I thought about that," Marge said. "But we can counter by saying it must have been quite a lot of blood to survive a professional cleaning. Also, Dresden's cover story is fishy—that he left the top down in a rain. It had to have been quite a downpour because the interior was not only soaked beyond redemption but infested with mold."

"When did he bring the car in to the shop?"

"About a month after the crash."

"So check that date against the local weather reports. Let's see if it was raining around that time. If it wasn't, we've punched a hole in that alibi."

"I've already put Oliver on that as well. The weather was L.A. consistent—partly cloudy with burn-off in the afternoons. No precipitation in the area other than morning dew. I also had Scott check farther up north and east in the mountains. There was some light rain in San Bernardino, but the system passed through pretty quickly. I'm no mycologist, but for it to smell that bad, it sounds like the interior was soaked. I think Dresden took a hose and drowned the interior, trying to wash away evidence."

"Makes sense. Let's see if we can get some bright blue splotches to back it up."

"Where are you now?"

"I'm back in my hotel room packing up. I've got a little spare time, so I'll probably grab some lunch and then drive back to Albuquerque. I'll make sure my cell is charged, but reception on the ride back isn't always so great. If you don't get me, just leave a message. Call as soon as you know anything."

"I will. Have you decided on where to eat?"

"Anywhere I can walk. Any suggestions?"

"Pasquals on Water Street. It's casual, it's comfortable, and the food is terrific. Be sure to ask for both red and green chili on the side. Man, that'll give your taste buds a workout."

"I could use a good meal. Thanks for the tip."

"I'll give you another one. Instead of asking for red and green chili, just ask for Christmas chili. It'll mark you as a local."

DECKER HAD THE option of a private table with a thirty-minute wait or immediate seating at a round communal table. He was tired and starved, so he opted for the latter. His tablemates included a retired stockbroker with a passion for fly-fishing, a ceramic artist, a family of tourists with two young children, and a couple from Texas who owned a second home somewhere in the mountains. When the stockbroker asked about him and what he did for a living, Decker told the table that he was a lawyer and was in Santa Fe on business. The two sentences, stated separately, were the truth. It was only putting them together that turned his words into a little white lie.

He had just closed the door on his rental car when his cell went off. It was a restricted number, which meant it was probably Rina.

"Yo," Decker said. "I'm on my way home."

"Uh . . . I'm looking for Lieutenant Decker."

The voice was male and official. Decker switched gears. "This is Lieutenant Decker. Who am I talking to, please?"

"This is Detective Newt Berry from San Jose Police Department."

That got his attention. "Yes, Detective Berry, what's going on?"

"About twenty minutes ago, I got a call from a woman named Lindie Holmes. She said she'd like to talk to us, that she has a lot to say about her husband, Raymond, who, as you well know, is still in our custody."

"Thanks for calling. I'd love to talk to her."

"Figured as much. I think it might be a good idea for you to fly up here and do just that."

Decker said, "I'm in New Mexico, but I'm on my way to the airport. I'll see if they offer any flights into Oakland or San Francisco. Did she ask for me specifically?"

"She asked for whoever was in charge of her husband's investigation. She says she has a lot to say about that."

"Even if I can find an immediate flight up north, it's going to take me at least three hours to get there and that's with a one-hour time gain. Do you think she'd be willing to come in to the station house in the evening?"

"Tell me your schedule once you know it, and I'll call her back. Right now the woman seemed very eager to unload on her rotten husband. She kept on saying that she has information that would interest us."

"Sounds promising . . . if she tells the truth."

"Yeah, I thought about that. From speaking to her, I can't tell you if she's gonna lie to us because she's mad at the bastard and wants revenge, or if she's finally coming forward with the truth because she's mad at the bastard and wants revenge. What I *can* you tell is that she's pissed with a capital *P.*"

42

WITH A LITTLE shuffling around, Decker managed to secure a flight that put him into Oakland at six in the evening. Newt Berry was waiting for him at the baggage claim. The San Jose detective topped out at six feet, thin and bald, with a long equine face, brown eyes, and a ski-sloped nose. The two men shook hands and walked to the parking lot in silence. When they got into the car, Berry said, "You found a direct flight?"

"Two stops. A little roundabout, but I'm here."

"What's up in Santa Fe?"

"My main witness against Raymond Holmes. I think he's getting cold feet." Decker brought Berry up-to-date. It took the entire ride over to police headquarters. "I'm wondering how much Lindie Holmes knew about Ray's past."

"Well, I'm sure you'll find out. The woman is on a mission."

"Seek and destroy?" Decker said.

"Just destroy. She kept going on and on about how much she hated the son of a bitch. I didn't ask anything too specific because I knew you were coming down."

"Smart. Where is she now?"

"By now, she should be at the station. Over the phone, she asked if we could get her a decaf grande nonfat latte and vanilla syrup. She says she talks much better over a cup of coffee. I told her it wouldn't be a problem."

"Not at all. If it's only coffee and revenge she wants, we'll get away cheap."

LINDIE HOLMES WAS crunchy granola: a petite woman in jeans, a T-shirt, athletic sneakers, and a hooded jacket. She had straight, shoulder-length salt-and-pepper hair with bangs cut across her forehead, and a face free of any kind of makeup. Her skin was clear and held some wrinkles around her brown eyes. Her mouth was small and hard set, giving her an angry expression. Her right hand was clutched around a paper coffee cup; her left was clenched in fury, with a ring finger encircled by a light patch of skin that had once been covered with a wedding band. Decker didn't need a prod to get her to talk. She was out of the gate before the gun went off.

"The son-of-a-bitch bastard! He swore to me that there was no one and I believed him. How dumb is that!"

How dumb, indeed. Her husband was going to go before a grand jury on charges of capital murder and she was irate about his mistress.

"Jesus, I just want to ring his neck!"

Decker nodded. "I need to ask you a few basic questions. Who are you referring to when you say 'no one.'"

Lindie rolled her eyes. "His little chippie. The missing flight attendant. Roseanne Dresser or something like that. From what I could get out of the blubbering idiot, he met her on a flight from San Jose to Burbank. The bastard told me he had a project in L.A. about a year ago. Turns out he was coming down south just to screw her. It would be one thing if he just screwed her and that was that. But the idiot gave her gifts! Over ten thousand dollars! I've been clipping coupons and he's been spending money on a whore."

"How'd you find out about the money?"

"I have an account with Smithson/Janey."

"The brokerage house."

Lindie nodded. "We have a few accounts with them, but I have a savings account that I keep in case of emergencies. I've been building it for years—a few dollars here and there. But it adds up. When Ray called and asked me to get bail and lawyer money, I immediately called up our broker to withdraw money from my account. I mean, if this didn't qualify as an emergency, what would, right?"

"Right."

"So I call up the broker and guess what?"

"What?"

"The account has a grand total of five thousand and seventy-one dollars. I tell him, 'Excuse me? Last I heard I had almost twenty thousand dollars in there. Check again.' And he does. Then he starts telling me about all these withdrawals that I made about a year ago. I say, 'There must be some mistake. I never made any withdrawals from that account a year ago. I've never made any withdrawals from that account, period!'"

She slapped her forehead.

"And then it hits me like a rock! About a year ago, Ray suggested that he be a cosigner on the account in case something happens to me. Like if I get in a car accident and can't withdraw the money, he can do it. I thought it was a little funny, but then he countered my suspicions by taking out a disability insurance policy on himself in case something happened to him. Then I would have money. He showed me the policy. I think to myself, 'What a guy,' and told him yeah, it would be a good idea. I mean who would think that the asshole would be stealing from me after twenty years of marriage."

"How did you come to the conclusion that he took out the money?"

Lindie said, "When I received copies of the checks made out on that account, it became very clear *where* he was spending the money. Six made out to Benman's Fine Jewelers. Occasionally, Ray bought me a necklace or a bracelet for special occasions—Mother's Day, my birthday, Christmas—that kind of stuff. But six checks? Uh-uh, no way Ray wrote those checks. Then I noticed that they had invoice numbers on them. When I called up the store to ask about the invoices, I got the shock of my life. My first thought, naively, was that someone had gotten into the account. Logical, right?"

"Right."

"Someone must have forged Ray's signature. But then in talking to the owner of the shop actually, he remembered Ray because the bastard bought a fucking Chopard and had it inscribed on the back. *'To Roseanne with my deepest love from Ray.'* I felt so sick I just wanted to throw up!"

"Spending *your* money for his girlfriend," Decker said.

"Like they say in limbo, how low can you go." A long sip of the latte. "Can you believe that?" She held up the paper cup. "Can I get another one of these?"

"Sure." He looked at the camera. "Another special-order latte for Mrs. Holmes, please?"

Lindie was muttering. It took about ten minutes to get her designer coffee. Within a couple of sips, she became talkative again. "And then he has the nerve to ask me to post bail? What a schmuck!"

"It's a lot of money . . . his bail."

"It's over a quarter-million dollars. Even at ten percent, I would still have to take out a second on the house. Not to mention the lawyers' fees. He can rot in prison, for all I care. I want to file charges. I want my money back! I'm going to need every penny. I have kids. Thank God he couldn't touch the college fund."

She leaned over and looked at Decker intently.

"How do I get my money back?"

So that was her agenda. Maybe Decker could work with it. "Mrs. Holmes, what your husband did was despicable."

"You said it!"

"It's morally reprehensible."

"Damn right."

"Unfortunately, it isn't a crime."

"What?" Lindie screamed. "The bastard stole money from me!"

"Technically, he didn't steal anything because his name was on the account."

"But only in emergencies and if I was incapacitated!"

"I know what the intent was, Mrs. Holmes. And you're right. He was clearly taking money from you and using it in an inappropriate way—"

"He was spending *my* money on *his* mistress."

"I realize that. It's terrible, it's immoral, it's just plain wrong." Decker winced. "But it isn't illegal."

"That's ridiculous. Can't I can file a police report for theft or something?"

"I'm sure a savvy lawyer and you could come up with a plan . . . sue him for fraud in civil court. Maybe that would work."

"I can't afford a lawyer right now."

"There are people who might take the case pro bono," Decker lied. "Maybe you can tap into your husband's life-insurance policy or something. I don't think he has a lot of spare cash at the moment. Mr. Holmes is in pretty bad shape right now."

"Fuck the bastard!"

Decker took a deep breath and let it out. "You've been through hell, Mrs. Holmes. My heart goes out to you. Surely, you don't want to be dragged down by your husband any more than you already have been, right?"

Her eyes got wary. "What do you mean?"

"I mean that if you are aware of any other crimes that Mr. Holmes might have done, I'd be happy to listen."

For the first time, the woman was silent.

Decker quickly added, "Of course you know that as Mr. Holmes's wife, you're not required to expose any crimes that your husband may have done and confided in you—"

"I know, Lieutenant. That's called the Fifth Amendment."

It was clear that she and Holmes had talked before. "Exactly," Decker said. "But if you're willing to talk . . . get it off your chest . . . I'll be willing to listen."

Her eyes met Decker's and she studied his face for a long time. "I take it that you think Ray had something to do with the missing flight attendant."

"What I think is that Ray is in a heap of trouble. He's going before a grand jury on capital murder charges against his former sister-in-law, Isabela Devargas."

She shrugged, but her body had stiffened. Color had drained from her face.

"You know that Ray was born Belize Hernandez. That his brother and sister-in-law went missing over thirty years ago. Ray was involved. You know that."

Another shrug. Decker regarded the woman. She was more than happy to level fraud charges against Holmes, but she balked at murder.

Decker said, "It's all going to come out. Now's the time for you to tell me your side of the story."

"Nothing to tell," Lindie said.

"I'm not interested in giving you any more grief, Mrs. Holmes. I'm just interested in getting at the truth."

Again, Decker was met with silence. He said, "Would you like another latte?"

"Yeah, actually, I would. Thank you."

"How about something to go along with it?"

"Just the latte."

The request was entered. Again, another coffee was brought in to her. Decker neglected to tell the camera decaf and Lindie didn't correct him. That was good. He wanted her awake and edgy. After a few sips, she started talking again.

"I can't believe he took my money."

"I can completely believe it," Decker said. "Your husband has a past."

"Don't we all?"

The words twanged Decker's antennae. He tried to be subtle, but he found himself studying her face. She was around Holmes's age, and Decker could easily imagine her as a hippie in the seventies.

"You were a member of the church, weren't you?" Before she could answer, Decker said, "And don't tell me you don't know what I'm talking about. We've already located two of the church's former members—Alyssa Bright Mapplethorpe and Christian Woodhouse. They'll have no trouble identifying you as one of their own. I'd like to hear your side of the story."

She took another sip of coffee and said, "I have no side of the story. I don't know what you're talking about."

"You expect me to believe that?" Decker said. "You honestly expect me to believe that you, as a member of the Church of the Sunland, didn't know about the disappearance of Beth and Manny. You expect me to believe that you didn't know about the stolen money. You honestly expect me to believe that you didn't know your husband was there when Beth Devargas was murdered. You know what, Mrs. Holmes? I don't believe you. And if I don't believe you, I think a grand jury won't believe you, either. So either you tell me your side of the story or you're on your own."

Not a word was spoken, but the tears streaming down the woman's face spoke volumes. Finally she whispered, "I was twenty years old, Lieutenant."

"You were very young, and it was a long time ago," he said gently. "So as best as you can, tell me what happened that night."

She was sobbing now. "I don't know what happened because I wasn't there."

"You were an innocent victim caught up in something that you didn't do."

"Exactly!" More tears. "Oh God, that's always been my problem. My stupid naïveté. My daughter's the same way."

Decker reached over and patted her hand. She grabbed it and gave it a squeeze. "I was in love with him. That must make me the biggest sucker in the world."

"He's a smooth-talking guy." Decker removed his hand from hers, then went for the jugular. "Lindie, why don't you start from the beginning and tell me the whole story? Get it off your chest once and for all."

And then she started talking.

43

"OH GOD!" LINDIE Holmes sat back in the chair and looked at the ceiling. The tears were coming freely now, her brown eyes muddied with sadness. "I feel like I did back then . . . when everything came crashing down."

"I'm hear to listen, so why don't you start from the beginning?" Decker had several notepads. Pen poised, he said, "Tell me about yourself, Lindie."

"Nothing to tell. I was a good kid from a nice family. It was the times."

"Crazy times. Lots of good kids got swept away. Where'd you go to college?"

"Kentmore College in Pasadena. Do you know where that is?"

"Absolutely," Decker stated as he wrote. "It was started by the Reverend William Coolidge Jones. It was a bastion of conservatism during very turbulent times."

"Exactly. Most of us came from conservative homes. That's where I met Christian Woodhouse. We started dating with the intention of getting married. I had the wedding planned out in my mind. Then one day at a party, he met Alyssa Bright, who later added the Mapplethorpe, the pretentious twit. After he met her, things radically changed."

"How so?"

"Alyssa was a transplant to UCLA and Berkeley. She introduced Christian to a social conscience, but mostly she introduced Christian to sex and drugs." She shrugged. "I was in love with Christian, so I went along for the ride. He didn't have to prod me too much. It was a hell of a lot more fun than organic chemistry."

Decker nodded, his hand cramping as he wrote as fast as he could. He got a slight break as she finished up her third latte and asked for another.

"All the drugs and partying took its toll. Technically, we dropped out of college, but if we hadn't left, we would have flunked out. Both Christian and Alyssa came from more money than me, but I had some savings in the bank. We pooled our resources and rented some crash pad in the East Valley. Its biggest claim to fame was that it had a lot of bedrooms. To make ends meet, we took in boarders, dropout students like us. We weren't picky about who they were as long as they could pay the rent. In the end, there were twelve of us in the one little house. Drugs flowed, sex flowed, life was one big party." She stared at Decker. "You're around that age. You must know exactly what I'm talking about."

"I know exactly what you're talking about."

"See?" A smile through her tears. "Even cops have a past."

Not much of one. In the early seventies, Decker was a father, a husband, and, most important, a traumatized vet, working as a beat cop in Gainesville, Florida. Still, he gave her a smile. She perked up when her fourth latte appeared. It gave her fortification.

She sipped and said, "After a while all the mindless stuff got boring, so we slipped into the next obvious stage. This was around '73 or '74, I guess. The Beatles and the Stones had discovered the Eastern religions. Now there was a purpose to being stoned. It led to spiritual enlightenment, but when we tried it out, something was lacking. Then

Alyssa brought in Beth and Manny. Things changed. We found our real purpose."

"Let me back it up a moment," Decker said. "How did Alyssa meet Beth?"

"At the coffee shop where they both worked. Alyssa invited her to one of our meditation parties. Beth and Manny happened to be somewhat religious . . . Catholic by birth, but they also had included many Native American customs in their worship. It led to the perfect solution. We created a service that was familiar, but now we had the cachet of including Indian lore. We were entranced. Manny and Beth joined our group. We started our own spin on meditation. Hence the birth of the Church of the Sunland."

Decker wrote and wrote. "Okay, then what?"

"With Manny as our leader, we pulled in some new members. He gave our little group some focus and much-needed gravitas. Otherwise we were just a bunch of white American kids rejecting what we grew up with. People started coming to hear Manny speak. It was Beth's idea to start charging money for the good of the group. She also found the storefront and that made the church a real entity. Beth and Manny used to spin the Indian tales and folklore. Beth taught us all how to cook traditional New Mexican dishes and we held all these potlucks that drew even more people. Beth also gave demonstrations in ceramics and charged for lessons. We used one of the bowls for sacramental wine, and another for an incense burner. It was all very exotic."

"I understand."

"Manny was the natural leader, but Beth was the creative one. She also came up with the idea of buying an organic farm to give the group some real purpose. We all thought it was a fabulous idea. This was before the hard-core organic-food craze, but a lot of hippies were into health food. We were all psyched on the idea. We finally had some goals in our pathetic lives. It was all going so well!" Lindie sighed and drank more latte. "Then Belize showed up."

Decker nodded. "Trouble?"

"With a capital *T*." She wiped away tears. "If Manny and Beth were exotic, Belize was the king of glamour. Belize not only had Indian blood, but he had actually served time in jail. At that time, you've got to remember that there were no such things as criminals, just political prisoners. This was the decade when the Indians took over Alcatraz. Native Americans were hot. Belize was hot. He caught everyone's eye when Manny brought him in one day. Manny worshipped Belize. Their old man was sentenced to something like forty years in prison for murder. Belize took over the role as Manny's father figure."

"Belize took an instant liking to me. Believe it or not, I was cute when I was young. I wish I had had warts on my nose. It would have saved me a lifetime of misery."

Yet she had stuck it out with the guy. Decker said, "He made a play for you?"

"Yes."

"And it flattered you."

"You have to understand, I was always second fiddle . . . more like third fiddle. First in the alpha female position was Beth, then Alyssa, then me, and then some of the others. All of a sudden this exotic, mysterious guy was coming on to me. Instantly, I gained a new stature."

"What happened to Christian as your boyfriend?"

"That broke up a long time ago. He was part of the group, but we were no longer an item. It was a free-for-all." She paused. "Do you know what happened to Christian?"

"He's a headmaster of a very exclusive private school back east."

She rolled her eyes. "Talk about a sellout."

"Maybe he felt he could serve best by educating young minds," Decker said.

"Maybe he fell into the job because that's what his father did. Christian used to deride his dad because he received all these expensive birthday and holiday gifts. Now he's doing the same thing. I use the word 'hypocrite', but look at me. Soccer mom complete with the brownies and the SUV."

"You're raising your children in a wholesome environment. What's wrong with that?"

She gave him a tearful smile. "Thanks."

Decker said, "When you say that it was a free-for-all, I assume you mean all the partying?"

"Of course."

"What about Beth and Manny. Did they get into the partying?"

Her eyes looked past the physical walls that she gazed upon. "For some reason, I remember the two of them as being kind of spiritual. I know they smoked a lot of weed, that I can remember really well. But I don't recall them fucking around a lot. Beth and Manny took their roles as leaders pretty seriously. I remember Manny being more into drugs and food than sex."

Consistent with what Alyssa Bright Mapplethorpe had told Marge. "How long was Belize with the church before things went wrong?"

"He was never really with the church, which is amazing." She blew out air. "In roughly two weeks' time, Belize managed to ruin all of our careful planning and hard work."

"What happened?"

"The man was a goat . . . insatiable . . . some things never change." She blotted tears. "I guess I didn't satisfy him. Or maybe I just wasn't around. He was living with Beth and Manny and Manny wasn't always around. Beth was a beautiful girl."

Decker thought a moment. "He made a pass at Beth?"

"Truly incredible, huh? Why I didn't leave him years ago . . . I'm such an idiot!"

"People get caught in situations," Decker said.

Lindie let out a small laugh. "You do a great job at playing 'good cop.' If I weren't so distraught, I'd probably fall for you."

Decker smiled. "I take it Beth told Manny about Belize's pass?"

"She did. Manny was forgiving of his brother's roving eye, but Beth wasn't. She insisted that Belize move out and get his own place. Belize didn't want to move out. He didn't want to have to pay rent, he wasn't paying for food, mostly he was lazy. And he really resented Beth telling him what to do. The two of them began to argue constantly. Manny tried to keep peace but it was useless. It was inevitable that things would come to a head."

Decker nodded. "Tell me about it. I need to hear your side of the story."

Her eyes moistened. "I don't know what happened because I wasn't there."

"So tell me what you do know."

Her tears had returned. "Something went awry . . . horribly out of control. Belize told me that he . . . he and Beth were arguing . . ." She started to pant. "That the argument got very heated . . . that Beth wouldn't quit . . . that things escalated. They got physical. There was pushing and shoving and the next thing he knew . . ."

She took in a quick breath and forced it out.

"He told me that Beth had hit her head on the wall. He told me that I needed to come over and help him clean up the mess."

"Mess?"

"That's what I asked him. What mess?" She blinked repeatedly to rid her eyes of all the tears—like bailing out a sinking ship. Her voice was barely audible. "He *begged* me to come over. I never heard such desperation. Of course how well did I know him? Something like three weeks?"

"Did you go over to the apartment?"

She nodded slowly. "It was horrible . . . horrific. I didn't know people had that much blood inside of them."

"Describe the scene to me."

"Blood was . . . everywhere. On the walls, on the floor, on the ceiling." She regarded Decker with a trembling lip. "I think I threw up. It was sickening. It was the most . . . I had nightmares for years. I still have them. That's why I remember everything so clearly."

"Poor you," Decker said, and meant it.

She started sobbing. "Thank you for saying that."

Decker let her weep openly until her breathing had slowed to an acceptable rate. Then he said, "The scene wasn't what you expected."

"I don't know what I expected. All I knew is that something horrible had happened. What I should have done was run like hell, drive back to my parents' house, and call the police. Instead, I . . ." Her voice trailed off.

Decker said, "Who was at the apartment when you got there?"

"By the time I arrived, Manny and Beth were gone. Belize was making some pathetic attempt to scrub down the walls."

"Did you ask him what happened?"

"No . . . not at that time. I couldn't speak. I was in a state of shock and Belize was shaken to the core. He pleaded with me to help him clean up the mess. I took a rag and started wiping the blood from the walls. It was nauseating. The smell of fresh blood and knowing that something real bad happened. My punishment for all the hell I put my parents through."

"You can't blame yourself for someone else's crime, Lindie."

Again, she started crying. "I should have seen it coming! I should have left. I should have insisted that Belize leave! I should have, I should have, I should have."

Decker had no words of solace. He waited a few moments then continued. "Did Manny return to the apartment?"

A long, suffering sigh. "He came back about four hours later. By then, Belize and I managed to clean most of it up . . . but it still reeked."

She swallowed hard.

"Manny told us the apartment wasn't clean enough. He said it needed to be spotless before we left. He also said that he needed to pack up his belongings and Beth's as well. His plan was to wait until morning and make it look like he and Beth disappeared with the church funds. He said that he'd take out the money first thing in the morning and then we'd all take off together."

"And what did Belize say to that?"

"Belize did whatever Manny told him to do."

"I thought it was Manny who adored Belize."

"Suddenly the roles reversed and Manny was telling us what to do. He was the only one who was thinking that night . . . preternaturally calm, actually. Maybe it was nerves. Mostly, I remember that he was very pissed at Belize. Unforgivingly so."

"How could you tell?"

"Belize was constantly trying to talk to him and Manny didn't answer. Finally Manny told Belize to shut the fuck up. Manny was always kind of a nice guy . . . seeing him like that, I was terrified. I don't know who killed Beth; either one could have done it. Of course, I was way too petrified to ask."

Decker was battling off a terrible hand cramp. "Tell me what happened next."

Lindie kept shaking her head, trying to rid herself of the dreadful images. "We spent the entire night cleaning the place up. By morning, you could have eaten off the floor, it was that clean. As soon as the bank opened, Manny took out his own money that he had saved with Beth plus the church's savings. We piled into Manny's truck and headed for Vegas. We drove the entire six hours in total silence."

She blew out air.

"I stayed in the hotel room, terrified, panicked, horrified, catatonic . . . waiting for the other shoe to drop. Manny and Belize spent the entire week gambling and getting drunk. Both men were constantly in bad moods and several times I had to lock myself in the bathroom to avoid being a punching bag. Mostly, it was Manny. He was acting like a wild man. Then . . ."

She turned away from Decker. Her profile showed tears running down her cheeks."

"This is so hard." Another swallow. "Toward the end of the week . . . around two in the morning, Belize came back to the hotel in a panic. He ordered me to pack the bags . . . that we had to leave. I was so scared and numb, I just mindlessly obeyed. I was constantly afraid that the police were going to arrest us. I thought they had finally caught up. In a way, I was relieved. But that wasn't what happened at all."

Decker waited.

"Manny got stabbed in a bar fight and the knife went right through the heart. He didn't stand a chance. Belize had his brother's body in the pickup. We needed to get rid of it before someone reported the incident.

"We were out in a flash. We drove and drove into the middle of the Mohave Desert. We buried him somewhere in the middle of nowhere. By the time we finished, it was close to daybreak. We left Nevada and drove to New Mexico because that's where Belize wanted to go. As he drove he told me what had happened that night. He said that Beth had become enraged and suddenly charged Manny with a knife. That Manny reached for the first thing he could find just to fend her off. He s٢١d that Manny killed Beth in self-defense."

"What did Belize say that Manny used to fend her off?" Decker asked.

"He didn't say. He kept saying it was self-defense, but the law wouldn't see it that way. Especially now that Manny was gone, it would look like the both of us killed Manny and Beth in order to steal the church money. He had this way of making me feel that I was part of it all, that I had no choice but to stick by him or else we'd both go down together."

"Do you actually believe that Manny killed Beth?"

She shrugged haplessly. "I don't know who killed Beth. I never questioned Ray's story."

"And do you also believe that Manny died in a bar fight?"

"Totally." Lindie was on surer ground. "Manny was drinking really heavily and was acting really belligerent. He was picking fights with everyone he met. I think it was his way of atoning for what happened . . . his personal method of suicide."

Decker nodded, although he suspected that Lindie was now speaking as the loyal wife. It was clear to him that Belize Hernandez had killed Beth. Now he was just wondering if he killed his brother as well.

Lindie was still talking. ". . . kept saying he would rather die than to go back to prison. He told me I needed to help him, that we needed to start a new life together . . . from scratch. From where I was standing, that sounded like a great idea."

Decker nodded.

"Belize actually convinced me that it was better that Manny had died. Now it looked like Manny and Beth had stolen the church money and disappeared together. I know now that I should have run when I had the chance back in Vegas. But you have to realize that I was scared out of my wits. What if Belize or Manny got mad and hunted me down? I knew that one of them had brutally killed Beth. I was convinced that they would have murdered me without blinking an eyelash."

"Still, you went with Belize to southern New Mexico?"

"He had convinced me it was Manny who was the killer. It was very convenient for me to believe that."

"Do you still believe that?"

"I never asked, Lieutenant. I'm not going to start now."

Decker understood. "So you went with Belize to New Mexico."

"Yes. We stayed there for about two years. As soon as we got there, Belize changed his name to Raymond Holmes. That was *fine* with me. Ray took odd jobs in construction. Then we moved to Arizona, where the building trade was booming. He worked for a firm and learned the business inside and out. My husband's a smart man."

"When did you become Mrs. Holmes?"

"About a year after we moved to Arizona. We settled down into some kind of parody of a normal existence. When Silicon Valley started its construction boom, we moved to San Jose. Ray began a business renovating old homes. He did very well financially. We had kids. We joined a real church. We never spoke about the incidents again."

"And you never thought about leaving him?"

"I thought about leaving him all the time, Lieutenant. I thought about leaving him when I suspected he was having an affair with that flight attendant. It turns out I was right. I knew he was lying. For all his being a criminal, Ray was always a terrible liar. I could always tell when he was trying to snow me. I knew in my heart of hearts, he was lying about the flight attendant. I suppose I just chose not to believe the truth. You have to understand that I was very good at denying what I didn't want to deal with. Staying with him was easier than divorce. And

I think in the back of my mind, I didn't know what Ray might do if I tried to divorce him and take half of my rightful assets."

"You thought he might get violent?"

"Maybe. We had this weird relationship, Lieutenant. We were stuck with each other forever simply because neither of us trusted the other one out of our sight."

44

THE INTERVIEW LASTED close to eight hours. By the time the statement was typed up and signed by Lindie, it was time for breakfast. Decker had been up for thirty hours, kept awake by the sheer energy that comes with solution. Although he was sure in his mind that Belize Hernandez had murdered Beth Devargas, there wasn't enough current evidence to sustain murder beyond a reasonable doubt. There was enough proof to assign Belize some degree of culpability in his brother and sister-in-law's demise. New evidence might be uncovered, but the case was over thirty years old. People die, things get destroyed, memories fade . . .

Lindie Holmes would probably accept some kind of plea to lesser charges in exchange for her statement and testimony. Decker believed her when she stated unequivocally that she hadn't been involved in either Beth's or Manny's murder, but the assignment of charges was up to the district attorney's office. Lindie probably wasn't looking at any jail time because of her cooperation. Why she chose to cooperate when she wasn't required to do so was left up to speculation. Decker figured she had finally had enough of Raymond Holmes. The verification of her husband's affair with Roseanne Dresden, the pilfering of her hard-earned cash, and thirty years of gnawing guilt had finally pushed her to the point of no return. She had confessed freely without much prompting. She not only wanted to be rid of the bastard, but she craved absolution for her part in the horrific past events. Decker couldn't give her that kind of forgiveness. Neither could the Devargases, although their clemency would mean more than Decker's. The only person who could truly exonerate Lindie Holms was dead.

The Holmes/Hernandez case would move past the grand jury: that much was certain. Decker had done all he could do. The rest was up to a good prosecutor and twelve intelligent people.

While Lindie was talking to the D.A., working out a deal to finally disentangle herself from her husband, Decker had a chance to catch up on his cell phone messages.

The news from Marge was good. "It glowed as blue as South Pacific. If there was that much protein after a cleaning, Lord only knew how much was originally there. We're going after a warrant for the car. We expect something first thing in the morning."

Decker glanced at his watch. It was already past "the first thing in the morning." He called Marge on his cell. "Yo."

"It's been a while," Marge said. "You must have had a productive evening."

"I finished up about ten minutes ago."

"Good stuff?"

"Yes, but it's complicated. I'll probably be back in L.A. around two. Did you pull the warrant?"

"We pulled the warrant, we have the car. Things are looking up."

"Great. We'll talk about it later. Cell lines aren't protected, and for all I know, we're being secretly taped by the enemy."

"Who's the enemy?"

"That remains to be seen."

———

AS SOON AS the plane took off, Decker fell asleep. He didn't stir until he felt a slight shaking, courtesy of a flight attendant. He roused himself to a state of semistupor, and was barely conscious enough to drive home from Burbank. He was too tired to notice that he had accidentally driven to his house in the West Valley instead of the station house. Rina took one look at him.

"Go immediately to bed. Do not pass go, do not collect two hundred dollars."

"Can't."

"How long have you been up?"

"Awhile."

"You're the living dead."

"I've got to go back to work. I probably shouldn't be driving. Can you take me back to the precinct?"

"You're asking me to be an accomplice in this folly?"

"I'm *finally* getting somewhere with both cases. I can't stop now."

Rina sighed. "Did you eat?"

"Just tanked up on coffee and even that's not working anymore. Maybe some protein will help."

"Salami sandwich?"

"Way too strong."

"Egg salad?"

"That would be terrific, but only if it's no inconvenience."

"Not at all. Go take a shower and I'll make you some lunch. You'll feel better after you've changed clothes and have eaten."

A shower and food were exactly what he needed. He dragged himself into the bedroom. By the time he'd cleaned up, he felt slightly renewed. He knew he shouldn't waste time by eating at home, but he needed a few moments with his wife to center his aching body. "So tell me what's new?"

"Your daughter made Model UN."

"Really. That's great!"

"Hannah was very proud, although I'm not surprised. The kid could debate her way to the Supreme Court."

"Ain't that the truth? Have you spoken to Cindy and Koby?"

"They're doing fine."

"How's the construction going?"

"Quote, unquote—Mike is a godsend. If you're going to be conscious this weekend, I'll have them over for Shabbos."

"That would be wonderful. To prove my gratitude, I'll make ribs."

"Yum, but don't make promises you can't keep."

"Yeah, you're right about that." He finished off his sandwich. "This really hit the spot." Rina knew him very well. She had made him a second one without even asking. Sheepishly, he picked it up. "Thank you so much."

"You're welcome." She leaned over and kissed his forehead. "Food always tastes better when you're hungry. I take it the case is going well?"

"Not perfect, but good enough." He gave her the salient details, leaving out the gory parts.

"Do you have enough to get it past the grand jury?" Rina asked.

"Yes, I'm pretty sure of that."

"And you believe that the wife wasn't there when it happened?"

"I do."

"So where does that leave you in the case against Raymond Holmes?"

"You mean what do we have against him?"

Rina nodded.

"We have a signed statement given by Holmes's father. In it, Ray told his father that he pushed Beth, and that's how she died. Unfortunately, the father is now backtracking, claiming his memory is fuzzy. He's now saying that it could have been Manny who pushed Beth and being that the guy is close to eighty, maybe he was confused."

"And what do you think?"

"First of all, Beth didn't die by hitting the back of her head against a wall. She died because someone bashed in her head with a blunt object. According to Lindie, there was spatter everywhere."

"Ugh!"

"Sorry."

"That's okay. I should be used to it by now. So who do you think hit Beth Devargas?"

"Not that my opinion matters in a court of law, but I *know* it was Raymond Holmes. Manny wasn't described as being violent or having a hairtrigger temper. By the accounts of those who knew him, he was a pretty decent guy who smoked a lot of weed and ate a lot of food. I think after Ray killed Beth, Manny couldn't bring himself to turn in his brother."

"Or maybe he was frightened of his brother."

"Could be, but I don't think so. According to Lindie, after Beth was murdered, Manny took over. Lindie described Manny as being very calm, probably more shock than anything else. After it wore off and Manny realized that he had buried his murdered wife, I think the boy was overcome with guilt. He had lost everything—his father, his brother, his wife. He was despondent. He drank himself into a fatal bar fight: his own brand of suicide."

"Poor man. Trapped by being born into the wrong family."

"Still, people make bad choices," Decker told her. "He should have known his brother was bad news."

"At least Manny was related to Ray. They had a history together. What was Lindie Holmes's excuse?"

"Just plain dumbness."

"And you really don't think she was involved in the murder?"

"Not in the murder, no, but she did help Ray or Belize clean up the mess after Beth was killed. She also helped bury her brother-in-law in the desert."

"So you'll charge her with what? Tampering with evidence?"

"Exactly."

"Suspended sentence."

"Two for two."

"And what about Roseanne Dresden? Do you think Holmes had anything to do with her disappearance?"

"That's an open question." Decker told her about the disposed carpet mats that shone blue with blood protein after being sprayed with lumi-nol. "I haven't ruled out Holmes, especially considering who he is, but he's down on the list. After his arrest, we got access to his credit cards. I turned up a receipt with his signature on it, putting Holmes in San Jose at ten-fifteen on the morning of the crash."

"You found him an alibi."

"I did. There is no way Holmes could have murdered Roseanne that morning, disposed of the body, and then hopped a plane back to San Jose and signed that receipt at ten-fifteen on that same morning."

"Could Holmes have hired someone?"

"The next question, and it's a very good question. So far we don't have any evidence that proves or disproves that theory."

"So that brings you back to Ivan," Rina said. "All that blood on the car mats . . . and Ivan took in the car to be completely reupholstered. There's a logical connection."

"Logic doesn't always enter into the picture, but we do what we can." He looked at his wristwatch. "Ready?"

"Whenever you are."

"That's never." He stood up. "But tuition is expensive and I've got to make a buck, though Lord knows there are easier ways."

"But you love your job," Rina said.

"Sometimes," Decker admitted. "It's rewarding when you solve some perplexing cases and put away some real bad people. But most of the time, the work is a lot of drudgery and just plain sad."

MARGE WAS WAITING for him, a cup of coffee in her hand. "We've got news."

She wasn't smiling but she wasn't frowning. He'd just have to wait for the verdict. Decker pulled out the key to his office. "It's been that kind of week." He opened the door. "Come in and tell me all about it."

She handed him the coffee and stared at his ravaged face. "When was the last time you had some sleep?"

"A while back."

"Go home, Decker," Marge told him. "We can execute warrants without you."

Oliver walked into the office and regarded Decker's puffy face. "You need sleep, Loo."

"I do, but as long as I'm here, you two might as well bring me up to speed. Then one of you has the privilege of taking me home."

"I can do it," Oliver said. "I'm ready to pack it in myself."

"What happened to your car?" Marge asked.

"Rina drove me. I'm not alert enough to be behind a wheel."

"Good call." Oliver leaned against the wall and looked at Decker. "You want to go first?"

Decker sipped coffee. By now, his gut was on fire from all the acid, but being conscious took precedence over comfort. "I have a quick question, first, and then I want you two to tell me what's going on. My question is: Are we still considering Raymond Holmes as a suspect in Roseanne Dresden's murder?"

"Why?" Marge said. "Do you have anything new that would point us in that direction?"

"No, but I'll add this. If Holmes did it, it would most likely have to be a murder for hire. A credit-card receipt puts him in San Jose at ten-fifteen on the morning of the crash. So I'm flinging the question back to you. Do you have any indication that he was involved?"

Oliver and Marge exchanged looks. Then she said, "I'll repeat what you told me over the phone. It's complicated."

"This is not what I wanted to hear," Decker said. "Okay, what do we know so far?"

"We are pretty sure that the Beemer was a kill spot," Oliver said. "Forensics stripped off the new carpet, went down to the original metal, and sprayed it with luminol."

"It lit up like blue fireworks," Marge said. "There was a big pool of blue on the rear floor behind the driver's seat, but there was also a lot of fluorescent spatter."

"On the steering wheel, on the dash, on the gauges, on the gearshift, on the convertible roof, which wasn't replaced, just cleaned."

"There was a steady stream that fluoresced on the glove compartment. It looks like the initial spurt that might come from a stab wound that hit a major artery."

Decker said, "Do we know if the blood is Roseanne's?"

"Not yet," Oliver said. "We called up Shareen Lodestone and asked her if she might have something that contains her daughter's DNA, like an old hairbrush or an old toothbrush."

"No go on the toothbrush, but she does have an old hairbrush," Marge said.

"We need a hair with a root," Decker said.

"Yes, that would help," Oliver said. "But even if we don't find a hair with a root, we can always do a mitochondrial DNA. If Shareen's mitochondrial DNA a is perfect match to the mitochondrial DNA extracted from the blood, we can establish that the blood has to have come from a female progeny of Shareen. The woman doesn't have any other daughters. I think the conclusion is obvious."

"Can we extract mitochondrial DNA from the samples we have?"

"According to forensics, definitely," Marge told him. "The samples are not that old and not that degraded. Plus they found what they think might be tissue."

"Excellent." Decker smoothed his mustache. "So if there's a match, we can be almost certain that she was murdered in her car."

"With that much fluorescence, it's a safe bet," Marge told him.

"Can we put Ivan at the scene?"

Marge said, "We found some latent bloody prints. Several partials on the dash and a lovely right thumbprint on the steering wheel itself."

Oliver said, "Meaning that the prints were made at the time Roseanne was murdered in her car."

"You're hesitating. What is it? The prints aren't Ivan's?" Marge and Oliver shrugged. Decker swore. "Do you have *anything* that links Ivan to the bloody scene?"

Oliver said, "We have his prints all over the place, but since he's been driving the car for over six months that proves nothing."

"Damn!" Decker told himself to backtrack. Let the evidence point to the suspect and not the other way around. "Where is Ivan right now?"

Marge shrugged. "We have a warrant to search his car for blood, Loo, not one for his arrest."

"We're working on that," Oliver told him. "As soon as the blood is determined to be Roseanne's, we'll get a warrant for his arrest."

"In the meantime, he goes south of the border?" Decker said.

"Wanda Bontemps and Lee Wang are watching him."

"Where is he?" Decker repeated. When the question was met with silence, Decker said, "Scott, call Wanda and find out where Mr. Dresden is currently parking his ass."

Oliver left wordlessly. Decker looked at Marge. "I take it you're running the prints through AFIS?"

Marge answered, "George Kasabian is on it, and he'll call either way."

"He's good," Decker said. "How long has he had the prints?"

"About an hour."

"Let's hope he's contemplating something." No one spoke for a moment. Then Decker said, "Do you have Kasabian's number?"

Marge read it off of her cell. Decker put the phone line on speaker and punched in the number. George announced himself after picking up on the fourth ring.

"Hi, George, it's Pete Decker from West Valley."

"Welcome back, Lieutenant," Kasabian told him. "I was just about to call you. Actually, I was just about to call Marge Dunn."

"I'm right here, George," Marge answered. "What's the good word?"

"If you have a pencil, I have a name."

Two shocked but spontaneous grins. Decker gave his hands a loud clap and said go into the speakerphone.

"The thumbprint belongs to Patricia Childress." He spelled the last name and gave them Childress's date of birth. "These particular prints were taken when she was arrested for prostitution seven years ago."

"God bless vice." Decker handed the information to Marge. "Dunn is going to feed her information into the computer. Thanks, George. You made my day."

"I made my own day."

Decker hung up and rushed over to the computer. Marge had input-ted the data and the information on Patricia Childress popped up on the monitor. Two arrests for soliciting, two drunk-and-disorderlies, one misdemeanor drug possession, meaning less than an ounce of weed. At the time of her first arrest, she had been nineteen years of age, five six, 105 pounds, blue eyes, and dark brown hair. Her expression was fear masked by contempt.

"Her last known address isn't too far from here," Marge said. "I'll get a warrant, and if she still lives there, we'll pay her a visit and bring her in." She pressed the print button to get copies of her mug shot. Decker picked up one of the sheets and stared at the face. "Who are you, Ms. Childress?"

Oliver walked over to where Marge was working. "According to Wanda Bontemps, Ivan Dresden is eating dinner at Sage with a couple of buddies." He looked at the monitor and became excited. "George found a match to the bloody fingerprint?"

"He did." Marge handed him the printed mug shot. "Meet the owner, Ms. Patricia Childress."

Oliver snapped his head back when he saw the picture. "Patricia Childress?"

Decker said, "You've seen her before?"

"I've *met* her before. She was using the name of Marina Alfonse. She's a lap dancer at Leather and Lace. More important, she's Ivan Dresden's girlfriend."

45

O LIVER POINTED OUT a sleek blonde in pasties and a rhine-
stone-studded thong, grinding away at a customer. "That's her."
Marge nodded. "Let's do it."

The two of them walked over to Patricia Childress a.k.a. Marina Alfonse and pulled her off the lap of a sweaty bald man in his late fifties.
He was incensed but not as mad as she was. "What the fuck?"

Marge flashed her badge. "Police, Ms. Childress. You need to come
with us."

"I'm clean!" she cried. "I swear I'm clean!"

"We believe you," Marge said. "We're not from narcotics."

"Homicide," Oliver answered.

The owner of the club came rushing over and asked what was going
on. Oliver showed him the shield and said, "Hello, Mr. Michelli, nice
to see you again. We have a warrant for the arrest of Marina Alfonse—
whose real name is Patricia Childress—"

"You!" Recognition of Oliver's face in the dancer's eyes. She had
turned ashen. "I had nothing to do with it. It was all Ivan's idea!"

Michelli said, "Can we do this in a more private place?" He regarded the confused look on the customer's face. "You'll get every penny back, sir." To the cops, Michelli said, "This way."

The detectives followed Michelli, guiding a furious dancer between them, until they stepped into the common makeup and dressing room. The owner waited until after Marge had Mirandized his dancer. Then he said, "You're fired, Marina. Pack up your things and go."

"But I swear I didn't *do* anything, Mr. Michelli!" Patricia cried out.

Michelli glared at the dancer. "Get her out of here!"

By now, Patricia was sobbing. Her makeup was smeared, black streaks of mascara running tracks down her cheeks. She moved slowly, taking off her thong and her pasties until she was stark naked. With effort, she poured herself into her street clothes—a low-cut pink T-shirt, skintight jeans, spike-heel sandals, and a hooded sweater jacket. Since she was still wearing loads of cheap rhinestone jewelry around her neck and arms, she looked like a streetwalker. Patricia had stuffed her working clothes into a giant handbag and looped it over her shoulder. Tears were still washing her face. "It was all *his* idea."

"You can tell us all about it at the station house." Oliver grabbed one of Patricia's arms and Marge grabbed the other. They led her out the back door, into the parking lot, and toward the unmarked car. Oliver let go of her arm to pull out the handcuffs. As soon as he did this, Marge turned Patricia until she was looking at the dancer's back, pulling one of her arms behind her in anticipation of snapping on cuffs. That's when something metallic winked at her.

It could have been the jewelry, but Marge didn't stop to figure out what it was. She threw the woman down to the ground and pounced on top of her.

A .32 Smith & Wesson skittered out of Patricia's hand, fell to the ground, and discharged, the bullet slicing through the car's rear passenger tire. Immediately, the car sank off balance. Marge stared at the hapless vehicle.

What was it with her and flat tires at the most inconvenient times?

By now Marge was riding Patricia's back and had yanked her arms around as Oliver clamped on the manacles.

"That was dumb." He straightened up and picked up the dancer's purse. "What else do you have in here, Patricia?"

"My name is Marina and I don't have anything in there!"

"You have Mace."

"A girl needs protection!"

"What the hell is this?" Carefully Oliver pulled out a leather sheath. Inside was a seven-inch boning knife. He handled it gingerly, knowing that he could be looking at a murder weapon. "A gun *and* a knife and *Mace*? Are you planning to take on some terrorists?"

"I didn't *do* anything!"

"Lady, you just tried to *shoot* me!" Marge exclaimed.

"I wasn't trying to shoot anyone," Patricia yelled back. "If you wouldn't have jumped me, the gun wouldn't have gone off!"

"Oh my God!" Marge's heart was beating like a hummingbird. She didn't want to say anything she'd regret, so she kept silent.

Patricia was yelling. "I was just trying to get rid of the gun so I wouldn't get into trouble."

Marge got off the dancer's back and jerked her to her feet. "Guess what, Patricia! It didn't work!"

DECKER WAS GRATEFUL that he had gone home instead of straight to work. It had forced him to shower, change, and eat and made him much more presentable for the long hours needed for the upcoming interviews. Patricia Childress a.k.a. Marina Alfonse had been charged with capital murder, ADW, weapons possession, as well as resisting arrest. She wasn't going anywhere. Ivan Dresden was another story. He had been asked to come in voluntarily to answer a few routine questions about the Beemer, using the pretense that the police were planning to return it shortly.

Decker wanted to see whose story best fit the forensic facts. He figured that both of them were in on the crime. Whoever was deemed the more reliable would be tapped as the state's witness against the other. It was possible that neither one would qualify, but he wouldn't know that until he had heard both sides.

Since Oliver had dealt with Patricia before and since it was likely that Patricia favored men over women, he was elected the primary interviewer of the stripper. Decker would try his luck with Ivan Dresden. He was relieved when Dresden walked into the station house without his lawyer—not likely to remain that way once the questioning got started. It was Decker's job to put Dresden in a talkative mood.

"Thanks so much for coming in, Mr. Dresden." He did a quick once-over of his prey. The stockbroker had on a black muscle T, a pair of black jogging pants, and a sweat jacket. Athletic shoes on his feet. His hair was combed back and he was newly shaven. The man appeared comfortable and that was good. To make him even more comfortable, Decker had brought in two cups of coffee with packets of powder and sugar and laid them on the steel table: that along with three steel chairs composed the furniture in the room. He sat down, took a sip from one of the paper cups, then loosened his tie and tried to appear casual. "Just in case you want some coffee."

"No." Dresden was dour. "How long is this going to take?"

"How about some water?"

"You didn't answer my question."

"I know." Decker grinned. "That's a police technique we learn at the academy. Never answer questions."

Dresden wasn't biting. "When do I get my car back?"

"Aren't you curious why we took it in the first place?"

Dresden said, "Is that also a technique? To answer a question with a question?"

"You caught me." Decker pulled out a pad of paper and his pen. "We're trying to rule out the possibility that you had anything to do with your wife's disappearance. We checked your condo and that was clean. Next step was the car."

"Then why did you bother with a warrant?" Dresden sulked. "Why not just ask me? You could have checked the car."

Decker wrote as he spoke. "We just like to do everything by the book."

"And what book is that? The comic book?" Dresden shook his head. "You said you had a few questions and then I'd get my car back. I came here without my lawyer. I'm trying to be cooperative, but everyone has a limit."

"Then I'll sum things up for you," Decker said. "We talked to Jimbo Jim Franco at Jim's upholstery. You had the entire car redone about a month after the crash. I'm curious about that."

"First of all, I didn't redo the entire car," Dresden said. "I changed the carpets and the upholstery. Roseanne had some kind of whitey, creamy color that looked too feminine for my taste." He looked down at the tabletop. "Also the car reminded me too much of Roseanne. I wanted to keep the car, but I didn't want a ghost riding around with me. Plus, I sold my own car to pay some debts. So if that's a crime, sue me."

"The upholstery was cream but the carpets were black. Why replace black carpets with new black carpets?"

Dresden's eyes shifted. "Didn't Jimbo tell you the whole story?"

"Jimbo doesn't talk a lot. Why don't you tell me?"

An exasperated sigh and a glance at his watch. "How long is this going to take? Am I under arrest or something?"

"Why do you ask?"

"I mean I can just walk out right now, right?"

"You don't want to do that, Ivan." Decker leaned forward and pushed the coffee in front of him. "Just tell me about your car and we can all go home."

Reluctantly Ivan picked up the coffee and began to dress it to his liking. It gave him something to do. "I loaned the car to someone who left it out in the rain with the top down. Everything got ruined. Moldy and wet and smelly. That's why I had it done."

"Who'd you loan it to?"

"Does it matter?"

"Yes, it does. We need names to verify your stories."

Ivan's eyes narrowed. "This was precisely why I didn't want to come in here. Not only are you hounding me, you're going to get someone else involved."

"And you'd rather not get someone else involved?"

"I know why I'm here." Dresden glared at Decker. "You think I hurt my wife."

Decker said, "You sound outraged!"

"Of course I'm outraged. Not only did I lose my wife, but you idio— You people think I had something to do with her disappearance."

"Do you have any idea what happened to her!"

"How many times do I have to tell you? I don't know what happened to Roseanne!"

"I believe you, Ivan." Decker leaned in again. "I really do and that's precisely why I insisted that we call you up and have you come in voluntarily. So you can explain the problem we have." He paused, giving the words a chance to sink into Dresden's brain. "We found stuff in the car, Ivan. We need some help with that."

"What do you mean by stuff?" His eyes got big. "Oh shit! The cops planted drugs—"

"Not drugs, Ivan." Decker shook his head in earnest. "No drugs whatsoever. We found blood, Ivan. Roseanne's blood."

Dresden went white. "What?"

"We found Roseanne's blood in the car, Ivan." Decker sincerely hoped that his words were the truth. He certainly didn't want to deal with the possibility that the blood was from someone else. "Lots of blood, and that's troubling. That's why I brought you in. Out of respect. Because I believe you when you say you don't know what happened to Roseanne. That's why I have to hear your side of the story."

Dresden's eyes went from side to side. "I don't know what you're talking about."

"So let me explain the situation to you. We know that nothing bad happened to Roseanne in your condo. We searched it and it looked okay. So right away, we didn't suspect that you did anything bad to her. Are you with me, buddy?"

Dresden nodded.

"But here's the problem. Roseanne didn't die in the crash, Ivan. Recovery has unearthed things or remains belonging to everyone involved in the crash *except* Roseanne. Nothing, *nothing,* puts Roseanne at the crash sight. And this is a problem for us. What happened to Roseanne? I assume because she's your wife, it's a problem for you, too. I mean not that you're a ghoul, but you are entitled to insurance money once we clear up her disappearance."

Decker waited for a response but nothing came.

"I'm sure you would like to put this entire episode behind you. And I'm trying to help you do that."

"You're not trying to help me. You're trying to trap me to say something I shouldn't say."

"Then don't talk for a moment and just listen. I'm thinking to myself that if nothing bad happened to Roseanne in the condo and Roseanne wasn't in the crash, maybe . . . just maybe . . . something bad happened in her car. My detective and I were attacking the problem from every angle we could think of. We've been relentless: going back over our notes, knocking on door after door after door, reinterviewing witnesses."

"What witnesses?"

"I'm getting to that. All I'm saying right now is we've been working nonstop on your wife's disappearance and it finally paid off. We caught a break. On the day of the crash, the day that Roseanne disappeared, we found a witness who saw Roseanne's car flying out of the condo parking structure at around sevenish in the morning."

Dresden paled, but remained silent. Decker didn't know how much longer he had before Dresden lawyered up. He tried not to sound too accusing, but the implication was clear.

"Ivan, this is the kicker. Roseanne wasn't driving." He didn't know that for a fact, but Ivan didn't have to know that, either. Decker leaned in close. "We did hard-nosed investigating, and we found out that you had the car reupholstered. No big deal concerning that. I accept your explanation. But just for the sake of completion, we learned that you told Jim Franco to throw away the original car mats from Roseanne's

BMW. I think the words you used were 'to chuck them in the garbage.' Do you remember telling Jim Franco that?"

"No."

"Well, Jimbo remembers you telling him that. He's willing to swear to it in court."

Dresden was quiet.

Decker said, "Jimbo's a businessman, Ivan. He doesn't like to throw away money. So instead of chucking them, he cleaned them and sold them to someone on e-Bay. I think you know where this is leading." Decker nodded. "We tracked that person down, found the carpets, and tested them for blood. They tested positive . . . very, very positive. Once the mats tested positive, that's when we got a warrant for the car to see if it was just the mats were covered in blood or maybe there had been more blood where that came from. See, I really need to find out what happened to Roseanne. Taxpayers are giving me good money to do my job and I take it seriously. Now, I'm trying to get you out of this mess. So bear with me a moment, okay?"

Again, Dresden didn't answer. Decker noticed his skin color had turned slightly green. He sipped coffee.

"The next step after we tested the mats was to test the car for blood. We stripped the car down and sprayed it with luminol and it lit up bright blue. That means forensics found lots of blood protein. We also found patterns—blood spurting, blood pooling, blood spraying."

Dresden buried his head in his hands. "I'm feeling a little sick."

"Yeah, it's pretty sickening. You feel light-headed?"

"A little."

"Can I get a paper bag, some water, and some paper towels, please?" Decker asked the video camera. A minute later, the supplies were delivered. He told Ivan to breathe into the bag while Decker mopped up his brow. "Try to breathe slowly—"

"Just leave me alone for a few seconds, okay?"

Decker complied. After the minutes passed, Dresden raised his head. He looked pale and dank. Decker offered him water and the stockbroker eagerly drank it up. "How are you holding up?"

"I want to go home."

"Just let me finish and then we can talk about that."

"I still feel sick."

"I'm sure you do. It's nauseating to hear all this, but for your own protection, you should know what's going on. I'm trying to clue you in so you know what we're after, okay?" Dresden nodded, although his eyes looked a bit dazed. "We know that something bad happened in that car. We know that for sure. We know that because we found other things besides the blood."

Dresden stared at him, sweat pouring down his brow. Decker offered him a paper towel.

"We found fingerprints, Ivan. Not just your normal fingerprints, because we know that you drive the car. We expected to find your fingerprints. But we found *bloody* fingerprints."

Decker began to tick off his fingers.

"We've got witnesses that saw Roseanne's car speeding away, we've got Roseanne's blood all over her car, we've got fingerprints, *and* we have your stripper girlfriend, Marina Alfonse, in the next room who is talking as fast as a hurricane—"

"*What?*"

"She's not feeling very kindly to you right now—"

"I don't know what that bitch is saying, but she's a pathological liar!" Dresden blurted out. "She's been arrested for prostitution! She's on drugs!"

Decker said, "You see, that's precisely why I want to hear your side of what happened. Because what she's been telling us isn't good for you. So set the record straight and tell me what happened."

"I don't *know* what happened," Ivan yelled out. "Why don't you believe me?"

"I do believe you, Ivan," Decker said. "So let's go back to my first couple of questions. Tell me why you got the car reupholstered."

"I told you; because Marina left it out in the rain."

"So you gave the car to Marina?"

"No, she took it . . . she . . ."

Decker said, "Ivan, why don't you start at the beginning?"

Suddenly Dresden's eyes watered. He slumped in the chair and shook his head. The next time he spoke, his voice was soft and defeated.

"What's the dif? You won't believe me anyway."

"Why don't you start with the truth and let me decide. Despite what Marina's been saying, I haven't arrested you. I'm a fair guy. Help me out so I can help you out."

Dresden took in a deep breath then let it out. "This is all I know, okay? And it isn't much."

Decker waved his hand, signaling for him to continue.

"After Roseanne died in the crash—"

"She didn't die in the crash, Ivan."

"I know, I know." Dresden mopped up his sweaty face with the provided paper towels. He took another drink of water. "After I *thought* she died in the crash, I was a basket case, you know. Everything was like a blur. Especially . . ." He held up his hand and swallowed with difficulty. "Especially because Roseanne and I had just gotten into a big fight . . . well, not a big noisy fight. It was a silent fight . . ."

He buried his head in his hands, holding up a single finger indicating he needed a minute. Decker waited him out. Again, he lifted up his face.

"Roseanne wasn't supposed to come back from San Jose until later in the afternoon. She called me the night before and left a message on the machine, telling me that . . . that she'd be home tomorrow around two. When I played back the message and heard it, I was with . . ." Another swallow. "I was . . . Marina was over the condo. We both heard the message, so Marina decided that rather than have me take her home . . . it was pretty late and she doesn't live all that close . . . well, we decided that she should just sleep over and I'd take her home early the following morning."

Decker nodded encouragingly. "Makes total sense."

"Yeah, that's what I thought. But . . ." Dresden shook his head. "Roseanne must have changed her schedule and didn't tell me about it. She came home at six-thirty in the morning and found us together."

"Where?"

"In the condo."

"I mean what room?"

"Oh . . . not in bed," Dresden told him. "Thank God for that. I had to go into work early that morning . . . I told the police that."

"Yes, you did."

"So we were already dressed and I was making coffee when she came in. But then she saw Marina and saw that her hair was wet. Roseanne assumed the worst."

Way more than just a simple assumption, Decker thought. "What happened next?"

"The marriage was over anyway," Dresden said. "But I didn't want it to end . . . I didn't want her having ammunition against me in divorce court, actually. And if that sounds bad, well, she wasn't the saint that everyone says she was. She was fucking around on me just as much as I was screwing around on her."

"I know that," Decker said. "So what did Roseanne do when she saw you two together . . . and Marina's wet hair?"

"She made some little snide comment about how she hoped I liked my whore because I was going to need a place to stay very soon." He shook his head. "I went nuts. I grabbed her. I shouldn't have done it, but I was angry. Like I said, she was fucking around, too."

"I understand. She got your goat."

"Man, did she ever, the little bitch! So I grabbed her and shook her hard and said something like, 'Talk about whores.'" His eyes welled up. "I don't remember what happened after that. My recollections get a little fuzzy. I was furious and she was furious. I remember that we tussled. I think I must have pushed her. Her purse fell to the ground and opened up . . . that must have been when her phone dropped out. I don't remember if she said anything to me . . . maybe she whispered 'bastard.' But as soon as she was free, she picked up her purse and stormed out of the condo."

He was breathing hard.

"I was so mad I was shaking. I wanted to *kill* her!"

He looked at Decker.

"But I *didn't*. I remember Marina telling me to calm down and that she'd handle it. Then she picked up her own purse and left. I sat down on the couch, waiting for Marina to come back. I was trying to get a grip on myself. A few minutes passed, a few more passed. I suddenly realized that my shirt buttons had popped off and there were scratch marks on my chest. Roseanne must have attacked me with her nails and that's why I pushed her . . . to get her off of me."

Decker nodded. He had taken two confessions in two days. His hand was going to fall off soon from writing so much. "You pushed her to get her off, not to hurt her."

"No, not to hurt her." He glared at Decker. "And I *didn't* hurt her. She was fine when she left. I mean she was mad but she wasn't hurt. I went into the bedroom to change my shirt. I was starting to focus on what happened. Then I realized that about a half hour had passed and neither one of the bitches had come back. After I changed my shirt, I put on my suit jacket and decided to go to work. I looked around the condo's parking lot before I left. There was no sign of Marina or Roseanne or Roseanne's car."

He shrugged.

"I went to work. About a half hour later I heard about the crash. I think a coworker told me. I don't remember too clearly. I went numb when I heard the news! I wasn't sure where Roseanne was. I didn't think automatically that she was on the flight, but I wasn't sure."

Decker said, "So what did you do?"

"I tried calling Roseanne, of course. I must have called her about twenty times in a row until finally I get this incoming call from Marina, who's calling me to tell me how sorry she was. I asked her what she meant."

He swallowed again.

"At the time, I wasn't thinking that Roseanne had been on the plane, only that it was a WestAir crash and maybe she needed me for support."

"You honestly thought that?"

"She was still my wife." He drank more water. "I really don't know what I was thinking! But then Marina told me that Roseanne was on the plane. I felt faint. I asked her how she knew that. She said that she had talked to Roseanne in the condo parking lot . . . that they agreed to talk later, woman-to-woman, but that Roseanne couldn't talk at the moment because she had to catch the flight that crashed . . ."

Again, he buried his head. Decker waited for him to resurface.

"I blacked out. When I came to I was sick, I was confused, I was . . . it didn't make any sense to me. If Roseanne was going back to San Jose right away, why would she go home first? But then I thought about the fight and maybe that was why . . ."

More tears.

"I was too stunned to question Marina's story. On some level, it made sense. I couldn't get hold of Roseanne and now Marina was telling me she was on that plane."

Tears ran down his face.

"I was in a stupor for a long time afterward. I didn't go to work, I didn't go out, I didn't call anyone, and I didn't answer any calls. I drank a lot because I was a wreck." He shook his head. "I was a zombie."

"I'm sure you were," Decker said. "And I feel very bad for you. But we still have the car problem, Ivan. How did Roseanne's blood get all over the car?"

"I don't know!" Dresden protested. "I don't have any idea."

"You say that when you went out to the parking lot that morning, Roseanne's car was gone."

"Yes."

"So how'd you get it back?"

Dresden furrowed his brow, trying to bring back the memory. "I think . . . I . . . oh, wait. Okay. This is what happened. A few days later, or maybe it was a day later—it was after the airport reopened—Marina came back with Roseanne's car, saying that she picked it up at the airport for me. She said she didn't want me to have to think about something so trivial, so she did me the favor."

"How'd she get the keys to the car, Ivan?"

"I don't *know* how she got the keys unless she took them from Rose-anne."

Bingo, Decker thought.

"But why would I think that? I was still thinking that Roseanne died in flight 1324."

"So she brought you the car a few days later?"

"No . . . No . . . wait . . ." He thought a few moments. "Okay, this is what happened. Marina said she had the car. Then she asked if she could borrow it for a while. At first, I told her no, that it would be a very bad idea for her to drive it. You know, that it would look weird for my girlfriend to be driving my wife's car a few days after she died. That's when she told me that she had actually picked up the car from the airport after the crash and that it smelled funky . . . that some old food had been left inside and she wanted to take it to the car wash or have it professionally cleaned or something like that. I think I asked her where the car was now and she told me it was at her apartment. So I told her return it to me as soon as it was clean. I also told her that we shouldn't see each other right after Roseanne died. Man, did she get pissed! It wasn't like I was planning to dump her. I just needed some time to myself."

"Totally understandable. So what did she say to you when you wanted to cool it for a while?"

"I don't remember the exact words, just that she was going on and on about how she was going to tell everyone about the affair and that I wasn't worth her time and that she was going to ruin me. I *finally* shut her up by promising her some insurance money once the whole thing was settled."

"And calmed her down?"

"A little. I don't know. I don't remember anything too well." He rubbed his forehead. "I think it took about a month for her to finally bring me back the car. It reeked of mold. I asked her what the hell happened. She told me she was really sorry, but she left it out in the rain with the top down. But then she handed me twenty-five hundred bucks in cash and told me to get the car reupholstered the way I liked. She gave me Jim Franco's name and told me that he'd do a great job and after all I'd been through didn't I deserve a little something for me?"

"You weren't suspicious?"

"Man, those days were such a haze. I had taken a leave of absence for a month and I wasn't doing anything except drinking . . . smoking, if you get my drift."

"Got it."

"So Marina gives me twenty-five big ones and tells me to clean up Roseanne's Beemer, I figured that the bitch actually had a good idea. So that's what I did. I changed the car inside and out . . . it was a real mess . . . and that's the last I thought about it. Then you guys started sniffing around, telling me that Roseanne didn't die in the crash. The second the police got involved, I knew Roseanne's father-in-law must have said something. The man absolutely hates my guts. That's okay. I don't like him, either. So I wasn't concerned because why should I be nervous? I didn't do anything wrong . . . I mean, I cheated on my wife, but she cheated on me. I certainly didn't hurt her. Even after that lady detective found the phone, I still figure so what? It's only a phone."

"Why didn't you just give it to the police instead of destroying it?"

"Because, I don't know . . . I was shocked to see it. Like I told you, it must have fallen out of Roseanne's purse when I pushed her. You guys were already on my case. I wasn't going to admit to a bad fight on the morning she died. You can understand that."

"I do."

"Anyway, when the search of the condo came up dry for you, I thought, 'Finally, that's that!' Then you started in on my car . . . I called my lawyer up as soon as you executed the warrant to search my car. He asked me if I had anything to worry about and I told him no, I didn't. So he told me not to say anything if the police ask me questions, and that I should call him if things got hairy. When you called me up, saying that there were just a few questions you needed to ask, I figured why should I pay that jerk two-fifty an hour just to answer a few questions?"

A moment of silence.

"I probably should have called him up." He paused. "But I didn't *do* anything. Why do I need a lawyer? I don't *know* what happened to Roseanne!"

"She was murdered in her car."

"I wasn't *there*. I didn't run after her. *Marina* ran after her. Why don't you ask her what happened? She may actually have an answer for you!"

46

AS IT TURNED out, Patricia Childress a.k.a. Marina Alfonse had absolutely nothing to say. Thirty seconds into the questioning, she sobered up enough to ask for a lawyer—exactly what Dresden should have done. Decker thought that maybe he hadn't asked for representation because he had actually thought he had done nothing wrong. And since there was no physical evidence that linked him to the murder scene in the car, maybe he was telling the truth when he insisted he wasn't there. Dresden was eventually charged with tampering with evidence—suspended sentence and two years' probation. Although the law may have allowed him to slip through the cracks, insurance wasn't going to play so gently. He'd be tied up for years in court before he'd see a single red cent from his wife's death.

Patricia Childress wasn't going anywhere. The police had her bloody fingerprint at the scene, but most important, the knife that Oliver had pulled out of Childress's purse had minute amounts of Roseanne Dresden's blood on it. She had been charged with premeditated murder. Since she faced a possible death sentence, she pleaded guilty to murder two and a minimum sentence of twenty-four years in prison in exchange for her full confession, telling police exactly what happened in Roseanne's Beemer, and also where she had buried the body.

At the personal invitation of the Lodestones, Decker flew up to Fresno to attend Roseanne's funeral. Afterward, Farley, somber and uncomfortable in a black suit, thanked him with a firm handshake and a whisper of a job well done. Shareen squeezed his hand, and with tears running down her face, thanked him profusely for all his hard work. He flew back down to L.A. on the same day and never heard from either one of them again.

IT WAS STILL an hour away from Shabbos when Rina rushed out of the kitchen to answer the knock on the door. She was having a crowd tonight. Hannah had invited two friends to sleep over, and Jacob, on semester break, had brought home a couple of college buddies. She had also invited her parents, plus another couple who were new in the area. Counting Koby and Cindy and Peter—if he made it home from work on time—she was cooking for thirteen.

She couldn't imagine Cindy and Koby coming this early. Maybe it was one of Hannah's friends. She wiped her hands on her apron, threw open the door, and found herself looking at two strangers in their seventies.

The man was wearing an ill-fitting suit and tie; the woman was wearing a green dress, black orthopedic shoes, and had her gray hair knotted into a bun. They were dark-skinned Hispanics with wrinkled faces that had endured lots of sun damage. The woman was carrying an old-fashioned, patent-leather structured bag that was looped around her arm. She was also holding a plate of fresh and dried fruit. They looked as if they had just come back from church—fifty years ago.

"Hi." Rina smiled. "Can I help you?"

The woman spoke. "We're looking for Lieutenant Decker."

Rina kept smiling, wondering what she should do. Peter was always telling her to be very careful, that things happened when they were least expected. For all Rina knew, the two of them could be A-list terrorists.

A terrorist with a fruit plate?

"I believe he's still at work," Rina told them. "Would you like me to give you the address of the police station?"

"We called," the man groused out. "They said he'd left for the day."

"Oh." Again, Rina smiled but still didn't let them inside the door. "So he must be on his way home. Is there something I can help you with?"

The woman's eyes watered. "Your husband was very kind to us."

"And you are?"

"Sandra and Peter Devargas."

Immediate recognition. Rina said, "Oh, please come in."

"We can wait outside," Peter grumped.

"You look very busy," Sandra said.

"I'm always busy," Rina said. "Please come in." She stepped away from the threshold. "I insist!"

Reluctantly, the couple walked inside the living room. The woman said, "This is for your husband and you. Just a little something."

"Thank you so much." Rina relieved her of the fruit plate. "Please sit. Would you like something to drink? Water? Iced tea?"

"Something smells good," Devargas said. "I guess anything would smell good after eating fast food for the last twenty-four hours." His wife poked him in the ribs. The man said, "What?"

Rina smiled. "Thank you for the compliment. I happen to be cooking for our Sabbath, which we observe on Friday night. I made plenty of food. Would you like to stay for dinner?"

Devargas said, "That sound—" Another poke. "What? The woman asked us."

"We're fine, but thank you," Sandra said.

Rina chuckled. "Honestly, it's not a problem."

Devargas shrugged, but Sandra was reluctant. Having dealt with older, ethnic women her entire life, Rina felt something click inside her head. "Really, do stay. I'm having a lot of people. I could always use another pair of hands."

Sandra's knuckles were white from clutching her purse. "Well, if you need some help, I'd be delighted to help you."

"Great. You can make the salad. Just leave your coat and handbag on the couch. Peter will hang it up."

"Where do I hang it?" Devargas asked.

"Sorry, I meant Lieutenant Decker. He can do it when he gets home, which should be pretty soon. Mr. Devargas, you sit down and relax while you can. There are going to be a lot of people coming in and out in the next half hour. If you wouldn't mind catching the door, it would h lp me out."

"Of course he wouldn't mind." Sandra followed her into the kitchen. As soon as she stepped into the warm, humid space, the old woman relaxed. "Just point me in the right direction."

Rina gave her salad vegetables, a big bowl, and a knife. Sandra washed her hands meticulously and began slicing vegetables. They worked a few moments without speaking. Then Sandra said, "I'm so sorry to be barging in on you like this."

"Please. My house is a bus station," Rina said. "People in and out. They follow the food."

"Yes, wherever there is family, there's a meal." The old woman sliced and diced the tomatoes with practiced skill. "Please understand my husband's frankness. He isn't used to fast food. I love to cook and I cook for him. And he is right. Everything does smell very good."

"Thank you."

"What are you making?"

"Well, this here is called a kugel, which is just a Yiddish word for pudding. Yiddish is the language that the Jews spoke in Europe. I made two kinds of kugel tonight—a sweet noodle pudding and a potato pudding."

"Oh, it all looks so wonderful."

"And this big pot here is a stew for tomorrow's lunch. It's called chulent. Jews aren't allowed to cook on Saturday, but if we start the dish on Friday, then we can eat it hot on Saturday."

"That's interesting. What's in it?"

"Meat, potatoes, beans, barley . . . but really you can put whatever you want in it."

"So your husband doesn't eat it?"

"No, Peter eats chulent. He loves chulent."

"But how does he eat it if he's a vegetarian?"

Uh-oh. Rina smiled. "He isn't really a vegetarian, Mrs. Devargas. We're kosher. We can't eat meat unless it has been ritually slaughtered according to our laws. So he tells people he's a vegetarian whenever he's in a bind and doesn't want to insult anyone."

"Oh . . . oh, I see." Sandra nodded. "Well, it was nice of him to tell me that, then."

"He told me that the food you served him was absolutely fantastic. Now that you're here, I'll ask you for the recipes."

"It was just simple cooking."

"That's the best kind."

Sandra smiled and blushed. "Slow cooking. We do a lot of slow cooking, too, especially on Feast Day. For the Santa Clara Indians, it's August twelfth. If you're ever in Santa Fe at that time, you must come and eat with us so we can return the favor." She paused. "I'll make sure that there will be lots of vegetarian dishes that you can eat."

"That would be great. What do you cook?"

"So many dishes you can't even imagine. The dancing goes on from dawn to dusk. The climax is a beautiful corn dance. My daughters . . ." Sandra looked the other way. "My daughters are very good dancers."

"Do you dance?"

A hint of a smile. "Sometimes. Do you?"

"I kick up a storm at weddings."

"Best time to dance."

"Absolutely."

Sandra finished the tomatoes and went on to the cucumbers. "It's nice of you not to ask why we're here."

Rina said, "I try not to get involved in my husband's business."

"But you know who we are."

"Yes. The case made headlines and Peter . . . Lieutenant Decker was very involved."

"He helped us so much . . . with the situation."

"Thank you, I'm sure he'll appreciate hearing that."

"Yes, I don't think I ever thanked him properly."

"That isn't what I meant at all," Rina said. "I'm sure you thanked him profusely, but you just don't remember."

"Maybe you're right." Sandra put down the knife. "But we didn't come here to thank him, Mrs. Decker. We came because . . ." A sigh. "We need his help." Sandra looked at Rina. "Maybe you can help. I have to say that it's easier for me to talk to a woman than a man . . . even your husband. So if you don't mind, maybe I can talk to you."

"I don't mind at all."

Sandra set her shoulders square and began to talk. "This is the situation. As you know, my daughter, Beth, was murdered. There's no debate on that. The problem seems to be who did it. The case never even got to trial. Belize Hernandez pleaded guilty to a lot of lesser charges and he is serving some time in prison . . . not as much as he would have if he had been convicted of murder, though."

"It must be so painful for you."

"God will take care of him and those who deserve to be punished. I firmly believe that even if my husband doesn't."

"Faith is a wonderful thing."

"It is, isn't it? But that's not the problem we have, Mrs. Decker. Last week, we received a phone call from the state police in Nevada that a group of hikers in the Mohave Desert found some bones *right* around the same area where Belize Hernandez told authorities that he had buried his brother, Manny. I don't know how the searchers missed it the first time. They must have gone over that spot fifty times. But maybe the recent rains washed the bones up or maybe an animal finally unearthed them. The desert is a very fluid thing. It gives and it takes. I suppose that's life really." She fluttered her hands. "I'm just talking silly."

"Not at all."

"I'm running off at the mouth because I'm nervous."

"You're perfectly articulate. Go on. I'm listening."

"Thank you. You see we have Manny's dental chart. The same dentist who kept Beth's records kept Manny's X-rays as well. It was a miracle that he had Manny's because the boy only had one cavity his entire life. Good diet. Not a lot of sugar and lots of whole grains. Not like today's diet, where everything is refined. But that's an old lady talking."

"I agree."

"Anyway, we took the X-ray over to the police in Nevada. Right now they are trying to use it to positively identify the bones."

"I see." A kitchen timer went off. "Excuse me, one second." Rina opened the oven door and took out two broccoli quiches. "Sorry about that."

"Oh, please. I'm sorry for interrupting you."

"It's no problem. So what's going to happen to the bones if they are Manny's?"

"That's the problem." She sighed. "We are the closest of kin other than that person locked up in prison and his father, who doesn't want anything to do with his dead son. It's up to us to decide what to do with the remains."

"Yes, that is a problem."

"We can leave them with the police and let them keep them or dispose of them. That's an option." She paused. "But I seem to recall . . . that the last time we spoke to your husband, Lieutenant Decker seemed to be convinced that Manny didn't do it . . . the murder."

"Okay."

"Do you think he was telling us the truth or was he just trying to make us feel better?"

"If Peter thinks Manny didn't do it, then I would believe him."

Sandra looked intently at Rina. "You said the case made the news. What do *you* think? Was your husband just being nice or do you think Manny was truly innocent of Beth's murder?"

Rina gave the question some thought. She sat down at the kitchen table and so did Sandra. Finally, she said. "All right. This is what I think.

Sometimes Lieutenant Decker does say things that may soften a blow. But in this case, everyone who knew Beth and Manny, everyone who Lieutenant Decker talked to, the former waitresses who worked with Beth, all the old church members who came out of the woodwork to give their opinion, they *all* remembered Beth and Manny as a very loving and spiritual couple. Maybe they smoked a little marijuana, maybe they had some unconventional ideas about God, but they were very sincere in their beliefs and in their love for each other. Manny seemed to take his job as church leader very seriously. And Beth was very keen on organic farming. For her, farming for wholesomeness and goodness was a religious thing."

Rina got up and stirred a pot of curried chicken soup.

"Actually, Beth was way ahead of the time. Or maybe she just grew up with a mother who knew all about food that was nutritious as well as delicious."

Sandra rose and started chopping red peppers. "So you don't think he did it . . . Manny?"

"I know, Mrs. Devargas, that nice people can do bad things. But from what my husband has said, from what the newspapers have said, and from what the people who were there have said, I think Manny and Beth were a committed married couple. Personally, I have a much easier time believing it was Belize rather than Manny."

"But of course we'll never know unless he confesses and that's not likely unless he's on his deathbed." Her face became troubled. "And that's not going to be in my lifetime!" She gasped and stuck her finger in her mouth. She had cut herself with the paring knife. "I'm such a klutz."

"If you cook a lot, you cut yourself. I do that all the time." Rina opened the cupboard and took out a bandage. "Here you go."

Sandra put on the bandage and continued to work in silence. A few minutes later, she said, "I think what we'll do is take home the remains and give my son-in-law a proper burial." She nodded. "We'll bury him next to Beth. That's where he should go."

Rina felt her throat clog. "A husband and wife should be buried next to one another."

"I think so, too."

Rina heard male voices coming from the living room. Moments later, the two Peters came into the kitchen. She felt instant relief.

Decker said, "Thanks for inviting them, Rina. We had to do something to pay Tía Sandy back for all the meals she gave me in Santa Fe."

"Please!" Sandra protested.

"My wife is an excellent cook. So is her mother. You'll meet her in about . . . five minutes. How long before Shabbos?"

"A half hour."

"So I'd better shower and shave—"

Devargas cleared his throat. Everyone looked at him. "First, before you do anything, I want to apologize for us barging in like this."

"It's absolutely fine, Peter," Decker said. "Really."

"No, it isn't fine. It's not proper and we both know it. But you also must know me a little by now, Lieutenant Decker. I wouldn't have done it to be friendly. Unfortunately, we've come here because we have a problem."

Sandra elbowed him in the ribs. "No, we don't have a problem."

"Yes, we do have a problem," Devargas insisted.

Sandra gave him an intense "hush-up" look. "No, we *don't* have a problem."

No one spoke.

"I thought we had a problem." Devargas regarded his wife, a confused expression on his face. "I guess we don't."

"No, we don't!" Sandra said firmly. "We don't have any problem at all."

Again there was silence. The doorbell rang.

"I'll get it," Decker said.

Devargas said, "No, I'll get it. That's my job." He looked at Rina. "Right?"

"Right."

"Then I'll get it." He walked out of the kitchen, shaking his head.

Rina said, "Peter, why don't you see if that's my parents. I think Mr. Devargas would get along great with Papa."

"They probably would." Decker left.

To Sandra, Rina said, "Thanks for the fruit plate. We'll use it for dessert."

"I would have baked a cake, but it doesn't travel well."

Rina laughed. "Cake baking is my mother's department. I'm sure she brought several of them. You'll like her."

"You're close to your mother?"

"Very close."

"That's nice," Sandra said, dry-eyed. "Mothers and daughters . . . that's very, very nice."